CHAOS HOUSE

By Annie Pearson

Chaos House

Demons & Destiny [forthcoming]

RESTORATION RULES SERIES

No One Dies

Reap Justice

Call the Reavers

RAIN CITY INCIDENTS SERIES

The Grrrl of Limberlost

Artemis in the Desert

Nine Volt Heart

The Pirate King

CHAOS HOUSE

by
Annie Pearson

Published by Jūgum Press
Seattle, Washington U.S.A.
Ebook versions at www.jugumpress.net
Print ISBN: 979-8988286219

Cover design by Jacyn Stewart.

Cover landscape art began as a painting by Elinacious; Red Tailed Hawk Flying photograph by rck953; both licensed via depositphotos.

Ink wash bird illustration by boykotapaint plus other cover-art elements licensed via Shutterstock.

Contents

For Susan Urban, who reads and writes so very well.

CHAOS HOUSE

PART I:
Summer's End

September 1983

The Chaos House that can be named
is not the eternal chaos.
— Molly Eliot

1: Dust

THE HEAVENLY IMMORTALS HAD NOT arranged the day to suit me. Their penchant for the random almost always runs counter to my needs.

The day after Labor Day in the Siskiyous, it's too hot to run after eight in the morning, but I'd had to wait on a phone call with my mother's doctor to review her meds, only to hear, "We'll just stay the course, Mr. Eliot. It's disappointing that modern medicine can offer only palliative treatments. Let's schedule Ruby's next checkup for October."

I said goodbye without reassuring the doctor that it's a long time since I'd held any hope that could be disappointed. The only thing close to disappointment: that call meant it was later than I wished by the time I'd run only four miles up the trail, so the temperature was already well over eighty degrees. I got lost inside my head without fully enjoying the run.

Then, on my way down the trail from the Ashland Watershed, a gap in a stand of second-growth ponderosa pines revealed Grizzly Peak, a blur in the late summer haze, hinting at a sublime world, like in a painting from the Song dynasty.

Inspired, I picked up my pace. This day could still unfold differently. Maybe it could be made special despite the Immortals' randomizing tendencies.

Skreeeee!

A hawk's cry echoed up the mountainside.

A red-tail hawk circled overhead, then dove after vermin, lost to my sight beyond a ragged patch of golden chinquapin and buckbrush. Someone I once loved claimed that hawks are angels bearing messages from the Heavenly Immortals who were our ancestors. I don't receive messages from the Immortals because they are only metaphors for chance forces in the universe. To me, *skreeeee* is a wild creature's exaltation. Yet instead of joining that rapture, my undisciplined thoughts strayed after a love long gone.

The red-tail beat its wings, then soared up Mt. Ashland.

Watching it, I stumbled on a divot in the trail, then dodged a cluster of poison oak. A mountain quail, its plume standing straight up in alarm, scurried with its chicks to hide in a clump of mahogany. Just as startled, I forced my focus back to my breath and pace. A saltwater stream ran down my spine, drenching the waistband of my shorts. My damp t-shirt clung from pecs to belly.

A mélange of odors—sunbaked sumac, madrones, manzanita—changed every ten paces, the strong scents penetrating the bandana tied over my face to guard against breathing trail dust. I smelled the pending surrender of summer to fall. As the ancient poets wrote, the dying season's perfume evokes melancholy for an ending endured and a new beginning anticipated.

Coming back down the trail, my legs had that jelly feeling. I left the dusty foot trails and hit the first unpaved road where fingers of the town reach up into the forested mountainside. Yet the steep upper lanes are not smoother than the trails. They're graded rather than paved, and it's been a while since the city could afford that. Gravelly dust has scattered into the buckbrush, leaving ruts and potholes. My well-worn running shoes crunched on the sandy roadbed.

Jelly legs aside, I felt good. I'd been an asthmatic child, rescued by modern drugs, so I have a sense of victory in running for miles. I cut over to Terrace and then to Meade Street, where a dozen cedar waxwings flitted in a lichen-encrusted crabapple tree. Flocking up, ready to fly halfway across the world.

That'll be me next year.

Descending Meade, I smelled fallen apples and mint.

Once again, I heard my grandfather's voice as he drove these streets in his Chevrolet Bel-Air with its plush velvet seats:

> Look over there, Ricky. That's where Nabokov lived while he finished *Lolita.* I had dinner with him twice last year, once up in the hills at Callahan's. You can always count on good quality food up there.

Then he'd roll down the car window and light a Chesterfield King. We shared a name, Aldrik Alexander Eliot, but he was Lex Eliot on the cover of his Zane Grey knockoffs, and I was Ricky to my family. Two streets farther up Terrace, Grandfather would say:

> I've published a baker's dozen more books than Vladimir. And I stuck to living in my own country. That's the way to do it, Ricky. Stay where you belong.

Grandfather must have popped a gasket when my mother Ruby moved us all to Hong Kong. Our father's job managing an export business landed us in a community with U.S. and Brit expats and international corporate employees. The ten years there formed most of my childhood memories.

Yet I'd best shake off letting the past roam through my mind. On a long run like today, I want only to give my heart to the hawks. My flittering thoughts narrowed.

A drink of water. A shower.

Forget exaltation and return to the mundane.

Get to my temp teaching gig on time.

I'm responsible for twin nieces and an infirm mother. I'm also a single gay man living in a town that's stuck in a never-ending recession, the timber economy in freefall. Like most everyone here, I must patch together multiple gigs to keep food on the table.

For only the length of one more school year.

Then I'll be a scholar again.

I dodged a pothole. Should've taken a path down through Lithia Park, since Meade Street is too steep, too rutted. Hard on the knees. Passing the Oregon Shakespeare Festival's fake Globe Theatre, I headed for the paved pedestrian passageway by the modern concrete-and-metal Angus Bowmer Theatre.

My bandana had done its job, catching beads of sweat, and was now a damp, dust-crusted veil. My soaked hair fed the salt stream running down my spine. Sweat-wetted dust coated my bare arms and legs like clay, so I must resemble a crude ceramic mud-man in a Chinatown shop window. Except I am a real boy.

"Hey, Rik! Morning, sunshine."

Becca Lee waved from the corner by the Festival offices. A sturdy Norse blonde with a snub nose, Becca lives at Chaos House, where I rent rooms to boarders. We often talk late into the night in a mutual effort to steer rocky thoughts to fertile ground. She's like an ideal sister, comforting and provoking. Sadly, my real sister, Wendy, has been missing from my life for a decade. Every year at Christmas, I ask her to at least visit, but she won't do it. Because Ruby, our mother, lives in the house.

"Playing Jesse James today?" Becca motioned for me to pull down my bandana mask. She looked cool and professional in linen trousers and a blazer.

I left my mask on and trotted in place. "Gotta go. Dying."

"You're thirty-three, Rik, not sixty-three. You can't die from running up the Watershed."

"It's the heat, not the frailty of this human vessel. Do you need me to do something?"

"It's what I've done for you. I arranged for a significant contribution to a worthy cause." Becca writes and administers grants for the Festival. She tapped her lip, as if repressing a sly grin, which meant she was teasing. It's how she shows affection, the opposite of how teasing was used in my family.

"I secured funds for Rik Eliot's great escape to glorious cosmopolitan Hong Kong." She waved her hand to indicate the theatres behind us. "The Festival is renting all three of your guest cottages till the end of October."

As my best friend, Becca knows more than most people about my Return to Hong Kong savings effort.

"Thanks," I said. "Hope they aren't problematic. The last actors in the cottages left a hundred empty wine coolers. The refund for hauling them back to the store didn't cover my time. It's why I prefer to rent to long-stay tourists."

"It's a visiting director with his small entourage. He's here to plan a production for next spring. And I told the bookkeeper that you raised your rates."

"Do I get a security deposit and a contract to protect me?"

"I'll bring it home tonight. Your new guests chose the catered breakfast option. I added 20 percent to the fee you charged your summer guests."

"Okay, but there aren't choices for breakfast. I'm not a short-order cook. I'll stock snacks in the kitchens."

"They requested muesli, goat's milk yogurt, and pu'er tea."

Jogging backward away from Becca, I called, "Cripes, am I renting to another bunch of the Festival's artistes? Call me this afternoon with the whole list."

Then, rounding the corner of the Festival offices, I nearly collided with one such artiste near an arched doorway.

Fercrissakes. It's Xavier.

Xavier freaking Torres.

Wearing creased jeans and a starched oxford shirt.

California tan, square jaw, expensive hair.

Aviator sunglasses.

I couldn't swallow. A firethorn blossomed in my throat. I've never had a real firethorn in my throat, just one that claws at the notion of Xavier Torres. I wanted to spit yet had vowed not to waste any of life's energy on the man. As I jogged past, my head down, I caught sight of a familiar motion. Xavier wagged his index finger—Xavier's idea of a cute gesture—admonishing a man in ragged cutoffs and flipflops who leaned inside the archway, his face hidden. What I could see: he had longer and much better legs than Xavier. In fact, the nicest legs I'd seen in quite a while. Except he had Superman Band-Aids on both his knees.

My breath hitched at that brief image. It stirred a rasp in my chest. No, not asthma. A jagged outline of a memory, something tender and raw.

Xavier took a predator's step to stand closer to those lazily lounging legs. The legs' owner moved back, dodging Xavier's approach. Ah, no need to shout a warning about Xavier to Skinned-Knee Guy. I jogged past, a sweating masked mud-man.

Stephen Garland stood smoking out behind his café, staring into the distance, a wry smile on his face. He owns the town's only French bistro, though he can't cook and speaks scant French. Since his wife split last winter, he's roomed at Chaos House, which is a lodestone for people who find themselves unexpectedly needing a new place in the world.

"Bonjour, Stephen!" I pronounced his name in the French manner because it makes him smile. *"C'est un plaisir de te voir!"*

"Hi, Rik! Joining us tonight?" He lets his friends hang at the café bar after hours.

"Mais oui, bien sûr, mon ami! Do you have possession of your house yet?"

"Just days away now. Can't wait to hang drywall with you again, *mon ami."*

"You're at the top of my handyman schedule this fall."

In June, Becca said Stephen looked like Serge Gainsbourg if Serge got baked in the Ashland sun and rolled down Sad Street in a domestic dump truck. Now, Stephen is much better, as seen in that wry smile while he smoked behind Café Margot. Last night

Becca and I had a typical conversation. Yes, we gossip about our friends. It's a particular way of caring:

> Becca: I think Stephen's in love. He's changed.
>
> Me: How? Stephen has only been at the café and here at the house all summer.
>
> Becca: That narrows the possibility to only about 20 percent of Ashland.
>
> Me: You're hopeless, Becca Lee. You want everyone to be in love.
>
> Becca: Not everyone. And it doesn't need to be love. You certainly need some basic action. How long since you went on a date?
>
> Me: How long since you've been in love?
>
> Becca: I might have some of that coming. Do you?

Besides having kids and all the work I can manage, I have no wish for any kind of action, especially after the unfortunate mistake with Xavier a couple of years ago. A run in the hills, that's all the pleasure I need or desire.

—

No, what I desired at the moment: a decent pace to finish my run. No potholes. A drink of water. A shower.

When I reached Water Street, four short blocks from home, my mental discipline collapsed. An image from two years ago haunted me. I stood in the San Francisco airport, Xavier wagging his finger, admonishing me. It wasn't cute.

"You still have a boyish figure, Ricky, and beautiful porcelain skin. But you're near the end of your shelf life. You can't always play rent-boy for free rides to the big city. Soon, you'll have to pretend to love the men who pay your way."

I had the perfect response, never once regretting it.

"Fuck that, Xavier. You didn't pay for one thing. And you never did prove you're the world's greatest fuck."

No, I have one meager regret.

I hadn't noticed my fifteen-year-old nieces standing right there, waiting to fly home with me after visiting their cousin in Berkeley. Ramona, tall and swanlike, wore all-black, like a City Lights barista. The much-smaller Molly wore baggy jeans and a t-shirt with the cover of the Ramones' *Road to Ruin.* Yeah, it was a band shirt, but at that moment it read as a caution.

"Not even," the forthright Molly said. "Fuck that, Xavier."

Ramona, the quieter sister, said, "It's more of an art than a science, Xavier. Or so they say."

In my mind, the geometric maroon-and-turquoise carpet in SFO Departures muffled the sound as the wall shattered between my very private life and my life as the girls' guardian.

Like their mother, Wendy, the twins are smarter than me. And I shouldn't have been surprised to see them. My sister-in-law Claudia had told me by phone that she was sending the girls home a week early, to fly with me so she could avoid the fee for unaccompanied minors. The girls arrived at the drop-off curb just in time to speak the truth of innocents and then play rock-paper-scissors to select who got the window seat.

Xavier's play at the Festival that summer, *A Street Car Named Desire,* hadn't been a critical success. Whyever had Xavier been invited back? I guess the people making decisions weren't privy to the twins' wise words.

Fuck that, Xavier.

After I crossed the Plaza and reached Water Street, I spit more of the imagined firethorn that clawed inside my throat.

—

Almost home, I passed those three Twenties-era guest cottages, just west of Chaos House. They had nearly disintegrated by the time I ended up stuck in Ashland. I'd undertaken major wiring, carpentry, and plumbing on my part to raise the quality of the cottages above D-minus student-grade housing. Now Becca says they're cute. I rent to tourists on extended-stay vacations, Festival actors and artists, or graduate students. When I pass the cottages, I privately salute how, through my own sweat, I'd halted the slide of the Eliot family's abysmal finances.

At Chaos House (named after my grandfather's bestselling Rogue River western), I found an empty envelope tucked inside the front screen door, "thank you" scrawled across it. Earlier I'd left a key in that envelope for Inez Saint's ceramics studio, two houses down Water Street. When Inez left for a sabbatical in Italy, she rented her house to her work-study assistant at the local college but loaned her studio to the stand-in for her fall ceramics classes. She'd left me a note with the key: *I told him you're good at raku kiln work and cited an hourly wage that's twice your usual. The guy's here on a grant and can afford it.*

A lucky windfall for me. I keep us all afloat because I'm good at figuring out how things work and fixing them (except for cars). I make money doing whatever I'm reasonably good at: serving as Inez's kiln jockey, acting as Chaos House concierge, playing handyman for neighbors, gigging as a substitute math teacher. After all the bills, I add any spare mite to my Return to Hong Kong fund, which Becca teases me about: *How will we all take care of ourselves if you really decide to run back to Hong Kong?*

But I did really decide, and it's a return, not some kind of running away. I have a robust plan for the future. This December, my dissertation will be approved (Chinese Literature in Translation), at which point I'll finally be a PhD rather than a perpetual candidate. The week after my nieces graduate in May, we'll leave Ashland for Hong Kong, so I can show them where I lived from age five to fifteen. Then they'll be off to school in Boston, and I'll find a teaching position at a Hong Kong university. This plan will carry me up to the turn of the millennium when the

British lease on Hong Kong expires. No one knows what that will mean, so no use planning too far ahead now.

What returning to Hong Kong represents for me is that, by next fall, I will live as my true self, teaching in a cosmopolitan city, unencumbered by children. It's not that Hong Kong will be as freeing as San Francisco is when I visit, but the external landscape will more closely match my internal world.

Right now, I am focused on two objectives crucial to my goal. One: finish my PhD by mid-December, when my supervisor retires and when the university's timeline expires for finishing my PhD work. The other: secure future finances for my family. The girls have trust funds from my grandfather for college, but they'll need other funds until they're fully fledged. I'll need to move my mother to a care home and fund my life in Hong Kong until I have a paycheck as a professor. Those key objectives make decisions easy amid everyday turmoil with teenagers, home health care workers, and my cadre of boarders.

When I got back to Chaos House, I remembered that Ramona had vacuumed the floors the previous day. To avoid tracking dust through the house, I came around to the back, stopping on the porch to stuff my socks, shirt, shorts, running shoes, and bandana into the washer. The machine groaned as it awakened. I pray the Heavenly Immortals might preserve this machine until we're done with it.

In my skivvies, I took the back stairs two at a time to jump in the shower. I should *not* have started the washing machine since this house doesn't have good water pressure. As hot water trickled over my sweat-drenched hair, I dropped the shampoo bottle. While retrieving it, I saw Watershed dust swirling down the drain. Did that mean plumbing problems in the future? Maybe. Probably. Everything goes wrong in this aged four thousand square-foot Victorian monstrosity with only me and no money to keep it from collapsing in on itself.

I scrubbed my hair, the Dr. Bronner's smelling like the gardens on Meade Street. I rinsed away the lather, now clean enough that my thoughts turned to the afternoon chores.

"Muesli and goat's milk yogurt for the artistes."

As I muttered the words, I dropped the shampoo again, hitting my toes and inducing outsized pain. Before I finished swearing, reality hit hard. My new artist-guests in the cottages must be Xavier Torres plus whoever else he dragged into town with him. Skinned-Knee Man?

Why would Xavier choose my guest cottages for any reason other than to annoy me? Why make me deliver his damned breakfast every morning? To pretend that I'm his servant?

No, no. I won't do it. My nieces can trade off breakfast duty. A before-school chore will get Molly and Ramona up and ready without my prodding.

Out of the shower, I put on my watch and saw it was getting late. In an early-morning phone call, the vice principal had offered me a substitute position, Activities Chaperone for an after-school civic project. I can't say no to such offers since I always need the money. Now I was due at the high school by noon for my part in registration-day orientation meetings.

When I was first stuck in small-town Ashland and had to cobble together a family economy, my master's degree in mathematics had the best earning potential. Chinese Literature in Translation did not have a strong economic future in Ashland. I got a teaching certificate, which took only six months because I had extensive academic credits as a long-time professional student. For the past seven years I've been the preferred substitute for middle-school and high-school mathematics and French in Ashland Public Schools. I can't teach full time—because of Ruby, because of the house, because of the kids (at least when they were younger). And my handyman jobs pay double a substitute's hourly wage (and under the table).

After the shower, I dressed in my substitute-teacher costume: a button-down shirt, a tie, and chinos. I slipped on my blue blazer despite the heat. My *Dress for Success* uniform serves as a power signal to students and keeps me as closeted as I need to be in this town. Once I loved someone who insisted I'm a human chameleon, always camouflaged. No one here knows me intimately enough to offer that kind of observation, not even Becca. Yet I do have friends and I'm no longer sad about once-upon-a-time lovers.

At the front door, I grabbed my teacher loafers from the shoe rack, unworn since June. Since I'd bashed my toe during my eureka moment in the shower, I tugged on socks and shoes gently, blaming Xavier Torres for my still-painful toe. I expect he'll be the author of all irritations until that guest-cottage contract ends.

My aged white Datsun 510, parked in the driveway beside the house, has been an avian public restroom since mid-July. I can't do anything about it because the telephone wires that cross the driveway make a perfect birdy swing and outhouse. I'd washed the car last Saturday, but it already needed it again. When I opened the car door, it was hot as Hades inside.

While letting the Datsun cool for a minute, I spit to be rid of the firethorn gnawing my throat, then got in to drive to school, with barely ten minutes until noon, when the student orientation session would begin for my new Activities Chaperone gig.

2: The Chaperone

THE HIGH SCHOOL'S READERBOARD NO longer advised students to READ! for summer vacation, but the board was still excited:

> Welcome students & teachers!
> 1983–84 year starts Sept 7!
> Orientation Sept 6!
> Go Grizzlies!!

I found the last guest parking spot and emerged into the midday heat ready to play Activities Chaperone. I grabbed permission slips from the office and sought the classroom assigned for orientation. It was ninety degrees outside, the room even warmer. I switched off the overhead lights and opened the windows.

I knew each of the dozen senior students there. Half these kids ate at the Chaos House dinner table regularly. The others I'd had in a math class for at least a week in the past year. At the front of the classroom, Ramona and Molly whispered to each other, a surprise to me that they'd chosen this after-school project. The tennis coach will definitely telephone me later to complain, since the girls had done well last season.

For being twins, the girls are opposites, and not just tall versus small. Molly brushes her shoulder-length hair back wet, treats it like it's a nagging hassle, so it's usually a wild bush. Ramona wears a pert ponytail and looks like her mother, though I'd never say that where Ramona might hear. She has strong features, like that portrait of Virginia Woolf. Molly is five foot two and looks like me, fine featured and too thin. Or so Ramona says.

On the other hand, Molly wears so much eye liner, how can Ramona know there's a resemblance? No one has photos from my brief punk-glam phase, just after Bowie released *Life on Mars*. Someone I loved back then said it was incongruous with my true self, so I abandoned eye liner before anyone snapped a Polaroid.

My belly clenched at that stray thought, inappropriate to the task at hand.

I straightened my tie and blazer, then went to the back of the room to shake hands with the parents, most of whom I'd met at after-school events over the years. By the time kids are seniors in a town this size, most parents know each other. Students typically fail to carry papers home, so I gave the parents the mimeographed permission slips. They all brimmed with curiosity about why their kids were so excited. The hum I overheard:

> Mrs. Helman, Zooey's mother: They say the funding comes from everywhere. Oregon artist-in-the-schools. The Festival. A couple of foundations.
>
> Mrs. Hargadine, Quinn's mother: My boy claims I'm out of it because I don't watch late-night MTV, or I'd know what's going on. It makes me feel so old.

Like a dummy, I hadn't asked the vice principal for details about this gig other than the payrate. I was artfully weaseling out of answering parents' questions when Xavier Torres entered the room, pompous as fuck.

An entire bouquet of firethorns bloomed in my throat.

What the hell? The vice principal said this gig was for a civic project, not a drama thing.

Xavier, leaning on the portable lectern atop the front table, told a long story about how he'd been invited back to the Festival to prepare a new *King Lear* production. He rambled on about the importance of *Lear* in Western civilization and passed out cheap copies of the play, encouraging them—"with every fiber of my being"—to read it. Then he offered paeons for project funders, as if he were raising money for public television.

My ears resisted the torture of his voice. Mastering the impulse to run away, I did what I'd learned to do when my heart races at inopportune moments: inhale four counts; hold for four counts; exhale for four counts; hold again. It only ever takes two cycles before I'm bored spitless with my irrationality.

While I was counting breaths, I noticed the twins exchange glances, fluttering mascaraed eyelashes at each other and pursing their lips. Judging. They had not forgotten Xavier Torres.

So. I cannot ask them to deliver cottage breakfasts just because I'm loath to encounter old demons. Also, who in their right mind chose to put Xavier in charge of high school kids? Did I need money badly enough to be Xavier's Activities Chaperone? What tortures might he inflict? And could I afford to decline that guest-cottage contract with the Festival? Doubtless it'd be better to rent it to college students, even at a lower monthly rate.

"Ah." Xavier interrupted his efforts to suck all the air out of the room. "Here's the artist. He's never been late before."

"Gosh, I'm so sorry." The artist called from the hallway, out of breath. "I couldn't find parking."

Smiling, Xavier wagged his finger at the man still in the hallway, so I guessed it'd be Skinned-Knee Man.

The kids stirred collectively, like an excitable covey of quail, the twins' friend Quinn more excited than the others.

"Ladies and gentlemen," Xavier said, "allow me to introduce Jade Solberg, the creative ceramic genius and mural artist you have the privilege to work with on a new masterpiece."

When the genius came through the door, the kids sighed.

Me, I couldn't get my breath. Like when I tripped once at the end of a half marathon and had the wind knocked out of me. Tripped and left breathless this time by my own wild past.

Xavier hung his arm around the artist's shoulder while reciting accolades, then slid his arm down to the waist of the artist's jeans. The artist stepped away and took charge of the lectern, spreading his arms to claim the entire table as his.

"Hi, everyone." Jade waved.

The kids shuffled again in their seats, starstruck. I took my first startled breath at hearing the cello-like tone of his voice, then got my breathing under control, since I might be the sole person in the room who knew he'd once been gangly Jimmy Solberg from Scio, Oregon, who went to court on his twenty-first birthday to shed the most common first name in our age cohort.

How did this happen? How did we get here?

Jade smiled.

The kind of smile that foments chaos around him. He's an agent of pandemonium, like Monkey King. Or Coyote. Or Loki.

Jade once sublet a room in the house I rented during grad school at the University of Washington. His hair, long then, was the color of the sundried tall grasses in the upper hills, but now it barely reached below his ears. He still wore Chuck Taylors, and his ripped jeans revealed the Band-Aids over both knees. His t-shirt—"Sky River Rock Festival and Lighter Than Air Fair"—had been washed so often it was threadbare, the stretched neckband exposing the sharp bones of his clavicle. Also, it had originally been my shirt, scrounged at a University District street fair.

"Good grief," he said, "now we have only fifteen minutes for this meeting. I said I was sorry, but I also promise to never waste your time again. What's most important to discuss first?"

"What's the project?" one parent asked.

"It's a mural!" three kids called. Another said, "A mosaic!"

"Yes," Jade said. "We're doing a twenty-foot mural on the wall behind the Angus Bowmer Theatre."

"Then tell us about safety," a parent in the back said.

"Gosh, yes, a wise place to start." Jade held up a hand with a splinted little finger. "I'm here to tell you, safety first."

The kids all laughed. The parents all looked wary.

After the laughter died out, Jade said, "Despite my poor first impression, I pledge to do everything possible to ensure everyone's safety. We'll start with my worksite rules."

Jade motioned for Xavier to pass around a stack of yellow fliers, but Xavier made a brief excuse and left the room. Too inglorious a task for a director with a growing international reputation? No matter. I'm always glad to see the back of that man as he retreats from wherever I am.

A parent took the paper monitor role. I didn't step up for the task, still recovering from stifled respiration. I hadn't been seen or introduced, so I still pondered giving up this gig.

Jade paused, one finger on his lips in contemplation. "The worksite will have a first-aid kit. Plus I'll be nagging you all the time, like your old granny." His voice shifted to a falsetto. "'Don't run with scissors, children. Follow the rules. Don't be a dolt like Jade.'" His voice shifted back to normal. "I broke this pinky by being a dolt and not paying attention. And I mean no offense to any of you who might be proud dolts."

He had the kids laughing again. The rasp in my chest stirred. I wanted to call out a caution: *He's a wild man. He's always got banged fingers and knees and toes.*

Jade thumbed his lip again, a sign of thinking seriously. Those full lips, though, looked chapped from too much sun. "I've been told that not everyone sees the world the same way. But for this project, my way is the only way. All of you are merely," he grinned as he rubbed his hands together, the splinted finger sticking out, "instruments in my quest for world domination."

Even the parents laughed. Five minutes in, and these kids would follow him over a cliff. Long ago I'd been there, at the edge, excited for the next adventure.

But later, I stood on atop a different cliff far away from wherever the Monkey King had journeyed to.

"Questions?" Jade held up his bandaged hand.

"Where is the project?" asked the woman who'd distributed the yellow safety sheets. Since I hung in the back, I'd received the last sheet.

"Behind the Angus Bowmer theatre," Jade said, then he again focused only on the kids. "We'll meet here tomorrow to go over the site rules and how we'll collaborate to make art." He began to pass around more sheets, pink ones. "Tonight, please have your adult sign the permission slip, including the sections on transportation and scaffold work."

"Scaffold?" Zooey Helman, the girl seated by Quinn, voiced my alarm. I'd worked on a couple of Jade's large installations while he finished his MFA at the UW. I'd learned about courage versus caution, and I still apply those lessons when I have to fix a roof or paint a tall house. But twelve kids on a scaffold?

Jade said, "The scaffold is only eight feet high, with guard rails. It's not like the tall scaffolds I used in Paris, if you've seen pictures of that project. If you don't like heights, tell your adult not to sign that part. No blame, no shame."

"Mr. Solberg, who's our adult?" Quinn asked.

"Please call me Jade." The kids stirred again. Teachers didn't allow use of their first names in the classroom. However, I felt jealous as a teacher for how he'd enthralled these kids so quickly. "It's the person who signs your absence excuses. I don't say 'parents' since not everyone has those."

Most kids nodded, murmuring. The twins sat still at first, then Ramona furtively glanced in my direction.

"When do we start work?" Quinn again, the most forward of the crew.

"You're asking a question after my own heart." Jade tapped his chest. "I salute your desire to get to the business of making art."

Quinn had been excited before then; Jade set him on fire with twenty words.

"On Thursday," Jade said, "we'll meet at the project site. I'll give you a ride if your adult signs that part of the permission slip."

A parent asked, "Can kids drive to the site?"

He shook his head. "Neither the school nor the Festival wants that. Ride with me to the site." He circled his finger to encompass the kids in front of him, a gesture I knew in our UW days, enlisting people to join his crew on a new adventure. "Or ride a bike. Or run if you want. You'll have to get home on your own." He held up his hand, like he was firing a starter pistol. "Can you do it?"

His crew cried, "Yes!" as if answering a coach getting his team game ready.

But then, most of Jade's crew hangs in upper Lithia Park after school, so of course they could get themselves home.

"Goodness, look at the clock. I'm supposed to make sure people can catch the bus."

Jade was ending the meeting. He'd said nothing further about the nature of the mural project, yet the kids remained excited as they stood to leave.

"Gosh, wait! I forgot!" Jade drew their attention back. "While we're working, there's to be no visitors to the site. No friends, guardians, or onlookers. I require your full attention while we're making art out in the wild world."

The kids nodded, but Quinn once again spoke up. "Mr. E has to be there. He's the activity chaperone."

Molly said, "We have to have a chaperone. And he has to be there to get paid."

"But don't worry, Mr. Solberg," Quinn said. "He won't rat you out to the vice principal."

"Unless you drink," one boy said.

"Or toke weed," piped another. "Or, you know, do the touching thing. Then, wham, you're dead."

"Gee, I'll definitely keep all that in mind." Jade shaded his eyes and scanned the room. "Who is Mr. E?"

"It's Mr. Eliot," Quinn said.

"They call him Rik in the teacher's lounge," Ramona said. "But kids can only call him that at his house."

Did Jade blink? I didn't see it, though I'd watched his eyes all through the meeting. The edges of his contact lenses caught the overhead fluorescent light, so I saw Loki behind those shining eyes.

"He tends to have a cow if you break the rules," Molly said.

"That's not true." Quinn defended me. "Mr. E only goes off if you break big rules. The ones that matter."

"Is Mr. E here now?" Jade peered into the back of the room.

Half the kids pointed in my direction. Since I was in the shadows, I stood, though I wanted to disappear. Like a ghost in a Chinese folktale, slipping through the wall. I'd been clenching my hands, so my palms were slick, but I managed to drop my arms, pretending to relax.

"Oh, gosh. Hello." Jade tipped his head. Then, likely only I understood his next word. "Sasha."

That rasp in my chest again. I felt my pocket, seeking my inhaler, then stopped. That rasp wasn't asthma. Curious and panicky at the same time, I didn't see how to avoid this unexpected invitation to wild chaos. Not a state children should see.

"Yikes!" a boy exclaimed. "The buses are here."

"Goodness, go!" Jade said. "But I'll stay to answer questions." He still stared my way. I couldn't read his expression.

Since I was near the door at the back, I sought to get out of the room ahead of any parents or kids. Xavier blocked the way. He didn't notice me as he headed straight for his artist, shuffling for position among the six kids who'd stayed to ask questions. The twins, despite years of inspecting me closely for my reaction to every damned thing, didn't notice me hurrying to leave.

"Whoa! Slow down," Jade cried. I made myself not turn around. Then his voice became soothing. "Help me understand your question so I can answer."

I glanced back. He was speaking with a girl, Zooey Helman, who literally hopped in place. He offered her that smile, like the Monkey King in comics I'd read in grade school.

She said a few words I couldn't hear. Jade said, "Okay, I understand. I'm sure you can do this. Please trust me and don't worry about failure. I'm known as Mr. Positive Mental Energy, and I'm always right when I guess who will succeed."

For a Trickster, Jade is at least open and honest while beguiling people into his adventures. No demon juju, only earnest charm: *Gosh. Goodness. Gee.*

As I headed down the hall to get out of the building, Quinn's mother tapped my elbow.

"Rik, I'm so glad it's you who's chaperoning. I've never seen Quinn this excited about anything other than his guitar."

"Uh, thanks, Mrs. Hargadine."

I shoved the panic bar to open the door that leads to the guest parking lot. I can take care of Chaos House just fine, but I dislike messiness, like when my past life collides with my current life. And two collisions in one day—first Xavier, then Jade—must be seen as beyond messy.

It's like finding a well in the deep, dark woods that hasn't been covered to keep people from falling in.

Quick, everyone, follow Lassie! Ricky's fallen in the well. Who will save him from drowning in memories?

Me, I'll save myself. Since I ended up in Ashland, I've learned multiple ways to keep from being pulled into a deep hole, to avoid that which I prefer to forget. I wasn't about to fall in now. I have goals, objectives, and chores I must attend to.

3: Thrifting

SASHA. HE GAVE ME THAT NICKNAME, riffing off my middle name, Alexander, when we knew each other in Seattle.

Oh hang the interfering Heavenly Immortals and their haphazard ways! He'll be living in one of the cottages, like Xavier.

And that Trickster had rented my garage. I'd told Inez Saint that her sabbatical stand-in at the college was welcome to use it. That I'd gladly work as his kiln jockey. Why hadn't I asked Inez who her stand-in was?

And he'd been inside Chaos House once before. And he knew I still lived there when he picked up the envelope with the key earlier.

Worse, he's working with Xavier at the Festival. As part of Xavier's personal entourage? Jade Solberg, that chaos genie, once claimed to be able to sniff out asshole imposter artists from fifty yards. He'd been blasted on acid at the time, but has he lost his detection abilities since then?

Cripes, had Xavier, that human lizard, talked about me?

I cannot abide either man living right beside me. Both spawn chaos as they go through the world, which I know from past experience.

"*Shushu!*" Molly called to me.

Just as I reached my car in the school's guest lot, the twins materialized. Molly hadn't called me that before this moment. These two employ the handful of Chinese words they know in only two cases: to express affection, or to soften me up if they think I might say no to a request.

"*Shushu,* we need fifteen dollars," Ramona said.

"Each, *shushu.* Fifteen dollars each," Molly said.

So softening me up this time.

"You heard *shushu* at the fight movie last Friday," I said. "It's Mandarin and means father's younger brother. I'm your mother's younger brother. In Hong Kong dialect, you'd probably say *kaukau.*"

Ramona wrinkled her nose. "*Kaukau* sounds like yuck candy they only sell at the movies. Or a dog's name."

"A really cute dog," Molly said. "But the kind that barks too much, like our neighbor's new dog."

Ramona said, "And it scratches at the door in the dark of night when ghost-demons come for the Shaolin temple master."

"To extract retribution for offending the Immortal demi-gods." Molly nodded her affirmation.

I should never have taken them to fight movies. Or told them the comic-book ghost stories I translated in my dissertation.

"I thought I gave you enough cash for the activity fees."

"You did, *kaukau,*" Molly said. "And there's no fee for the civic arts project."

"Then why do you need so much money?"

"Isn't it, like, totally obvious?" Molly rolled her eyes. "The end of our childhood begins tomorrow."

"We need clothes for the first day of class," Ramona said. "Especially since it's our last year. We also need #2 pencils, Bic pens, and new Trapper Keepers."

"Can't you use last year's? I bet there are erasers left on all your pencils." My teasing served to elevate their creativity.

Ramona said, "We cannot endure the shame of being seen by our peers as neglected urchins."

"Or pitied by our teachers as penurious waifs," Molly said.

"As if you'd care," I said, "in either case."

"Impossible not to care," Molly arched her eyebrows, "when everyone in this tiny town gets in your business and judges."

"Our business," Ramona said, "being our own private business, not fodder for gossiping Socs."

They'd read about Socs—the Socials in *The Outsiders*—and saw the movie last summer. They now scorn the local Socs, though to my certain knowledge there are no class-warfare gangs in Ashland. Just cliques with firm borders.

When the girls came here in the fourth grade, they worked hard to be anonymous, to look like everyone else. When they began to develop independent styles, I saw it as proof they felt secure at last. Through junior high and high school, they cultivated an anti-hippie style. In tenth grade, Molly convinced Ramona to join her in ordering school uniforms from the Sears catalog. Then last year, they abandoned Peter Pan collars and skirts. After watching *Funny Face* one Saturday afternoon, a friend remarked that Ramona looks like the shop girl—meaning Audrey Hepburn in fake beatnik clothes. Ramona took to black turtlenecks and pegged her jeans like it was 1966 all over again, and she wears black flats, which are in fact kung-fu shoes from a Chinatown shop. The Hepburn ponytail suits her.

Molly, however, had an intellectually meaningful friendship with a boy from Venice Beach. He lived in Ashland for just five months before his parents resolved whatever custody issues they had, and he returned to California. But Molly still wears baggy jeans and loose black t-shirts with mysterious symbols or band album covers. All her shoes are suitable for a skate deck, whatever the weather.

Ramona said, "The Medford Goodwill is refreshing its racks today. Becca told us that by tomorrow, the Festival's costume crew will have it all picked over."

It's my good fortune that the girls shop thrift stores. Becca says designer jeans, the most desired fashion at Ashland High, cost over thirty dollars. But my girls prefer five-ninety-nine jeans from the Blackbird surplus store in Medford.

"Do you need more than another pair of jeans and a couple of used t-shirts? Winter coats?"

"We might find treasures." Molly looked up at me with hopeful, pathetic eyes (but faking it).

I handed each of them three five-dollar bills, happy to get off easy for this year's school shopping. "I need the car for the rest of the day. I can't take you to Medford."

"Thank you. We'll take the bus," Molly said.

"You are so sweet." Ramona kissed my cheek. "See you at dinner, *kaukau*."

Was I imagining that Ramona is now so tall she stooped for that peck on my cheek? Given her physical similarity to Wendy, her mother, one might expect sarcasm and a flash-fire temper. But no, the diminutive Molly got all that. Ramona is too kind for this world. For example, when they were nine and came under my care (after what I call our Specially Bad Christmas), I enrolled them at Briscoe Elementary. Two weeks later, I had to pay the school library for all its copies of *Old Yeller* and *Sounder* because Ramona destroyed them—though testing had shown they read at only second-grade level. My question still remains: why teach children's books where animals die for a cheesy emotional hit?

Or, as Molly says whenever the *Sounder* destruction story is retold: "In a just world, no moral person puts Bambi's dead mother in a child's Little Golden Book."

How did I get off on that maudlin rumination?

Oh, it was Molly's quip—*The end of our childhood begins tomorrow*—while I was shaking off the sense of falling into a memory well. Yet the end of the twins' childhood was the key marker for my Return to Hong Kong plan. Just one more school year before I no longer had a crucial place in their daily life.

I unlocked my car and held the door open to cool the inside.

Ramona came running back. "Uncle Rik, the artist asked for you when he finished answering questions."

"Why?"

"Dunno." Ramona shrugged.

"Well, he knows where to find me." It's not a mystery.

"Do you know him, *kaukau?*"

"We were both in grad school at the UW."

And boy-oh-boy, did that understate the case. But it satisfied Ramona, who then ran to catch up with Molly.

—

I climbed into the Datsun's roasting interior, which smelled of hot dust and, vaguely, Windex. Shifting into reverse, then forward out of the lot, I took care not to squeal the tires in my haste to get away.

While driving down Siskiyou Boulevard, I fell into the deep well of memory that Molly's quip had opened. Stray thoughts of how they'd thrived under my care brought a warm sense of comfort; they must feel it too.

Last week, they'd returned from Berkeley with expensive shoes and good secondhand leather coats. These were, as I understand it, thank-you gifts from their Aunt Claudia for accompanying their cousin Alex home via Greyhound after he'd spent the summer playing guitar in our garage. All-black Adidas Superstars for Ramona and white Nike Air Force Ones for Molly, already scuffed from skateboarding. My sister-in-law Claudia seeks to outfit them in popular styles, not having noticed that they don't care. Or is Claudia poking at me since I could never afford those shoes? I prefer to think better of people, so I hope that's not true.

There'd been a controversy over their recent trip to Berkeley: they had not asked permission to go. I learned they were gone when I went to cook dinner and found Ramona's note, which offered a heart-wrenching tale about Alex being scared to travel alone, even on the bus, so it was the twins' duty to provide moral support for his journey. However, for some reason, Claudia reported their sudden adventure to Wendy, who called me to say, "If they did a runner because of Ruby, it's better if they come live with me, not Claudia."

"No worries. They didn't run away," I'd said, gently. "You could call and talk with them."

"I did. But I just want to make sure Ruby isn't getting up in their shit, like she always did with me."

This many years later, Ruby seems to still be Wendy's bête noire. My sister is a fragile person whom I love deeply and who forever gives me reasons to worry. She has never fully recovered from any of her successive life crises. Eight years before, under extreme emotional stress, she had begged me to take the girls while she went abroad to teach. That launched one of the greatest experiences in my life. Wendy returned to the U.S. after four years abroad but has met with us in person just once. She calls the girls a couple of times a year.

In the last couple of calls, Wendy has offered to have the twins come live with her: *But only if they want to.* They have never expressed such a desire. Currently, that'd mean living with Wendy and her current lover, Jophiel, the incarnation of one of the Ascended Masters, on a goat farm run by a Human Potential collective up a dirt road in Big Sur.

I'd repeated Wendy's offer with sensitivity, letting the twins know it'd be their free choice.

"It's not where I'd choose to live," Ramona said.

"Yeah, even if a nuclear holocaust wiped out life as we know it." Molly shrugged. "I'm not a fan of goats."

I'd also explored in family counseling sessions how they felt about Wendy leaving them in my care and about not knowing their father. We've stopped those sessions at their request: *It's not relevant to real life.* Lucky for me, the twins don't ask about their father, because I have no clue who he is, much less how to find him.

Musing about that particular stranger, my mind wandered further until a sudden thought caused me to brake abruptly at the traffic light where Lithia Way crosses Pioneer Street.

Molly and Ramona hadn't recognized Jade.

When Wendy left them with me, had they been too young—or too traumatized—to remember details from that time? Or had the Heavenly Immortals blessed everyone but me with the ability to forget?

That rasp rattled deep in my chest, and I again felt for my pocket inhaler. Yet my breathing had been fine while running that morning. This hitch in my chest didn't come from a failure of modern medicine.

Likely it's a character defect.

A guy up Ashland Mine Road, who follows the teachings of Wilhelm Reich, assured me of such a defect when I had an asthma attack while tearing out old insulation in his house. He showed me his box for trapping orgone energy, explaining: *Scientifically speaking, you must have a rigid structural resistance of the ego, and it blocks your awareness of buried emotions.*

Yeah, I built that structure myself, using old-fashioned hand tools. And I now wear a good respirator during demolition. It's not *my* character defect that makes it impossible to swallow the idea of historic agents of chaos living next door to me.

—

When I got out of my car at Chaos House, the local scrub jay dived at my head from the large white oak next door. It's been after me all summer, long past breeding season. And California scrub jays, the kind we have in Ashland, don't migrate. I'll get no respite.

My guess about the source of this one-sided hostility: I caged the backyard bird feeder, so only songbirds dine there, not scrub jays. This jay knows me to be the local elemental demi-god of the feeder, but it won't bow down. Instead, it dive-bombs me, then sits on a branch to screech its existential resentment.

If I spoke scrub jay, I'd advise: *Bitching will get you nothing. I know from experience.* I tried explaining my demi-god nature in Cantonese, but the scrub jay flitted high up in the locust tree and bitched at me from there. But I shall not relent. If I take the cage off the feeder, the scrub jay will invite its extended corvid family from as far as Medford to party, bankrupting me over birdseed. The demi-god of the feeder carries a heavy burden.

The paving stones from the driveway to Chaos House are lined with herbs and smell of mint and thyme, the same scents as Meade Street. Which got me wondering once more why my grandfather, with his grandkids in the backseat, drove along Meade Street so often. The road goes nowhere special. My grandfather's growling proclamation about writing more books than Nabokov is one of my few memories of the old man, little me thinking: *Here we go again, another Nabokov story.* I didn't know Nabokov from Nabisco at four years old. The butterflies were the interesting part, to my poor recollection. Then we left Ashland to live in Hong Kong for ten years, so I never heard more about the butterflies or Old Man Eliot's adventures hanging on the edge of Nabokov's social circle.

I never read *Lolita* as a mathematics undergrad. However, not long after I began my Chinese Lit master's work, I saw the movie in a repertory theatre off University Avenue in Seattle. That tiny theatre had retained the accumulated odors of each person who'd ever sat in the banks of forty-year-old maroon-velvet folding seats. I'd come with someone I once loved. After the movie, I babbled all across the U District that my grandfather must have been jealous of Nabokov's ability to describe and evoke passion.

"In my grandfather's westerns, every story is a thin soup with no emotion voiced beyond 'Consarn you, Black Bart.' Thirty-five books full of persistent jerking but never coming."

I was about to say that my mother Ruby wrote terrible rage-filled *Peyton Place* imitations. But my companion said, "You're lucky you got to know your grandfather. I'm jealous."

My emotions collapsed into self-doubt—like everything then. I had a crush that I wanted to be more than private longing, but it felt problematic between us. I was relatively rich (back then); he was poor. My family constantly said cruel things to each other; he was an orphan. I knew I wasn't straight; he dated female grad students. I thought then, as now: *I cannot have what I want.*

Consarn that rasp in my chest.

I walked up the Chaos House driveway to the back porch, where I found another envelope, this one taped to the screen door:

For Mr. Richard Eliot

Ah, yet another note from my Disputatious Neighbor, whom Molly dubbed Mean Mr. Mustard. My friends call me Rik, which is what it says on the mailbox. My legal first name is Aldrik. Yet messages from my Disputatious Neighbor address me as Richard, likely because in the distant past he'd heard Ruby call me Ricky. Without opening the envelope, I knew I'd be upbraided for being a bad neighbor, like in all messages before it. For example:

Crowds of rowdy teenagers fill your garage late at night, smoking cigarettes and playing loud music.
(Under Rik's Rules, the music stops at nine o'clock, the best that can be expected.)

Some of your garbage, specifically a Sara Lee wrapper, blew into my yard after Tuesday's trash pickup.
(I have never once bought anything labeled Sara Lee.)

Your cat uses my marigolds as a toilet.
(We don't have a cat. I'm allergic.)

Et cetera.

I am a considerate neighbor. I have never said a word about his rooster, which crows at four a.m., nor about the new chihuahua, which once it starts cannot stop barking. Yet since the week I'd ended up stuck in Ashland, my Disputatious Neighbor has taped scolds to the Chaos House back door. He's compelled to walk around the fence that divides our properties, pass by my front door, slink down the narrow walkway into my backyard, and post his baseless screeds on my rattling wood-framed door, further denting the screen with each scolding message.

I have to replace that screen. At least by next spring.

Being accused of miscreant pets is especially egregious because the twins would very much like to have pets. That lack is down to my allergies to dander and feathers, and also, I don't want to hold any more funerals for fish or turtles. Last time, they played Bob Marley's 'Waiting in Vain' as funeral music, so I ended up weeping with them over a two-inch turtle that ran away and died in the dust bunnies under Molly's dresser.

I left my Disputatious Neighbor's envelope on the kitchen table and headed for my mother's room, greeting the woman who is the six a.m.-to-two p.m. caretaker.

"Good afternoon, Mrs. Adams."

She stood to greet me. "Hello, Mr. Eliot. If you're here to sit with Ruby, I'll read in the garden for a few minutes."

A narrow, tidy person, she prefers formal address, though she's been in this house almost daily for five years. She's as careful and kind as a Julie Andrews version of a nanny.

If the weather permits, Mrs. Adams takes her breaks on the patio behind the house, under the shade of the maple and locust trees. Here in Ashland, she can sit out back three hundred days of the year, though some days demand a good winter coat. The two-to-ten-o'clock helper, Howard Curtis, is built like a lumberjack and seldom feels a need for a winter coat.

I took off my *Dress for Success* blazer and went to sit by Ruby, who was in her lounge chair, covered by an afghan despite the day's heat. "Hello, Mother."

"Shh." She pointed to the TV. "*General Hospital.*"

I begin our midday ritual by rubbing lavender-scented lotion on the papery skin of Ruby's age-spotted hands.

"Look at the yellow rose." I direct Ruby's attention away from the TV, although the window screen blurs the view into the backyard. No breeze stirs the stale air, yet a single bloom scratches at the screen, likely shaken by a neighbor's cat seeking shade.

"My goodness, Chris. It's rained all day, but the first rose of spring is unbowed. It makes you believe in the redeeming love of God, doesn't it?"

"Yes, Mother."

Except it's the last rose of summer. The screen is mottled with late-summer dust.

And my mother has never, to my knowledge, believed in God or redemption. However, since July, Ruby has attended daycare sessions at the city's senior center for three days a week. A van with a wheelchair ramp picks her up and brings her back three hours later. It's government sponsored, yet lunch seems to include songs of redemption. And not the Bob Marley kind.

Also, my brother Christopher died over a decade ago in a traffic accident near Oakland Army Base, just before he was due to be discharged. Christopher, Wendy, and I resemble each other, our faces inherited from Ruby. Only Christopher and Wendy got my father's height.

I'd learned early in this adventure not to correct Ruby's faulty memories. It just confuses or frightens her.

September doesn't care if it's mistaken for April.

Dust doesn't care if a frail woman mistakes it for rain.

It hurts no one if she believes Christopher is her guardian.

The liver spots, though, must cause perpetual rage. Ruby kept her press clippings, especially those where she'd been called a beauty. Now, she's sixty-three but looks eighty-three.

I perform my chores as familial duty, not filial piety, which I don't believe is possible in my world. When Ruby last called me Ricky, it was with hateful anger. I managed the phases of her decline by remembering that decades earlier I was loved by her, or at least comforted. Now I'm forgotten. None of that is her fault. Her brain robbed her body of the spirit of the woman she'd hoped to be, as a girl, as a mother, as a writer. I focus on other crucial elements of life, especially supporting Ramona and Molly, where I've made a difference.

When Mrs. Adams came back to Ruby's room, she twisted the knob on the TV to turn up the volume. *Days of Our Lives* was playing, not *General Hospital.*

The TV also doesn't care what Ruby thinks she's watching.

I set off to make tea, all I can do for either of them just then.

Ruby isn't unhappy. Terrors sometimes bubble up in nightmares, but usually she lives in the moment. She's far into her decline, so she's forgotten her immense anger at how life treated her and how inadequate her children proved to be. And I've exhausted my grief and dismay over what life dealt her and what she dealt out to the rest of us.

Ancient poets declare such travails of life to be the tyranny of Heaven.

I can bear the tyranny of the Heavenly Immortals, those randomizing a-holes. It's no greater than what I encounter in the mundane world, where I must make sure the washing machine works every single day and must sometimes crawl under the house with the spiders to fix broken plumbing.

4: Chopping Wood

IN THE KITCHEN TUESDAY AFTERNOON, I washed my hands in the sink since lavender isn't my favorite scent. While water boiled for tea, I moved the laundry from the washer, after first checking for the tree frog that keeps invading the dryer, where there's nothing to eat and nothing to mate with. But my efforts to find its entry point have failed, and he (she?) returns to the dryer, no matter how far I walk down the creek to place the frog in a better habitat.

After I delivered the tea to Ruby's room, I opened the latest scolding note from my Disputatious Neighbor:

> Mr. Eliot, respectfully, I understand from Dr. Inez Saint that she designated you as her studio's custodian while she's absent. Today, a ragged stranger who appears to be using her studio has parked a derelict vehicle in front of my house. I trust you'll instruct Dr. Saint's tenant on respectful behavior in our neighborhood.
>
> Sincerely, J.J. Smith, Lt. Col. (retd)

Why didn't Mean Mr. Mustard tape his scold on the derelict vehicle and leave me out of it? It offers a new opportunity to exercise his daily aggressions without involving me.

The phone rang.

"Rik? It's Becca."

"I'd never have guessed."

"Busy day. Hey, I forgot to tell you this morning that the light went out in my bathroom. Can you fix it?"

"I can." Her bathroom is a converted closet, created the first year I took over managing this house. Her two rooms are small, but she has the east balcony with its view of Grizzly Peak.

"Can your new cottage tenants move in now?"

"In a couple of hours. After I stock the kitchens."

"Then this evening, for sure? Wait till you meet the actor. He's like a Greek god. And nice. I swear you'll fall in love and forget your monk-like ways."

Impatient, I ignored that and jumped on to my questions. "Is the new guest Xavier Torres? And Jade Solberg?"

"Yes! How'd you guess? The Festival is so lucky to get Xavier again. And Jade Solberg is doing Xavier's set design, besides the grant for his mural on the south wall. I managed a good windfall for you, didn't I?"

"Yeah, I'm lucky." I lied. Becca and I share important confidences. I had not, however, shared my previous experiences with Xavier. "What's on the guests' snack list?"

As she read it to me, I jotted items on my grocery list.

"That's it," she said. "The Festival cut a check for September and October. I'll bring it home tonight with the contract. Now, I gotta go."

"Bye, Becca."

She didn't hang up. "Uh, Rik? I'm telling you, it's time to let down your guard. The Festival might have contracted to house your soulmate right next door. This actor—he's called Timothy—is beautiful enough to deserve you."

When a click ended the call, my belly tightened, as if to defend against a punch.

Becca's friendly notion comes from her belief in soulmates. She's tested a few false candidates yet is still waiting for the Heavens to deliver hers. Me? Experience plus my dissertation research into T'ang poetry have together pointed out that the Heavenly Immortals are more inclined to fuck things up than deliver a soulmate. And I foresaw enough unwanted chaos with two of the new guests, I didn't need a third added to the disruption.

On my list of the day's tasks, I checked off the finished items, then drew a line and began a list for tomorrow. Daily, I make lists of the tasks required as part of my pieced-together economic life.

Until next May, when I'll be free to return to Hong Kong.

I didn't need paper and pencil to do the math that's been nagging at me. I'd been doing it in my head since I left that classroom. The arithmetic answer was so grim that I drew too heavy a line under the grocery list and tore the paper.

I cannot afford to *not* rent the cottages to the Festival. Or *not* be Activities Chaperone. Or *not* be kiln jockey. I can afford only to cough up that rasp, swallow that firethorn, and get on with life.

I headed out to the food co-op, which would have muesli and cow's milk yogurt. There's no goat's milk in Ashland, even at the co-op. And nowhere in town will I find pu'er tea.

I will repeat: fuck Xavier Torres and his entire pretentious, self-centered being.

However, I quelled the little bitch that lives behind my rock-hard heart. I did not toss the plainest brisk tea into my cart. Instead, I bought gunpowder tea, South American yerba mate, and (my personal favorite) lapsang souchong. That should be enough pungent choices to stand in for pu'er.

When I returned from shopping, I spied the derelict vehicle parked in front of my Disputatious Neighbor's house. It's an International Harvester crummy, a twelve-passenger vehicle built to haul logging crews over rugged forestry roads. Like most crummies, it had once been bumblebee yellow, but now, a third of it was rust-colored—and too large for the short driveway by Inez's studio. Contractors' trucks were parked along Water Street because a California immigrant is remodeling a two-story Victorian. With no other parking on this street, the crummy had cleanly avoided my neighbor's driveway.

Sadly, J.J. Smith, Lt. Col. (retd) must dwell in a tortured underworld, with no possible relief from his torments.

I now foresaw two months of being scolded for all transgressions made by Inez Saint's chaos-spawning stand-in, who has driven into my life in a logger's crummy large enough to carry major baggage from my past life. I shall cling to a hope that Xavier knows nothing of the wild adventures that Jade and I shared in grad school. Not one of my Ashland friends knows that history.

And I don't have time for a pair of chaotic intruders. So I stuck the rigid structural resistance of my ego into a box along with the groceries from the co-op.

—

It only took thirty minutes to stock the cottage kitchens. Each cottage was ready for guests since I'd cleaned on Monday after the last of the summer tourists departed.

The cottages are one-story, two-room Craftsman bungalows from the first era of tourism in Ashland. To the east, Chaos House looms over them, set just a few yards off Water Street. It's four stories if you count the daylight basement below the over-sized front porch. A late-Victorian behemoth from the first era of the lumber barons, the house has all the elements of West Coast mansions from that time, like mail-order cupolas and leaded glass windows. The two balconies visible from the street are out of proportion to the rest of the house.

After burning, scraping, and power-washing the house's crumbling exterior paint, I'd painted it a color that my friend Frankie says matches several old houses in historic Jacksonville. Frankie works in the college printshop, since paid work as a historiographer is rare around here. She's researched and written monographs for the historical society in Jacksonville, which is digging deeper into its Gold Rush history. And that's why I relied on her declaration: *Paint it creamy yellow.*

The inside of the house took more out of me. Replacing the lead-pipe plumbing and the knob-and-tube wiring meant tearing out lath-and-plaster walls to keep us from falling sick or setting the place on fire. The first floor has two studios, one for Ruby and the other for the nighttime caretaker, plus Stephen Garland has a two-room flat with its own entrance in the back of the house. On the second floor, Molly and Ramona share a large room. Becca has one of the two-room flats, and the other is rented by Valerie Ortega, who has a four-year-old son, Julio. My room and its study are under the eaves on the third floor, along with attics and a guest room suitable for an exceedingly small person. They each have a private bath. And it's past time for me to stop complaining about how that plumbing work hindered my spiritual cultivation.

At the back of the property, the cottages share a strip of concrete patio. Our house has a ramp down to its larger patio, and a path runs into a little wilderness along Ashland Creek.

Despite the never-ending recession, I hope all my work incites a significant sale price to a California immigrant when spring comes. The realtor will tell each potential buyer that the babbling creek can be heard from the patio and even from the kitchen if the window is open.

As long as no one is tearing down lath-and-plaster walls.

—

After finishing my chores in the guest cottages, it was time to make dinner. It's common to have one, two, or six extra kids at the Chaos House dinner table. Since it's the first school night in months, I made what I know kids like. I appreciate that the twins' friends feel comfortable at our table. In Hong Kong, I'd learned that the family dinner table is a sanctified space, and an evening meal is a source of comfort and pleasure. I've tried to recreate that here.

I didn't learn it at my own family table. In Hong Kong, the school I attended ran on the English model. Quite early, I showed an aptitude and passion for mathematics, which was noticed by my math teacher, Master Chan, a Hong Kong native who held a degree from Cambridge University. His full name is Chan Wei Wen—"a great literate of the old Chan family." The English-born teachers called him Wade, an anglicized name he first chose in England. While visiting outside of school, I first addressed him as Chan-sinsang since he was my teacher. Because we met almost every day, we became friends, and he said I could call him Chan-suk, "uncle" being a term of respect. I've never had any other uncle, and he remains a dear friend who kindly reviews draft chapters of my dissertation. Last year Chan-suk introduced me to his brother-in-law, who has dangled the strong possibility of a university teaching position when I return to Hong Kong.

In those days, my mother paid Chan-suk extra fees to tutor me in more advanced math than I'd get in the school's primary classes. That meant a session in my master's study every afternoon while his son Kai did his homework beside me at the study table. I was often invited to dinner, and a quick call to my mother always resulted in permission to stay.

The most important thing I learned in the Chan family house was the many deeper meanings of filial piety, beyond burning joss sticks for dead relatives. As Chan-suk taught, it also means dining together with respectful conversation. Peace at the end of the day. He presided at one end of the table, with Kai's two sisters on one side, Kai and me on the other, and Madam Chan at the end beside her wheelchair-confined mother. The elder Madam had suffered a stroke, but sat with the family every night, being fed by her daughter.

This was my introduction to filial piety as a Confucian virtue. Master Chen—my guide to the ancient and modern ways of Hong Kong society—explained that he and his wife sought more than repaying the burden that their parents had borne. I'd heard it more than once: *Care of our elders is the root of being human. More than an obligation, it's the foundation for cultivation of righteousness.*

Dining often with the Chan family also led me to recognize by age twelve that my family was cuckoo, long before someone I loved warned me that my family was toxic and didn't care about me. Oddly, that warning warmed my core being because it came from deep kindness. I'd understood my family's wackiness before we left Hong Kong since I could compare our family table with the Chan family table. It's best to recognize while you're young that your family is totally nuts instead of it slowly dawning on you later.

In the Chaos House kitchen, I started the rice cooker and began chopping onions. When I first learned to cook, I found that kneading bread and chopping vegetables contribute to a calm, meditative mind space—which I needed after the day's havoc.

Except at some point between sautéing fresh garlic and shredding cold beef, I lost focus and let my mind wander back to Xavier's rent-boy insult. That summer, Xavier somehow found his way to Chez Margot after hours, where he flirted with me incessantly all of August. Not knowing him, I was flattered. I said farewell one night:

> Me: I might not see you again. I'm off to hear music in San Francisco.
>
> Xavier: I'm going there this weekend for a film festival. Why don't you come with me?

He moved closer, inviting me to be his guest at that festival, which was previewing his documentary (behind the scenes at an L.A. production of *The Dresser*). I pleaded poverty (no lie there) and previous commitments. He implored me to be his guest. The film festival was covering his airfare, hotel, and meals, and would comp him for a guest. I'd be the plus-one, like on a wedding invitation.

After I agreed and showed up in San Francisco with him, I found that I had to rent a tux and buy new shoes, which cost more than a roundtrip economy ticket to the city. Before Xavier's invitation, I had planned to stay with my friend Michael and his partner, who'd feed me and let me crash like they do when I join them for Gay Freedom Day or other visits to the Bay Area.

It's likely I'm protesting too much when I insist that I did not seek or receive compensation for being left adrift in the modest crowds of Xavier's admirers, abandoned except for a few tortuous scenes where I played arm candy. But the emotional tone of that weekend went beyond boredom and incompatibility, and it provoked an outright quarrel when I split to meet friends to see the Blasters live at the Greek Theatre in Berkeley—my original reason for coming to the city. I had one issue in that argument: how can anyone be expected to miss a Blasters show, even if it means showing up in a tux?

We did not, I'm happy to say, sleep together. We fumbled in his hotel room, and I left after a quarrel about condoms. So I do not know from personal experience that Xavier isn't the greatest fuck. I just had preliminary evidence.

However, I remain satisfied with my response to Xavier's unwarranted insult. I also believe the girls remain happy with their response. When the *Sunday New York Times* included a piece on Xavier after he won a Tony for a soapy stage drama, Molly penciled, "Fuck you, Xavier" across the one-column story, using a #2 pencil. It prompted a warm feeling, the kind when you know that the people closest to you have your back. Even if they don't know exactly what's going on.

The Chaos kitchen was too warm—and had been since July. I'd opened all the windows but had to stop dinner prep a couple of times and wipe my face with a wet kerchief. When I added the onions to the hot oil in the wok, the lachrymatory agent released by the onions finally got to me, uniting with the irritation of the firethorn in my throat.

5: A Dating Game

"DINNER SMELLS BETTER THAN GREAT, boss. Fried rice, right?"

Howard, Ruby's afternoon-through-evening caretaker, pulled her special Blue Willow bowl from the cupboard. As usual, he wore blue orderly scrubs over his extra-tall extra-sized t-shirt and sweatpants. He wears scrubs, he says, to help Ruby feel she's being taken care of properly.

"Yes, with shredded beef from Sunday's roast." I hadn't dished up the rice yet, since no one else was there for dinner.

"So kids' style, huh? It's too bad that the Dahlia brainwashed kids into thinking fried rice is bland."

"I'm expecting the twins will bring several others to dinner." Kids in Ashland, including mine, had eaten too often at the Dahlia, the Chinese restaurant on Lithia Plaza, and they all think fried rice should have frozen peas and carrots.

"Too bad for me, boss. I like it when you load it up with garlic and ginger and your chili oil." Howard dished up Ruby's plate and began picking out the carrot cubes. I know she doesn't like them. Where had my head drifted that I hadn't already done that?

"Howard, you are again going beyond what the job calls for. Let me take care of that."

He held up his huge hand, stopping me. "It's not a problem, boss. And Ruby's watching a rerun of that *Gilligan's Island* movie, which I cannot abide. Can I add some chili oil from that little jar you keep? To mine, I mean, Ruby can't tolerate food that tastes like something."

While Howard sat at the kitchen table and gobbled his fried rice, I made a plate of cookies that Ruby likes and prepared a pitcher of lemonade. When Howard took dinner to Ruby's room, his booming voice carried down the hall.

"How you doing, sweetheart? Ready for dinner? It's yummy tonight, just the way you like it."

Howard and Mrs. Adams look after Ruby better than I do. Mrs. Adams says it's because they're trained to do it. Howard is adamant: *Hey, boss man, you do the cooking and go to work every day. Leave Ruby to us professionals.*

I wiped the kitchen table again, then set out a stack of plates for whoever showed up for dinner. I believe deeply in the Chaos House kitchen table, endeavoring to imitate my Hong Kong experience. Lately though, the adult boarders had been scarce. Becca only eats breakfast with us, then dines on crew food at the Festival. Stephen tends to eat at his café. Danielle, Ruby's nighttime caretaker, is a nursing student and seldom eats more than breakfast with us.

And the twins had yet to return from Medford.

This day had shaken things up in novel ways, and I didn't relish sitting alone at the dinner table. Fortunately, Valerie Ortega, the other second-floor boarder, almost always eats here. She rushed in right after Howard rejoined Ruby. She's always rushing. In the morning, she drops her four-year-old son Julio at daycare; later, she picks him up after her day as a Festival seamstress.

After Valerie reminded Julio to kick off his shoes at the door and then coaxed him into washing his hands, Becca came in. Without saying a word, she grabbed the keys to the cottages and ran out the door. Back in three minutes, she kicked off her shoes and called hello to Julio and Valerie. I got a hug.

"Wait till you see what I have to show you. Besides this." Becca waved a check for me to take from her. Then she handed Valerie a copy of *ArtForum.* "I brought this home, like I promised."

Valerie began thumbing through the magazine after she got Julio up to the table.

Having three people joining me at the dinner table lifted my raw mood. Before I served the bowl of fried rice on the table, I set down a small dish of plain rice for Julio. He eats only potatoes, pasta, or rice with butter at dinner. Every day at breakfast, he eats Cheerios and must pour the milk himself. I don't judge Julio for this. I had been a finicky eater before we lived in Hong Kong. For example, at the Specially Bad Eliot Family Christmas, Ruby barked at Wendy for letting the twins skip eating their vegetables; my sister wielded me as defense:

> *Little Ricky ate only toast and jam for months. You let him be a spectacularly picky eater while the rest of us had to clean our plates. So back off. Go bug Ricky. Look how skinny he is.*

"What do you say?" Valerie prompted her son.

"May I have butter please?" He looked up at me. I held out his special bunny plate with spoonfuls of soft butter. He grinned. "Thank you, Uncle Rik."

Valerie had fretted about what Julio should call me, but Julio's choice was a reasonable solution.

As I spooned butter onto Julio's rice, Stephen Garland rambled in. Julio stood on the bench. "Uncle Stephen, sit by me."

Stephen got Julio to scoot over and sat beside him, rubbing the kid's head, offering a high-five. He dished fried rice onto his own plate when the bowl was passed. "Ah, mild style. May I ask, is there chili oil?"

"*Oui, mon ami.* And may I say, I'm surprised to see you at this hour. But I'm glad." I rose to fetch the serving jar of hot oil.

Stephen shrugged. "We're training a new bartender. It was suggested that he'd be less nervous if I was gone for a bit."

He added considerable heat to his plate, then passed the jar over Julio's head to Valerie, who took some, then passed it across the table to Becca, who declined. I reached for the jar and poured chili oil on my rice.

"So good," Stephen said. He dished up more fried rice and more chili oil. The others hummed agreement. "You are the people's hero, Rik. Where will I get food like this if you go back to Hong Kong?"

Valerie said, "Maybe you can learn how Rik makes chili oil."

Stephen looked thoughtful. "I suppose. But truly, Rik, I'll miss you like a lost limb if you really do run off to Hong Kong."

Sweet. I felt it. So I didn't say: *I'm really leaving.*

"Where are the twins?" Becca said. "Wasn't orientation today? Why isn't the house full of kids guessing which teachers suck and which teachers give easy As?"

"The girls went shopping in Medford on your advice, Becca." I was nonchalant yet remained distracted about the twins' absence.

Stephen began telling us about Eddie, his new bartender, and Becca asked if Chez Margot had enough business once tourist season slowed to require new staff, and…

And I lost track of the story, still fretting that the twins hadn't at least called. I forced my attention to Stephen, like a good friend should. Stephen was the first friend I made in Ashland. He'd arrived about when I did, but he was fresh out of the army (stationed safely in Germany) and newly flush with family money. He bought a greasy spoon on Main Street that had been there even before my grandfather began stalking Vladimir Nabokov.

Stephen hired me when I answered his ad in the *Daily Tidings* for help to gut the old coffeeshop. I'm not so good with a sledgehammer, but I'm great with a pry bar. Stephen and I became good friends while smashing old plaster and discarding ducts, walls, and ceilings imbued with an unspeakable amount of smokey grease. We did that hippie thing, calling each other brother, my-family-is-your-family. Though I can't say that his (former) wife was ever happy to see me when I took Stephen hiking in the hills on Sunday mornings.

"I feel pretty mellow after that meal." Stephen finished his second helping. "If you could cook French food, I'd hire you, Rik."

"Chez Margot's food is outside my skill range."

"It feels good tonight, everyone eating together," Valerie said. "We've been too busy all summer."

We weren't all together. The twins were missing.

When my friends pushed back their empty plates, I swooped down to move dishes to the sink. We had brownies with whipped cream for dessert. Julio wanted only whipped cream. As expected.

"Becca, what did you bring for Rik?" Valerie asked. "I hope it's good. He's so solemn, even after fried rice and brownies."

"He looks fine to me," Stephen said. He tapped a wiggling Julio on the noggin. "I-spy-with-my-little-eye...a cat." He started the game we play to keep Julio at the table longer than the five minutes it takes him to eat seven bites of white starch.

"I *am* fine," I said softly, not wanting their attention.

"There!" Julio shouted, drawing everyone's attention, thank the Immortals. He pointed to the Felix the Cat clock over the kitchen sink, which I'd salvaged from that greasy spoon. Its swiveling eyes and twitching tail ticked at the same beat as my edginess over the twins' absence.

Becca said, "I brought the publicity sheets for Rik's new guests." She spread them out on the table. "Let's play *The Dating Game* to choose a date for Rik. I already have a favorite."

She nudged a sheet my way, which pushed Jade's sheet to the floor. I bent to retrieve it, thoughts ricocheting like pinballs.

"This is the actor, isn't it?" Valerie had her finger on the sheet Becca shoved at me. "I met him in the break room. He seems nice."

"Yes," Becca said. "We need to talk Rik into dating him."

"I don't date."

"Leave Rik alone," Stephen said. "Do either of you know what he wants? Women should never try to set men up."

"Thank you, *mon ami*," I said.

"We'll let Julio choose." He set the PR sheets in front of the boy. "Which one should be Uncle Rik's special friend?"

"See?" Becca tapped my hand. "We all want to help."

"Expect to be evicted tomorrow." I folded my arms.

She laughed. "Oh, Rik! You know I'm teasing."

Valerie glanced between us, smiling hesitantly. "But if he doesn't like it..."

"It's okay," I said. "At least Becca didn't put me on the street with a For Sale sign."

Stephen straightened the sheets while Julio studied them. Julio pushed Xavier's picture away. "He's bad. Like Oscar."

"Who's that?" Stephen frowned with concern. "Is someone being bad to you?"

"Oscar on *Sesame Street?*" Valerie asked. Julio nodded.

Good job, Julio.

Then Stephen lifted Julio and scooted down the bench, switching places so that he sat beside Valerie. He stroked her hand. Ah, that's why Stephen was smiling on the Chez Margot back steps this morning. I don't know what's going on in my own house.

"Okay, Julio. What about this guy?" Stephen pointed to the one who must be the actor I hadn't met yet.

Julio looked up at Stephen. "Is he fun to play with, like Ken? Do girls get mad if you play with him?"

"Is Ken at your school?" Stephen asked.

Julio nodded. "We have four now, so we don't fight. But the girls still get mad."

"Four Kens?" Stephen looked puzzled.

"I think," Valerie said, "he means four Ken dolls."

"We're done now, right?" I gave Becca a stern look. "Time to do the dishes."

Julio had the third sheet, the one with Jade's picture. "He's nice. But he's my friend, not Uncle Rik's."

"How do you know him?" Stephen asked.

"He's the car man."

"Like *Herbie the Love Bug?*" his mother asked.

"No, the big yellow car." Julio pointed out to the street, where Jade's crummy had been parked. "This morning I said hello and he said, 'Morning, cowboy,' and he made me promise to have a good day." He turned to me. "Did he call *you* a cowboy, Uncle Rik?" When I shook my head, he said, "See? *I'm* the cowboy and *I'm* his friend."

"Like I told you," Stephen pushed the papers over to Becca, "you have no idea what men want." Then, may the Immortals bless him, he tapped Julio and said, "I spy something yellow."

Julio shifted to look around, then pointed to the kitchen wall. "Telephone!"

I was waiting for it to ring, not just to get out of an awkward dinner conversation, but for the twins to say where they were. It's our deal. Rik's Rules:

> Be free. But call if you're late.
> Keep a dime in your pocket to call.
> Keep five dollars in your shoe in case you miss the bus.

I ask little in my modified version of familial duty, besides household chores, basic respect, and kindness for each other.

The phone rang. I jumped to answer it.

But it was the tennis coach, asking how she'd lost two good team members. I explained that the girls chose the civic arts project. "They might be back for tennis in the spring," I said. Then I had to say no, she couldn't talk with them because they weren't home.

It was an awkward phone call, but it ended *The Dating Game*. No contestants won. People rose for their night's business.

Stephen ruffled Julio's hair, said, "Good night, cowboy," and headed back to his café.

Valerie said, "Time for a bath and books, Julio." When she left, she passed me that copy of *ArtForum.*

Becca said she had a meeting at the Festival, but when she was putting on her shoes by the door, she said, "I'm sorry we teased you, Rik. I honestly believed you'd think it funny."

"No harm. Julio saved me."

"What's going on with you? Not to be nosy—"

"Except you are."

"Please think of it as caring. Tonight, you are…not happy."

"The twins said they'd be back in time for supper."

"However, they aren't ten years old."

"Still, it is what's bothering me."

"And that's why you're pale under your summer tan? You looked your usual self this morning. Except extra dusty."

"What could you see? I had a bandana over my face."

"Still…"

"Can I tell you about it another time, Becca?"

"Good idea. I'm late." At last, she gave up plaguing me and rushed out.

Alone at the table, I thumbed through *ArtForum,* fearing I'd get another dose of Xavier Torres and be dragged back into all that irritation. But it was the edition that described Jade Solberg's artwork in Barcelona, Istanbul, and Paris, focusing on his ceramic mural in Paris, *The Temptation of Paris,* with the apple in real gold, commissioned by a rich dude who owned the building. The twist: Jade had gotten arrested while working on it because the rich dude's assistants failed to inform the local police about the permit for street closure. Jade was released after just two hours in jail, but he received enough press attention that the contretemps and the resulting video became a feature in *ArtForum.*

The creation of Jade's Paris mural had been documented by an auteur director who sought to simulate 1930s Jean Renoir, but it more strongly resembled the havoc in *A Hard Day's Night.* Just the kind of chaos Jade attracted in grad school. The video is only seven minutes long and dubbed with music by the Cocteau Twins attempting medieval chants.

I'd been at the film festival when that video premiered in San Francisco. With Xavier-freaking-Torment. I'd left when the video ended, before they brought Jade Solberg on stage for an ask-the-artist session. Xavier wanted to meet the artist in the after-party, but I'd reached my limit and wanted to see the Blasters instead. I didn't tell Xavier that I knew the artist, that I'd worked on large-scale projects with him in grad school. I'm no longer interested in that world of ultra-ambitious artistes.

However, that video must be why kids are thrilled that Jade Solberg is here in Ashland.

While I cleaned the kitchen, cooler evening air wafted down from the Watershed. I moved through the first floor, closing several windows that provide Ashland-style air conditioning. The sound of guests moving into the cottages drifted in the windows.

Strangely, after spending the day in a bitchy mood, I found those sounds comforting. It meant I had paying guests. Also, it filled the silence beyond the ticking of Felix the Clock. Eight. Eight fifteen. Eight thirty. I couldn't make up my mind what number on the clock might indicate that it was time to worry.

6: A New Tenant

TUESDAY NIGHT, THE FIRST STARS flickered in the darkening sky when the twins returned on the last bus from Medford. I'd taught myself before now to be happy to see the girls when they're tardy, rather than being ticked off. There's nothing to be gained with teenagers if you merely act in the way they expect you will. I prepared to be more upbeat than I felt.

They came in the front door with their cousin Alex trailing behind, dragging a guitar, a skateboard, and a stuffed-to-bursting army surplus duffle. He'd been here all summer, so he knew to kick off his shoes at the door.

"Hello, Uncle Rik." Head bent, he mumbled a greeting.

The boy is taller than me and stocky like Christopher had been, but Alex's face is round like his mother's. His blond hair is always tousled, and, unlike Christopher, Alex was born smiling; his current apprehensive expression was foreboding. I didn't need three graduate classes in childhood development to recognize a kid in crisis. Likely, Alex would be staying a while.

"Hi, Alex. You're in luck. The basement studio isn't rented yet. But an artist from the Festival rented the garage, so you can't rehearse there."

"But it's okay to crash in the basement?" Alex looked heartbreakingly hopeful.

When he fills out the frame he inherited from Christopher, he'll be a good-sized guy. But unlike Christopher, Alex is timid. He'd undertaken a brave act, leaving home, riding BART to the airport, and flying here alone. All the signs of an emergency.

"Yes, Alex. Of course. For as long as you want. But first, call your mother."

"I left her a note."

"Call to say you got here safely."

The girls had retreated to the breakfast nook, having more practice than Alex at reading my reaction to whatever they'd lobbed my way. For my part, I'd gotten good during their freshman year at withholding advance notice of my thoughts when we're at odds with each other.

Alex made the call, speaking only two sentences before holding out the phone. "She wants to talk to you, Uncle Rik."

Our household phone hangs on the wall in the kitchen. It's yellow, princess style, with a fifteen-foot coiled cord that allows pacing while talking. I have no memory of how a yellow princess phone came to be here. Thrift store? Garage sale? It's the wrong shade against the pale lemon yellow I painted the kitchen walls.

"Hello, Claudia. I hope you're well."

"You did this." Claudia has a deep voice, from genetics as well as cigarettes. The tenor made her words more threatening than panicked, though I guessed the force came from agitation. Panic is what I'd feel if my kids disappeared.

"I am innocent of Alex's flight," I said, "and as surprised as you. If he wanted to stay here, he could have asked last week instead of getting on the Greyhound."

"You turned my son gay." This was unexpected. "You and the depraved inmates at Chaos House."

"Claudia, people are born that way. I'm not sure he is, just on your say-so."

I had only noticed over the summer that Alex had spent 90 percent of every day playing music in the garage. And every night hanging out with the twins and their friends in upper Lithia Park. I didn't notice anything about his sexuality.

Claudia's voice dropped a note lower. "Send Alex home. Put him on a plane tomorrow."

"Let me talk with him, Claudia. I'll call you back."

I hung up without waiting for her answer.

Alex said, "Don't make me go back." Quietly, not defiantly. "She yells at me day and night, and she locked up my guitar. She says I have to go to military school."

"Claudia won't do that."

"She already wrote a check for fall quarter. Says it has to be military school since I refused to go to conversion therapy at a church camp in Redding. Which is heinous."

I said, "But Claudia is an atheist," which wasn't to the point.

All three kids watched me, solemn faced, as if waiting for me to pass judgment. Alex was holding his breath.

Hence, I called Claudia back in less than two minutes.

"Alex is fine here. He'll start school tomorrow. Can you please send his vaccination card and school records?"

That had been the big hang-up at school when I first had charge of the girls. But Alex waved his hand for attention. "I have my vax card with me."

Claudia growled. "Alex cannot live in that circus you keep. He's too impressionable. Now he's come home thinking he's gay."

I said, "Another reason, Claudia, why he should not go to military school."

"I know what's best for my son."

"Not if you send him to a military school."

"I want him to be safe while I'm in Europe for six weeks. Military school is the best option."

"Do you know what happens in virtually every boys-only boarding school?" I'd thought she was a sophisticated, cosmopolitan person. Where had all this come from?

"Send him home, Rik."

"Not if you're plaguing him. My mother plagued Christopher, so he ran away to college, got married, and then joined the army. Don't do things that will destroy your bond with him."

Was it emotional blackmail to mention my brother in this call? Who cares. I had my eye on the dejected, worried Alex.

"Is that your excuse, Rik? Your mother?" Claudia pitched her cigarette voice like nails on a chalkboard.

"My mother nagged a hole in my soul, but she didn't make me gay. Give Alex time to find his way. He's safe here."

"You have no right to meddle, Rik. Put him on a plane and send him home."

"I won't do that. If you want Alex home, come and get him."

"I have to be in Europe in two days. I can't fetch him."

"Then you can't manage his school and other needs, can you, Claudia? Since you'll be gone, he should stay here."

"He needs to be in the right environment, so—"

"So you can scream at him? Or send him to the wrong school? Or take away his music—which is essential to him?"

"I know what's best for him." She kept repeating her chorus. "Put him on a plane tomorrow."

I took a breath. "You're proving you don't know him. Alex is afraid to fly. Coming here was the bravest thing he's ever done."

"I certainly do know my son." She took a huge breath, so I thought she'd say more. But she'd just lit a cigarette.

"But you aren't respecting him. And I will do everything possible to protect him from being tortured for who he is. Alex shall not endure what I did."

She breathed so hard in my ear, it felt like the heat might come through the wire and set my hair on fire.

"Claudia, I promise he won't become a drug-addled rentboy by Thanksgiving. Or even by Christmas."

"You can't promise that. You seldom behave like a supervising adult with those girls. They've become hellions."

"What do you perceive as hellion-like in their behavior? They are kind, self-directed, and on the honor roll." Annoyance crowded out my other feelings. "Childhood development was part of my last master's degree, Claudia. I prefer guidance to dictatorial supervision, with demonstrable benefits for the twins."

She sucked air through her teeth. "That reminds me, Rik. Grandfather Eliot's Patek Philippe watch? It should have come to Christopher. Tradition demands that you give it to Alex."

What, as my grandfather often said, in tarnation?

"Okay. I'm sure he'll appreciate that, Claudia. Until you come back from Europe, Alex stays with me. And if he wants to, he can wear a ten-thousand-dollar watch to school every day."

"We aren't done, Rik Eliot. You will hear from my attorney. Whom I will instruct to take immediate action." She hung up, but at least didn't slam the receiver into the phone's cradle.

No, he won't wear it. He's freakin' sixteen and wears a Swatch watch. Plus, I need to keep my grandfather's watch to pawn when I'm strapped for cash.

—

When I hung up, Alex wanted to smile but wasn't yet able to.

"I can stay?"

I nodded, keeping quiet about my sure knowledge: whenever my adult relatives start talking about inheritances or money, they are about to fly off into cloud cuckoo land.

Molly, however, darted a finger at me, pretending to scold. "Rent-boy? How can you talk like that, Uncle Rik? It's so irresponsible of you."

Ramona joined in the faux chastisement. "Uncle Rik, you're supposed to be the adult here. You probably gave Aunt Claudia a heart attack."

"Not like the heart attack I gave Ruby when I..."

The three kids gawped at me, waiting for my next words. I had that feeling, which a lover once described as left over from ninth grade, when you accidentally expose who you are. Or when you inadvertently tell children—well, they're almost adults—what their grandmother had done to her offspring, back before rapidly advancing dementia made her forget.

"There's leftover fried rice in the fridge," I said. "Heat it up in the frying pan. Clean up when you're done, then get to bed. Come morning, I will neither nag you to be on time nor write tardy excuses. I am not an alarm clock."

"We won't even ask for a ride to school," Molly said.

"I can't give you one anyway." I had other plans for early morning. "I'll be at school at eight-thirty to get Alex registered. Make your lunches tonight. There's cheese, eggs, and bread. Else, eat in the cafeteria. Our free-lunch approval lasts until Friday." I'd better apply for this year while getting Alex registered. "Alex, if you don't want a sack lunch, the cafeteria costs seventy-five cents, plus a nickel for milk."

"Only babies drink milk," Alex said.

How I understood his response: he's shell-shocked.

Ramona said, "Can you register Alex when you aren't his guardian? Every year, you have to prove you're our guardian."

"That's only because," Molly said, "there's a new guidance counselor every year, who mistakes Uncle Rik for a student."

I said, "Claudia sent a medical consent form last summer in case Alex's asthma acted up. That'll do until we figure it out."

Alex's asthma hadn't acted up all summer, as I'd reassured Claudia weekly. There'd been no wheezing; I didn't say there'd been no clove cigarettes. Because that would be a lie.

Ramona said, "Uncle Rik, be chill. Don't show up at school like you're Alex's bodyguard."

"Lots of kids met Alex this summer," Molly said. "Quinn can introduce him to the other kids."

"Yeah, Quinn will vouch for me," Alex said.

Quinn? Curiosity got the better of me.

I asked, "Alex, how did you get crosswise with Claudia? Did she overhear something? Or did you *tell* Claudia you're gay?"

That might be the most honest tack, but it hadn't worked for me when Ruby learned of my first crush.

Alex said, "I was talking to Quinn on the phone. Just before I hung up, I said, 'I love you too, man. Miss you.' Then I got the Spanish Inquisition."

He stood there, as forlorn as any human might be, looking like he very much needed a hug. I squeezed his shoulder.

"Eat something, Alex. At least grab a snack."

He nodded. "Okay. Can I call Quinn to tell him I'm here?"

Quinn lived over on B Street, Ashland's modest version of the other side of the tracks. He'd also spent the summer playing music in my garage. Would Quinn's mother be calling me too?

Someone I once loved insisted: *A simple crush can wreak havoc even before it becomes a broken heart.* That memory rattled around, making it hard to gather my thoughts. Had there been signs over the summer of crushes and broken hearts among these kids? No, there'd been no sign of either longing or actual romance. They'd all been too busy teaching Alex how to be cool.

> Ramona: Isn't there anybody who's cool in your school?
>
> Molly: It's Aunt Claudia's fault, making you go to the kind of school where you have to wear a uniform.
>
> Alex: Only a tie, white shirt, and chinos.
>
> Quinn: Ew!
>
> Me: Chinos are a legacy of the Spanish-American War. The U.S. bought the fabric from China. Hence, chinos.
>
> Molly: No true rebel wears the legacy of U.S. imperialism. So sad.

Alex had arrived at our house in June not knowing how to be a teenager, and so spent the summer learning to paint hooded sweatshirts and rip t-shirts in artful ways, and smoking clove cigarettes with the twins' friends in upper Lithia Park. Skateboards were involved, though Ashland has too few sidewalks and too many potholed streets. And, as my Disputatious Neighbor pointed out, my garage often held more people than just a pair of practicing musicians.

I could identify with Alex's situation. I was an outsider at the English school I attended in Hong Kong, where I had one real friend. Then I'd gone from tenth grade to being a freshman in a UW dorm, where math students from Taiwan and Hong Kong wore slide rules in leather holsters on their belts, so I soon had enough friends to stop feeling homesick for Hong Kong. I spent my undergrad years as a pure, unadulterated geek.

"It's nine thirty," I said. That's the hour at which, by tradition, I claim the rest of the night for myself. "Finish up in the kitchen. Then say goodnight to Ruby if she's awake."

"What if—" Molly began.

"I know she won't recognize you," I said. Ruby hadn't recognized me since 1978; life had gotten better since then. "It's a human kindness. You might want such kindness in sixty years."

After they finished in the kitchen, Alex headed downstairs. I stopped the girls before they escaped to their room.

Ramona held up her hands, a defensive motion. "I know, we should have called at dinner time. We made you worry."

"No. I mean, yes, you should have called. But I want to say I'm proud of what you did for Alex, getting him here safely."

Molly grimaced as if still hesitant. "You aren't mad that we helped him run away?"

"No, because you saw this as a special case." I couldn't make it past her folded arms to hug her, so I just said, "You did good. I'm proud of you both."

7: Immortals Hidden on Earth

WHEN I WENT UPSTAIRS TO my study, I forgot to make my evening tea while worrying about the scope of "sixty years." Ruby was diagnosed in 1975 with early-onset dementia, but the signs—the drastic personality change—began when she was forty-five. I'm thirty-three. Then, if it's hereditary, do I have only twelve good years ahead? Not forty? Certainly not sixty. No use fretting.

For the next four months, all I can worry about is getting my dissertation past my advisory committee.

Plus, I have the new burden of worrying about Alex.

No. Alex is not a burden.

Chaos House is sheltering one more resident who seeks to feel safe. I already know how much it costs to feed a sixteen-year-old boy. Would Claudia get over her ridiculous panic and send money for his food and school needs?

It hurts my well-hidden soul that Claudia is being horrible to her son. I'm likely the only one Alex knows who can help sort this out. And I'll need help from a lawyer to succeed.

Upstairs, I put the Eurythmics' *Sweet Dreams (Are Made of This)* on the tape player. I slipped into the robe I wear while writing. The one I wear in summer is thin red silk. When it gets cold, I wear one my friend Kai sent me, double layers of black silk. Secretly, I'm posing as a T'ang scholar.

This is my closeted self in this town, being a scholar. Few friends here know me this way, not even Becca. She knows I retreat at night to write my dissertation, but not that I become my truest self while deep in this work.

Alas, no tea. That drama with the kids had interrupted my evening ritual. Yet I wasn't going to get dressed and wander back down through the whole house in pursuit of lapsang souchong and hot water. I focused on the work, determined not to dwell on the hornets' nest Claudia knocked loose or the chaos likely to be unleashed by Xavier Torres and his entourage.

What I intended for the night's work was to validate each printed page of my current draft so I could submit it to my committee for approval. That is the penultimate step on the tortuous road to finishing my PhD.

My dissertation advisor claims that my translation challenges stem from how I learned Chinese—from the dialect spoken where I lived in Hong Kong. When we moved there (when my mother loved me), Ruby enjoyed having servants plus tutors for her children, which was why I learned to read and write Cantonese at a young age. I learned Mandarin at university, too late in life.

Yue Chinese is what Western scholars call the dialect group that includes Cantonese. My dissertation discusses the peculiarities of Written Cantonese and Hong Kong dialects and the related challenges for English translation. That material has been revised, reviewed, and edited thoroughly. I no longer revisit those pages, but I did publish them as a monograph with my advisor.

My language skills are due to my math tutor, Chan-suk, and his son, Kai. My friend's name, Chan Kai Xiang, means rich, literate, and victorious. People at school could pronounce his Chinese name, so his English name is just Kai Chan—though every year on the first day of school, he had to say, "It's Kai like high, not kay." Kai and I began in the same grade, born the same year. After math tutelage and homework, he and I read Chinese comics and cheap novels while Chan-suk corrected papers. After our study session, we were free until six o'clock, since my mother preserved her writing time until evening and then wanted the hour before dinner with my father. If he came home.

Those three hours after our studies—plus every Saturday afternoon—Kai and I did what boys do. Me being an awkward math boy, I had only Kai as a friend. We were both rotten at team sports, but played a modified version of jianzi, which is like hacky sack and has been played across the ages everywhere, even among the Immortals. On rainy days, we watched TV, alternating between programs in Cantonese, where Kai translated dialog, and English programs, where I helped him with nuances. On Saturdays, we went to the movies, preferring wuxia, the ancient martial hero stories, which are the equivalent of American westerns. Later, we liked Hong Kong and Taiwanese fight movies, the kind with subtitles in four languages.

We also knew the best shops for comics and illustrated magazines. We advanced to kung fu magazines before Bruce Lee made kung fu popular in the West. I didn't see manga until my family returned to the States, because all of Hong Kong still resented the Japanese. When I returned to the U.S., Kai often sent me comics and pirated books and, after cassette tapes became available, bootleg copies of fight movie soundtracks.

To conclude this digression, I learned written and spoken Cantonese from comics, movies, and the streets of Hong Kong, including neighborhoods where we were not supposed to go. Kai and I read the equivalent of dime novels meant for youth and untutored readers: ghost stories; wandering adventurers (which Kai and I longed to be); heroic tales from feudal eras when one dynasty fell and another struggled to rise.

Hence, I began my Chinese Literature academic career with Cantonese learned solely from popular culture. My PhD dissertation does not feature lofty translations of poetry and Daoist or Confucian texts. My work focuses on the last fifty years of popular culture in Hong Kong. When I began, no one else was doing anything similar in U.S. universities, so I had that valuable scholar's prize, a novel topic.

My work that Tuesday night was straightforward: gather my chapters, check the order and page numbering, and ensure the entire manuscript was ready to be photocopied the next day. Then I'd mail it to my advisor and Chan-suk.

This was the third draft I'd prepared on my Eagle PC, a cast-off from Claudia, whose published-writer budget allows a new computer and printer every year. An IBM Correcting Selectric had supported my first several drafts. I'd obtained daisywheels for the printer through Chan-suk and got the knack of entering accented characters. The pages now require few manual emendations. At my advisor's request, I added a synopsis of my dissertation topic. I can appreciate that over eight years of drafts, he needed a precis to remind him what I've been doing.

This night I was taking a monumental step closer to the goal for the next part of my life, when I'd become a Wandering Scholar, free of endless chopping wood and carrying water to keep people alive who aren't yet old enough to do it for themselves. Plus one who'd never again be able to care for herself.

I cannot claim I am at all like a scholar in the Western Zhou era, collecting songs and poems for the emperor to know what the common people were thinking. That scholar's collection is still read in *Shi-Jing,* often called the *Book of Songs* in English. Children learn to chant four-character sayings from the collected poetry. For my scholarly purposes, I debate whether the use of a snatch from a modern Cantonese story or song captures the ancients' meaning. Or do the words in Cantonese popular media represent a twentieth-century snark on a commonplace saying?

I'd switched majors after finishing my math master's, yet I retained a mathematician's inability to read ancient poetry as anything more than music and rhythm. More than a couple of scholars in my department are transported by the mystical powers of Li Po and Lao Tzu to an ancient world where people move like dancers through a divine landscape.

I first heard fragments of Li Po shouted by kids quoting lines from fight movies. I didn't know it was poetry until Kai and I were calling lines to each other, imitating wuxia fighters. Chan-suk said he was pleased to see us take an interest in classical literature: *They teach Shakespeare at our school but don't spend time with Lao Tzu or Li Po. It's good you found it on your own.*

Kai and I read the texts Chan-suk showed us and, as know-it-alls, cited literary sources when other kids chanted rhymes from movies. Then we wondered why our classmates always wanted to beat us up. The Heavens know I was the little ass-muncher who started it. Kai just stuck beside me because he'd be censured by his father if he let me get beaten on the street.

In the closet that I'd turned into an office on the third floor of Chaos House, no one can beat me up—except, of course, my dissertation committee. May the Heavenly Immortals open their hearts to this scholar's modest submission.

After I packed my validated manuscript in a stationery box, ready to be copied and mailed in the morning, I wanted a reward. Eight years' travail was wrapped in that box. I went downstairs, which meant dressing again in jeans and a t-shirt. The brownies were all gone.

If I wanted a late-night reward for eight years' work, I'd have to leave the house.

8: The Ones Who Almost Know Me

AT ELEVEN O'CLOCK, WHEN I WALKED up to Chez Margot, I fell to pondering the conversation I needed to have with Alex. I'd start by relating what I learned from furtively kissing Kai in Hong Kong. And then I'd repeat what someone I once loved said: *Before you make a move, strive to know how the person you want to kiss feels about it. Best way to avoid heartache.*

Heavenly Immortals! Was Alex like Kai during my last week in Hong Kong? Did a naïve boy like teenage Rik kiss him? I'll only find out if Alex tells me.

I shivered, but it wasn't because the air cools quickly after sunset in September, rushing down the narrow valleys from the mountain top. I'd sprung loose unhelpful memories of ancient crushes where my striving to know did not avoid heartache. Yet the night air smelled sweet, felt gently caressing. Most of downtown had locked its doors and doused its lights. Half of a long block up Main Street from Lithia Fountain, Chez Margot's wood-clad front glowed warmly amid the blocky stone-faced stores surrounding it.

The café's front transom windows hung open. Warm, sultry odors of butter and garlic wafted out along with the sanitizer used to clean tables and the lemon-oil polish used on the bar. Stephen had transformed this space with chandeliers, honey-colored wainscoting and millwork, and checkered tile floor, creating the inviting feel of a traditional French bistro. Though I only know French bistros from post-WWII movies.

While Stephen created this café scene, with just twelve tables and an elegant bar, he gave me badly needed work. Also, he quickly made new friends, dragging me along. These new friends filled the loneliness that almost drowned me when I'd washed ashore here.

Tuesday night, when I opened the café's heavy carved door, people turned from the bar and called out a greeting or waved. A physical sensation washed over me, like being borne aloft by a warm ocean wave. These are the people I most trust in this town.

The usuals were all there except Inez, off in Italy, and Becca, still at Festival meetings. These friends had all spent time living at Chaos House, except for Nick Lawrence, the beefy jock among them, who is also my attorney.

Gaye Verlaine, the after-midnight DJ on the college radio station, now lives in a band house on Mountain Avenue, where she's the band's sound engineer.

Frankie Weiss, manager of the college printshop, lived in my house after the women's collective on Oak Street turned vegetarian. It was not the diet but the non-consensus decision that drove her out. (She's a red diaper baby.) She now lives in a consensus-driven household on Iowa Street.

Kevin Emery, the regular bartender, came to town with a lover who soon became an ex, so he lived at my house for a couple of years. He's a stranded liberal arts scholar like me and as happy to be a half-time bartender as I am to be a substitute teacher. Unlike me, Kevin still has long hair left over from grad school, tied back at work in a samurai headband.

When I stopped beside Nick at the service bay, the new bartender carded me.

"Sure." I fished my wallet from my jeans pocket. "I'm Rik Eliot. You must be Eddie."

Kevin waved away my ID.

"Don't card Rik. He's a friend of the house. Also, his looks are deceiving. He's old enough to be your father."

Gaye gasped. "Eddie's mother assaulted Rik when he was ten?" She has a sing-song Minnesota accent but looks like she came from Prince's side of Minneapolis, with chopped black hair and a narrow frame.

"In Oregon," Nick said, "you get jail for interfering with a minor. Poor Eddie, growing up without a mother." Nick held a schooner of Oly. He went to a midwestern law school where they drank Pabst and Rolling Rock, and then adopted Olympia beer after he moved to Ashland.

"Consider how traumatic it was for Rik," Frankie said.

I gave Eddie a grimacing smile. "They're good people."

"He's been warned about the afterhours circus." Kevin picked a glass from the shelf in front of the mirror, handing it to Eddie. "Give Rik an Old-Fashioned with a half shot of E&J brandy. Trust me, he can't drink more and cannot appreciate better liquor."

Gaye motioned me over. "I brought back a present for you from San Francisco, Rik. It's California morels plus imported Matsutake and lion's mane mushrooms. And wonton wrappers, the kind you like."

"Wow! How kind of you, Gaye. Thank you."

"No, it's you I'm thanking. You did a fantastic job with the electrical in the band house studio. Makes life better."

"Glad it worked. I'll cook Sichuan mushrooms one night soon. Let me know when you're free."

"Soon. I will miss such fare when you run off to Hong Kong. Which I wish you wouldn't do, my friend." Gaye dropped her voice as she handed me a bulging paper bag. She glanced at the front door again, looking wistful. "Have you seen Becca?"

"She was at dinner. But you know Becca. A short workday is twelve hours."

"They don't pay what she's worth." Gaye scowled. "She promised to talk with me about a sound project but never has time. Because they suck every waking hour out of her."

That tone in her voice held a note of more than just *Becca's late.* Do I ask what's going on? No, I hate it when Becca pries into my business. Best wait till someone tells me.

I said, "If you can figure out what night Becca is free, that's when we'll have spicy mushrooms."

"Will do. Can I play a request for you tonight? What do you want to hear?"

"'Straight to Hell,' please. This has been quite a day."

"Golden oldies from the Clash?" She gave me a wry look. "Doncha know, Rik, that song isn't about personal melancholy?"

"I did read that somewhere."

I'm not melancholy, just distracted after a chaotic day.

Stephen came in from the kitchen. He leaned on the bar near the serving station, making Eddie nervous. Stephen didn't notice.

"Did the twins get home on time?" he asked. "Must have, or else you'd be out beating the bushes."

"They went to fetch their cousin at the airport. Looks like I have another boarder, maybe for the school year."

"That's good news," Stephen said. "Julio likes Alex."

When had Sad Serge become Julio's champion? Stephen hadn't turned happy only because he and Valerie both live in Chaos House. No matter. I'm happy that he's happy after a rough year.

"Alex is your nephew?" Gaye asked. "That boy who played guitar in the garage all summer? He's a decent musician."

"Need my help again, Rik?" Nick asked. He'd saved me years before when I had to quickly become guardian for parts of my family that needed guarding.

"Most likely," I said. Definitely. "But I can pay you." Last time he'd served as my lawyer, I'd remodeled the bungalow on

Siskiyou Boulevard that he uses as his office. There was no way then that I'd have money for a lawyer. This time...maybe?

"Naw." Nick shook his head, spilling drops of his Oly. "I need new windows on the south side of my office. Let's swap." He lowered his voice. "Because doing family law for you is like wading in tar. Not worth the money." He slapped me on the back, like jocks do, even when they have a law degree and a license to practice law in Oregon. "Call me tomorrow."

After I got my drink, Frankie motioned for me to sit by her.

Kevin was pouring Frankie a shot of Jack Daniels. He asked, "Softball season over? Did I miss the last game?"

"Yeah, too many players have kids in school," she said. "Wrecks things for kid-free adults." Frankie plays second base on the top women's softball team in Jackson County. She's only five-one but has great peripheral vision and a good arm.

She once again pointed to the tall stool at her side. "Have you heard from Inez yet?"

"Not since I took her to the airport Saturday morning. But she left a book I'm supposed to give you." I took the indicated seat. "I'll bring it tomorrow when I show up at your printshop. I'll be on my knees, begging you once more."

"Another dissertation draft to copy?" She smiled, which makes her eyes crinkle at the corners. "Be at the printshop by noon or you'll have to wait till Thursday. We have a big print project scheduled for tomorrow afternoon."

"Not another draft," I said. "The final draft."

Frankie whooped, slamming her open hand on the bar. The others glanced our way, curious.

She held my hand aloft. "I'm buying this man's drink tonight. It's the end of an era. And I am proud to have contributed to his great scholarship." She rose, took a bow, still holding my arm. "I faithfully sneaked in-kind support from the college printshop for each draft. Now Rik has finished his dissertation. Raise your glasses."

Everyone clinked with whomever was closest. People shuffled by until everyone, even Kevin, clinked my glass. He had a glass of Perrier behind the bar and poured another for Eddie, pushing him into a second round of toasts.

"Here's to making the impossible manifest." Kevin toasted me. He knows exactly how much work a dissertation takes.

My face burned because I'm shy about attention. But by the time people set their drinks on the highly polished bar, I felt warm and full, this being the reward I'd really wanted. With people who matter to me.

While clearing away emptied glasses, Kevin said, "Be aware, though. Rik still has to defend his dissertation. The millstone remains around his neck." He and I nodded to each other. Our shared reality: all but dissertation; a PhD so close, yet just out of reach. "So we have a couple more chances for toasts. Champagne next time."

Gaye said, "Forgive me, Rik, but tell me again what your dissertation is about."

Frankie said, "'Pair-bonded Friends in Cantonese Pop Culture.' I've seen that mammoth masterpiece dropping from the big copier a half-dozen times."

She fractured the title, but a correction would be meaningless. As it was, Gaye's eyes glazed over, her lips parted as if incapable of speech. The reaction I'm used to when people ask.

Stephen repeated what people always ask next. "But what's it *about?* Exactly?"

"Brother-like bonding in Chinese adventure stories. In both medieval and modern times."

"Like brothers-in-arms war stories?" Stephen asked.

"While fighting monsters or political enemies," I said.

"Is pair-bonding like finding a soulmate?" Gaye asked.

"Sort of." That's the usual place people jump to next.

Kevin said, "Sounds gay."

I nodded. "Maybe?"

But Kevin knows. He's read and commented on three different drafts of my dissertation. A true sign of friendship.

After a pause, Stephen said, "I believed that the first person I made love to must be my soulmate. Did you feel that?" He gestured, asking everyone.

Feeling exposed by the question, I stepped back, hiding behind Frankie. And why do people start thinking about who they'd slept with whenever the word "soulmate" is uttered?

"Yes, definitely," Nick said. "But I was thirteen, and she was seventeen. I was too young to have a clue."

"Thirteen?" I croaked. "I can't imagine."

Frankie said, "My brother was twelve, and the girl was fourteen. She claimed they were soulmates all summer. He didn't agree. I've never believed in that soulmate nonsense."

Though chronically honest, Frankie looked down when she said that. So I don't believe her.

Gaye sighed. "At band camp after high school, I felt sure the camp's bad boy was my soulmate. Later, I found lots of other people to fall in love with." She sipped her Perrier. "But then, it was a church camp, where bad boys aren't very bad. And life-long relationships are strongly encouraged, though you aren't supposed to do the sweet thing beforehand. I've always wondered how you could know without trying first."

We had gotten a long way from the notion of pair-bonding. The more my personal discomfort grew, the more people continued to share too much information. My friends had turned solemn and weren't even teasing each other.

"I had such a notion of bonding once," Kevin said. "For a few moments, I wanted to believe we were soulmates. But I was wrong. What about you, Rik?"

I shrugged, my discomfort like a lump of dough in my throat. It was, however, an opportunity to drag people back toward what pair-bonding means. I offered another "first time" story like people had been telling, but a PG-13 version of my bonded comradeship with Kai at fifteen.

"We were avowed friends forever, like in *Legends of the Condor Heroes,* which we'd just read. Then I had a mistaken idea and kissed him. Sadly, he didn't want *that* kind of bonding."

Kevin said, "I feel you, brother."

"Kai and I stayed friends, but it took me five years to get over the embarrassment."

Everyone murmured, as if commiserating.

I was saying, "To double the embarrassment, his father came in," when Becca pushed open the café's back door.

Gaye sat up straight and pointed to the seat by her.

Following behind Becca: Xavier Torres and a young actor. But not Jade.

The Chez Margot team is a rather tight clique. However, if Becca brings a guest, they're welcomed. Too bad it was Xavier.

Becca introduced him, though it wasn't his first time among us. "Xavier is directing *King Lear* next season. Do you remember his *Streetcar* from two years ago?"

Everyone but me lifted a hand in greeting.

"And this is Timothy Bonham-Day," Becca said. "He's new to Ashland and new to the Festival."

Frankie and Gaye waved. The men nodded a greeting.

"Are you British, Timothy?" Frankie asked.

The actor blushed, his baby-blue eyes shiny under the chandelier. "The Screen Actors Guild requires a unique professional name. So I added my mother's maiden name."

"Congratulations," Kevin said. "Joining SAG is a major milestone, isn't it? I heard the Festival will be an Equity house soon."

Timothy seemed shy; he nodded and smiled.

Becca introduced our crew, finishing with me. "The urchin at the end of the bar is Rik Eliot, who is your landlord."

"We've met." Xavier spoke icily. Kevin didn't need to shake the Manhattan he was preparing; Xavier could self-chill his drink when it passed his lips.

The chill didn't reach me. I was in a warm, safe place with friends. However, Becca blinked several times, casting an accusing you-never-said look my way.

Gaye again motioned for Becca to sit by her. And people began drawing Timothy out of his shell.

Frankie: Where are you from?
Gaye: Are you liking Ashland?
Kevin: What have you appeared in?

I alone observed Xavier's baffled surprise at not being the center of attention since a sweet young man outshined him. Xavier kept drawing Timothy closer, only to lose contact in two heartbeats when Timothy responded to the kind attention from the Chez Margot crew. He was handsome like a young Paul Newman, but with a nonthreatening, low-level sexuality that was more like teen pop stars. Shyness shone through all his charm. Watching Timothy struggle with that paradox, I decided that he must be a good actor. But he also looked like Eddie should card him.

Close to midnight, Stephen shooed us all out, insisting he had to close up.

Gaye had departed for her midnight shift ten minutes earlier, so Becca left with me, slipping her hand into the crook of my elbow after we waved goodbye to our friends.

I didn't check back to see if Xavier watched us leave. He hadn't glanced my way once, which was just fine. Also, the look on his face while Timothy held everyone's attention? So worth walking up to the café to see.

—

Chez Margot's carved wooden door had barely closed behind us before Becca burst forth.

"When I gave them the keys to the cottages, do you know what Xavier told Timothy?" She didn't wait for my answer. "That the landlord is a frigid fairy who uses people! Who is incapable of giving either pleasure or comfort!"

"Was the…set designer there?" I eased out of Becca's hold on my elbow to juggle Gaye's shopping bag full of mushrooms.

"Jade? No. He was up at the Festival. Probably still is."

Not a big deal then. My shoulders relaxed. "I've been called worse." I tried carrying the bag at my side, then switched to cradling it in my arms like a baby. "And it's not as if he said it in front of the PTA or the school board."

"Don't you get it?" She stamped her foot, her fists clenched. "I was standing right there. Xavier wanted me to hear."

"Yeah, and he wanted you to tell me." I laughed. How else to respond? "I could have warned you. Xavier is a colossal jerk."

"I know that now. When he said it, I stuck up for you, Rik." *Oh no.* Becca can't be expected to just be quiet. "I said, 'Rik Eliot is a hot date who loves to flirt, but he only makes a move three days before his date leaves town.'"

"Thanks for sticking up for me, Becca. You are a true pal." Still, overall, it was better than being called rent-boy.

"It's true though. Or it was until you became a monk."

"You've made a few assumptions with no foundation, Becca."

She dismissed that with a wave. "Anyway, Xavier scowled and Timothy laughed, like he was nervous. He's nice, but I think he's shy and pretends not to be."

"Timothy is also too beautiful. Someone should warn him about Xavier. Is that you?"

"I don't see how it could be. What do I know?"

We'd crossed Main Street with its two-story stone-and-concrete buildings and mercury-vapor lamplights, a clichéd small town. After we crossed Lithia Way, the modest nighttime breeze loosened September's odors from sunbaked trees. As soon as we stepped off the main drag, I told Becca about the debacle with Xavier two years earlier, in the middle of SFO Departures with its revolting maroon-and-turquoise carpet. I included the twins' vigorous defense.

"How vile," she said. "Xavier, I mean, not the twins."

We walked on in companionable silence, until I couldn't stand it and so also shared the I'm-not-a-rent-boy part of the story, while trying not to sound defensive.

"Fuck Xavier Torres," she said. "Do you have any more excruciating stories about your new guests in the cottages?"

"No. That'll do it."

That's the only story I'll tell, even to Becca. My chaotic experiences with Jade happened years ago on a planet far away, at a time when I liked acid better than mushrooms. No one tells such stories once university years are in the rearview mirror.

Our shoes scrunched on the gritty granite sand that dusted Water Street.

Becca sighed mightily. "We haven't indulged our late-night ramblings since summer began. Let's talk soon. Do we have to make appointments to see each other?"

I murmured something about Saturday.

"And I promise," she said, "not to waste time complaining about my lack of a love life."

"Feel free to complain. Just don't take it as a personal failing. Because it's—"

"Yeah, yeah. It's Ashland. But at least these days I have a crush. One that's actually heating up."

"Who?"

"I'm not telling." She zipped her lips. "Do you ever tell me about your crushes?"

"No, and I won't." I repeated a truism we'd shared before: anyone who moves to this town quickly perceives that everyone has slept with everyone else. And most know who their previous crush is now sleeping with.

"Have you ever had a real crush, Rik Eliot?"

"No." Not in this town.

In the Chaos kitchen, I set water to boil and made chamomile tea. I'd come away from Chez Margot feeling keyed up, and Becca lingered with me.

"Let's see if Gaye is doing her job." Becca turned on the radio. The last chords of a Clash song played, followed by more strong background music.

Becca and I bonded years ago over late-night conversations in this kitchen. She's lived here since I first invited renters in. We help each other think and goad each other to act. Our initial late-night discussions considered what it means to be out in a small town like Ashland (well, more or less out). This was back in the day—the Seventies encompassed at least seven separate historic eras—when such long conversations included shifting contemporary reflection:

> *Family birth-order and related syndromes.*
>
> I was a pampered baby; Becca, a bossy only child.
>
> *Found family versus birth family.*
>
> Many post-college discussions move to that. The Seventies featured roiled family lives for lots of us.
>
> *Our trauma as gifted children.*
>
> Our recent discussions of a popular book led to painful explorations of our similar childhood experiences.
>
> *Whether a true feminist can allow males in her life.*
>
> Harsh. But Gaye, Frankie, and Becca had struggled with the issue in several households before landing here.

Whether "soulmate" is only a patriarchal notion of romance. We shared opinions but neither of us had experiences to guide any exploration of the question. (Or in my case, I didn't share experiences.)

Presentation of self in everyday…anywhere. This started with a text that wasn't self-help. We applied the know-and-show-your-true-self notions to our friends, then were privately introspective.

We skipped the issues around "adult children of alcoholics," since that wasn't in our family experiences. We also discarded *I'm OK You're OK,* because we judged that pop phenomenon as belonging to a different generation, a different world than ours. Also, we didn't either of us feel okay.

That night, apropos of nothing, Becca said, "I wish I could take safe, short-term paramours. I don't possess sufficient glamor. Or courage. How do you do it? I mean, how did you used to do it before you became a monk?"

"Paramours? Like in a novel from the Twenties?" I discounted the glamor part and didn't speak to it.

She dolloped honey into her teacup. "How long since you enjoyed a weekend with a beautiful person?"

"I'm no longer interested, I guess."

"I don't think so." She shook her head. "You watched Timothy like a hawk at the bar."

"I resent that predatory metaphor. I have never in this life preyed upon or stalked another person." Almost 100 percent true. Close enough.

"If you say so. However, you've been cultivating loneliness like…like…"

"No, you're wrong." I cut off whatever twisted metaphor Becca might invent. "I can squeeze one run and a couple of hours of writing into each day. I don't have time for paramours."

"Did you quit dating because of Xavier Torres?"

"Xavier has not influenced my life choices." As true as a line that continually approaches a given curve and never reaches it.

"Yet you didn't like seeing Xavier's hand on Timothy's butt."

"Xavier is a monster. We should protect the innocent."

"Okay, Mr. Soul. Don't ever change." She yawned. "That's enough for tonight. We've confessed at least some things to each other. G'night, my dear friend."

I rinsed our teacups and went upstairs.

I refused the wave of feelings that threatened to drown me. Between now and my return to Hong Kong, I want no more disruptions like the grenade set off by the failed big-city weekend with Xavier. I've buried the adolescent notion of mystical connections with another human. It's not possible outside of a 1950s wuxia novel published serially in the newspaper. I won't end up living my best life in Hong Kong if I waste time with other people's chaos.

9: Trapper Keeper

WEDNESDAY MORNING, I RAN AT five thirty, then showered and prepared breakfast. Alex volunteered for chores as soon as he came into the kitchen.

"I'll do anything you need," he said, his face open and eager, but also still nervous. I hope that was about having undertaken a huge change, not about intruding on me or Chaos House. It hurts seeing him strive so hard to do the right thing, a wary innocent.

The chore I had for him was easy: deliver breakfast bento boxes to the guest cottages. Which also meant I didn't spend the day silently bitching about having to serve Xavier freakin' Torres.

With their chores done, the Eliot trio of cousins prepared to depart for school. As a former professional student, I was jealous. An organic instinct flows through me every first day of school. I want new pencils. A fresh notebook. A new beginning.

Also, I don't brag much, but I'm proud of these kids. They've almost made it through the years of hell, psyches intact. So I see the first day of school as a celebratory holiday. Hence, I was in the kitchen, happy, drinking a second cup of tea.

Someone knocked on the front door.

I am confident that Xavier Torres will never knock on my door, even if he catches on fire. That firethorn rasped in my chest, though my breathing had been fine while I ran that morning.

Alex answered, then called back to the kitchen, "Uncle Rik, this guy says he rented the garage. He wants the key."

I wheezed. That rasp must come from an old injury.

"Give it to him. It's hanging on the hook," I called. Pathetically, I was not prepared to speak with Jade Solberg over morning tea. I vowed to do better. It's not like he was asking me to score acid or something. "And give him that box of light bulbs by the door. Go along to show him which outlets to avoid."

"I put duct tape over the bad ones," Alex said.

"Go anyway. Make sure he knows what not to do."

I'd intended to fix the wiring last week, after Alex's summer rehearsals ended, but didn't get to it. Likely as not, it'll be freezing in the garage come December before I fix those outlets.

Alex was back in five minutes, beating dust off his jeans before he came inside. Ramona stopped him from slipping off his shoes. "If we leave right now, we can walk with Quinn."

Looking eager, Alex nodded. The trio hoisted their backpacks, ready to go.

I said, "I have errands later this morning, so I have to drive. Alex, I'll meet you at the counselor's office before the bell rings."

They set off down the stone walkway to the street.

"Be careful out there." I called the traditional farewell. "Don't forget to follow Rik's Rules."

"Rik has fewer than ten rules," Molly said to Alex. "First is, 'Don't get pregnant.'"

"Not your problem." Ramona patted Alex's shoulder.

"'Don't go with college boys. Don't get arrested.'" Molly chanted more Rules.

Ramona said, "'Don't do psychedelics until you're eighteen.' Which is in three months."

"New Rule," I called. The kids were on the street, so my Disputatious Neighbor must have heard all this. "Recent scientific reports indicate that it's prudent to avoid psychedelics until you're twenty-five. Wait till your brain is fully formed."

"As soon as we're eighteen, you can't tell us what to do."

I couldn't tell if that was from Molly or Ramona. Alex walked backward, checking my reaction, his brow knitted. He hadn't yet learned all our traditions.

Serving as the twins' guardian became much easier after they turned sixteen. I'd guided them closely for the first six years we were together, to prevent any possibility that they might fall off the rails. For two years now, I'd been loosening that hold, letting them practice things on their own, like fledglings. Or was I getting myself ready to let go? Anyway, I'm proud that they have more common sense and intelligence than many of their peers. Now, what help might Alex need in the coming months, beyond me engaging Nick over legal issues?

Instead of swimming in a soup of first-day-of-school emotions, I had to prepare for my first task as Alex's guardian. Then I'd go be a scholar in the bright light of a September day, which meant running the copier in Frankie's printshop.

—

I parked just off Siskiyou Boulevard in one of the high school's guest spaces. When I pulled open the metal-and-glass door near the school offices, the heady chemical smell of freshly waxed floors evoked the sense of returning to school after the holidays, with Kai and me nervous about what the new term might bring.

The bell having not yet rung, kids still milled in the hall. When I passed the vice principal's office, Jacqueline Urquell called to me, dousing that irrelevant memory of Hong Kong.

"Rik, you are a hero, taking on that chaperone job."

"Hardly," I said. "It's only two months and twelve kids."

"A walk in the park for you, then."

I teased. "Upper Lithia, where the skateboard crew hangs out? Or behind the Shakespeare Theatre, where no kids go?"

She laughed. "Yeah, behind the Theatre. Come back when you're done with the guidance counselor. I have a question."

I went in search of the counselor, who was new (just as Molly predicted). Alex sat in front of her desk, his hands folded. I introduced myself and we quickly resolved relationships.

"Likely Alex has told you why he's in Ashland," I said. Alex nodded, folding and unfolding his hands. Let's hope our stories match. "Alex is staying with us while his mother is on an extended business trip in Europe. If we're lucky, he'll be with us all year." I did not add that I will pay Nick Lawrence to make that be true if Claudia can't fix herself.

The counselor and Alex nodded in agreement, so we were off to a good start. We got through several crucial questions, while she kept Alex involved instead of speaking only to me. Kids hate it when you only talk to their adults, as if they're inert.

"Alex, as we discussed before your uncle arrived, we have to wait for your transcript. Still, from the details you shared," now she turned to me, "we can place Alex as a senior. Math is his sole barrier to graduating this year. Can you help, Mr. Eliot?"

"I can, if it's what he chooses." For the past three summers, Claudia begged me to tutor him, but he'd refused. "Alex, do you want to commit to graduating this year?"

I wanted to say: *C'mon, Alex. You can do it.* But I wasn't about to pressure him because of my goals for next spring.

"Yes, Uncle Rik," he said. "Whatever." Spoken just as shyly as when he'd asked for morning chores.

The counselor said, "Is that a commitment? 'Whatever'?"

"I mean," Alex looked at me, pleading, "whatever it takes. Anything I have to do, I'll do it."

After Alex left for class, I asked the counselor to make sure his teachers called him Alex. I'm a solemn witness to what happens when teachers say "Aldrik Eliot" at roll call.

Then I stopped back by the vice principal's office to sign the substitute contract for this school year.

Jacqueline said, "I want to ask…" She paused for too long.

"Is it good news or bad? I can't stand the suspense."

Her pause proved to be a tease.

"Sally Ogden is expecting a baby in late December. Then she's taking four months off. Do you want to sub for her, December through April?"

"That's good timing for me." I hoped the *ca-ching* of my mental cash register couldn't be heard. I'd often subbed for Sally. Since she's taught math for fifteen years, her lesson plans are meticulous. I could do that job in my sleep—heh, except for having to worry about one hundred twenty-five students' success. "Which classes does she have this year?"

"Two sections of remedial math. Two of Algebra II. One of Calculus, mostly seniors and a handful of juniors. Two prep periods, since that load means so many papers to correct."

"Yes!" I said, enthused.

It didn't mean that much paperwork for me, given how I manage tests and homework. I calculated the payrate per hour. It'd make a weighty addition to my Hong Kong fund.

So I signed this year's contract. The first assignment: spend every weekday afternoon haunted by ghosts from the past. I focused on the *ca-ching* of coins falling into my savings.

10: Carrying Water

ANXIOUS FOR MY NEXT TASK of the day, I drove to the college, my manuscript in a box on the floor.

"Hey, Rik!" Frankie called over the noise of the offset printer, copiers, and paper joggers. "How's the first day of school?"

"Swell so far." I still felt cheery about those kids walking down B Street together. The change in schools was sure to be good for Alex, along with his new goal: to graduate this year. "With my nephew back and Festival people in the cottages, I'm cooking huge breakfasts now."

"Have you met the artist who rented Inez's studio?" Then her voice turned wistful. "It's so weird to think of a stranger working in her private space."

"She only left me a note." I moved on to what I believed she really wanted to ask: *Any news about Inez?* Becca wouldn't tell me who her crush was; meanwhile, Frankie incarnated *Crushing Woman.* "And she left me something I'm supposed to give you."

I had to set my manuscript box on the shop counter to be able to dig into my messenger bag. The package was wrapped in tissue, but a hardcover book is unmistakable.

Frankie took it from my hands as if it were delicate. She folded back the tissue and drew a breath: Mary Oliver's *American Primitive.* I recognized it because Becca bought a copy as soon as it appeared in McCarley's bookstore. That accounts for only two copies and so does not statistically prove that it's *the* favorite book among Ashland's lesbians.

"How thoughtful." Frankie tucked it behind her, looking cool. "How did she manage this when she must have been so busy getting ready to leave? She already thanked me for helping with her art book project last spring."

Considering Inez's expression when she asked me to deliver the book, and Frankie's reaction upon receiving it, I took a chance.

"Is there more going on than mere gratitude between book collaborators? You didn't look that way when you and I worked on your Chinese laborer project for the historical society."

"Yeah, it's..." She set the book carefully on the counter. "I helped Inez pack up her studio Friday night. She'd come to all my softball games in August. It suddenly felt like more might be happening. But there wasn't time to figure it out."

A bookmark hung from the book's pages. When I pointed to it, Frankie flipped open the book. I barely saw the title—"The Sea"—before Frankie snatched it. I matched her enthusiasm.

"'More happening'? That's good."

Frankie laughed. "Get real. She won't be back until late April."

"Still," I said.

"Yeah. That inner golden core you wrote about in your dissertation? Mine is now in suspended animation."

I nodded, acknowledging her dilemma. Frankie left to answer a work-study student's plea for help with the offset printer. That turned out to be complicated. I got busy with my task, watching the pages of my dissertation fall out of the copy machine.

Last night, I'd prepared that beast of a manuscript to send it to my advisor. I'd also send it to my most important reviewer, my dear friend Chan-suk, who always has the most useful comments. I most want him to declare that my dissertation is ready. My advisor will urge me to submit it immediately, so it can be defended and accepted before he retires in December. That's also when I hit a hard deadline. My PhD program allows ten years to complete all requirements. Those ten years expire in December.

I felt true joy copying this final version. Having to change the ink canister and fix three paper jams didn't irritate me.

"It's a bad batch of paper," Frankie called from where she still worked on the offset printer problem. "Got damp somehow."

We had no more opportunity to talk about Inez when I had my copies in hand. I bowed my silent thanks from across the room and waved farewell.

Then I went to the post office and sent my advisor's copy by overnight mail. That was easy. An International airmail package, however, is never easy. The task might have been more complicated because my fingers tingled with excitement after I handed the packages to the lady at the counter and paid for postage.

Of course, as soon as I let go of the two packages, I began to think of a half-dozen word choices and turns of phrase that I should improve.

No. The previous night's decision was to make no more revisions unless demanded by my advisor or recommended by Chan-suk. My sole job was to push that sucker to the finish line by December. I'm a marathon runner who's run low on energy one hundred paces beyond the last refreshment station. Just finish.

I went back to my car, wiping ideas of future revisions from my mind, thinking how this last draft was taking me to the end of my long journey as a professional student.

—

That journey began in Hong Kong, like everything else.

After our father left us, we'd stayed on for another year. My asthma worsened, and my mother retreated further into her writing, though she published nothing from that era. We returned to the U.S. when she was too broke to keep a maid and a cook, landing at my grandfather's house in Ashland.

The first dinner back at Chaos House, Grandfather berated Ruby for not having published a book for ten years.

"How can I write?" Ruby whined, her voice sinking into the register of a young teenager. "I had three kids inflicted on me. They demolished my intellectual life. They killed my muse."

Right then, I understood why she resented my father's desertion: she'd have preferred to be the one to leave us.

Beginning the day we arrived in Ashland, my grandfather said three times each day that we owed our future to his hard work and talent. One month after we returned to Ashland, he died. We were left with trust funds for college, which our mother controlled.

The day after Grandfather's funeral, Christopher ran off to school at San Francisco State. Later, he married a woman six years older than him, joined the army, and had a kid. He and I were never close. After he left Ashland, we never had an opportunity to speak again, so I'm vague about details in Christopher's story. Claudia never speaks of him except in abstract ways.

I lasted two more months in Ashland because I was too young to figure out how to escape as quickly as Christopher did. I did have the good fortune to have been admitted to the UW in Seattle for fall term. Chan-suk had helped me apply the previous fall, saying: *You have a mathematical brilliance that must be nurtured.* He believed that no American high school could meet my educational needs, so he helped prepare my college application.

When I describe to friends how I left Ashland as a fifteen-year-old, I unfairly omit the part my sister Wendy played. She helped me out the door while having a much harder time escaping. Waiting to leave for Seattle, I avoided being home as much as I could. I didn't know a soul in town, so this meant roaming the hills or hanging out at the town's Carnegie library or the one at the college. I avoided home because the battle between Ruby and Wendy echoed everywhere in the house, no matter where I tried to shelter in the creaky old place. They fought night and day. A rough transcription:

Ruby: You do not get one penny from that trust fund unless you live in this house and go to college here. Forget going to Boston, like I did.

Wendy: I'm going to Stanford. I'm already admitted.

Ruby (never listening): Forget going to Boston, like your grandfather planned for you. The very idea makes me laugh. Just look at you. You are utterly incapable of taking care of yourself.

Wendy: It's *my* trust fund. I'll do what I want.

Ruby: I control it until you turn twenty-five or graduate. You'll stay right here until then.

Wendy: I'm going to be a writer. No one who goes to college here becomes a writer.

Ruby: You, a writer? You can't pass a spelling test. You're a total nothing. You've never lived.

Wendy: I cannot go to college in Bumfuck, Oregon.

Ruby: Wendy Joyce Eliot!

This exchange is bowdlerized, since they were filthy and cruel with each other. Whenever I remember it, I wish I'd been adept enough to intervene, like Wendy did whenever Ruby got all over my case. I never did learn to stand up to Ruby.

Also, just now I omitted a key issue in their vile exchanges: Wendy was pregnant. If I do the math now—premature twins born in December; we returned in May—it must have happened immediately upon our return to the U.S. Or she managed it before we left Hong Kong.

Wendy, brilliant and talented, could have successfully gone to Stanford, like she wanted to. What she did do: have twins, publish three books, and finish an English BA in Ashland, all in three years. She told me that she'd paid a significant portion of her trust fund to Mimi, a live-in nanny. Irritating Ruby by succeeding must have been one of Wendy's key motivations.

The day I left home, I had to catch the Greyhound to Seattle. Ruby harassed me to fly but didn't offer to buy my ticket, and I was already marshalling every dollar of my trust-fund allowance. On the final day in Ashland, I shouldered my duffel and called "Bye, I'm going now." I got no reply. I was a block up Water Street when the front door slammed and Wendy joined me.

"*Sailou,* you rat." Whenever she called me *little brother,* she shrieked it. "You're only get to go to Seattle because Ruby is too busy wrecking my life to pay attention to you. You lucky bastard."

She admonished me, then talked rapidly and without pause all the way to the bus stop. Her advice: keep out of Ruby's sight; pretend to agree; don't ever tell her you want to be a writer.

"Stay safe. Don't come back home." She pecked my cheek just as the Greyhound bus arrived. "If Ruby doesn't see you, she won't think of you."

At the UW, which I immediately learned to call the U Dub, I met my first classmates while standing in line to register for two math classes. My five brand-new friends, all Chinese from various places, gave me two important pieces of advice. First, choose the international dormitory because its cafeteria has an Asian food line. Second, take the #7 bus to the International District where two theatres show Hong Kong and Taiwanese fight movies. The dorm food was so-so, though better than at Grandfather's house. I made friends (and cash) tutoring English.

My Hong Kong homesickness abated, given that my time was filled with classes, fight movies, and frequent dinners in Chinatown with my new math freak friends. Yet I still missed Kai, Chan-suk, and the Chan family table.

My mother's sole contribution to getting me into college? She'd signed every document I placed in front of her. From the time my father left, she'd come to hate me, so my departure to Seattle was a relief for both of us. Also, my asthma disappeared.

Ruby never published another book, even with her children gone from home and Grandfather no longer nagging her. Much later, she forgot I was one of her children. We were gone and forgotten, both of which were good outcomes for me. In heartbreaking ways, Wendy had a harder time leaving. I don't know how much she's forgotten about what happened, but I hope she has found her own good outcome now.

—

Driving home from the college printshop, I stopped for the traffic light on Lithia Way at the Pioneer Street crossing. Like everyone else in town, I felt that particular stoplight did not need to be so long. On Pioneer, there's a row of one-story Fifties shops and cafés leading up to Main Street, plus a modest faux-Tudor on the southeast corner, coated in September's dust.

Three male figures walked along Pioneer Street toward the Festival buildings. The man in the middle, obviously Xavier, rested his arm on the shoulder of the taller figure to his right. Jade. Xavier's arm slid down to his companion's waist, but Jade stepped a foot away. Xavier then rested his other arm on the slight figure to his left, the actor I'd met the night before.

What was his name? Ah, Timothy.

Rather than stepping away from Xavier, the actor seemed bent under the weight. Then Timothy stopped, gesturing back the way they'd come, and walked rapidly away.

By the time a car's horn warned that the signal light had changed, I'd reached a conclusion: no need to warn the innocent about Xavier Torres.

At home, I began trading calls with Nick to figure out a legal strategy for Alex. Nick sounded surprised.

"His mom thinks he's gay? But she doesn't want him with you? Strange. I'd leave my gay kids with you in a heartbeat."

"You don't have kids, Nick."

"It's hypothetical. I have relevant experiences since I made the unwise decision to practice family law in a small town."

"I feel bad about benefitting from your career decision."

"Does Claudia know you carried Molly and Ramona out of hell on your back? And built the good life they now have?"

"Claudia was present when my sister Wendy left the twins with me. I had no idea Claudia could panic about gay men."

"Is Alex gay?"

"My guess? No. A boy kissed him this summer. I'm waiting for him to ask me specific questions before I unload all the advice I have to give."

"Can we meet at ten tomorrow morning? My office?"

I'd gladly run over to his office right at that moment, but I had chores. "Yes, I'll see you then."

My mother left at midday for the senior center, which freed the core of my day for chores ahead of the chaperone gig. I started a pot of soup for dinner that night. I'd made broth from chicken bones on Sunday and now added soy sauce, chili sauce, and ginger. Then I stuffed wontons with veggies, using the wrappers Gaye gave me. I'd add the wontons to the soup at dinner time. Kai's mother always served wonton soup on the first day of school, and Alex loves wontons. It's the perfect comfort food for a time when he must need it. After my second day as chaperone, I'll want comfort food too.

I seek to recreate a sense of home as I knew it in Hong Kong. Many people crave their mother's cooking when in need of comfort. I crave food from the Chan family table. I don't think I've ever eaten one thing prepared by my mother. I learned to cook for a crowd during grad school, since five other students lived in the house I rented. I started with spaghetti and pizza, then tried the chicken soup and wok veggie fry I'd seen prepared in Madam Chan's kitchen. At Chaos House, I exchanged many letters with

Madam Chan to learn to prepare the more complex food I'd enjoyed at the Chan family table.

It didn't take long for cooking at Chaos House to become as easy as laundry. I built the table, which runs the length of the kitchen and seats twelve. I enjoy that it often holds more than the twins and boarders since it represents what I learned about filial duty from Chan-suk: physical care, respect, service.

After starting dinner, I stocked pantry shelves with after-school provisions for starving kids and organized what we'd need for the short week's breakfasts and dinners. Thursday, by tradition, is *dan dan mian*—fried noodles with minced pork. Friday will be spaghetti, since several other kids are usually at the table. I'd figure out the weekend and next week's meals while doing the Saturday shopping.

I'd make a great housewife, plus I have good chainsaw and plumbing skills learned while scratching out an income.

—

The cottages, just west of Chaos House, share a continuous back-yard with the main house, though no path invites guests into the narrow wilderness by Ashland Creek.

For the last midday chore, I went to retrieve the breakfast bento boxes. Signs in the cottage kitchens ask for the boxes to be left in the milk delivery crates on the front stoop.

Timothy was moving baggage between cottages. He dropped the duffle he held when I inadvertently startled him. I endeavored to be reassuring and offered to shake his hand.

"Hi. You're Timothy, right? I'm Rik Eliot. We met briefly last night. Can I help you with that?"

"Thank you, Mr. Eliot. I'm almost done." He shook my hand. He wore Paco Rabanne cologne, which senior boys had taken to wearing last year, drenching my classroom with it.

"Call me Rik. I came to pick up the breakfast things."

"Oh, they're in the milk crate, like the sign says."

Timothy's friendly smile makes you believe you are the center of his attention. I've met a half dozen actors with that sparkling charisma in the past eight years.

Becca and I had guessed right, though. Timothy is shy and striving to hide it. I'd been worrying about Alex's shy discomfort that morning, never thinking I'd have to put one of the cottage guests at ease, much less a member of the Screen Actors Guild. Yet I felt a duty to make an extra effort over his comfort, since Timothy had heard about me from Xavier—and Becca. The best course: identify neutral ground.

"Have people told you how to find things to do in a small logging town?"

"Not really." Timothy hesitated. I chalked it up to yesterday's Xavier-and-Becca gossip. "I won't have much time. Xavier wants me to see every play at least three times before the season ends next month. And I'm supposed to meet all the lead actors, to learn what it takes to be on stage every night."

"You haven't done live stage before?"

"Not since college. My agent wants me to learn more about expressing human emotion. That's why he got me this gig."

No use expressing my unkind thoughts about Xavier's miniscule knowledge of human emotion. I asked, "You're watching stage plays to learn about human emotions?"

He nodded, paused, shook his head, then changed the subject. "So what do you do here for fun? Take walks in Lithia Park?"

"I'm only in the park when I run," I said. "Ashland is on the West Coast circuit for touring musicians, so we go hear live music when it comes to town. Robert Cray is here this weekend if you like to dance. Or if you like the blues, which are a fantastic way to learn about the depths of human emotion."

"Are you asking me out?"

How abrupt. I said, "No, I'm just cataloging entertainment options for you."

"Because I'm not out." He said this without using his charm. "My agent insists that the world isn't ready for gay actors. Especially with AIDS in the news."

"I'm not out either, beyond my friends," I said. "I teach at the high school my kids go to, so I am discreet."

"And I'm bi, not gay."

"Timothy." When I said his name, his eyes darted to me with trepidation, then he offered his star-quality smile. "I know what Xavier and Becca said about me. Neither is true."

Becca's defense of me came fairly close though.

"Is Becca the dyke who took us to the bar last night?"

"Uh, yes." I couldn't tell if he spoke of her as someone on the same team.

"She seems nice." He stood there, holding a duffle bag.

"Becca said the same about you, which is a compliment."

"Does this town share lots of gossip?"

"Yes. It's pretty much like small towns in any movie you've seen. Except prettier." I retreated to neutral ground. "As for what to do here, Xavier knows where actors hang out. There's a bar on Lithia Way that has disco dancing on Fridays and Saturdays. I prefer punk and retro Bowie, so I've never been there. And my kids claim it's wrong to even call it disco in a small West Coast town."

"I never go dancing alone," he said.

Not information I needed. I went on with more ideas. "There are fight movies at the Varsity Theatre after midnight on Fridays and Saturdays. Hong Kong and samurai mostly. And the usher doesn't check whether you're carrying a flask."

"I don't drink. My agent says—"

"Of course. Me neither, mostly."

Timothy shuffled, stumbling over the duffle he'd set down while we talked.

"Are you sure you don't want my help?" I asked. "It looks like you're doing a removal."

"No, I'm about done. We just traded rooms because…" He hesitated, but I was getting used to him faltering like an uncomfortable Jimmy Stewart. "I claimed this room because it gets the most morning sun. The wall curtain was pulled shut at first, so I didn't know what I was getting into. My friend Jade offered to switch cottages."

*My friend Jade…*I rubbed at the hollow spot in my chest.

"Yeah," I agreed. "The *Raising of Lazarus* isn't everyone's cup of tea."

"How did it get there? Everything else in the cottage is so normal. Tasteful."

"Years ago, an artist staying in the cottage saw that Alec Guinness movie, *The Horse's Mouth.* He set out to recreate the *Raising of Lazarus* like in the movie." Timothy and I had just done a bit of personal revelation, so I plunged ahead with the true story. "The artist enlisted my help, and for five nights, we ate Owsley acid with supper and then worked on the painting all night."

Timothy raised his eyebrows in the way of someone who didn't go to college in the Seventies.

"Of course," I said, "I was a different person then, but weren't we all?"

A few months after the painting of *Lazarus,* I began repairing the derelict cottages. In the Lazarus Cottage, I installed a curtain across the wall so guests who don't appreciate it, like Timothy, don't have to look at it. Still, he's swapping rooms to avoid it. And, apparently, he hadn't looked at the artist's signature on the painting, which is clearly visible when the curtain is pulled open.

"I'll see you around," I said. "Let me know if you want to go with my friends to hear Robert Cray on Saturday. The club is just up the street."

Timothy gave me an automatic wave, lost in thought. Did his agent caution him about not doing acid for five straight days? It's a personal preference that I never recommend to others. Me, my daily cautious self sometimes misses the old walk on the wild side. This afternoon, for example, I have to dress in a substitute teacher's costume and show up for that chaperone gig. The one I can't afford to turn down.

As I remember it, though, one reason not to recommend five straight nights of acid is that all the serotonin activity is exhausting. It ends with a few days of flat emotions and empty dreams.

11: Site Rules

WHEN I ENTERED THE CLASSROOM that afternoon, Alex was sitting in the first row with Quinn, the twins behind them. I counted heads. One of the original girls was absent. Alex had lucked into the last slot. I tucked myself into the far back of the room. Students don't like a chaperone hanging over them.

Jade came in, again wearing ripped jeans and that threadbare t-shirt. He closed the classroom door. Must be that he's never had a classroom of teenagers at end of day, else he'd never have closed the door. Several had PE last period and rushed here sans showers. And we were all toasty in the early September heat.

"Ready to begin, my friends?" Jade held up a notebook. "Please sign the roster sheet on Page One of my journal. Add your adult's phone number so I can call in case of accidents or cancellations. Then write down your favorite album."

"Why?" Three kids spoke at once.

"Because otherwise, you'll be listening to my music while we work, which means krautrock and Spandau Ballet. Some of you won't appreciate that." This evoked mixed responses. Alex nodded, rocking in his seat, his arms wrapped tightly around his torso. "You are joining this project at the creative end, at the holy moment of execution. To do the work, you need the mind of a Zen disciple raking gravel in a garden. For the Zen of mural work, we must have music."

His last large mural in Seattle, as I remember it, was executed with the Zen sounds of Bob Marley, Queen, and *Diamond*

Dogs, the volume two notches down from blowing the amplifier's tubes, the bass buzzing in the speakers.

Molly said, "We aren't chanting *Hari Krishna* or *Om mani padme hum,* are we? A dude came to town last year and got people chanting to attract wealth. It was dumb."

"And isn't Zen a cliché that mostly means homemade bread and Danish furniture?" Ramona asked.

"I am positive that I'm using the word correctly," Jade said. "Now, my new best friends, are you ready to learn how we will collaborate?"

He passed around a couple dozen eight-by-ten drawings of portions of the mosaic they'd be working on plus enlarged photos of his murals in several U.S. and European cities.

While the kids looked at the pictures, Jade taped a large drawing on chalkboard. He explained the grids and color-coding that'd guide the work, which was to be a scene from *King Lear.*

Then he demonstrated how to handle the tiles, all the size of my little toenail. He showed them the palettes—which looked like aluminum TV dinner trays—and the palette knives they'd use with thin-set cement to "glue" tiles into place.

The kids listened earnestly.

"Now, I'm going to be depressingly honest. This will be fun, but it's serious, painstaking work." Hands behind his back, Jade rocked heel to toe while he spoke. He never could stand still. "We must finish before freezing weather sets in. To achieve that, you will abide by my rules, which supersede all your school rules. The chaperone," he didn't look my way, hadn't looked my way once, "will never have a chance to report to the vice principal—"

"Mr. E never would!" Quinn said.

"He won't," Jade said, "because I will ban you from the site if you break even one of my rules one time. It's not just no smoking of any kind. If you show up high—and don't think I won't know—you're banned and gone."

Sighs and shuffling feet.

I shall pass to the underworld and become a ghost before ever revealing how high we'd been while working on most grad school projects. It's a wonder no one ever fell into the raku kiln.

"Goodness, can you believe it? I have even more rules," Jade said. "No pictures, aside from formal shots made by the Festival staff. No interviews if a reporter approaches you."

"Wow," someone whispered. "It's a secret?"

"Yes," Jade said. "The Festival wants to control all contact with the press. Do you understand why?"

"No bootleg MTV videos!" Quinn answered, excited.

Jade nodded, tapping his nose. "A minimum standard."

Every kid murmured an assent, including my typically taciturn twins. Excitement rippled over them, as if a wind blew. He now had deft control of his crew.

"Next, my friends, and this is critically important." Jade waved a copy of the rule sheet he'd handed out. "You will wear hard hats and eye protection at all times on site. You will seek first aid for even the smallest cut or scrape."

"Is the work dangerous?" Ramona spoke softly. Molly jabbed her elbow and shook her head.

"You will get cuts and scrapes." Jade held up his hand with the splinted little finger. "You can avoid severe accidents by following the rules and taking good care."

"Severe like what?" Ramona asked.

"Falling off the scaffolding. Which I advise against."

People were reading the rules closely.

"We'll form teams now," Jade said. "The teams will build the mosaic from opposite sides and from the middle out."

He passed around blue, red, yellow, and green tiles, then used them to form teams, splitting friends (and the twins) into different teams. Alex didn't receive a tile and had a heartbreaking expression, like an abandoned waif. Jade quickly noticed—"Gosh, sorry, man, my bad"—and assigned him to the middle section.

"Each day, one team will mix cement, because it's better if it's delivered in small batches. That team rotates every day. How to mix cement is the first demonstration on site tomorrow."

"What if we make a mistake and place a tile wrong?" Alex asked. That lost-puppy look had disappeared. Quinn's arm hung on the back of Alex's chair. They both slumped comfortably, legs spread before them, like boys do.

Jade tipped his head, then laughed. "When you bring your grandchildren to see our work, you can point out your mistake, because it will be there forever. My projects in Barcelona, Istanbul, and London all contain mistakes for the entire world to see. We take great care, but shit happens."

Zooey Helman opened her eyes wide, then looked around and saw that *shit* hadn't stirred the others.

Alex said, "It'll be like the cough that got left on that Pink Floyd album."

Jade jutted a finger at him, but not like Xavier's rude pointing. Rather, Jade confirmed with a broad, gleaming smile that he knew which Pink Floyd album. Alex sat back, folding his arms, pleased to be correct. I hadn't noticed until then that Jade's twisted dog tooth had been repaired.

When Jade ended the session, the only kids who left had to catch their rides home. My kids remained with the others who helped Jade reassemble his drawings and photos. Students still tagged after Jade while departing the classroom. I stayed to switch off the lights and close the door after the last stragglers.

Driving home, I determined that my blue blazer and chinos would not survive the job site. Best to wear the Carhartt canvas jacket Molly and Ramona gave me for Christmas. Or would the kids think I'm trying too hard to be cool, undoing my power-dressing teacher moves? Should I wear Red Wing boots or Converse?

I'd listened in years past to Jade Solberg describing how people collaborate to make art. Since then, Jade had become a relaxed, skilled teacher, showing no trace of his former quick-tempered impatience with volunteers who didn't understand what he required. And for all of the past two hours, Jade hadn't glanced once to where I lurked at the back of the room. After the kinds of things that happened in Seattle, me turning up as his project chaperone must be as much of a surprising flash from the past for him as it was for me.

I wanted to congratulate myself on my own achievements. The second day after seeing him in Ashland, I'd listened to Jade speaking without watching the bob of his Adam's apple. For my next achievement, I must quit telling myself stories from the past that include that aside, *someone I once loved.*

Since it's Jade Solberg in every single story.

It's his signature on the corner of *The Raising of Lazarus.*

It's the sole person I've spent more than a weekend beside.

For the first year after I ended up in Ashland, I'd have sold whatever soul I possess to be called Sasha again, the name Jade spoke when he first saw me in the classroom. But that's as long ago as the Zhou dynasty. I'd gotten over hearing *Sasha* whispered by a ghost knocking on my door in the wee hours.

There are no ghosts, only culture-specific folk tales that scholars and young boys like to read, the kind that nurtured my young teen soul. And which I'd resurrected in my dissertation, to stave off the soul-sucking sense of loss when Jade departed from my world.

It's not as if the old whispering ghost has moved into Lazarus Cottage, thirty feet from my bedroom window. Jade no longer incarnates the force of chaos that upset my life long ago. Working close to Jade now is only a tiny piece of the plan that will take me back to Hong Kong.

12: Homework

WHEN I GOT HOME, THE KITCHEN smelled comfortingly of Madam Chan's chicken soup. I dished a bowl for Howard, then another for my mother and set it on a tray for Howard to collect. I inhaled that odor, thick with memories of dinner with the Chan family.

Yet I too prepare a good family table. I'd made a batch of water dough on Monday and refrigerated it, so I rolled it out and set *lo por paeng* to bake. Most everyone likes these Hong Kong-style wife biscuits. I figured out how to substitute honeydew melon for the filling, since winter melon isn't ever at the food co-op. For Julio's sake, I left the sesame seeds off a few of the biscuits.

At six thirty, I was removing the wife biscuits from the oven when my crew came home, along with Quinn and Zooey. Lack of warning is never a problem. There's always plenty. I dropped wontons in the soup while the kids scarfed hot wife biscuits, drowning them in butter and honey. Even Julio liked his biscuit after Valerie let him butter it himself.

The topic at the table was, of course, Jade's project. Or rather, Jade himself. One voice after another:

> Quinn: He blows my mind, how he always gets where you're going when you ask a question.
>
> Ramona: Can you believe he'd take so much time?
>
> Alex: What he promised is, like, unbelievable.

Busy ladling soup into bowls, I endeavored to withstand not knowing about the promise, but failed. "What's so unbelievable?"

Ramona said, "Jade promised that he would critique our portfolios and offer advice if we ask."

"Even if we aren't planning to major in art," Quinn said.

Alex said, "Then he asked what schools we're applying to. He knew at least one professor at every school."

"And he promised to write recommendations for anyone who wants one." Quinn sat back, happy.

"What's he like?" Valerie had been coaxing Julio into trying the soup. She accepted failure when Julio began buttering a second biscuit. "I've seen the video, but that doesn't say much about him as a person or as an artist."

Alex said, "He makes art seem like the most important thing in the world."

Yes, Jade always had that ability. But I'd never heard Alex sound that passionate—outside describing music he admired.

"He's pretty handsome," Zooey said, "for an old man."

"He's only thirty-three." I didn't mean to say it aloud, but we share a birthday. Date and year. Our draft number was 366.

The phone rang before anyone could ask how I knew Jade's age. Ramona rushed to answer it, stepping into the living room, as if she expected a private conversation. But she called, "Uncle Rik, it's for you. It's Quinn's mother."

Yikes, here it was. Claudia had fomented disaster, and the next brick in the wall was falling on me. I crossed the kitchen, circling the long way around the table, preparing to redirect yet another wild accusation: *You turned my son gay!*

I had anticipated this call, but not eagerly.

"Hi, this is Rik Eliot. Can I help you, Mrs. Hargadine? Do you want me to send Quinn home?"

Quinn bore the surname of a city founder, though they live on B Street.

"Is it true?" she asked. "That artist has been in jail? Is he the kind of person our children should be involved with?"

It's not about Alex.

Relief rolled off me, like Sisyphus setting down his boulder.

"Do you mean Jade…Mr. Solberg? I'm absolutely sure the kids are safe with him."

Fercrissakes. I'm calling him Mr. Solberg? In this lifetime, and not in some alternate universe?

Yet hearing me say *Jade,* all five kids at the table turned my way. Listening.

"Last night," the voice in my ear was breathless, "Quinn said that man had been arrested. Called him a hero and a rebel. And you saw the way he was dressed at orientation."

"I'll send a copy of *ArtForum* home with Quinn." I looked at Quinn as I said this, silently thanking Becca for bringing home that copy. "It was a minor administrative mistake that occurred when Mr. Solberg was mounting a mural in Paris."

"Then Quinn and the others are safe?" She wanted reassurance in the way that desperate kids I tutor in remedial math ask: *Will I pass this course?*

"I promise you, both Mr. Solberg and I take the kids' safety quite seriously."

We said goodbye with the usual niceties and hung up. A subtle guilt crept up my spine. The version of Jade that the kids met in their high school classroom? Yes, safe as a walk in Lower Lithia Park. The Jade I knew in Seattle? Like Loki or the Monkey King, so wild that he wasn't always safe to be around. Here in Ashland? The only glimpse people had of his wild nature was the splinted little finger. And Superman Band-Aids on his knees.

When I returned, Alex declared, while Julio crawled into his lap, "Jade Solberg is the best thing to ever happened to me."

"Second best," Ramona said. "After our *kaukau.*"

Sweet. She wasn't even trying to soften me up.

"We get to work with Jade Solberg." Quinn sighed.

"Every single day," Alex said, his smile beatific. "The best thing ever."

I coughed. Coughed again. The rasp in my chest was so bad I had to drink water. Standing at the sink, I tried again to analyze the rattle. Not asthma.

No, more like broken remnants of glass rubbing on each other. Like a handful of Dragon's Blood crystals from a Haight-Ashbury head shop, rattling in a hollow between my lungs and heart.

—

After dinner and dishes, Quinn and Zooey departed. Valerie and Julio retreated to her room. I sat at the table with the kids to review their schedules. Only Alex had a math class. The twins took calculus last year, ending their math career at Ashland High. They'd refused to take physics this year, so had nothing I'd call a hard class for fall quarter.

"We need to be free," Molly said, "to enjoy our senior year. Homecoming. Tolo dance. Senior prom."

I about sprung my eyes out of their sockets, rolling them.

"It's the happiest time of our lives," Ramona said. "Isn't that what they say?"

"Whoever 'they' are," I said, "in my experience they're as senseless as a stone."

"Which experience was that, Uncle Rik?" Ramona asked, her face masked in innocence. "You were never a senior. You went to college without a high school diploma."

"We should have finished last year and be in college now," Molly said to Alex. "We suffer from abject child cruelty."

Alex's eyes bugged wide open. Even after living here all last summer, he's still often bewildered by how they teased me.

"Our cruel Uncle Rik wouldn't let us skip a grade," Ramona said. "Not seventh or tenth grade, which were both useless repetition of the same lessons as the year before."

Yeah, I didn't permit a grade skip. I'm manifest evidence for why a fifteen-year-old shouldn't be at university. Except for the whole "avoided living with my dreadful mother" thing.

"But you're letting Alex skip a grade," Molly said. "You're even encouraging him to do it. Not that I'm complaining about your failure to adhere to core principles. I'm merely astonished."

She was complaining.

"The kind of high school Alex formerly attended…" How to explain this? His school charged outrageous tuition while promising admission to top colleges yet couldn't help an intelligent guy like Alex gain a decent grasp of mathematics.

"It's just daycare for snotty rich kids," Alex said. Then he went off. "I couldn't get into orchestra because everyone else who tried out started doing Suzuki with the director's wife when they were, like, four. Claudia only let me take one art class, and that was just freakin' Life Drawing. I've had the same witch of a math teacher for three years. She makes you say your quiz scores out loud in class."

Yes, only a witch would do that.

Molly said, "Since you'll graduate in spring, ask the counselor for an application to take the SAT exam."

Ramona said, "Sign up for the October date. You have to say on the form which colleges should receive your scores. It costs more for every college you list."

I almost cried "Not October!" but resisted the impulse to tell Alex to wait until we could raise his score on the math section. But then, he could take the SAT a second time.

"We're going to Boston University," Molly said. "You too?"

"That's where my mother went," Alex said. "But I want to go to San Francisco State, like my father did."

My task list was on the table, so I added a note to talk to the counselor about the steps for getting three kids into college—part of my robust plan for leaving Ashland.

When the girls went upstairs to practice French, I reviewed Alex's math homework with him, to evaluate how well he understood it. He moved closer on the bench beside me. He's the kind of teenager who showers after PE but then douses himself in English Leather cologne. I'd wait to speak to him another time about how much scent is enough, since at that moment he was nervous about showing me his homework.

I will never complain to a student, a parent, or another teacher about any instructor's methods. Yet when I tutor kids with math troubles, I have to help them understand the concepts and how to cope with their teacher's style. I'd subbed for Alex's new math teacher a dozen times. He's retired military, so I expect that Alex might require coping-with-teacher skills besides concept reviews.

"Let's spend time Sunday on the coaching I promised," I said. "If you're free Sunday morning."

"I'll be free. I've thought about it all day, Uncle Rik. I'm, like, totally into graduating this year. I'll do whatever it takes."

When I rose to leave the table, Alex looked up. "Aren't you going to check the rest of my homework?"

"Do you want help with other subjects?"

"No, but Claudia checks all my work every day. To make sure I followed the teachers' instructions."

"Let me know if you need help, Alex. Otherwise, your homework is your private business, between you and your teachers. It's one of Rik's Rules."

Alex again knitted his brow, the way he had when the twins and I teased each other. He and I had more business to discuss, but he had yet to open the way. So I handed him my grandfather's watch. When Alex didn't take it, I set it on the table.

"Claudia said I should give this to you."

He glanced down, then imitated Claudia's smokey tones. "'It should be your legacy from your grandfather.' However, I will not tie that to my arm."

"But she's right. And I prefer my Timex." Which doesn't make me feel like there's a bank vault strapped to my wrist.

"Uncle Rik, Claudia only told you that because of what I said when she yelled that I'd turn gay over her dead body."

"Uh, should I ask?" I sat back down at the table. "Did you say, 'People don't turn gay. They're born that way'?"

"I said…uh…I planned to be a better fag than a skinny old guy who wears a big watch." He bent his head. "Sorry."

I couldn't laugh but wasn't about to scold. "You're built like your father. You'll never be skinny. And you don't have to wear the watch. Keep it because it's valuable. We can put it in a safe deposit box at the bank, so you can claim it later."

Alex shuffled his math papers, not looking at me. "That was really bad of me. I always say the wrong thing when Claudia picks a fight and yells at me. Sorry, Uncle Rik."

"Don't apologize. Try not to dwell on things said under pressure." I was struggling, trying not to remember being trashed at high volume by my mother.

"Still, I'm sorry." He swallowed. "I'll call my mom and tell her I'm not gay. I only said it because she got up in my shit."

"Are you sure you want to do that?"

"Don't you think I should just tell her, Uncle Rik? Then she'll quit harassing you and I can stay in Ashland."

"Don't worry about me," I said. "And don't just say what you think your mother wants to hear."

Okay, it's clear to me that Alex isn't gay, but he didn't ask my opinion. I believe Alex needs to work it all out on his own, separate from Claudia's twisted demands.

"Molly told me to stop making Claudia act crazy until I turn eighteen. Until then, Molly says I should just fake it."

I pulled out my wallet. "Here's five dollars if you'll take my advice instead of Molly's."

He laughed and brushed the bill away. "Claudia has no clue who I am. I've been faking it for years. If I just keep faking it, she won't go off her nut."

I was the grownup here, but each thing Alex said resurrected ancient arguments with Ruby.

"As your adult," I used Jade's term, "I'm required to argue for speaking the truth."

He laughed again, then shrugged, nervous and shy again. "What's the use? Whatever I tell my mother, she'll go off her nut."

"And no one else will get hurt if she does?"

"Huh?" He was surprised by the idea. "Like you? Do you think she might hurt you for letting me stay here?"

"No, like anyone you might…have feelings for."

He had the same look as when he couldn't figure a math problem. Then it dawned on him. "Like a girl? No, I don't."

"Will Claudia call someone else's mother, being angry?"

"Oh. No," Alex said. "She knows about Quinn, but he'd just fall down laughing if Claudia called his mother to say he's gay."

"Still, don't lie to Claudia. We'll figure out what it takes for you to stay here. Meanwhile, both of us should avoid winding her clock. But let's not tell lies."

"Okay." Alex shoved the watch over to me. "I'll tell her you gave me Great-Grandfather's watch. But I don't want it. It'd look okay if you wear it, Uncle Rik, but I'd look like a freak."

Well, yes, he would.

I put the watch in my pocket. I think Alex and I understood each other better, though we needed a great deal more conversation. Meanwhile, the long-term planning portion of my brain intended to stuff the watch into the back of my sock drawer in case any emergency requires me to pawn it again for quick cash.

13: Fox Spirit Becomes Human

I WENT UPSTAIRS AFTER OUR homework session, tea in hand this time, and set to work on a translation project for a U.S. engineering company that wants to do business in Hong Kong. That's the kind of work one can find with a Chinese Literature master's degree while living in a small town out in the back of beyond.

Then, at the edge of the well of remembrance, I failed to resist falling into the memories roused by Jade's reappearance.

When I started graduate school in mathematics, my thesis advisor gave me a long-term lease on a five-bedroom house at the edge of the U District. On Fifty-fourth Street Northeast, to be exact. He was insane to do that since I'd just turned nineteen. He reimbursed expenses and knocked off part of the month's rent for any repairs I made. So I made many trips to Hardwick's, the hardware store on Roosevelt Avenue, where I could ask what tool to use and how to fix what had most recently broken. I didn't, however, learn plumbing or basic electricity until I had to keep Chaos House from flooding or burning.

With my landlord's permission, I rented the other rooms to math freaks like me or a stray physics major. We called it Fermat's Last House. It was only a party house on nights when I made pizza. We'd crack a two-liter bottle of Dr Pepper and play Mastermind or PanzerBlitz until midnight.

Besides offering the guys in the house cheap rent, I kept the refrigerator stocked and cooked meals at night. The math freaks subletting from me couldn't boil ramen. That's where I learned to cook for more than two people, which made for another income stream. (My math prof advised me to charge time and materials.)

All through my undergraduate years, I'd clung to memories of my Hong Kong crush. We wrote to each other frequently. When I first returned to the U.S., I wrote at length about a British TV show called *The Avengers,* which wasn't like any comic we'd read but owed much to the kung fu traditions we knew. Kai wrote that his father had convinced him to sell his comics collection for his college fund. But he saved the #8 *Amazing Spider-Man* I gave him when I left Hong Kong, plus a few from the Avengers and Fantastic Four series. I begged Kai to come to school at the UW, though I'd be starting graduate school when he'd be a freshman. I explained all the advantages the U Dub has as an institution. I never once mentioned that awkward day.

However, Kai did as his father had done and went to Cambridge in the U.K. I still missed him and held on to a childishly romantic notion of friendship. As a consequence, for the last two terms of my master's work in math, I signed up to study abroad—at Cambridge, a holy site for us math freaks.

It poured cold English rain when I stepped off the train from London onto the Cambridge platform where Kai promised to meet me. I found two things: Kai had become a very handsome man since I'd last seen him, and he was engaged to an English girl named Victoria, who considered him her property. She went everywhere with us the whole time I studied at Cambridge. Whenever I spoke to Kai in Chinese, she'd say, "English, please," and Kai would apologize for being rude.

A long rainy English winter was spent getting rid of my last hopes for a second chance. But more than hope died in Cambridge. After I came home from England, I spent one term working on my PhD in mathematics. Then I switched majors. Life in Cambridge drove a spike into my brain, killing the part that cared passionately about mathematics. When I switched majors, my math advisor declared that I'd broken his heart (Chan-suk said the same), but he also noted that I wasn't the first math prodigy to burn out young.

Then I chose what seemed to be the easiest alternative. I became a Chinese Literature major. Which marked the beginning of my life as a professional student. What I didn't do: initiate new flirtations or replace the secret crush I'd carried since Hong Kong, and I was seldom anywhere that someone might flirt with me. It was just school, study, and house chores. One might think my life was ever thus.

As a newly launched liberal arts major, I lacked a substantial liberal arts foundation. I was no longer the smartest person in the room, having switched rooms. I'd never been the smartest one in the math room either, just over-praised for my abilities. That praise had been anodyne after Hong Kong since succor could not be had from my family.

With no liberal arts background other than 100-level freshman requirements, I had to do all the coursework for another master's degree. I had a half-baked notion of focusing my thesis on the motif of smashing pottery in contemporary Chinese cinema, and argued with my new advisor that I should learn about Chinese ceramics as a foundation. That's why I took a pass-no pass ceramics course as an elective.

The teaching assistant for the ceramics course was Jade. On the first day of class, he asked the class for leads on a room to rent. I needed another housemate to make the arithmetic of my household expenses work properly.

So Jade rented a room at Fermat's Last House.

And proceeded to serve as a catalyst for a great change in my life, greater than leaving Hong Kong.

When he moved in, I had a brush cut and wore a madras shirt (pressed) and wheat jeans (also pressed). But two months later, I was in navy surplus thirteen-button bell bottoms and a t-shirt from the Sky River rock festival. My hair had crawled over my ears and was on its way to my collar.

My friends describe their experiences between ages fifteen and twenty as filled with emotional jaggedness and self-doubt, worrying about how others perceived them, falling in and out of love. I didn't experience those emotional travails until I was twenty-one, because I didn't finish puberty until I quit math and met Jade. Then I grew four inches in eighteen months, which was quite painful. I became intensely self-conscious, lost in daydreams, and emotionally explosive when alone in my room. After all, I'd learned with Kai about the perils of disclosing one's private obsessions.

Life at Fermat's Last House went on for four more years after I dropped out of my mathematics PhD program. In fact, I managed Fermat's Last House until I left Seattle. I wonder who has that house now? Has my math advisor retired? I should look for him when I'm in Seattle to defend my dissertation.

When I came to Ashland, I accidentally ended up with a second chance to create a house that offers more than mere shelter. But there's no second chance in this world for creating the wild experiences possible during college years.

As I bent over the translation work in my study, it quickly became late, and I'd meditated for too long on the non-scholarly part of my university years. However, I did make modest progress on my translation project before folding it away for the night.

Before bed, I finished my list of the next day's chores.

14: Outside the Wall

EARLY THURSDAY MORNING, I AGAIN started my run at dawn, up Water Street to where the street loops around Lithia Fountain and its eight spigots for sipping sulfurous water. That paved oval of the Plaza is surrounded by two-story commercial buildings, spruced up since they were born in the first half of the century. These include a dry-goods store, a Chinese restaurant, and a dive bar that is horrifically unfriendly to tourists. The two-story stone-façade police station squats on the corner that leads up to Main Street in one direction, to the park in the other.

With all the granite foundations and stone facings on the buildings, this part of town is like a Fifties movie set with women in wide-skirted dresses and men in Stetson hats. But no one is out this early in the morning. Even the cop shop is silent.

I ran past the fake lake with its native mallards and non-native mute swans, and then up into the park. I passed only three other early-morning runners. Being alone in the early hours in a man-made forest lets loose fantasies of journeying as a lone warrior through spirit-drenched T'ang landscapes. I'm not a spiritual person but running into the Watershed's upper reaches lets me feel the connection between ancient land and modern strivings.

I should cut back on excess consumption of kung fu movies.

When I came back down from the hills, I passed that sad old zoo near the upper pond. I'd signed a petition last year that begged the City to remove all the old caging and free the bedraggled, depressed eagle in the aviary. Every time I run past it, I think it's too bad my Disputatious Neighbor can't put his contentious nature to work for civic good.

Then, just down the trail, I smelled weed, though it was far too early for people to be smoking in the upper park. Tomcat pee? Two more paces, and I knew that rotten cabbage smell. A dog had frightened a skunk, and I'd just jogged through a memory of the encounter. Likely the dog ran away thinking it won and still hasn't come to grips with the existential abyss where it now abides, while its owner compulsively washes the poor dog with tomato juice. I don't know much about dogs, but I do know about the existential abyss. In my personal abyss, I now smelled worse than boys in a closed-door classroom after PE.

I came down Pioneer Street into town, glimpsing the two ribbons of road through the commercial core. Beyond, the eastern strands of the town dipped down to the grass fields and marshlands along Bear Creek. On the street where I ran, song sparrows and house finches fought for breakfast at birdfeeders.

Curiosity had plagued me since the project launch meetings with Jade, so I paused above the wall where a mosaic King Lear mural was to be mounted. And where I'd be spending every afternoon until Halloween. The wall had been part of the beehive-shaped Chautauqua building, Ashland's manifestation of the turn-of-the-century self-improvement movement. Now reinforced, the wall remained through the many changes made after Angus Bowmer got a Shakespearean bee in his Tudor bonnet.

The first year I was in town, and stone broke, Becca showed me where to sneak over the safety fence to watch plays from atop the wall. Sneaking over the fence again, I looked down the fifteen feet from the wall's edge to the brick-lined plaza below, where Jade's scaffolding was in place. I wiped sweat from my face with the tail of my t-shirt, wondering if I should bury my clothes in the backyard for a week, like I had to do the last time I ran through skunk scent.

"Don't jump." A deep, warm voice called from close by.

Jade came up beside me, grinning. He held out his hand to grasp my hot, sweaty palm, then put his other hand on the shoulder of my drenched t-shirt. The hand with the splinted finger.

I stepped away, too conscious of my skunk taint.

Jade first came to Fermat's Last House during a drenching Seattle downpour. I'd opened the door to a tall guy with soft golden stubble and long, out-all-night hair, a duffle over his shoulder. He was softly singing 'Here Comes the Sun' while tinkling the Chinese wind chimes on my porch. He never could sing well, but that didn't stop him. Instead of hello, I'd said, "Dinner is just now on the table." He offered a brilliant smile, as if that filled him with joy. Now, here in Ashland, Jade smiles the same warm way, whether he's meeting me or total strangers.

Jade said, "I broke my finger trying to see what happens if anyone falls. That's why the onsite rules forbid flipflops. Or stepping over the safety fence." He released my hand. "Gosh, can you believe I'm still that much of a dolt?"

"I'd only call it rash." I coughed to clear my throat. Or was it in my chest?

"No, Sasha, it's totally broken. Not just scraped."

Sasha. The dragon crystals rattled beneath my sweaty t-shirt.

"I mean, your impulse to jump was rash."

He laughed, tipping his head back, exposing his throat. "I don't deserve my own luck. When I heard that a chaperone was required, I dreaded having to coach a stranger on how to collaborate on a work site. But the angels delivered you! Goodness, what a surprise!"

He grasped my shoulder again, the metal splint scraping my smelly t-shirt.

"Caught me by surprise too." My heart beat too hard. He must feel it through my shirt. I swayed, took a step back from the edge of the wall for safety's sake. Buckbrush scratched my bare legs.

Jade grinned again. "I'm also lucky since this is my first gig with high school kids. When I ask for help, you'll know I don't have a clue what to do. A stranger wouldn't be able to guess."

I hadn't foreseen how blasted awkward I'd feel when we stood close, talking to each other—without even considering my scent-drenched t-shirt. I fingered the side seams of my shorts to keep my hands from shaking.

"That's my job," I rasped. "I'm paid to keep the kids from wandering off if you lose their attention."

"I want more from you, Sasha." He sounded wistful. Then he shook his head. "Can you help me as a teacher?"

The crunching crystals threatened to crack my breastbone.

He had come so close that I smelled the woody sweet-spice scent of bay rum. I once more wiped my face with my dog-and-skunk-fight shirt. Jade might think the scent is weed. Except maybe he remembers that I don't smoke. Makes me paranoid.

Then I got paranoid at that moment about having lifted my shirt and exposing myself.

I said, "I've never worked on a grid-and-color-matching project. I can't help teach that."

"Sasha, I'm scared I'll fuck up." He ran his hand through his much shorter hair. Was he feeling awkward too?

"You were a great TA. You've had plenty of experience since then, haven't you?"

"But with graduate students. You know what that's like."

"What do you think is different with high school seniors? Except they all think they know more than they do."

"That's just it, Sasha. How do I criticize young kids? How to avoid busting their spirit?"

"You'll see a light when you do it right." I wasn't prepared for pedagogy at dawn with a guy who kept repeating a nickname I hadn't heard for eight years. I wanted to run home and bury my t shirt. "A kid's eyes shade over if you get it wrong."

"Gosh, I hope I only see the dawning." He pushed his hair back again, which distracted me. Before, he wore a hippie ponytail except during kiln work, when he tied it up like Toshiro Mifune going to battle.

I said, "You already won over your crew. They think you're the best thing since David Bowie." Nervous, I couldn't stop. "And Bowie only drew pictures. Didn't know one thing about ceramics or large-scale mountings."

"But it's only due to that wacko video." Jade dug his hands into his jeans pockets, the splinted finger left hanging. "Kids think I'm cool for running from the gendarmes. Not for making art."

"Not true. And they think you're at least better than a poke in the eye with a sharp stick."

That's what he used to say when forced to make do with the worst kiln or inadequate space on the ceramics drying racks.

"Ha! You do know me, Sasha." He tossed his hands in the air. The morning breeze coming off the mountain slammed *you do know me* into my chest. "I'm just a freak trying to get what's inside my head out into the world. With no one getting hurt."

"Including you?" I pointed to his splinted little finger.

"Goodness." He stuck that hand behind his back. "I'm still working on impulse control. Any tips for teaching teenagers?"

I believed my rational mind was in control, but I offered intimate advice that I'd never dream of giving the twins. "Don't wear shirts that reveal so much."

"You want me deep in the closet?" He mistook my meaning. "Imagine *you* admonishing *me* about that."

Years ago, just after we met, Jade said: *You wear madras shirts like a disguise.* But he'd meant it kindly.

"You asked for tips," I said. "It's what my supervisor said when I was a student teacher. Some young girls cannot yet differentiate their own projections from men's signals. Or even when there aren't any signals."

His eyes flitted. He still didn't get it.

"Jade, remember that Ceramics 101 section? I think it was Fall quarter 1972, when that girl misread the situation when you offered guidance with the pottery wheel?"

At last he nodded. "Yeah, I remember. I haven't touched any students since then."

"Your Sky River t-shirt is too old and thin."

He beamed. "Do you remember it? The shirt, I mean. I know you missed the festival."

"Not the point. It shows…every bone underneath. A teen child might misconstrue what that means." Not me. I know how attractive he is in t-shirt and jeans. I can just look away. "One parent already complained to me last night."

"Oh. Gosh." He was so slow to understand. "I suppose I can wear teacher clothes like you do."

"You don't have to go that far. But it's High School Teacher 101. Don't wear clothes that are…um…revealing."

"Thanks, Sasha." He grinned. "It's good, isn't it? That we can talk like this again? You and I don't need to take weeks to get to know each other."

"Yeah." *Crunch.* I froze my face, masking the pain coursing through me.

"I'm glad that luck brought us together," Jade said. "So we're friends again."

"Yeah. I have to go. I should be cooking breakfast by now."

"Sure, Sasha. Glad we got to talk. Xavier said you'd be at Chez Margot last night, but I missed you. I did get a chance to talk with Becca though. She seems nice."

Worthless faithless feckless Immortals, providing no protection! Freaking Xavier talked about me. That news destroyed what had been a decent morning run.

"Uh, Jade?" I felt compelled to speak my one truth. "I ran through old skunk scent. I don't smell like this."

He laughed. "I know. I'm from the Cascade foothills."

I stepped back over the fence onto the street. Safe.

Then he called after me. "Do you think I don't know what you really smell like, Sasha? See you later."

Breathless, I ran home to Chaos House, the Dragon's Blood crunch interfering with my pace. I should have been prepared for close contact. The night before I'd talked myself into the proper mind space for being in the same world again.

But I was not ready. Especially in my skunk shirt.

Jade, however, showed no problem acting normal.

At home, I stuffed my reeking clothes into the washer and started the hot-water cycle, then ran through the house wrapped in a towel from the dryer. After a two-minute shower, I was dressed and then down in the kitchen, brewing coffee, making a frittata, filling bento boxes, pouring orange juice. Greeting Mrs. Adams when she came into the kitchen for Ruby's breakfast.

All that crunchy nervousness and self-doubt washed away in the shower, but I had no solitude for deeper reflection. Everyone was in the kitchen, drinking coffee, hurrying through the morning meal, making sure Julio ate his Cheerios, packing bento boxes. Alex again went out to deliver breakfast.

He was gone so long, his frittata got cold, and it was time to leave for school. When he came in, he was elated.

"Guys! Jade Solberg lives next door! Why didn't you tell us, Uncle Rik?"

I shrugged. "You gave him light bulbs for the garage. Didn't it dawn on you when he walked into class yesterday?"

Then breakfast, like the previous night's dinner, was eaten amid the excitement spawned by having Jade Solberg as a teacher and a neighbor.

No one noticed me doing a superior job of cleaning the kitchen while silently congratulating myself. That I'd done it. I'd had an intimate conversation with Jade. Stood close to him in the early morning light.

Then I again fell into the deep well I try hard to avoid: the shaft deep underground that holds memories of when we first became friends. That one time when the Heavenly Immortals had scrambled the world in my favor.

15: Sons as Rebels

ON JADE'S FIRST NIGHT AT Fermat's Last House, I showed off after dinner while making tea for him, using the tea set that had been Chan-suk's farewell present to my mother. She never opened the box, so it came to Seattle with me after I'd been home for Christmas my sophomore year. (The last time for a decade.)

Of course, I acted like a nitwit, explaining to my Ceramics TA about Ru Glaze Gaiwan and how the glaze crackled under the heat when used for tea. "My uncle in Hong Kong said it's a Song dynasty technique."

"You have a Chinese uncle?"

"I call him Chan-suk, as if he were my uncle. He tutored me in mathematics and continues to teach me a great deal about language and culture."

"When did you live in China?"

"Hong Kong. For a decade."

"With communists?"

"No, it's a British colony." Which I thought everyone knew.

"Boy am I jealous," Jade said. "I grew up in Scio. Do you know where that is?"

"No." We both had holes in our knowledge of geography.

"It's in the Cascades foothills in Oregon. The town has five hundred people. My family had five acres on the edge of town, but my father made his living as a logger."

"So," I tried humor, since I hadn't made an impression with my cracked-glaze teapot, "you're Scio's most famous artist?"

"Definitely. I left town the day after I graduated. My parents had died a few months earlier and—"

"I'm sorry. How sad."

"It was. But we weren't close. It's outrageous to say, but ending up at the UW was easier without my father to interfere. He'd been insisting on Oregon State University."

"That's a cow college." Was that rude of me to say? "You quarreled over it?"

Jade said, "That, and everything else, most every day. First, my dad would go silent, then he'd blow his stack and hit me, but only with his open palm. From what I've read since then, he had what the Brits called shell shock. But I don't know for sure, since he didn't tell me what he'd done in Europe during World War II."

"Did you resent it?" I wanted my new friend to say more. My method for managing a perpetually angry parent was to give myself amnesia and never go home.

"I bear no grudges," Jade said. "I did cry when my old man died, but I walked away from Scio with a check from his lawyer that got me through three terms of tuition and art supplies. Once I was a Washington resident, I won scholarships and stipends."

"Wouldn't an Oregon school have been cheaper?"

"There's no ceramics scene like at the UW. Our profs are changing everything about ceramics in the western hemisphere."

We sipped tea from the elegant cracked-glaze cups.

I'd also won scholarships for my performance in mathematics. However, after switching majors, I had to rely on the trust fund from my grandfather, plus my canny ability to manage Fermat's Last House. Jade's story humbled me. Through my irascible grandfather, I had the privilege of family wealth.

"Now, dear landlord." Jade had established the Bob Dylan joke five minutes after entering the house. "Tell me about your father. He's also named Aldrik Alexander Eliot?"

"No, that was my maternal grandfather. My mother changed our last name when she divorced my father."

"And she named you Aldrik? How cruel! Why don't you go by Alexander instead? Then I could call you Sasha, like the character in *Orlando.*"

Since I had virtually no liberal arts background before changing my major, I hadn't yet read *Orlando*—a good thing that night, since I had the sophistication of a twelve-year-old boy. I'd have been shocked.

I replied as a true innocent. "Call me Sasha. If you want to."

"Okay, Sasha. Why did your parents divorce?"

"My father often didn't come home. One night, he never came home again."

"Off with another woman? Or dead?"

"Who knows? If my mother does, she won't say. But he was alive when she divorced him." I shrugged. "About all I remember is the stink of his cigarettes. Pall Mall menthols. Mostly, he was a ghost. His kids weren't of value to him."

"Was he like my dad? Did he hit you a lot?"

"I don't remember that. All the lashings I remember came from my mother's tongue."

"It's sad he never knew you."

"He knew I was good at math."

"I mean, he never knew the actual you. You are kind and smart, which don't always go together."

Uh, wow. We had sort of just met.

He pushed further. "Do you think you'll ever see him again?"

I didn't know how to respond to his compliment. I answered the question instead. "No. I asked a friend in Hong Kong to check the public death and marriage records. There's nothing. Maybe we only imagined him and we're all the result of pathogenesis."

"You mean parthenogenesis?"

"No, I'm fairly certain it was pathological." That made Jade laugh. Which I liked and wanted to make happen again. But instead I said, "I've forgotten his face. All I gained from him is a desire to be a better man than he was."

That first conversation inaugurated a different university life than I'd known before, and not just because I'd never exchanged confidences with others at Fermat's Last House. From those late-night ramblings, I finally met my true self, following my Ceramics TA into the kind of wild student life others had been indulging since the Sixties. I was a late bloomer.

I can pretend that Jade lured me into that divergent journey, like the Monkey King. But I jumped and ran after him.

16: Normal Chaos

LATER THURSDAY MORNING, AFTER THE kids shouldered their backpacks and said farewell, I gathered papers in preparation for a depressing hour with Nick, who'd be acting as my attorney rather than recreational buddy.

Nick's office is in the front half of a modest Craftsman cottage he'd inherited from his father (along with the legal practice). When I came in, he glanced up from the papers he was reading. Rather than hello, he said, "Why did I think that family law would be a decent way to spend my life?"

"Alas." I held up my hands prayerfully. "Here I am."

When Nick pointed to the chair beside his big, old-fashioned oak desk, I sat and explained Alex's situation and indulged a few moments expressing my resentment for how Claudia was treating her son. Nick knows most of my family history. He first helped in early 1975, in the aftermath of the Eliot family's Specially Bad Christmas, when my family acted out a Tennessee Williams play updated for the Seventies. At that time, Ruby's role in the play was guided by phenobarbital and wine. For Wendy, it wasn't laudanum, just Excedrin, a puff of marijuana in the backyard, and the beginnings of an old-fashioned nervous breakdown. Claudia powers through every act with caffeine and over-confidence.

"Claudia's disrespect for Alex is a new development," I said. "And until now she's been friendly toward me, never rude. Suddenly she's afraid I'll turn Alex gay."

Nick began citing how we'd defend Alex's right not to be attacked by his mother. I listened, admiring how he remembers case law the same way he remembers which high school each NFL star came out of, with exacting detail.

"Since Alex isn't an Oregon resident, I'll enlist my old roommate as an advocate to file for guardianship in California."

"What if Claudia won't agree to it?"

"There'll be a hearing. Which will take time. We can run the clock out until he's eighteen."

"That's not for a year." I wrenched my hands with anguish, had to put them in my lap to stop.

"Buck up, buddy!" Nick tapped his desk. "Let's focus on the immediate future. We first need to know if Claudia will agree to you serving as guardian. That's the best result, the one we want."

"And the worst?"

"She might sue to have Alex returned to her care. Then we'll take steps to resist that."

"I want to tell Alex not to worry," I said. "Is that true?"

Nick said, "For now, tell him to let me worry about the legal side of things. You can help him with everyday worries."

"Okay, I can do that."

"I'd advise *you* not to worry, but I know you. I'd be wasting my breath. So let's talk about my fee." He pointed to the wall facing the street. "Those windows need to be replaced."

For thirty minutes, I took measurements and we discussed what kind of replacements he wanted (double-pane, double-hung wood windows).

We became fast friends after he tackled my family's legal affairs, though we're opposites. He believes Bruce Springsteen is a great musician and follows sports obsessively. He's a jock and begs me to play football on Saturdays with his friends—flag, he says, because we're getting old. He asks me to play tennis with his latest girlfriend and her roommate. Yet he won't run or hike with me in the upper hills. He goes with me to midnight fight movies at the Varsity Theatre only if he doesn't have another date.

"I'll call after I order the windows," I said, "to let you know when they might be ready."

"Before it freezes, I hope," he said. "The winter wind comes through these antiques like it has a grudge."

I walked home, talking myself into believing that Alex's problems would be easier to solve than Ruby's had been when Nick and I first met.

Before Ruby came out of the hospital after that Specially Bad Christmas, I began working with Nick to secure custody of the twins. It had become clear that Wendy would not be returning to Ashland. Perhaps just as well, since she wasn't in any mental or emotional state to act as their guardian, even if I could find her. After I attained supporting diagnoses from doctors about my mother's mental state, Nick helped me gain guardianship for Ruby. We then waded into quicksand, endeavoring to uncover how Ruby's money had disappeared. All that remained intact was her social security and the heavily mortgaged title to Chaos House. She had huge credit card debt and unpaid utility bills.

After staring at a pile of papers and receipts for a series of large cash withdrawals Ruby had made, Nick proposed the most likely answer: Ruby had had a lover who took everything. Who that might be, we found no evidence. The money from her father should have lasted beyond her natural life, but within the last six months, she'd become dead broke and was living alone in Palm Springs when she'd stolen my trust fund. That money disappeared from her bank account the day after it was posted.

My plan for 1975: finish my dissertation and find a teaching position at a university or get a Fulbright and begin the scholarly life I'd dreamed of. But no. I became a handyman and a substitute teacher, in part because an unknown man romanced my ill-tempered, dementia-impaired mother and stole all her money.

To recover from Ruby's past catastrophes and new hospital bills, I shouldered the mortgage. To pay it, I divided Chaos House into studios and two-room flats, beating back four decades of neglect. I also restored the slum-like cottages. The new rent contributed to Ruby's at-home care and my Return to Hong Kong fund. Nick made sure that Ruby's guardianship accounted for my sweat-equity as salary.

I did finish my dissertation, despite repeated interruptions. It just took eight tedious years instead of two.

—

After Thursday morning's unfulfilling meeting with Nick, the mailman brought me good news, despite his gruff greeting when he passed me coming down the steps. He hates our front stairs, which climb over the daylight basement. I perked up. If the postman came to the door, it meant he'd delivered important mail.

"A package or a certified letter?" I asked.

"International letter," he said, as taciturn as always. "And please tell your friends to use the mailbox only for mail with postage. It's illegal not to, and I almost carried it away."

Mrs. Adams had signed for the airmail letter and accepted the other envelope from the postman. While I kicked off my shoes, I found both letters on the hall table. That heavy, unstamped envelope had "garage rent" scrawled across it and held two hundred dollars in cash. The money should thrill me—it did thrill me. But Jade had left it in the mailbox instead of giving it to me directly. And it was four times as much rent as for the two months of mural construction. Like, it covered rent until late April.

When Inez returns from Italy.

That much rent means Jade plans to be in Ashland through Inez's entire sabbatical. Again, it bothered me that she hadn't told me it'd be Jade using her studio. My tardy internalization of Jade's long-term commitments left me feeling…

Like I'd rather not think about the garage rent. Instead, I eased open the thin blue letter. It was from Cheung Bai Shing, the brother-in-law Chan-suk had introduced me to. He's a professor at the university where I hope to teach in Hong Kong. He offered me my dream:

> My brother Chan Wei Wen shared the latest draft of your manuscript. I've shown it to others in my department. As you and I have discussed in previous correspondence, my colleagues are keen to advance a research and teaching position that focuses on Cantonese popular culture.

He proposed a mechanism for interviews via correspondence, followed by a live interview in December.

I could make December work. I could afford it if I found a bucket flight from a Chinatown travel agent. The interview via correspondence and then live, didn't pose a barrier. My rhetoric teacher at the school I attended in Hong Kong was an ex-Jesuit, so my written and oral communication skills are superlative.

This means that I could…have what I've wanted.

This was the first time since Tuesday that my pulse had raced due to joy rather than fear or trepidation. I paced around the living room and kitchen for ten minutes, until I stubbed my toe on the sofa and came back to the real world. Fortunately, I had my task list to guide my giddy self. As a first chore, I swapped the early-morning laundry into the dryer, taking care to transport the tree frog into the backyard.

When it was time for Mrs. Adams's lunch break, I read bits of *Pride and Prejudice* to Ruby. I then set out to retrieve the breakfast boxes from the cottages. I confess to watching the timing of Xavier's departures over the past two days in order to judge when I could perform my cottage-related chores without encountering him. I aim to stop feeling aggrieved just because he's in Ashland. And the thin blue letter left me feeling magnanimous for the entire world—minus Xavier F. Torres.

Thursday midday proved to be slightly cooler than the intense late-summer heat of the past several weeks. Stepping out of Chaos House, I inhaled the woody scents lingering on the still air. Becca says the turning of summer to fall instills a sense of mourning. For me, only Christmas weather plays with my emotions. I like the harbingers of autumn. I wish it were possible to bathe in the mélange of odors from the undergrowth in the Siskiyou ecology. The sun-heated vegetation after our no-moisture summer releases the best odors in the world. Chaparral in vacant lots. Mint species in rockeries. I took a breath. The scents lifted my spirits even further than the thin blue letter from Cheung Bai Shing.

The sole guest at home was again Timothy, who sat on the front stoop of the middle cottage, reading a script.

"Hi, Timothy." I had to step past him to retrieve the bento box from the shelter of the milk crate, where I found half of breakfast had been abandoned. Inquiring obliquely, I said, "I hope the meal was satisfactory."

Timothy chewed his lip for a second, then said, "I appreciate it. But I can't eat muffins or toast."

"I apologize. I didn't know you had a food allergy."

"It's not that. My agent recommended this No Bread No Pasta diet that's healthier than fasting before filming starts."

He's twenty-one—I saw his PR sheet. And he lacks about 10 percent of optimal body mass. I couldn't lead such a miserable life for love or money.

"Then no traditional chocolate chip pancakes for you on Sundays?" I teased but shouldn't have. His eyes went wild for a second. Timothy *wanted* chocolate chip pancakes. But then he shook his head, denying what he wanted.

He's signed up for twenty or thirty years of managed starvation if he becomes the star his agent wants him to be. His moment of hesitation made me wonder what Timothy truly wanted. But I didn't ask since we'd barely met.

"Seriously," I said, "you just need to balance calories consumed with exercise. Running? Air Force calisthenics?"

He looked at me as if I might be speaking Chinese.

He said, "I can't go dancing with your friends on Saturday. Thank you for the invitation, but there's a workshop that night at the Festival. Xavier insists I attend."

"That's too bad," I said. "But you like music, don't you? Who's your favorite?"

Timothy named performers. "Toto. Toni Basil. Billy Joel. Olivia Newton-John. The Go-Go's. Who's yours?"

We may have nothing in common. I tried for the middle of the road in case we might meet there. "Joy Division? Prince?"

Timothy's eyes darted up, thinking. "I've heard of him. He's from the Midwest, isn't he? Chicago?"

I tried harder. "David Bowie? The Clash? 'Should I Stay or Should I Go,' at least?"

Timothy shrugged. "I don't have to be at the afternoon workshop until later. So you can stay for a while."

Did he twitch because he thought I was coming on to him?

"Um, it's a Clash song. The other side of 'Straight to Hell.'"

He offered his charismatic star smile, but I could see that he didn't know the A side of anything from the B side. Further, he probably carried a Partridge Family lunchbox to school while I was finishing my math master's. That didn't make me feel old. But I mentally moved Timothy into the circle of adolescents I supervise after school.

I had all the breakfast bento boxes and thermoses in hand and was ready to head out.

"See you later," Timothy said.

I turned back.

"Timothy, I'll remember no bread and no pasta. But if your agent talks about dexies and whites, or suggests purging, then get a new agent. Seriously. Dexies do a bad number on people."

I harbored a suspicion that such substance abuse had been Wendy's new complication after she returned to the U.S. As far as I could tell from phone conversations, my sister never slept.

"Thanks," Timothy said. "But my friend Jade already warned me. Made me promise."

Your friend? I never knew that friend to give health warnings. The advice he gave me was more like: *Here, take this. The guy I got it from says it's only a hundred mics. You won't miss class.*

—

After chatting with Timothy, I walked down the driveway between Lazarus Cottage and Chaos House, intending to enter my house through the back door.

In the backyard that afternoon, under the dappled shade of an aging locust tree (which I need to cut down before it's even more of a problem), my mother sat in her wheelchair, holding hands with a man reciting the Serenity Prayer. Mrs. Adams, across the patio table, was reading *The Little Drummer Girl.*

The fellow caressed my mother's frail hands with his gnarled paws. He must be eighty, his nose and cheeks mottled with red veins. His liver-distended belly indicated a hard drinker—or, given that prayer, a former drinker. My shadow fell over them just as he said amen and Ruby echoed him. When he glanced up, the chihuahua at his feet began barking. He yelled several expletives to quiet the dog.

"Hello. You must be Chris." His voice, too loud for how close I stood, was etched by cigarettes. "Ruby told me so much about you. I'm Willie Smith from next door."

He stood and jutted out his hand in a jolly greeting, not noticing my arms were full of thermoses and bento boxes. I offered only my little finger to return his handshake.

"Smith? From next door?" That chihuahua explained the barking at night for the last few weeks. "Are you related to the lieutenant colonel?"

"My little brother, God bless him. Gave me shelter when my trailer burned up at Eagle Point last month."

"Retired logger?" I shifted my bento boxes, hugging them closer when one began to slip. The logging industry, even in this recession, is all that's ever happened in Eagle Point.

"Mill work. Fifty years. Served the country almost as good as the U.S. Army. 'Course, when I say that to my brother, he'd like to pop his eyeballs out." Willie slapped his thigh. "J.J. is one of those folks, you just love to get his goat."

"Indeed? Well, welcome to the neighborhood, Mr. Smith." And feel free to get your brother's goat twice a day and four times on Sunday, so he's too busy to pester me.

"Call me Willie, my friend. Mr. Smith was our daddy, God rest his soul. A good man. Your sweet, sweet mother is the only soul I've met who's a better person. You are a lucky boy, Chris."

I didn't expect this acquaintance to last long enough to be worth asserting my actual name. And I suspected that Willie-from-Eagle-Point might inhabit an alternate world closer to Ruby's than the one where I dwell.

"Mrs. Adams, a word please." I tipped my head toward the back porch. "If you have the time."

Mrs. Adams held a finger in her book to mark her place, and followed me up the long access ramp into the laundry room. I set my load of bento boxes and thermoses on the washing machine, which shook, spinning Ruby's daily laundry. I took a cleansing breath through my nose, let it out for four counts, my lungs assaulted by soap, lint, and mold from the utility porch.

"What in the ever-loving universe is *that* about?"

"They met at the senior center," she said. "He discovered they're neighbors when the van dropped them at home."

"What's he doing here?"

"He comes over in the afternoon when there's no lunch at the senior center. They've become good friends."

"Are you feeding him?" I'd counted the dishes on the patio table while Willie expounded on what a sweet mother I have.

"Ruby's manners are so ingrained, she asks every guest to share her lunch."

"But she only knows to eat when you put food on the table and then help her eat it. She doesn't know which meal it is or the time of day. How does she remember Willie from one day to the next?"

Ruby no longer has the physical ability to eat a sandwich without help. And she hasn't remembered me in years.

"You know how she pretends to remember," Mrs. Adams said. "I see no harm in his visits. And what's one more tuna sandwich?"

I could calculate the precise cost of a tuna sandwich, but it'd be a waste of my math degree. I took four more calming breaths, while Mrs. Adams looked woefully apologetic. Which made my irritation collapse.

"I'm sorry. Thanks for your excellent care of her, Mrs. Adams. Please let me know if you see any sign that fellow is trying to take advantage of her."

She nodded.

I scooped up the bento boxes, which needed to be washed before I dressed for my new gig. But I stopped, seeing Mrs. Adams stoop-shouldered, as if she'd been scolded.

"I feel bad," I said, "about being so ill-tempered. I'm not questioning your judgment. You do excellent work and are so very kind to Ruby. I am deeply grateful."

Mrs. Adams escaped, saying, "I'll bring her in now."

In the kitchen, as I washed bento boxes, I still felt bad about being curt with Mrs. Adams. The backyard scene had tipped me off balance. My recent recollection of Ruby's past troubles with an unknown man? A piss-poor excuse for being short-tempered.

I must again apologize to Mrs. Adams for being an asshole.

And I also must make sure Willie Smith knows that sweet Ruby has no money, though she lives in this big, beautiful house.

17: Collaboration

MIDAFTERNOON THURSDAY, I DRESSED IN worn jeans and Chuck Taylor high-tops and walked up for the first day's onsite mural work, intending to arrive ahead of the kids. My feet skittered on the granite sand along Water Street. I stumbled once on the curb at Main Street. On the hill climb, my legs felt like I'd run two-thirds of a marathon. But it wasn't fatigue. Just the return of trepidation.

Jade and I had had our first real encounter, so the worst was over. Yet what must he think of me, still stuck in Ashland? The most likely answer had to be: little to nothing at all.

I took five breaths to calm my emotions, like an ingénue fighting stage fright. I would not let my brain linger on stray thoughts. I've resolved that whenever I feel this way, I will focus on two truths: I finished my dissertation, and I have a job in Hong Kong as good as in hand.

The brick walkway by the Bowmer Theatre was warm from the afternoon sun, which had shifted at that hour, preparing to drop behind the western hills. Just outside the Festival offices, I ran into my friend Kevin, who wore what I'm sure is his sole tweed jacket. He's usually in leathers since his only transportation is his BMW bike. He leaned against a staff entrance to the Bowmer, so he wasn't out there on break from bartending at Chez Margot.

"Imagine seeing you here," I said.

"Indeed, it's such a big city. What an astounding coincidence." He grinned. "This is the gig I mentioned last week. I'm helping actors learn more about kabuki theatre, which is the interpretation planned for next season's *King Lear.*"

Kevin's dissertation topic, "Medieval Drama Traditions and Shakespeare," has proved more useful than mine since it gets him consulting gigs with the Festival.

"Can Xavier Torres imitate kabuki theatre?" I scoffed. "Can he pronounce it? He claimed Jean-Luc Godard as his stylistic model when he did *Streetcar* two years ago."

Kevin shrugged. "After he described his vision yesterday, I decided it'd be best to get to the actors before he does."

He took a key from his pocket and unlocked the staff door just as Timothy and two young women approached.

"Here for the kabuki workshop?" Kevin held up a hand in greeting, then motioned them to enter the open door. "There's a video viewing room here. I have three tapes of original Japanese productions to show you."

Nervously looking around, Timothy said, "We should wait for Xavier."

Kevin dipped his head as if sharing a confidence. "At university, you can leave a class if the professor's five minutes late. So let's start now."

"Uh..." Timothy *wanted* to go in the opened door.

"Let's go," Kevin urged. "It's very Shakespearean for the new generation to go behind the king's back to seize the future."

The two women—no one bothered to introduce us—readily followed Kevin. I'd have to ask later about the inclusion of women in the planned production. Except for its early beginnings, the kabuki tradition had all-male casts.

The door closed behind the quartet. The lock clicked.

Best of luck to them. Kevin had exaggerated the tardy rule: five minutes for a lesser credentialed assistant prof; fifteen for a full professor. At least, that was the rule of thumb at my university.

Wanting to hurry to the mural site, I ran straight into Xavier, the closest I'd come to him in two years. Reeking of the spice-and-licorice notes of Opium cologne, wearing a starched dress shirt and a freaking paisley ascot, he didn't recognize me for a second, since he was seeking his actors, his vision fogged by his steamy anger.

"Oh, it's you." Xavier stepped away.

"Sorry to disappoint."

"Have you seen my actor?" Note: singular; the two women didn't count.

"No," I said. "But it's grand that you have your own personal actor. Stanislowski's method? Stella Adler? Brechtian dialectics? Will he portray you as Everyman? Or as the anti-hero?"

"How humorous, Ricky. I'm looking for Timmy."

"Of course you are. They went that way." I turned to point in the opposite direction from where Kevin had stolen Xavier's actors. And stuck my finger in Jade's chest.

"Rik! You're here!" Jade exclaimed, hands up as if delighted. "Please come help me shift boxes."

With his hand only on the cuff of my shirt, he tugged me so that I loped with him up the brick pavement to the mural site.

"Move boxes?" I was relieved to leave Xavier, but the site now held multiple stacks of plastic-wrapped crates. "How much tile will this wall take?"

"Glass and stone." He automatically corrected me. "I didn't have you to help when I calculated the order. But this should be sufficient." His face open with pure joy, he dropped his voice. "From the look on Xavier's face, I guessed he was being rude to you. He's rude to everyone, but there's no time for indulging him. We need to get to work."

"In truth, I was being rude, so you just kept me from behaving badly to your friend."

"Professional associate. No more than that."

Then Jade spoke as rapidly as a person can, explaining more about what he'd introduced the day before. I got past my own trepidation when I saw how anxious he was about starting this work. I didn't have anything to do with his nervous vibration.

He'd done a huge amount of prep, from setting up the scaffolding to painting the grid on the wall. Precise white lines now marked off squares that matched the drawings he'd passed around in class. Each square had a painted alphanumeric identifier that matched the IDs on the drawings, which were now encased in plastic and taped to the brick plaza below the wall. Moveable fencing and yellow caution tape roped off the work area.

"I'm a paid child minder," I said. "Do I need to know this?"

"The kids know you. They'll ask you when they don't feel free to ask me. Here they come now." He pointed to where his crew headed our way up Pioneer Street. "I gave them a box of donuts on the ride over from school but wouldn't let them bring donuts onto the worksite. Crumbs attract sparrows."

Jade waved his crew onto the site. Over his shoulder, he said, "You were always so good at mural work, Sasha."

—

I greeted the kids too and joined them in examining the drawings laid out near the scaffolding. Xavier might be planning a kabuki *Lear,* but Jade's mural—which would be there for years beyond any memory of Xavier's artificial construct—was more Chinoiserie from the 1700s than kabuki. Stylized Daoist masters instead of overly painted dancers in kimonos.

Jade had assigned teams the day before, but reconfigured the pairs to accommodate those who wanted to avoid the scaffold. He made a show of tossing dice to assign which team had responsibility for a particular section of the mural. He then begged responses from his crew members.

"Tell me what you see in the drawings. Just shout out one or two words when I point to you."

He jutted his broken little finger at me. Startled, I blurted, "Chinese bandits."

"Gosh. Way cool." Jade nodded, then pointed to Molly.

"Ghosts in a nightmare."

"Wow." Jade nodded again, then waved his splinted little finger to elicit more from each team member.

Women in armor. Eerie horses. Trees like skeletons. Broken castles. A forest of spears.

"The Golden Rectangle."

That was Alex.

"Ah, way, way cool. We have a scholar," Jade said. "Will you take my penlight and trace it?" While Alex did that, Jade explained the golden ratio as a principle of composition.

He concluded, "Okay, my friends, this is the magic moment. Until now this art has been wholly mine. But you already have ideas different from what I had while drawing. From now on, this wall belongs to all of us. Congratulate yourself for joining a risky venture. We are now collaborating to make art."

He clapped first, motioning them to applaud each other.

Jade next demonstrated how to mix thin-set cement while promising he'd supervise each team's first cement rota. "It'll take you a few times to get a feel for it."

Everyone took turns feeling the consistency of the cement that Jade had mixed. Then he had them all in safety gear and up on the scaffolding, those who had signed permissions for it.

The first thing he instructed those on the scaffold: how not to fall off in the way I had the one time I fell. I was assigned to show the ground crew how to avoid being directly under the scaffold artists. The Festival had lent a few rope-and-pole sets used to control lines of attendees, now set to divide the work areas. Hence, my instruction was not technical: *Stay on your side of the rope.*

The Heavenly Immortals surely observed that I burned with jealousy for how Jade commanded kids' attention. I have never achieved that while striving to trick people out of hating math. As the session flew by, I learned:

> Jade still carries a pocket sketchbook and takes it out at least twice an hour to write or draw in it.

He focused intensely on the kids, spreading his attention evenly among them.

If kids are interested, they can focus for more than fifteen minutes. (I knew that from my own classroom.)

He has a different formula for thin-set cement. (Time passes. Things change.)

By five thirty, the kids sank into slow motion. A few sharp words were exchanged. Jade's donuts got them ready to work after school, but I'd best bring snacks for the day's finale, which I learned from the mothers who bring oranges and cookies to serve after tennis matches.

All my trepidation about working with him burned itself out. My morning encounter above the wall with Jade had felt awkward. These afternoons now promised to be sparked by the collaborating artists' enthusiasm. I forgot to be agitated.

At the end of the session, the crew members on the scaffold hung a grommeted tarp from spikes at the top of the wall, covering the work in progress.

After the crew departed the work site, I paused to pick up a pair of goggles that hadn't made it into the box of safety gear.

"It's going to work!" Jade, two inches away, grasped my elbow. He beamed, jubilant. "Thank you, Sasha!"

"I never doubted it."

"You are kind to say so." His hand ran down my arm until he let go. "But then, I didn't think you'd change."

I couldn't produce a sound but wanted to say: *Don't touch the chaperone. Because he'll misread the situation.*

He said, "When I read the roster on Tuesday, I saw your nieces' names. They're great kids. But you already know that."

"Yes. Alex is also mine. He's living with us."

"The one who keeps trying to pair up with Quinn? And yeah, I see that Quinn is my biggest fan. I hope I don't fuck up."

I seized an opportunity to shift the conversation. "Let the kids pair up with who they want. I didn't see even one lone wolf or wallflower who'd be left out if you let them choose partners."

"Do you think?" He tilted his head, then nodded. A typical gesture on his part.

"They all go to school together. They aren't strangers like you'd find in a Ceramics 101 class."

"Gosh, I'm so lucky you're here." He grabbed my elbow again. *Fercrissakes, don't do that when it means nothing.* "Oh, you'd say, 'Thank the Heavenly Immortals.'" He released my elbow. "I'll let you go. Becca left the Festival an hour ago. I bet everyone's waiting at home for you."

I escaped, hurrying to join my kids, who were halfway down Pioneer Street. I'd promised dinner to Quinn and two more kids who'd tagged along.

18: Golden

OUR CROWD FROM THE MURAL met Valerie and Julio in the driveway at home. Alex swung Julio around—five times, because Julio kept shouting for more.

As we all came up the Chaos House front steps, Becca was coming out with Gaye Verlaine, the pair deep in conversation. They didn't notice me on the porch until I spoke.

"Are you staying for dinner? I'll cook Gaye's mushrooms Sichuan style."

"Actually," Becca paused, trading glances with Gaye. "We have a date to use the Festival's recording studio."

Not an appointment. A date. So then, something *was* happening between those two. I liked the idea.

"Tomorrow?" I asked. "Are you free then, Gaye?"

They agreed and then were off, headed uptown.

My overfull day did not delay dinner. In the kitchen, I got the wok sizzling hot for *dan dan mian* and took the noodles and minced pork from the refrigerator. I can prepare pan-fried noodles as fast as any street vendor in Hong Kong. Or as fast as they were when I lived there. Ramona put people to work setting the table, since she knows it doesn't take me but a minute to fry noodles.

Everyone still talked excitedly about the mural, though they'd talked about it all the way home.

Alex said, "I can't get over everything I learned today."

"It was like the entire fall quarter of Mrs. Solon's art class," Ramona said. "But in three hours."

Julio tugged at me. "When's dinner, Uncle Rik?"

"Right now. Stay away from the stove when I'm frying noodles. Go wash your hands and sit down."

In response, Julio ran around the table twice calling for people to wash their hands and sit down. "Right now!"

I set Julio's plain buttered noodles on the table and then went back to add chili flakes to the *dan dan mian.* When I carried the wok to the table, people had switched from reviewing their recent art lesson to talking about Jade.

> Quinn: It's like he sees every movement on the site.
>
> Molly: Yeah, like how he spotted that reporter the instant the dude started up the pathway.
>
> Alex: Jade said one word and that reporter got lost.

Uh, no. I'd told the reporter that the site was closed. Sent him to the Festival offices. I'd be jealous of Jade's popularity if I weren't setting fried noodles on the table to great acclaim.

But after everyone had *dan dan mian* in their bowls, the conversation went right back to Jade.

"Jade's eyes are so weird," Zooey said. "They're golden."

"No, more like polished bronze," Ramona said. "Not a color in the ordinary world."

I shouldn't have listened. After three hours at the mural site, I'd prefer an evening that wasn't centered on Jade. Yet I said, "They're just brown, like old pennies. It's his contact lenses that make his eyes look odd."

I'd once called his eye color cinnamon, but Jade admonished me: *No, it's sienna. Or old pennies. Do not describe body parts as food. It's dehumanizing.*

The kitchen went silent, except for the ticking of that inane Felix the Cat clock, its tail wagging in judgment that I'd revealed more than I intended. So I said more.

"You can see light glittering on the edges of his contacts." Then I offered Zooey and Quinn the minor confession I'd given my kids earlier. "We went to the UW at the same time. I had a ceramics class with him."

"Oh, lucky you, Mr. E!" Zooey was enthusiastic.

Julio tugged my sleeve. "Uncle Rik, can I have more noodles?"

"What do you say?" Valerie prompted him.

"With butter?"

That gave me a reason to leave the table and avoid questions. After dinner, the guests helped clear the dishes, then headed home. Molly and Alex did the dishes while Ramona began baking for the next couple of days' breakfasts.

"Can you make those great peanut butter energy bars?" I suggested. "One of our guests doesn't eat bread or muffins."

"Sure. But can I add chocolate chips?"

"For half the batch."

Later, after the kids had finished homework and departed for their rooms, I began preparing tea to take upstairs as part of my evening routine. The phone rang.

"Hi, Rik. It's Gene Randolph."

My dissertation advisor's voice is distinctive, a warm tenor with silver tones.

"Good evening, Dr. Randolph. I hope you're well."

I clutched the phone so tightly, it's a wonder I didn't burst veins in my knuckles. *Make it good news. Please.*

"Better than well, Rik. Your package came at noon, so I've been reading to determine my final remarks."

Here it comes. Divine judgment. Or the closest thing to it in academia. I crossed my fingers like a superstitious child, protecting myself against hearing what I feared most: *Back to work Rik. You still have more to do.*

"Hah, are you holding your breath, my friend?" He chortled. I think it was laughter. "I've already made my final remarks. You are golden, Rik. I'll have my assistant contact your committee members to find a date for your defense."

I said—I'm not sure what. I hope it was at least "Thank you, sir." Or maybe "How did you read it so fast?"

He'd only read the changes, which I'd listed as a reference on a separate sheet.

My heart was beating too fast. My fingers tingled. A rush like the last time I ran to the top of Mt. Ashland. It's thirteen miles, with a full mile of altitude gain.

I did it. I finished. In this lifetime. All that's left is the defense.

Dr. Randolph said, "You know that my old roommate is the department chair at..."

This time I did hold my breath. I know who his old roommate is. My advisor has repeatedly said that I should have studied under his friend at the best Chinese studies program in the U.S.

"He has a post-doc funded for next year, Rik. It's perfect for you. He was quite enthusiastic when I shared your previous draft and asked him to serve as the external member of your committee. I'm sure he'll offer an interview right after your defense."

"That's kind of you." I did not say that the job I want is waiting for me in Hong Kong.

"You know I'm your chief cheerleader, Rik. Even though."

Even though.

> Though I've published only four papers in the last five years, all co-authored with Dr. Randolph.
>
> Though I haven't presented at or even attended conferences in the last four years.
>
> Though I'm a Caucasian American about to take an advanced degree in Chinese literature.
>
> Though my focus is modern Cantonese pop culture, but I haven't been in Hong Kong for eighteen years.

No matter. I should have told Dr. Randolph right then not to bother finding me a job. I'm going to Hong Kong. Not even the top program in the U.S. can draw me away from my plan.

I offered an effusive good-night and hung up the phone. Alex appeared suddenly.

"Was that my mom?"

"No, Claudia hasn't called back. It was my advisor, saying my dissertation is ready to defend." I grasped his shoulder. "You're the first person I get to tell."

That meant close to nothing to Alex. His mind was elsewhere. "She left for Europe today. Maybe she'll forget all about it and leave me alone."

I repeated Nick's advice.

"I met with my attorney today. He says he knows how to handle this, so let Nick worry about it." I gripped his shoulder again briefly. "It's going to be all right, Alex."

He nodded and headed down to his basement room.

I had no business saying that. I intended for it to be true, but I did not yet have control of the situation. I should say instead: *I'm trying to make it all right.*

I dumped my tea and made a new cup, since it had lost all its heat while Dr. Randolph proclaimed that the sun was shining on my academic fate.

19: Old Pennies

UP IN MY STUDY, I BEGAN Thursday night's work, making progress on translating that corporate technical paper. But after thirty minutes, I'd merely flipped pages and added two words to the glossary.

I fought against a groundswell of sadness leaking into my bones. Nothing about a glossary of engineering terms should invoke sweeping human emotions. I'd been sitting there, fingering a tea mug that had been made in Seattle. Staring at the pile of coins I'd emptied from my pocket when I put on my writing robe.

Old pennies.

Why had I watched the light play on Jade's eyes, recalling how he describes color? The Heavenly Immortals offered no clue.

Why had I let my feelings ride while meeting above the wall and then plunge when walking away from the wall after the day's work ended?

Why get hotly agitated about what Xavier might have said about me and then warmly confused when I'm complimented?

Why have an emotional response to being told I was always good at mural work?

I'm supposed to be happy—I am happy—because my dissertation is done. I have an invitation to interview for my dream job.

How are these old pennies bringing me to the edge of tears?

That Dragon's Blood rumble amped itself up to a wheeze. My neck muscles tried to do the work my lungs are supposed to. It feels like I can't get air in, but I know the etiology of asthma; I can't get air out. I cough, but it's all in my throat and rattles those crystals.

I tossed things around on my dresser, looking for my inhaler. I held the first puff for five counts, willing it to dilate my pitifully emotional bronchial tubes. I took a second puff, counting to five while recalling Dr. Randolph's kind words.

Be happy.

I'm getting everything I want.

It's years since I had any reason for being unhappy about what I cannot have.

The pager from Ruby's room buzzed. So I stopped pondering my unnamable emotions, took off my writing robe, dressed again in jeans and a t-shirt, and went downstairs.

Ruby thrashed in the throes of a nightmare, although it wasn't clear she was asleep. Struggling with Ruby in this state is too much for the night nurse, Danielle, to take care of on her own, so I begged Howard to stay longer to help me.

I always tiptoe around Ruby. Howard came back into her room, booming, "Hey, Ruby. How you doing, my girl? Doncha wanna sleep now, sweetheart? Here's some medicine for you."

Despite that dose of Valium, we didn't get Ruby settled until I held her in my arms and rocked her. Once she drifted into what might be sleep, Howard got Ruby back into her bed.

"That oughta do it, boss," Howard said.

We all said good night. Howard escaped to his own evening activities. Danielle returned to her studies, leaving her door open to listen for any further restlessness. I boiled another kettle of water and carried a fresh cup of tea upstairs, intending to resume my translation work. I put a tape in the player and turned it on.

When working on a technical translation like this current job, a certain portion of my brain takes over every other mental function. It knows when to reach for a different dictionary, when to leaf back through earlier pages. My translator's brain makes comparisons, adds to the glossary, checks each detail multiple times, dispassionately. This mode of work wasn't always possible while preparing my dissertation. Which is the other thing I like about technical translation work, besides the money: I don't have to wrestle with an undercurrent of emotion rising from my editorial judgment about the worth of my work. A translation is worth exactly what I'm paid to make it.

And yet, that night, I stopped my translation work several times, staring at the wall—well, pictures on the wall. I wasn't daydreaming so much as drifting in and out of a fugue, and not the kind that involves the mathematical principles of a music composition that interweaves repetitive elements. I had to climb out of my head and be more aware of my surroundings, beyond the source text and my translation.

No, what I had to do was stop the music on the tape player. *Stone Cold Crazy.* A bootleg tape of Queen in concert. Music Jade used to play. How did that tape surface? It'd been buried in an aging shoebox the last time I saw it. If I let it keep playing, I'd fall into long jags of crying. I'd end up on another round of tricyclic antidepressants.

I knew from experience how such bad nights begin, with Ruby's upset moments and me letting my attention drift. For example, I might be reading to Ruby from a book she'd read before 1975 or one that she'd written. Or we're watching one of her shows on the black-and-white TV in her room. *Happy Days* or *Three's Company.* I'm always cautious because anything more challenging leads my mother into confused emotions. Yet at times, ten minutes into a TV show that usually helps her sleep, Ruby pops up with a random memory. I can never tell what prompts it, and it's never an accurate memory.

The faulty memory she'd found while Howard and I tried to get her to sleep earlier tonight:

> Ruby: See how it is, Chris? I hate how that cowboy treats Ricky, his paws clutching at Ricky's shirt. Saw it with my own eyes. So horrible.

Christopher was lost years ago. I am the son formerly called Ricky, but not since we left Hong Kong two decades ago. She's never seen a man embrace me. I calmly divert her attention:

> Imaginary Chris: Look, Mother. You don't want to miss your favorite show.
>
> Ruby: I know that kind of man. Possessive. Lording it over a weaker lover. Ricky isn't strong like you.
>
> Imaginary Chris: You always know best, Mother.
>
> Ruby: Poor Ricky. You are never that way with women, are you, Chris?
>
> Me: Is it raining, Mother? I thought I heard rain. Can you hear it? The weather report said to expect rain tonight.

The original Christopher never obeyed her; he called her Ma, which she hated. Imaginary Chris is deferential and always calls her Mother. Why not? It doesn't hurt anything to be nice. But the faulty memories that Ruby conjured launched the steep decline of my well-wrought day. I want to argue with what Ruby imagines that she saw.

When my former lover held me in his arms, he clutched me like a man drowning, not as a possession. He said our hearts beat as one whenever we were close by each other. He wasn't a cowboy. He just inhabited a body that held a monumental soul.

If Ruby has a truly bad night, like tonight, she again misremembers the Specially Bad Christmas that fractured the structures of our lives. In her story she'd been a hero, rescuing her family. While I was working on my dissertation, such nights stopped any progress. I'd waste time merely reviewing my draft, checking every source, questioning every nuance to ensure I had it right. Until the clock freed me to leave off work for the night.

We all review scenes of our lives, like watching reruns on TV, similar to how Ruby replays our Bad Christmas.

Some people get their channel stuck on *Wild Adventure* or *Monday Night Football* or *Days of Our Lives.*

Some, like my sister Wendy, get stuck on endless reruns of *Gilligan's Island.* For Wendy's adventures, she first got stranded in Tunisia, then Barcelona, then came back to the U.S. and got stuck on a series of collective farms in the Southwest.

Some, like me, get stuck rolling a rock up hill, performing for the amusement of the Heavenly Immortals, who seem to enjoy watching their private *Sisyphus Struggles!* channel.

Ruby got stuck on the after-midnight test pattern, not knowing she has three spectacular grandkids who wish her goodnight before bed. She doesn't know her father's mansion has been restored to a semblance of its former glory and that the house sustains several people who need safe shelter.

A good life surrounds Ruby, yet she doesn't know it, which especially strikes me when she gets caught in a waking nightmare. I rock her in my arms and repeated comforting words:

It's going to be all right.
There's nothing to be afraid of.
You're safe.
We're all fine.

For the most part.

On Ruby's bad nights, I stew over things until one a.m.

Time to stop. I put away the translation work and picked up my pen to make a list of tomorrow's chores:

Back to the printshop for more dissertation copies.

Mail the copies to my supervisor's assistant, so she can send them to my committee.

Chores, meals, chaperoning, homework.

Repeat until spring comes and I fly away.

20: A Chance

EARLY FRIDAY MORNING, I SHOWED up at the college printshop brimming with eager energy to prepare copies for my committee. Frankie was there, alone, running sets of book-length copies.

She was, uncharacteristically, staring off into space. I had to call her name three times before she turned, and then it took a few heartbeats before she registered my presence.

"Rik! I'm going! I'm doing it!"

She stepped away from the printer to embrace me with all the strength of Jackson County's top second-base softball player.

"Where? What, Frankie?"

Her excitement forestalled my own announcement.

"Inez called me yesterday from Rome. It was past midnight her time. Can you imagine the expense?" Frankie wasn't seeking an answer. "Guess what she said."

"'Italian food is disappointing'? That's what people tell me."

Frankie punched me. "She said…oh lord, I am stunned. She said, 'I can't do this without you. Please come.' Do you believe it?"

"Yes. Are you going? How?"

The one thing that's true of all my boarders, past and present: they are broke. At this moment in history, most everyone in Ashland is broke for one common reason. We can't find employment that offers the remuneration our college counselors claimed we could expect.

Frankie tugged on my shirt sleeve, excited. "I said yes immediately. But I paced around my room all night. Can you tell I haven't slept? I'm still figuring out how to afford it."

"You'll give up your job?"

"Sort of. I've been here long enough that I can beg a leave of absence, then petition to return within a year. So I'm going!"

On Wednesday morning, Frankie had spoken about the uncertainty of what had recently passed between the two long-time friends. Now Inez had declared that she felt it too.

"I wish you the best of luck," I said, "and much happiness."

She gazed at me for a moment, like someone who hasn't slept. "You're worried that it might not work. Like Sarah." She named a friend we both socialize with. "She went to live with her one-true-love in New York but came back miserable a month later."

"I am absolutely not thinking that."

"You look weird."

Yeah. I was thinking about the year I'd spent hoping each time the phone rang that I'd receive a call like Frankie's.

Come be with me.

Frankie was so excited I had to give her a hug. I like Inez. I like seeing how happy she'd made Frankie, who intended to fly away in three days, not allowing time for a bon voyage party.

"I know you, Frankie. I know Inez. She has proposed the best of all possible worlds for both of you. Now, can I tell you about my own phone call?"

I repeated details of the happy call from my advisor. "Which is why I'm here to make ten copies of my manuscript. Academia is about to take a chance on me."

"So just when you've earned your big chance, I get my chance out of nowhere." Frankie gave me a high-five.

After I'd made the copies of my four-hundred-page manuscript, Frankie found an empty copier-paper carton and gave it to me to carry my huge stack of copied pages. Then I went to spend a small fortune at the U.S. Post Office. Being with the overjoyed Frankie had resurrected the good feeling from my advisor's phone call, so I carried a warm ball of friendship and academic achievement behind my breastbone.

That sense consumed my attention, leaving no room for jealousy over Frankie's call from Inez. Her happiness was infectious. No use allowing memory of my past losses to shade her sunshine.

In my car when I returned from my mailing task, the radio was playing 'It Won't Be Long.' Behind John Lennon's wailing plea, the scaling guitar riffs lifted my good mood into a reverie.

—

The Beatles played Hong Kong the day after my fourteenth birthday. Kai and I saved our spending money for tickets—to both shows. (I still have my ticket stubs for the two shows.) It took two weeks until we dared to persuade Chan-suk to allow Kai to go. Parental permission on my side required only that Chan-suk approved Kai going with me. We gave solemn vows about how we'd travel safely to and from Kowloon, forgetting that promise ten minutes later, because we had certain intentions.

We achieved all we wanted. Kai and I were at the airport when the Beatles arrived the day before the concert. We weren't either of us tall fourteen-year-olds, and we weren't comfortable being as aggressive as the crowd of ambitious girls, so we were shoved to the edge of the crowd. But that was our good luck. Kai and I were up against the rope right when the limo crept by. And I swear to this day, as a sober adult, that John winked at me. That night, and the next day, we were among those who staked out the President Hotel, where they stayed in Hong Kong. Kai and I were near the back entrance before dawn the day of the concert, and we still believe we saw a pair of Beatles sneaking in a service entrance. News stories later confirmed that it was a possibility, so me and Kai, we believe.

I clearly recall several parts of that day and the two concerts at the Princess Theatre: our feral, breathless roving in a crowd of mostly girls; the sobbing pain the crowd shared when we learned

Ringo couldn't perform; the girls' continuous screams, which we disdained, yet that prolonged treble shriek pierced our skulls along with the music; the chemical rush of shared anticipation and elation in a huge crowd. My only similar experiences were at a couple of mass antiwar demonstrations in Seattle where thousands of voices were raised in great passion.

Kai and I lived in that heightened reality for days, repeating to each other key moments, reciting the playlist, recreating every gesture on the stage. When adrenalin seizes your core in that way, you don't want to come down from the high. It's mystical, if not magical. It's as close as I've come to understanding what religious ecstasy might be.

Hence, June 9, 1964, remains one of a half-dozen significant markers in my life. The Princess Theatre in Kowloon is what I think of when people speak of hallowed spaces. And those two days remain precious amid memories that Kai and I still share, despite anything that's happened since then.

My sister Wendy calls June 9 the most significant day for our family, though neither she nor Christopher cared about the Beatles. It's the day our father left permanently, after having seldom been home for a couple of years. However, I was deep in my Beatles afterglow, which included that sweet subversive sense of succeeding at my first delinquent, freedom-seeking act. I didn't realize our father was gone until a week later.

My first thought when Wendy impressed our father's desertion upon me: that's why I didn't get in trouble for coming in at four in the morning. My father hadn't chastised me (which was only ever at my mother's bidding) because he wasn't there. My mother hadn't punished me because she didn't notice. She didn't notice much of anything for a few months. Looking back, I believe it was phenobarbital and wine. My siblings invented their own explanations:

Christopher: Our father had a lover for years. He left us for that woman. Or perhaps it was a man.

Wendy: He was a CIA spy, executed by communists who have infiltrated Hong Kong.

Me: Were we just a cover story? Are we really his kids?

Our mother wouldn't answer questions, saying, "It's not relevant to real life." After a couple of weeks, she just turned away with cold disdain for our puerile emotions, as if our questions rose from the same emotional realm as the girls screaming during a live performance of 'Love Me Do.'

I still regret one thing. I was fortunate to see the Beatles in the world-changing year of 1964, but Ringo was too ill to perform. And I feel bad for Jimmie Nicol, who played drums for screaming crowds that wanted a different man to be there.

In the driveway at Chaos House, I let 'It Won't Be Long' finish before I switched off the radio, although I had chores to attend to before playing chaperone at the mural site.

Those lyrics were wrong by a couple of words. It won't be *ever* till I belong to anyone. I'm like Jimmie Nicol, who has already lived through the brief days of his life's glory. I shrugged off any sense of jealousy over Frankie's happiness.

I came inside the house in time to answer the phone. It was Dr. Randolph's assistant, saying she had a date for my defense: October 21. I thanked her. Effusively. But I bet that's what she hears from every candidate she has to schedule for.

After I had a cup of tea and calmed down, I turned to my tasks. I'd promised Gaye a meal with Sichuan mushrooms, but Friday night always means more than the usual number of teenagers at the dinner table, so I'd better make macaroni and cheese for any kids who can't tolerate Sichuan peppercorns and dried red chilis. I had to get dinner prep done before going to my chaperone job, but I'd carried that Hong Kong reverie into the house and paired it with the promise of October 21. Together, they fueled my chores.

21: Obligations

SATURDAY MORNING AFTER MY RUN, I went into the kitchen to fix breakfast. Surprisingly, Becca, absent for the past several days, was at the kitchen table with Gaye. They had cups of tea and were drizzling honey into each other's cups. Gaye twisted a lock of Becca's hair, twirling it in the same direction she drizzled honey. I think they didn't notice me making waffles.

After breakfast, I went out into the backyard to clean up summer-deadened brush and sweep the patio. Down by the creek, a flock of gray bushtits scattered when I arrived. They flitted in their random way, congregating in the upper branches of a white oak, hiding their tiny plump bodies in the foliage, twittering.

Each year, five suspect cottonwood branches need trimming as soon as their leaves fall. Else, we'll have widow-makers when winter wind and snow arrive. From the edge of the creek, looking back up to our grand Victorian house, one wouldn't guess that it's a black hole of home maintenance. Most seasons in the year, I don't have time to do more than slash back dead grasses, poison oak, and the vines that threaten to swallow the house.

If I were to face reality—which I'd been disinclined to do several times over the last week—I'd make a plan to clean up the yard this fall, so the house will be ready to sell come spring. The future sale of the house is a key part of my master plan, so I began to assess the yard for work that had to be done.

The perennials blooming in the yard are charmingly vintage, mostly heirloom roses and hydrangeas. It looks like an old lady's garden because the design is my grandmother's original devising.

I never met her, and I'm guessing she copied what she'd seen in Boston without considering the southwestern Oregon climate. Then again, Grandmother Eliot would have known this climate, having been born here. When I last worked on the house title with Nick, we discovered that my grandmother had inherited this house. Which causes me to wonder if my grandfather married that woman for her money. One more family question for which we can never know the answer.

Behind our patio, I spied more tasks to add to my prepare-to-sell-the-house list. I needed to dismantle and remove the remains of our failed vegetable garden. One summer, the girls and I tried urban farming, since earthy hippies in Ashland have influenced everyone's view of food. The bugs got more to eat than we did, though most herbs did well. That project did work out for the girls when their joint seventh-grade science project won a blue ribbon for "Common Insects in a Rogue Valley Garden." Molly particularly enjoyed pinning bugs to the display board with steel pins from her great-grandmother's sewing kit. I'm sure it wasn't Ruby's kit because my mother never so much as sewed on a button. At least, not to my knowledge.

I raked a pile of brush and dead summer grass that I'd deal with after the leaves have fallen. Since Julio often plays in the back, I checked for poison oak down as far as the creek, finding several shiny leaves in the woodland below the guest cottages. So that day's yardwork concluded with me donning a costume for poison oak removal. Anyone who's ever contracted that malicious rash endeavors to never experience it again. Despite the late-summer heat, I put on two long-sleeved shirts (one, a turtleneck), two pairs of socks pulled up over the hem of my jeans, heavy-duty boots, a ball cap, my wrap-around woodworker eye protection, and a bandana tied over my nose and mouth Jesse James style. I decided against polluting my leather yardwork gloves and fetched pink dishwashing gloves from under the kitchen sink.

While I dug in the undergrowth, I heard the spotted towhee scratching in the leaf litter for his lunch. He returns every year—or sends his descendants. I know spring has arrived when I hear him mewling like a kitten while scratching in the duff for bugs.

I set to work destroying the future of poison oak in Grandmother Eliot's little wilderness by the creek. The physical exertion settled my jumble of unresolved thoughts. In a moment of honest self-examination, I must admit that the tangle I've wrestled with this week is emotion disguising itself as rational thought. Digging at those roots with a metaphoric knife, I praised my own successes:

> Met each of my obligations in a timely way, daily.
>
> Reached the intellectual summit of my professional scholasticism. Only the concluding rituals remain.
>
> Received an invitation to interview for a position in Hong Kong. How hard my heart beats when I think of it!
>
> Managed an unexpected family crisis.
>
> Cheered when Alex got a perfect score on his math quiz. He's actually been heard to laugh several times.
>
> Made twenty-four peanut butter sandwiches to put kids on even keel at the end of after-school mural work.
>
> Didn't feel put out when Jade became the hero on Friday by ordering pizza for everyone.
>
> Encountered Xavier Torres four times without ever once popping him in the nose for his supercilious expression whenever Jade or Timothy is nearby.
>
> Shifted the household to eating protein bars for breakfast so Timothy wouldn't starve himself. Even Julio ate one from the half batch that had chocolate chips. Fortunately, no one had a peanut or dairy allergy.
>
> Spent fourteen hours in Jade's company without significantly humiliating myself or hyperventilating.

That is to say, I'm fine. Everyone is fine.

While digging out the most pernicious poison oak roots, I did the math once again. For the sake of my Hong Kong fund, I can bear three hours a day being vaguely adjacent to a famous artist who unexpectedly moved into the same cottage as when he left this town ninety-two months ago. And I do not need Becca's advice for how to survive all this. She has no idea what happened in the long past. The sole adult in town who witnessed it is Ruby, who has forgotten.

In Saturday morning's knife-and-trowel endeavor, I successfully removed all traces of that devil's plant without getting poison oak goo on myself. However, I parboiled inside my defensive costume. The protective eyewear steamed up from the heat of my eyeballs. Sweat drenched the bandana. The two shirts turned into sopping biohazards. I couldn't assess the state of my socks until I hosed off my boots to avoid tracking any poison around.

After I finished poison oak patrol down by the creek, I came up behind the cottages. From the slim history I'd uncovered of my grandfather's properties, he purchased them in the mid-Forties. I'm guessing he did so to prevent having one of the Thirties-era "lithia spas" in his backyard, filled with tourists who came to drink nasty-tasting water to cure arthritis and migraines. After WWII he began renting to the swarm of students who were using the GI bill to attend what was then a teachers' college. I've uncovered no sign my grandfather performed even basic maintenance on the cottages after 1960.

I worked so quietly that the towhee came out of the undergrowth, scratching in the duff without a care in the world, my noble companion.

—

Below the guest cottages' shared patio, I found more of the demonic weed poking up at the base of a volunteer scrub oak. As I hacked with my hunting knife and garden trowel, the screen door of a cottage banged open and then banged shut. Voices drifted down from one of the patios.

First came a too-familiar California drawl. Xavier Torres.

"I know how to manage Timothy. I've directed a dozen like him. He's a man-child who must be led by a firm hand."

"You aren't doing right by him." It was Jade. "He came here to learn from you, but you're pestering and hounding him. You have obligations as his mentor."

"Should I be like you, promising your child laborers too much? You'll end up trapped by obligations. Look at Ricky Eliot. He carries obligations like a millstone around his neck."

"A millstone?" Jade sounded astonished.

I should not be listening.

I didn't want to listen.

But I was stuck eavesdropping like in a Shakespeare play, no way to leave without revealing my presence.

Xavier laughed in his remarkably obnoxious way. "Two kids and a bedridden mother, whom our Ricky uses as a shield against any possibility of normal human relations."

"Uh, no. And he's called Rik. Never Ricky."

"Oh come on, Jade. He let me call him Ricky when I was last in Ashland. He's compulsive, hiding behind those kids as his primary obligation. Has a holier-than-thou stick up his ass about it. You're being the same way with your child laborers."

"I'm obliged to keep the promises I made to my 'child laborers.'" Jade's voice dripped scorn. "Kids are a sacred trust, whether they're your relations or your students."

Wow, Jade offered a quote from my old teacher, Chan-suk.

"No need to sacrifice yourself like Ricky," Xavier said. "He's tied to a cross with his mother, like one of the crucified thieves."

"You are wrong. It's called filial piety. The ancient masters believed it's the divine essence of how order abides in the world."

Xavier coughed. Or stifled a laugh. "We didn't talk about our divine essences when I was dating Ricky."

Dating? Xavier is a freaking liar.

Now Jade will think I've been with Xavier.

An ill-natured part of me, which I tend to keep deeply buried, wishes I'd stuffed that ticket to SFO down Xavier's throat till he choked. I wanted my Red Wing work boots on his neck while he confessed that we never dated. We were in San Francisco one weekend when I was apparently the only guy Xavier could get to stand next to him in a tux.

"In fact," Xavier said, but I knew the next words would not be factual, "Ricky's family obligations destroyed our relationship. That's why I'm warning you about obligations with children. It will destroy your freedom."

"Shut it, Xavier." Jade voiced my thoughts, but more mildly than I would. "I have obligations to my students. I hold their hopes and trust in my hands. If I cannot help set them on a hopeful path, I must at least not bruise their spirits."

Xavier didn't respond.

My heart hammered hard enough to rip through both of my shirts. I wanted to forget Xavier existed and instead only think that Jade still believes as we had back then, when we'd talked into early-morning hours about our mutual desire to serve justice, art, and true scholarship.

Jade said more. "C'mon, Xavier. Don't you feel the same about directing? Especially with young actors at the Festival? Don't you hold their hopes as a sacred trust?"

Xavier coughed. No, it was laughter. "New Age blather. Sentiment dressed in bell bottoms and paisley shirts."

A chair scraped harshly on the concrete patio.

While unpleasant to overhear Xavier proving to be as scummy as I believed, it felt good to hear that Jade held the same values as when I'd last known him.

"Xavier, stop harassing Timothy."

"Did you catch Ricky's disease?"

"What disease?" Jade sounded exasperated.

Cripes. Condemned to hear what I don't want to hear.

"The no-fucking, no-sucking, no-fun disease. The essence of Ricky, don't you think?"

Not so bad. But untrue.

"Xavier, leave Timothy alone."

"Because I'm his director, Timothy belongs to me. You, Mr. Solberg, have no role in how that lad and I play out our autumn idyll. Unless you are perhaps a jealous lover?"

"Is that the only way you understand things? I'm telling you to stop teasing and harassing him."

"Or what? You'll be pissed at me?"

"I'm not threatening. Because you cannot show him respect, then think about it this way. Timothy is mine to protect."

Tmothy is mine.

The words reverberated through my little wilderness.

Xavier sneered. "Why should I respect Timothy? He's a child who doesn't know what's good for him."

"Thou shalt not trespass on the boundaries I am setting. Do you understand, Xavier?"

22: Importuning

I SLUNK THROUGH THE BRUSH down to the creek. Yes, slunk. Though it's *my* land. My poison oak-cleared wilderness.

Five minutes later, I stuffed the hacked-up poison oak into a plastic bag and buried the bag in the garbage bin in front of Chaos House. That scrub jay *cawked* at me from the locust tree but took the day off from divebombing my head.

From the back porch I called into the house, asking if anyone other than Ruby's caretaker was home, then wiggled out of my poison oak battle uniform and tossed it into the washer. I ran upstairs in my boxers to shower off any goo that might have come close to my skin, being liberal with Dr. Bronner's minty soap.

Did I not, just thirty minutes earlier, declare in a reverie that I'm fine? In the shower, I squeezed my eyes against feelings I did not want. The hot water did not fend off much of anything for long. I had to sort through what throbbed under the falling water.

Crying in the shower is so adolescent, even if I'd swallowed a bouquet of imagined firethorns, now being thrashed to bits by the Dragon's Blood crystals. It's worse than just being embarrassed about eavesdropping. It's what I'd heard: *Timothy is mine. I honor my promises.*

After showering, I came downstairs to see that the weekend caretaker had wheeled my mother out into the sun. I checked for my tree frog friend, then moved my laundry to the dryer and started a load of household laundry. A tickling breeze blew soap powder up my nose, sending me into paroxysm of coughing. I waved away the cloud of soap powder.

The screen door banged shut. The source of the breeze.

"Oh. Goodness." That voice. "I thought you waved for me to come in."

"Yes? Can I help?" I took two breaths. Then consoled myself that at least it wasn't my Disputatious Neighbor.

"If it's not a good time, I'll come back," Jade said.

"No, come in. Is there a problem in the cottages? I'll come by after I fix my mother's lunch."

"No. I came about mural and studio business. In fact, I'm importuning."

"Come in."

I fetched myself a drink of water from the kitchen, motioning an offer to Jade, who declined. Then I pocketed every bit of the last half hour's anguish, sat at the kitchen table, and indicated a place for him on the opposite bench. He wore flipflops, so I didn't ask him to take off his shoes.

He said, "I spoke with the Festival people yesterday, plus the school principal and several administrators. To finish the mural before it freezes, we need to work more hours than I'd planned. But I don't feel good about asking the kids for their time without reward."

"Your devoted workers will do whatever you want." My throat let the words out without betraying any jealousy about his popularity or his promises. "You are all-powerful."

"Ha! Very funny, Sasha." Like I was kidding. "But 'devotion' isn't a fair currency. Anyway, I won my argument with the school administration. They'll allow up to three credits for each kid, depending on attendance."

"Congratulations."

"But I'm also thinking of you, Sasha."

This time the rumble in my chest echoed the Heavenly Immortals' cry: *We know that cannot be.*

"No worries, Jade. The school pays me."

"But only as a chaperone. If the kids are earning credit, you need to be paid as a teacher. The project has funds for it."

"You mean I get paid more if I take roll call?" I grinned. Then didn't. It felt more like I was gritting my teeth because of what I'd overheard earlier.

"Yes. I wish it was more, Sasha." He pulled at the string around his wrist, slipped it off, began playing cat's cradle. He never could sit still for five minutes. "I'm lucky you're the chaperone, instead of a stranger."

My throat felt raw.

I drank from my water glass, preparing to speak. "I thought all Friday about proposing a change. Whatever the kids learn by mixing cement, it's time lost to one crew not working on the actual mosaic. I should mix the cement."

"Gosh, what a good idea." A light flickered on the edges of his contact lenses when he glanced my way. "It's as swell an idea as your peanut butter sandwiches. I'll make sure you're reimbursed for that, too."

"It's no big deal."

"Yeah, it is. Care and feeding of volunteers should have been in my original plan. Also, I have another change the administrators accepted. Students can choose to work on Saturdays, but it requires a school chaperone, so I asked for more money to be allocated out of the grant. Will you do it?"

"Today? Are you going there to work right now? I'll help." I stood up, ready to go. My insides felt like a watch that had gotten wound so tight, it couldn't tick.

"Not now, Sasha. Maybe tomorrow?"

"Sure. I can call to find who's available." Why was I volunteering? I had chores. "Or I'll ask Ramona and Alex to do it."

"That would be kind. I also came by hoping for a tour of Inez's studio today, but—"

"Sure." I stood up again.

"Don't you have to make your mother's lunch?"

Cripes. What is wrong with me? I pulled out the bench to sit back down at the table. "Yes, but it's just a tuna sandwich."

Through the back door, I saw movement in the yard.

"Not that turtle egg again!" I jumped up again, knocking over the bench.

Somewhere between the table and the back door, I heard that I was swearing in Cantonese. No one around here considers "turtle egg" to be the insult it is.

—

When I banged open the screen door, Willie looked up from gazing into Ruby's eyes. His dog was in her lap, turning in circles, preparing to sleep. Willie rose, his hand out for mine like a guided missile.

"Richard!" He had my hand in his big paw and pumped it with vigor. "My brother J.J. says you're called Richard, not Chris. Forgive me for misunderstanding your family nicknames."

"It's not a problem. Please call me Rik."

I sounded rational. Not at all like I'd been shot with an undiluted dose of adrenalin. The dog, meanwhile, calmed as Ruby petted it while watching Willie with her usual vacant smile.

Willie chuckled. "You wouldn't believe the nicknames J.J. and I had in school. I beat up three different guys over what they called my brother." That memory was a knee slapper. He had to wipe away tears before he said, "Of course, I'm sure your older brother got plenty of practice protecting you."

No, it was the reverse. Christopher sided with the bullies.

I headed back to the house. "While you chat with Ruby, I'll finish making her lunch."

"Thank you. That's mighty generous of you. Makes me feel right at home."

Not what I intended.

I slammed the screen door open and came inside so fast that Jade had to step back to let me pass.

I noisily made tuna sandwiches, then calmed down enough to trim the crusts off Ruby's sandwich.

"Do you want one?" I asked Jade, not sounding hospitable.

"No thanks."

It's my good fortune that Jade already knows how crazy my family is. No use pretending the tableau on the back patio wasn't weird. "I should write to Dear Abby for advice on how to dissuade gentleman callers from pursuing my mother."

"I'd offer to help, Sasha, but I'm not sure what to do."

"I can't figure it out. He just began appearing, and I don't want him here. I worry about men taking advantage of Ruby."

"I meant about helping to make lunch."

"Oh." *Way to overshare, Rik.* "There's lemonade in the refrigerator. Grab that pitcher and glasses from the cupboard. Please."

Jade said, "We can hover and look judgmental."

I set the sandwiches on the patio table, ready for the caretaker to assist with getting Ruby's lunch into her. Amazingly, the dog stayed asleep during the administration of the tuna sandwich.

Although I intended to steer Jade to the chairs on the other side of the patio, Willie had his massive paw out in greeting, grabbing Jade's elbow with his other hand.

"I'm Willie Smith from just next door. Retired from the mill now. I didn't catch your name."

Jade, smiling, shook hands. "I'm Jade. I'm a tile man."

"Like floors and bathrooms?"

"Yeah, just like that."

Ruby held up her mottled, frail hand. "Hello, dear. I'm Ruby. Tell me your name again."

Jade repeated his name, adding, "I'm new to town."

Which was true, in a way.

I had a rough moment, what with the whole morning being a bumpy ride, now worried that Ruby might recognize Jade and remember she'd once put him in a metaphorical discard basket. But at this encounter, Ruby was enthralled by Jade. She declared him charming, coerced Willie's agreement. Why not behave the opposite of when Jade last saw her?

Ruby didn't remember him and didn't get his name right.

"Oh James, I do wish you could meet my other son. You'd be perfect for each other."

I said, "Do you want lemonade, Ruby? How about you, Mr. Smith?" I poured drinks, knowing that ten seconds of distraction would derail whatever train she'd boarded.

But not this time.

"Hello, Chris. I was just telling James that it's too bad he can't meet Ricky. I bet they both like walking on the beach in the rain."

Neither Jade nor I liked walking in the rain. But I watched understanding dawn on him like a summer sunrise. Yes, Jade. My family is even more cuckoo than you remember.

"Gosh, I'd love to meet him." Jade charmed Ruby the way he charmed his students on first encounter. She was thrilled. There are no words in English for how trapped and embarrassed I felt.

Then she turned to Willie Smith, who'd been busy with his tuna sandwich. "Or do you think Ricky is too much of a faggot for James, who's such a beautiful boy?"

No, it was much like the last time she and Jade had met.

I glanced at Jade and shrugged an apology. But she didn't insult Jade this time. She saved that for Ricky.

Meanwhile, Willie didn't hear her question. He stood and towered over me.

"I asked your Mrs. Adams yesterday, and she thinks it best if I ask for your agreement."

He must have meant his towering stance to be intimidating, even with Jade right there. Was this Willie's clever strategy to keep me from being an asshole to him?

"What am I to agree to?" I smiled.

Jade chose that moment to pour more lemonade in my glass. I sipped from it, hating every moment of this.

Willie cleared his throat. "I'd like to take your mother with me to church on Sunday, Richard."

I nearly choked.

Willie wrung his hands as if from shy eagerness. "I'm a member of the fellowship at the Church of the Lord's Disciples. We testify to the Lord's coming return and the Millennial Reign."

My mother had not set foot in any church since the day she married. But I didn't want to be contrary. So I dodged.

"That's a nice thought, Willie. But can't drive her on Sunday morning, and her drivers must be licensed professionals."

"My church has a van to accommodate those of us in need. I'm sure the driver is licensed." Willie's eyes darted up to the right, as if checking his memory. "I'm sure."

I couldn't argue out of logic. "Fine, but I'll have to ask the night nurse, Danielle, to come along." Which meant paying her an extra ten dollars, because church is not her thing.

Soon after that agreement had been wrung out of me, I suggested, forcefully, that it was time for Ruby to come inside and rest. Willie lifted the dog from Ruby's lap, setting off a new burst of barking. My mother raised her hands, wordlessly seeking the return of the dog.

I ignored the gestures and hints that Willie be allowed a private farewell. Willie was, by my judgment, worse than his brother, my Disputatious Neighbor. I wanted to paste a note on J.J.'s door, telling him to keep his animals and his brother out of my yard.

Jade, who has better manners than Willie, helped the caretaker bring my mother inside while I fetched the plates, glasses, and lemonade. When I sat at the kitchen table and tried to gather my wits by writing the week's grocery list, Jade sat opposite me.

"Gosh, Sasha. I had no idea."

I waved an open-handed dismissal. "It is what it is."

"How long has she been like this?"

Eight effing years. You were lucky to miss all of it.

I said, "We got a proper diagnosis in 1975. The descent was quick, which I understand isn't uncommon."

"How awful for both of you, Sasha."

"She's seldom in pain. And did you notice? She lost her waspishness along with her memory."

As much as I tried to put him off, Jade persisted.

"She called you Chris. Isn't that your brother who died? That must be so upsetting."

"No, not really." I spoke quickly, trying not to say much. Jade's caring tone rubbed the wrong way, like a scab being picked loose. Unbearable. I yearned for it and didn't want it. "Ruby is content with the stray bits she remembers. Or misremembers."

"I just can't imagine," Jade said. Which lots of people say.

Then I couldn't stop, despite my intentions to keep all this to myself. "She lets me comfort her when she has nightmares. So I learned not to care what she calls me." I laughed. Poorly. Everything behind my breastbone burned with a throb worse than embarrassment. "And she hasn't mentioned that fellow she calls Ricky in the last five years. It's funny that she just now thought of...well, not me. I don't know what false memory cracked open."

"Goodness, I'm so sorry."

Well, hell, that heated my insides even worse.

"No need to be." I had to drink water to cool down the internal heat, but it could hardly make it past the swelling in my throat. "She has good caretakers. She isn't in pain." I again waved away Jade's concern. *Stop it. It doesn't help.* "Now, you said you want a tour of Inez's studio."

On the tour, Jade got excited about the shelving and various mechanisms I'd invented for her studio. He said, "I remember Inez's workshop from when we came to Ashland eight years ago. You've turned it into another world."

Our conversation was casual, I was wretched, and eventually Jade left for a meeting at the Festival.

The rest of my afternoon was consumed by shopping and restocking the snack cupboards.

Plus a great deal of self-recrimination rose, which I wanted to beat down with a stick. I wish I could tear out the poison vine wrapped around my insides, stuff it in a plastic bag, and chuck it in a garbage bin.

23: The Young Disciples

THE HOUSE WAS EMPTY WHILE I cooked Saturday night dinner and prepped food for the next week. Alone, I put the Cure on the turntable—*Faith*—and agonized.

When I restocked the cottage kitchens with beverages and snacks, I was nice to Timothy. But he still turned down my invitation to go hear the blues with my friends.

"Jade and I are going to a play tonight and then to a workshop afterwards."

Of course you are.

I took four deep breaths and returned to my chores. At one point, I forgot to turn off the water at the kitchen sink, because I confused the sound of the rushing flow with the memories coursing through me.

Not long after we met at the U Dub, I became Jade's acolyte, helping with large projects and loading the kiln for firings. He cheered my progress in the new-to-me liberal arts world. We ate dinner every night at the Fermat's Last House table, and we found new adventures weekly. But mind you, we were Spin and Marty, not Achilles and Patroclus.

By the end of that term, we were sharing the deepest and wildest friendship I've known. I completed my second master's degree in only nine months, during which I tortured my sorely immature self, burying the secret of my...infatuation. I didn't want to repeat the colossal mistake I'd made with Kai, where my confession harmed us both, dousing the sparks of our original friendship. I didn't want to do anything that might cause me to lose the thrilling everyday joy I knew with Jade.

Late one night we were celebrating the completion of Jade's largest work, a thirty-by-ten broken-ceramics mural of Patroclus outside the gates of Troy in Achilles's armor, featuring me as Patroclus. I wonder if that wall, owned by an emeritus classics professor, is still there. As usual when Jade led a project like this, no alcohol was involved. By two a.m., the Liberty Cap mushrooms had worn off. We were in Fermat's kitchen eating mint chocolate ice cream drenched in chocolate sauce and chopped peanuts.

I said, "If only it'd be like this till we're doddering old men."

Jade responded with a ludicrous grin, crazy and happy. I wiped chocolate from his upper lip and kissed him. Not a buss, but a deep, everything-I'd-longed-to-give kiss.

Then, because I was a foolish immature boy who'd gained no wisdom from past mistakes, much less one iota of common sense, I said, "I love you."

Jade moved away, watching me.

Time stood still, as they say.

I couldn't read his expression, since the kiss left chocolate smeared on his mouth. I couldn't interpret whether the flash of light in his eyes was residual Liberty Caps. My brain screamed: *Go back two minutes! Undo it!* I wished to be swept into the underworld with all the ghosts trapped by their errors.

Jade licked his lips, not catching all the chocolate.

"I've never been in love. If this is it, it's the best I've ever felt. So can we just go with it and see what happens?"

The heat rushing through my body was beyond gratitude for a great blessing from the Heavenly Immortals. A fire burned from a never-before-felt moment, knowing myself to be loved, to have permission to love where I'd only treasured secret longing.

Or maybe the mushrooms hadn't worn off.

After we'd kissed enough that our lips were swollen, Jade leaned back, looking at me.

"You have a beautiful smile," he said.

Because I had no practice at sustaining a moment, I said, "We enjoyed good orthodontia in Hong Kong."

He pulled me close again, whispering a question: *Is it time to consider the next act?*

It was. We fumbled, a pair of Gemini virgins who had a clue, but no experience. Trust me, we figured it out. We are both bright and creative.

He had pillowy lips. I retain a memory of what those lips felt like, beyond just kissing. And the rest...I'd had to teach myself to not let those remembered sensations overwhelm me. Still...

When we rolled apart for a moment at dawn, I asked Jade if he wanted breakfast.

"If it's no trouble," he said. "I'm starved."

We had the kitchen to ourselves since the Fermat denizens had all departed for their study carrels at Suzzallo Library. Jade lounged shirtless in jeans and barefoot, so I had to be extra careful with the knife while chopping onions and radishes to make *jianbing,* a savory and very eggy crepe the cook at our house in Hong Kong taught me to make. (She said: *Boys get hungry more often than meals are served. You have to know how to do it yourself.*)

Jade became grandiose. "Since we share a birthday, we are destined to live life as a new immortal pair."

"It is to be hoped," I said, "that we fare better than Achilles and Patroclus."

Jade began trading names of famous pairs. I'd advanced enough of my missing liberal arts education that I could contribute. We debated the merits of particular pairs.

> Oscar Wilde and Lord Alfred Douglas
> (We didn't either of us have a father, much less one who'd send his son's lover to the Reading Gaol.)

Michelangelo and Cavalieri
(Too great an age difference, plus he left Michelangelo for a wife—though do we really know who left whom?)

Emperor Hadrian and young Antinous
(I voted to omit that pair, disliking the idea of either of us dying in mysterious circumstances.)

Walt Whitman and Peter Doyle
("I'll be the streetcar conductor," Jade said.)

Alexander the Great and Hephaestion
("Ixnay." Jade tossed them aside. "Died too young.")

Fafhrd and the Gray Mouser
("Who?" Jade asked. For a liberal arts major, he had significant deficits in pop culture knowledge.)

Not long after that, at his first MFA gallery show, Jade sold the oil-crayon study for the Patroclus mural. I was disappointed, wanting to keep it. But Jade said, "Why? I can paint you dressed as anyone every day of the week."

It didn't turn out that way.

But it was nice for a while—all the way through my PhD coursework, until I had only to complete my dissertation. Because I'm a good and fast writer, I'd insisted it couldn't take more than two years, all while I played at being a ceramic artist's acolyte.

Like I'd told Timothy, we were all different people then.

—

After dinner on Saturday, the house emptied as soon as the kids finished the dishes. I sat with Becca to drink tea while she waited for Gaye. She stitched on a piece of embroidery, which she used to do often. Lately, she isn't home enough to practice homely arts.

When I put a record on the turntable—*Faith,* again—Becca drew a sharp breath.

"What?" I'd been inclined all day to feel judged.

"Are you okay? You've been downcast the entire week."

"I'm fine." I tried to sip my tea, but it was too hot. "I told you that my advisor says my dissertation is ready. He's scheduled my defense. And Cheung Bai Shing, my uncle's brother-in-law, invited me to interview for a teaching position."

"Why aren't you elated about getting every single thing you wanted?"

I didn't say: *Because I can't have what I most want.* I tried my tea again, but it hadn't cooled off in thirty seconds.

"I'm just preoccupied, worrying about Alex." Wait, am I hiding behind Alex? That'd be so wrong.

"It's more than worry. You're not happy." Becca threaded her embroidery needle with a new color. "The music you're playing cannot possibly help."

"The Cure? It's a fallacy that this song is about unrequited love. It's about the travails of an uncle trying to keep his naïve nephew out of military school because a boy kissed him."

We were not going to discuss that I was slipping into a deep, dark well because I'd overheard what I shouldn't have.

Mine.

"Claudia's trauma-inducing style of parenting must stress you." Becca hissed an inward breath, then examined the finger she must have pricked. "Given that your father disappeared and your mother took a one-way trip to la-la land."

"No psychoanalysis, please. I'm not an abandoned waif." That should be enough of a refusal, but she looked at me, her needle poised over her embroidery hoop. She has ways of coaxing me to say more. "I never knew my father. I do not miss him. I only blame him for ditching us with Ruby, who's always been a thoroughly bitter woman, which is likely why he left."

Becca set her embroidery aside. She was stitching an old-fashioned sampler, except for the words: *Eros harrows my heart.* Must be Sappho.

"Still, you're not happy," she said. "Does Xavier living next door bother you?"

"No. The Heavenly Immortals know he's just an asshole." I wiggled away from her examination, not wanting to explain feelings I expected to conquer by Monday morning. "I'm not unhappy. Things are coming together for me. By summer, I'll be doing what I've yearned to do, in the city where I long to live. Just the way I've planned it."

Becca cradled her cup of tea. "I feel like I'm watching a movie about a man who needs to be told he's beautiful and loved."

"I put too much garlic in the chicken alfredo. Yet it'll ward off demons and attract money, love, and success."

"C'mon, Rik. Tell the truth. You have an unrequited crush on someone, don't you? I recognize the signs. Who is it? Kevin?"

"What? No. Why would you think that?" I tried my tea, which was just about drinkable.

"You've been buddies since you met. You two can never start a conversation without it lasting an hour or more."

"Go find Gaye. Ask if *she* wants some mood therapy since I've declined." I drank my tea, raising my cup enough to keep Becca from glowering at me over its rim.

"I'm your friend, Rik. Tell me what's burdening you."

"That which burdens my entire academic cohort. We're in a recession that looks like a depression. The Age of Aquarius never happened. We're supposed to be zooming into our best adult lives, and none of us can launch."

"Fine. But when I came into the kitchen before dinner, you were about to cry. That's not generational existentialism."

"I was chopping garlic." I drained the last of the tea. It had not been a refreshing beverage.

"Too much garlic makes your sweat sticky. It doesn't make you cry. You're like the March of Dimes poster child for parental abandonment. If you'd had half the nurturing the twins got, you wouldn't be here moping on Saturday night."

"I'm not moping. We're going out dancing, aren't we?"

"Oh no!" Startled, Becca set her cup aside and stood. "I forgot to tell Gaye to dress for dancing."

With that, she left me blessedly alone. I rinsed my teacup and Becca's, then emptied and washed the teapot.

I was far beyond any need for parental nurturing. I wanted the wild other half of the pair I was born to. And there was no way I could have that again.

24: West Coast Blues

WHEN I CAME DOWNSTAIRS DRESSED to go dancing, I found Becca's note promising to meet me there. I hate going to clubs alone. It sends me off on a flight of should-I-stay-or-should-I-go qualms. Yet I wanted the great live music we can't get every night in Ashland. So I headed up Water Street for the club.

I like the blues, though I can't afford to collect records. A great deal of what I know comes from listening to Gaye on the radio after midnight. Like many of us children of the post-war era who appreciate the blues, we learned it via Liverpool. I was fortunate to see Paul Butterfield in Ashland, but I had to go to Eugene to hear Otis Rush and Albert Collins. Otherwise, among the bluesmen touring the West Coast, we get good shows from musicians like Paul DeLay and Curtis Salgado. But for me, nothing better comes along Highway 99 to play live in Ashland than Robert Cray, who practically lives on the road.

What I like best about being immersed in loud live blues is the elevation of emotion while in a trance of introspective solitude. Yet I have never stepped into a club alone and felt comfortable. Anyone can see I don't belong, no matter how I dress. That Saturday night, I was dressed pretty much the same as the musician: an open-collar shirt, neat jeans, a lightweight worn leather jacket. But Mr. Cray is an artist; he can get away with it. Me, I look like a dork who wandered away from a multilevel sales seminar for cleaning products. All my should-I-stay-or-go qualms renewed themselves, without the cool beat of the Clash.

If there's no free seat at a table, I should know to go to the bar. Yet I will always defer to anyone who wants to step in front of me. I feel like I'm a stranger in a strange land, though I've been here a dozen times in this year. Many people here know me. I approach the bar as if I'd crossed the border without a passport and will soon be detected, first by a barmaid who wants me to get out of the service bay so she can do her job.

By the time I wrangled a Coke and got comfortable with the tawdry smell of beer and bodies, the recorded music faded and the live music was introduced. Soon, I could move to the music, dancing with my Coke, the shuffle for when you've no one to dance with and your feet stick to last night's spilled beer. In the past, this hall spread sawdust on the floor and people cast down their peanut shells, so your feet wouldn't stick.

At last, the music took hold, strong enough to fill the many empty places behind my breastbone. I followed the walking bass into a trance. It's not lyrics that take me deeper. Rather, it's the mathematics of twelve bars and flattened pitches at thirds, fifths, or sevenths. I know people with synesthesia who see colors in music. I'd abandoned my math major, but once the music is loud enough to fill my body, I leave the mundane world for a higher sphere where mathematics takes the form of emotion.

Someone bumped into me. Hard. It was too loud to shout my apologies. But it proved to be Becca, towing Gaye, prodding me toward an empty table. They let me enjoy the music in my weird way while they bent their heads together, though how could they hear each other with the music at this volume?

When the band took a break, I found my Coke was empty. Before I waved to the barmaid, I looked to see if Becca and Gaye needed drinks too. They hadn't touched their schooners. They still had their noses in each other's ears, oblivious to the noise or crowd. Or me.

I was not surprised. Gaye had been distracted, waiting for Becca at Chez Margot on Tuesday. Becca had scarcely been home all week, save for Friday's mushroom dinner with Gaye. I saw her at breakfast only one morning.

"What's new?" Gaye at last noticed that I sat by them.

"Willie asked to take Ruby to the Apostolic Church of Ex-alcoholics come Sunday."

Gaye frowned. "Is there such a place in Ashland?"

"It's not called that, but I've been reassured that they serve grape juice at communion, just like Jesus drank."

"I never knew your mother was Sunday School." Gaye at last sipped her beer.

"She isn't. But she still attracts crazies." I fingered my empty Coke bottle.

Becca and Gaye began telling stories about elderly aunts who took up church with a vengeance late in life. I may have started the conversation, but I was nudged to the side.

Can I see it when people pair up? This was certainly it.

I signaled the barmaid for a Coke.

At the service bar, another barmaid loaded her tray with several tables' drink orders. Beside her, Jade put a friendly arm around Timothy, pulling him close to get out of the barmaid's way, a move for Jade that means camaraderie, not flirtation.

Or so I told myself.

He steered Timothy to a table, smiling broadly while folding his limbs to sit beside Timothy. A stranger sat too close on one side, but Jade's attention was only for Timothy.

Once that was me.

After Timothy spoke in his ear, Jade rubbed his other earlobe, then held up his finger with an idea.

The inner space that the blues had filled instantly emptied.

I disliked seeing that gesture. When Jade sleeps spooned with his lover, he has his thumb and forefinger on his lover's earlobe.

I think it's a gesture from infancy, like a babe in its mother's arms. It's too intimate.

Because it's no longer my earlobe.

I paid for the Coke, then found I didn't want it. I left when the musicians returned to the stage, unsure whether Becca and Gaye had heard my farewell.

—

I walked up to Granite Street, then followed it past the park's upper pond to where the street is compact granite sand. I'd been smart enough to wear tennis shoes out dancing. That familiar Ashland sound carried through the late and otherwise silent night: synthetic soles scratching over granite.

Up here, there were few porchlights and only a couple of yard lights, so the stars were free to shine. I walked far enough up into the Watershed that stars began to fill the spaces inside me that had emptied in the club.

No, that didn't happen. I don't have a poetic soul.

What I did was rub several childish sore points that needed metaphoric Flintstones Band-Aids. Timothy didn't accept my offer to hear the blues with my friends but leaned on Jade as his intimate friend. Becca, my closest friend, had tried to diagnose my existential moment, but I'd hidden all of it from her. It felt difficult for us to share secrets lately because Becca is in love and I'm stuck in my head.

I didn't get all I'd hoped from Robert Cray's sets at the club. Yet I can still celebrate the final path to my PhD and then to Hong Kong. My friends will celebrate with me, though perhaps only Chan-suk can appreciate how much it means to me.

In the middle of my walk on the upper streets, with the Milky Way overhead, I began to replay past psychedelic-fueled conversations, finding a deep connection under that strip of light across the night, wishing to cross the canyon between my private self and another person.

A memory echoed, that sense deep in the night, an hour or more after peaking, fumbling through sex, endeavoring to be present, performing with tenderness, murmuring soft words, feeling deep in one's thorax where the soul shelters that together you've crossed a barrier a millimeter thick and wide as a canyon.

I'd been privileged to feel that connection in this life. Few people gain a glimpse of that.

It had to be enough to have experienced it while knowing now that such a connection cannot be achieved again, probably not even with a couple hundred micrograms of clean LSD.

25: The Eight Gentlemen

WHILE SERVING CHOCOLATE CHIP PANCAKES and bacon, our usual Sunday breakfast, I repeated what Jade said about credit for students and the voluntary opportunity to work weekends.

"He's worried that we might not be finished before it freezes."

Ramona said, "How can he tell we're already behind?"

"Maybe he isn't good at math," I said. He definitely is not.

Becca said, "The Festival set the timetable. The grant called for the work to fit the schedule."

Despite the how-did-we-get-here discussion, the kids were eager to join weekend work. Even Ramona bounced with excitement. What I didn't expect: everyone else in the house wanted to participate. Then Becca made a point which cooled the eager crowd, that there was no use going to the site before the theatre crowd was inside for the one o'clock performance.

After breakfast, I paid Danielle to go to church with Ruby. The kids called other crew members to find who could work that afternoon. Alex and I spent fifty minutes on core math concepts, while the girls practiced for a French vocabulary quiz.

Later, everyone in the house got dressed to go work at the mural site. The kids went down B Street to rendezvous with their friends. I walked up to the site with Becca, who looked chipper in purple Zena jeans and a lavender polo shirt. Her hair, just barely long enough, was tied back with a rubber band.

"You look nice," I said. "Is Gaye coming?"

"Whyever did you unite those two ideas?" She put her hand on my arm, pretending to be startled by my question.

"Just commenting on the obvious, like people do."

Jade was working atop the center scaffold, which is what I'd expect. When I called hello, he turned around. "Sasha!" He leapt down, breaking the site rules about using the ladder.

I stepped right just as Becca stepped left, tripping over my foot. I caught her before she hit the bricks.

"Goodness, you came!" Jade cried

"I said I would." I shook off the hackles that rose every time I heard *goodness,* which was never in his Seattle vocabulary. "You know my friend Becca, right?"

She held her hand out like a genuine business administrator. "We've met. At Chez Margot, and over insurance disclaimers."

Jade grinned. "Gosh, we traded a dozen letters over the grant contracts, didn't we?"

"More like two dozen," she said.

He still held her hand. "You helped a lot with that business. I have to say...Whoa! My goodness."

My kids, Quinn, and Zooey were coming up Pioneer Street with Frankie, Stephen, Kevin, and Timothy.

Becca said, "Did you doubt the kids would come? This project is all they talk about at the kitchen table. The others are Chez Margot after-hours people. And Timothy. Xavier can't come."

Thank the Heavenly Immortals.

I did not say that out loud. And...Wait! Becca would never have invited Xavier.

Jade ran his hands through his hair. "I'll have to start all over with safety rules and how to mix cement."

"Don't do it." My substitute teacher instincts kicked in. "Pair the new workers with your usual crew and let them teach the rules." That's what every Ashland High teacher will do on Monday to help kids who missed the first week of school.

The volunteers congregated under the mid-September sun. Jade explained the basics of the work they were undertaking.

"We'll only work on background patterns today," he said.

After he paired guest workers with his crew, Jade prowled like a panther, listening in while kids with two days of experience taught their partners to wear safety goggles and explained how to cement tiny stones on assigned squares.

The weather was perfect. Warm, not hot. The trick of students-teaching-newcomers worked, and people settled in to enjoy their civic arts participation. I did twitch like a fool twice when Kevin called for more cement because I thought it was Jade who'd called and so I'd set off for the wrong end of the wall. Though, of course, Jade would call for Sasha, not Rik.

The one rough moment popped up twenty minutes after I'd begun delivering cement to the paired workers. Molly was paired with Timothy and guided him the way each crew member had been helping their partners. But as I passed, I heard that are-you-dumb-or-something tone in her voice that we'd worked on in seventh grade to remove from her repertoire.

"It's a repetition of spirals. No straight lines."

I paused close by, standing where Molly couldn't help but look my way and be subjected to my darkest avuncular gaze, since she had no excuse for being short with Timothy. However, she worked hard to avoid any glance my way.

Ramona came over. "Mr. Bonham-Day?"

He tilted his head back to see her. "It's Timothy, please."

"I'm working on the pattern around Edgar's face. Isn't that your part in *Lear* next spring? Why not come work with me?"

This was just like Ramona to rescue someone; yet I still couldn't see what was going on with Molly.

Frankie and Timothy changed partners, and that was the last ripple of tension on the work site. All Frankie wanted to talk about was Italy.

When I brought more cement, I said, "I'm surprised to see you here, Frankie."

"I packed yesterday," she said, "then jumped at the chance to do this today. Else I'd be pacing my room, trying to make the day go faster."

"Do you need a ride to the airport?"

"That's just like you to offer. But Stephen promised."

Frankie, being used to multiple manual tasks in the course of her day, picked up the knack of tile work faster than the other guest workers, so I was delivering thin-set cement to Molly and Frankie more often than to any of the other pairs, including Alex and Quinn, who were so hyped up on making art that Jade had to remind them twice to take more care while on the scaffold.

—

At three o'clock, Jade called people over to the shade along the Bowmer Theatre and poured water from a jug into paper cups for everyone, then passed around a package of Fig Newtons. The official crew warned the new volunteers not to bring food onto the mural site.

"No crumbs, no sparrows," Alex repeated.

People returned to work with good-humored bantering. As the hands on my watch moved toward four o'clock, the sun shifted behind the hills, so we worked in afternoon shade.

The change in the light might be why I homed in on what I'd noticed over the last few days: Molly and Ramona weren't speaking to each other. They didn't leave for school or arrive home together on Thursday or Friday. Alex became chatty at dinner, but the twins hadn't conversed during dinner or homework hours. This happens every few months and lasts for two or three days. Since I make it a rule not to stick my nose in their affairs without an invitation, I seldom learn what led to a rift. It's not my business. And what do I know about being twins?

One moment highlighted that rift when Molly left the site at four o'clock, walking off with a tall boy that I didn't recognize. He wasn't one of Alex and Quinn's garage visitors or one of the usual skate crew. More of a post-hippie Heathcliff in leathers and black jeans. When Molly walked away without a goodbye, a storm flashed in Ramona's eyes. Alex had been glancing between them during the earlier days of silence. He checked me when Molly walked away, his face tight with an expression similar to guilt. No, just trepidation. I recognized that look because I'd been battling such feelings for days. When I caught Alex's eye, I offered a nothing-to-do-about-it shrug. He nodded in agreement.

Except for those two Molly-shaped blips in the day, I admit to a certain kind of high from the raucous happy way everyone was cooperating on the mural. The sunbaked heat released from the plaza bricks and the soft hum of partners chatting induced a last-of-summer reverie. The mural crew acted out a motif from my dissertation: the tale of the Eight Gentlemen, guardians coming to rescue the community (not the gentleman scholars of the Western Han dynasty). I acknowledge that the threat of autumn frost didn't rise to the existential threat of bandits or northern raiders attacking the village. It wasn't *Seven Samurai,* but the last time I participated in an earnest community effort was filling sandbags when Ashland Creek flooded. This afternoon was more enjoyable. Also, my Disputatious Neighbor wasn't supervising, like he had during the sandbagging chore.

The ID tags on ten squares were now covered by swirls of opalescent white, sea foam, and shades-of-evening blue stones.

Like the clouds obscuring the Heavenly Immortals.

Valerie and Julio came up Pioneer Street, towing the twins' old Radio Flyer wagon, filled with snacks and drinks. When the pair arrived, the workers swarmed them. Alex was repeating the warning about no snacks on the work site when Jade pulled him and Quinn aside, saying something the rest of us didn't hear.

While people stood at a respectable distance to eat cookies and drink Fresca from aluminum cans, Alex and Quinn described how the Golden Rectangle served as the organizing form for the mural. With Jade's penlight in hand, Quinn pointed to squares taped onto the plaza as Alex explained the golden ratio and how it was repeated in elements of the mural.

"You can see it quite obviously," Alex said, "in the arrangement of horses and men in Lear's unruly knights."

Quinn added, "Their elongated forms enhance the tone of solemn distress."

It's bad of me to be surprised that Alex had read *King Lear.* I resolved to return to the text too. And the anxious, wound-up Alex who'd appeared at Chaos House last Tuesday? Gone. Before us stood two self-assured, almost beatific boys talking about art, while Jade stood on the side, his arms wrapping his torso as if trying to contain his own joy.

"And again with the evil sisters, Goneril and Regan, and their attendants," Alex said. Quinn shined the penlight over that group. "And also, each of the ghostly hilltop castles with their skeleton forests of trees."

Alex pointed, ahead of the penlight. "The lords who should support Lear form another Golden Rectangle inside the larger rectangle that is the mural's focus."

Quinn added, "Which is the king cradling his daughter."

"Hey!" Becca called. "You're giving away the whole plot before the audience gets inside the theatre."

"Don't forget Edgar," Timothy said.

"No, I won't," Alex said. "The Golden Rectangle is not so obvious in this drawing, because—"

"The people don't have faces yet," Frankie said.

"And Edgar is hunched up down at the bottom," Ramona said. "It's his face that will matter most for the overall tone."

Jade said, "We'll do faces last, when we all understand the full mural, its landscape, and the characters."

Kevin, who'd worked with Becca all afternoon, said in his acerbic way, "So will the mural have a happy ending, then?"

"No one gets a happy ending," Timothy said. "Haven't you read the play?"

Kevin, grinning, punched Timothy's shoulder. "It's a joke."

Timothy looked thoughtful. Didn't laugh.

After that snack, the regular crew explained cleanup to the guest workers, and the site was soon as immaculate as Jade's rules demanded. Cleanup was complete and the tarp covering hung before the afternoon audience departed the Bowmer Theatre.

Jade went around to thank each pair of the crew for coming. He ended up beside me and breathed right in my ear.

"Goodness, it's so great! It's what I've dreamed of. Thank you, Sasha." He grasped both my wrists. "Gosh, that thin-set cement will ruin your hands if you don't take care." He let go. I thought he was headed off, but he paused. "Becca is a genuinely special person, isn't she?"

"Yes, she is."

"I'm so glad for that. We can all be friends."

What the ever-loving…I do not need him sucking up to all my friends and spreading his special brand of chaos among them. Especially since I'm the only one who recognizes the chaos.

He set off to thank Becca and Frankie for coming, taking a long time to say goodbye to Becca.

Still feeling expansive despite that moment, I invited all of the Sunday mural gang to dinner at Chaos House. But Becca had a recording date with Gaye again. Jade wanted to finish prep work for Monday. Stephen invited Timothy and Frankie to eat at Chez Margot and made Jade promise to come to the café when he was ready for dinner.

I wished they'd all come back to my house since it'd be Frankie's last evening in Ashland for months, but there was no use being unhappy about it. Instead, I said farewell to the overly excited Frankie and wished her well.

Ramona, Alex, and Quinn came home with me, taking turns pulling Julio downhill in the wagon, which needed oil and a scrub with a wire brush.

I'd put a pot roast in the Dutch oven at noon, plus there was garlic bread left from the night before. Ramona whipped up an apple brown betty. I made a salad. The kids talked about the difference in making collaborative art versus working alone. All of life was great in the mellow late-summer evening.

Except Molly missed Sunday dinner.

—

Twilight had surrendered to night when I set out on a run. Possessing at least one lick of common sense, I ran the upper streets under the mercury-vapor lamps instead of the Watershed's dark woodland paths. I needed that run since I hadn't enjoyed the terpsichorean madness of the dance floor the night before.

I forgot my bandana. So toward the end of my run, I hacked up half a lung, discharging dust I wish I hadn't inhaled. Much more of this and I'd need my inhaler. Or maybe I needed to clean out blocked bad blood, like a Daoist cultivator.

What I did enjoy was a rational peaceful mind. In any moment of solitude since Saturday morning, my thoughts banged around like rocks in a tin can. Well, no. Ever since Tuesday noon. This run knocked all that out of mind. Long past dark, I came down Pioneer Street, pausing to glance over the wall at the mural site, dimly lit by streetlamps.

Jade lay on the plaza just beyond the scaffold.

I skirted the wall and ran to kneel beside him while my Red Cross training screamed instructions:

Clear passage?
Choking?
Breathing?
Pulse?
Bleeding?

He had a significant contusion at his hair line, but no streaks of blood. His right hand was a mess of scratches. I was saying what you're supposed to say, calmly begging for a response.

"Jade, are you okay? Can you hear me?"

He had a pulse and breathed. So, no mouth-to-mouth.

"*Kaukau,* what's wrong?" Molly was beside me, her tall guy friend back in the shadows.

"Jade fell," I said. "Go knock on the café back door. If Stephen isn't there, call him at home. We need to get Jade to the hospital."

Why do such crises have bright, sharp moments where every movement is filled with meaning, and then most are forgotten in the aftermath?

Stephen came. Yes, he'd parked his car on Pioneer.

Before moving Jade, I tried to rouse him, repeating first aid prompts to ensure he hadn't broken his neck or other bones. Molly and her friend put mural gear into the storage box, then disappeared into the night.

I might have overdone the repeated prompts and checks for a broken neck because Stephen poked me to say he was sure it was safe to move Jade. While we negotiated how to lift him, Jade roused enough to complain.

"I need to lock up the site."

"Already done," I said. We carried him to Stephen's car. I sat in the back, propping up Jade, who grasped my hand. For the entire ride, I kept asking questions to keep him awake. Each time Jade took so long to answer, my heart stopped. Unconscious again?

At the hospital up the hill, Stephen ran in for help. Once the ER crew arrived with a stretcher, I tugged at Jade to let go of my hand so they could get him out of Stephen's car.

At the admissions desk, I volunteered details.

"Are you a relation?" the nurse asked.

"His landlord." Sounded like a cold relationship. I immediately regretted that I didn't claim to be his brother. "He has no blood relatives."

"Who's responsible for payment?"

I gave my name. It felt too weird to be haggling when I most wanted to know what was happening behind the closed door in the ER treatment room down the hall.

Then Stephen and I waited. Tense. Too much silence. Stephen found coffee, so both of us set our stomachs on fire and our teeth to grinding. I was still in running shorts, though Stephen gave me a raggedy sweatshirt from the back of his car.

At one o'clock, they let Jade go, having wrapped his ankle and shoulder, bandaged his scraped hand, and given him a disposable ice pack for his head contusion. They had not decided whether he had a concussion. I listened to the care instructions since Jade was concerned only that no insurance claim or worker's comp claim would be filed for his accident.

He kept saying, "I'll just pay the bill. I don't want 'stumbling' on the site's safety records." No one argued, yet he persisted. "It's bad enough that my crew will figure out I broke the site rules."

Because I have kids, this was not the first time I'd been all keyed up leaving the ER, my fears not yet dissipated. The patient, however, blithely wanted a milkshake and fries from that midnight dive café across from the college.

Just like every time I've been in that café, 'Up on Cripple Creek' played on the jukebox. Jade got his burger so fast, I'm positive it had been cooked before we came in, intended for someone else. In the mirror by the door, Jade and I both looked like people you'd want to leave your late-night business as quickly as you could get them out the door.

26: A Haunted Protector

WHEN WE GOT BACK TO WATER Street, Jade wanted us to leave him at Lazarus Cottage. However, I had possession of the ER discharge papers, which had an exclamation mark by one item:

> A supervising adult must check the patient's pupils every 30 minutes for the next 6 hours. Return for emergency evaluation in the following cases:
> 1) Do one or both pupils not respond to light?
> 2) Is one pupil larger than the other?
> 3) Is the patient's speech incoherent?

"Let's ask Timothy to do it," Stephen said.

Jade said, "I don't want to bother anyone so late."

Stephen still had his arm around Jade after helping him out of the car. "Too late for that, compadre. Rik and I just spent three hours being bothered. Timothy can have a turn."

I knocked on Timothy's door. No one was home. Poking my thumb to indicate Chaos House, I said, "It'll have to be the sofa."

"C'mon, Jade," Stephen said. "Rik and I will take shifts to make sure you aren't dead or about to croak."

"I really want to sleep in my own bed," Jade said.

"But I don't want to sleep with you," Stephen said. They'd known each other for a week, yet already had a bantering relationship, like most of the Chez Margot crew. "And I am not spending the night in your papasan chair. You can try begging Rik, but do you really think he wants to sleep in your bed?"

That rasp in my chest woke up. Do the Heavenly Immortals laugh whenever my good friend tortures me, not out of malice but rather well-intentioned ignorance?

Stephen stood in the way, so I couldn't see Jade's face while he began to say, "Gosh, Sasha, I just…I just want—"

"No, do not beg him," Stephen said. "You need a shower. Badly. No one in the world wants to sleep with you. You can use my bath since it's on the first floor. Give me your key so I can get clean clothes for you."

While Stephen fetched fresh clothes, I had to help Jade take a shower. Got him out of his shirt. He could kick off his ragged Converse tennies, but I had to peel off his socks. I unbuttoned his jeans and held them while he stepped out. Then I draped plastic wrap from the kitchen over his shoulder bandage, using masking tape to hold it in place.

Then I stood outside Stephen's shower, per the aftercare instructions about preventing falls, all while blocking every thought and feeling provoked by touching him.

Stephen handed a change of clothes through the bathroom door, then declined his turn at dressing our patient. The clothes were well-worn, stretched-out sweats, so Jade mostly dressed himself. After removing the tape and plastic wrap, I had to pull the sweatshirt down over his torso while he hissed in pain.

When we emerged from the bathroom, Stephen was in the living room with a handful of clothes. He said, "I never figured you for such a slob, Jade. Or did thieves ransack your cottage?"

Not thieves. When I stocked the cottage kitchens, I'd seen that Jade's slovenly ways hadn't changed since Fermat's Last House.

"I'm tidy on the job, where it matters," Jade said. "Housework isn't my thing."

While I got a flashlight from the kitchen, Stephen tucked Jade under a blanket on the living room sofa. I heard Stephen's mellow baritone when I started upstairs to take a shower.

Stephen: The doctor is in. If you don't stop squinting, I'll just jerk your eyes open with my fat fingers.

Jade: That light is too bright. It hurts.

Stephen: You'll get a cherry lollipop if you're a good boy.

Jade: Are you saying I suck?

Stephen: No, I'd never judge. Ask Rik about that when he comes back. He's pretty forthright.

Where did Stephen get that idea? I've been ducking into closets all week—hiding while playing chaperone; hiding my emotions from my friends. What's the song that's been playing on the radio? 'Karma Chameleon'? Yeah, that's me. Never forthright. Busy fighting the memories that keep cascading over me.

And Jade doesn't suck. Rather, he's an electromagnet with only one attractor pole switched on. I must keep my anti-magnetism shield up when he's around.

—

After my own shower, I came downstairs still keyed up from the night's adventure and ER waiting-room coffee. I sent Stephen to bed. Jade had fallen asleep on the sofa, and I did what I could to coax him into the least stressful position.

His breathing had a husky tone. I listened for trouble, but it was just deep sleep. And a different sound from when I sit with Ruby after her nightmares. But thinking of Ruby and Jade's noisy breathing made me think of grief, provoking unwanted feelings.

I diverted myself, watching shadows of maple and locust branches dance on the wall. That awakened an ancient memory of being ill as a small child. Which parent cooled my fever with damp cloths and sat with me while I watched shadows dance? I recall only the dancing shadows, not a comforting parent. They probably paid someone to comfort me.

I roused Jade at two thirty to check his pupils.

He complained.

That must be some kind of aftershock symptom since everyone in this town knows Jade to be easygoing.

"Don't be such a baby," I said. "You insist that site rules must be obeyed. This is just another rule, a corollary to whatever site rule you broke that got you here."

I stubbed my toe on the sofa when checking his eyes. I keep bumping into things while wielding my anti-magnetism shield.

"I don't want to be a bother."

"Then shut up. Don't whine while I check your pupils."

"Yes, Mom."

Such banter between guys. I flashed the light. "This reminds me of a roommate I once had who refused to take his cough to the doctor. When it turned out to be walking pneumonia, I had to time the antibiotic doses, force chicken soup, find a humidifier, and then clean it every night."

"Point taken. Are you still bitter, Sasha?"

"No. I'm just at stage three of crisis response. With my kids, I'm so relieved once a child is no longer in jeopardy that I then get mad about the accident."

"Just like my mom. Sorry to have to say so."

Molly came in.

There was school come morning, so a broken curfew meant more than it did on a weekend. I'd been so worried about maybe-concussed Jade that I almost let it get by me. Except:

> Molly ditched Sunday dinner without saying a word.
>
> Ramona acted weird when Molly left with Tall Boy.
>
> Tall Boy didn't greet me at the mural site, hung back in the shadows, and disappeared without saying goodbye.

She reached the stairs, likely thinking she'd escaped.

"Please make breakfast in the morning," I said. "And I won't write a tardy excuse for school."

"Yes, *kaukau.*"

When Molly's door closed upstairs, Jade said, *"Kaukau?"*

"It means mother's younger brother. They learned a few words by osmosis while I was writing my dissertation. Or they get it from Hong Kong fight movies."

"They're exceptionally good kids," Jade said.

"I'm lucky."

"I wish I had smart, funny kids who called me uncle."

For a time, it was silent in the semi-dark. Shadows waved along the ceiling edges. I thought he'd gone back to sleep.

"Becca says your dissertation was accepted."

Becca talked to Jade about me? My best friend who knows most everything about me? Except she knows nothing about Jade in my life before Ashland, or about the Dragon's Blood crystals in my chest that I can't keep quiet.

"I submitted the final draft. But I still have to defend it. And my committee has to vote."

The silence again lasted so long I thought he'd gone to sleep.

"Forgive me, Sasha. I get so annoyed with people prying into my life, I resist prying into others' business. Still, I've been in town for eight days. I should have asked about your dissertation. Or congratulated you as soon as I heard about it."

"Thanks." I changed the subject. "Do you want an icepack for your shoulder?"

"Sasha, you should stop and congratulate yourself."

I'd failed to steer his attention away. "I'll throw a party after my defense is done."

"A big party. You once said our motto should be, 'Forward. Don't stop. No regrets.' This is a big milestone for going forward."

I said that? How blasted on acid were we that time?

"Sit up for a minute, Jade. Let me check your pupils again. Then you can sleep until three thirty."

"Thanks, Mom."

"Cut it out. No more unfunny comments about parents."

"You called me a baby."

"It was a metaphor. And I refrained from saying anything about grown men putting themselves in danger."

"It's just too bad that you and I didn't arrange to have father figures as good as you. Maybe in a future lifetime."

"I'm just an uncle, not a father."

Blessed silence for a while.

"Gosh, it's so good that we can be friends, Sasha."

I rallied my remaining strength to lift my shield. I'll need major help from the Heavenly Immortals to keep holding it up if he won't stop being so damned nice.

The Dragon's Blood crystals grew larger, like when we were kids and my brother Christopher poured ammonia and bluing on chunks of coal he'd found down by the train tracks.

At four o'clock, Danielle came in. "Rik, help me with Ruby. She's having a nightmare and I can't wake her."

"Coming."

First, I poked Jade awake to check his pupils. "I have to leave for a bit. Shall I get Stephen to sit with you?"

"I wonder where Timothy is," he mumbled.

"No idea." Far be it from me to recommend he get a better boyfriend. "If you need help before I get back, call for Stephen."

"I'm fine," he mumbled. I was four steps away when he called my name. "Sasha." When I looked back, he said, "I can't beat Becca. But I'm a good friend too, aren't I?"

"Sure."

How else was I supposed to respond to that? While I followed the mournful, frightened weeping to Ruby's room, I still struggled to turn off the bitchy voice in my head. It's just not like me unless I'm thinking about Xavier. But really, Jade: *Get a better boyfriend.*

Find one that shows up to check your pupils after a fall.

Or that at least appreciates the *Lazarus* wall.

27: The New Ordinary

"RIK, GO GET SOME SLEEP," Stephen whispered. He came in at six thirty to relieve me, just as daylight was exorcizing the ghostly branches waving on the ceiling. "I can make breakfast."

"Molly will make breakfast. You can start some coffee."

The tangled knot of energy in my gut told me I wouldn't sleep. Instead, I went to the kitchen to wait for coffee and sat at the table to plan out the week, which allowed me to be present but *not* glare while Molly made breakfast. After settling Ruby from her nightmares, I'd burned off all the censorious chemical that ran through my body in reaction to Jade putting himself in jeopardy and Molly coming home so late.

Stephen was filling my coffee cup and Molly was about to fill the bento boxes for the guest cottages when Timothy knocked on the front door.

"Have you seen Jade?" He frowned with worry. "He didn't come home last night."

Sheesh. Now you're worried about him.

"He's here," I said. "After—"

"I fell. Like a klutz." Jade came into the living room.

"What happened?" Timothy started into the house.

"Take your shoes off. It's a house rule." Jade pointed to the shoe rack. He leaned against the wall near the stairs, disheveled, the worn sweats sagging on torso and hips.

Timothy kicked off his shoes. "But what happened?"

"I fell from the scaffold. Stephen and Rik took me to the ER, then brought me home."

Stephen came in. "We had to check him every half hour for a concussion. You missed all the fun, Timothy."

"Sorry." Timothy was apologizing to Jade. "We closed down the bar. I didn't notice you were gone till this morning."

I clutched my coffee cup so tightly, my knuckles were white.

Not my business. I need to get a grip. It's Molly who should take a number and get in line to be scolded for breaking curfew. Not Jade's capricious young boyfriend.

Molly said, "Do you want to eat breakfast here? Or do we have to carry it out to the cottages?"

I might be the sole person present who heard are-you-dumb-or-something in her tone.

"Goodness, we can eat here," Jade said. *Goodness* had been gone when we talked in the wee hours; here it was again.

I said, "Coffee, Timothy?"

"Tea, please. If you have milk. I prefer Darjeeling."

"We only have lapsang souchong in the house."

"I don't know what that is," Timothy said. "I have Darjeeling in the cottage. I'll fetch it."

Becca came in just then, managing to say good morning.

I set water to boil, and then sat back down to finish my coffee just as Julio ran in ahead of Valerie and sat beside me.

"Howdy, amigo." I began our usual banter. "Molly made scrambled eggs for breakfast. Or do you prefer tofu?"

Julio scrunched up his nose. "No, thank you, Uncle Rik."

Jade slid onto the bench beside him. "Morning, cowboy. What are you having for breakfast? Beans and bacon?"

Julio shook his head. He hates beans, has probably never tasted bacon. "Cheerios, please. Uncle Rik knows how to do it. Did he tell you to come inside *right now* and eat?" He sounded just like me calling him in from the backyard.

"Molly asked us," Jade said. "It was very nice of her."

"We always eat here," Julio said.

"You are one lucky cowboy."

"If you ask Uncle Rik, he'll give you Cheerios. But you have to eat as much as you pour in your bowl. It's a *rule.*"

Again, Julio imitated me precisely.

When Timothy returned, Becca pointed out the tea kettle. He stood for a moment, uncertain. People moved around him. I could have reassured him that it was only the usual chaos:

> Becca and Stephen were there, silently drinking coffee, both staring off into space.
>
> All three kids were there, not silent.
>
> Valerie resisted taking over when I helped Julio with his Cheerios, spilling the usual amount of milk on the table.
>
> Danielle wandered in, seeking a cup of coffee, spoke only to Molly, then was gone.
>
> Molly insisted that people line up and serve themselves breakfast, *right now.*
>
> Becca, seeing me set out the jar of chili oil, exclaimed about blessings from the gods of Olympus, kissed me on the cheek, and declared that she loved me.

Timothy overcame his uncertainty and got into line for food, still a little twitchy. I find this kind of chaos comforting. That morning, Chaos House was just doing what it's supposed to, taking care of people. Unlike the nerve-wracking sort of chaos that Jade brought to town.

The phone rang. I picked Julio up and set him down beside Valerie before I grabbed the phone.

"Chaos House," I said, stepping into the living room so I could hear over the breakfast commotion.

"Rik? Thank goodness you're home." It was Jacqueline Urquell, the vice principal who corrals substitute teachers.

"You have a gig for me?" I'd had coffee. I could have more. I could take on a day's teaching gig with no sleep.

"It's the same gig we talked about last week. Sally Ogden's math classes."

"In December?" Was I about to lose that extra pay? I needed that money, probably to hand over to Nick for legal services. Repairing his windows might not cover it all.

"It starts today. Sally had an emergency last night, and her doctor has ordered bedrest."

"Oh good heavens. Is she okay?"

"She says yes, but I'm not sure. She always says she's fine, but she sounded shaky."

"Tell her not to worry about her classes. I'll be there."

That'll eliminate all the free time I've wasted moping and bitching about how the facetious Immortals did nothing to seize control of fate. Or complaining about other people's boyfriends.

Jacqueline said, "You know Sally. She insists she'll grade all the tests and homework. I think she's worried about being bored." Then she offered directions for finding Sally's lesson plans. "Sally wants you to call during prep period to learn details for specific students. Do call her, so she can stop worrying."

"I'll call now," I said. "And also later."

When I hung up after chatting with Sally, Ramona and Molly were right beside me, giving me scarcely room to move.

"You're subbing full time, Uncle Rik?" Molly asked. "For more than a day? A full week?"

"Through April."

Molly and Ramona looked at each other for the first time in several days.

"More cooking and housework for us?" Ramona said.

I shook my head. "You already do your fair share. This is no different from any teachers who have kids. We've done full-time before. It just means I can't do daytime handyman work."

"I'll lose my best drywall partner!" Stephen exclaimed.

"But the mural!" Alex said. "You can't quit that."

"Golly, I have to agree with that," Jade said.

I had, for the space of the call with Sally, forgotten about him being at the kitchen table. He was buzzing Julio with spoonfuls of Cheerios, spilling no more milk than usual on the table.

"I'm not quitting anything," I said. "Only adding to each day in a regular way."

Except I'd have to forego my lunch hour with Ruby. I had to check in with Mrs. Adams.

"This is fantastic news for your Hong Kong fund," Becca said. "I can hear the coins dropping."

"You're going on vacation?" Jade asked me.

But Alex jumped in to answer. "He's moving to Hong Kong as soon as we graduate. We get to come too, until August."

"That's the robust Return to Hong Kong plan," Becca said. "Becoming more real every single day."

"Are you going too?" Timothy asked. She was looking at her watch, not listening. She jumped up and headed out the door.

Ramona pointed to Alex since she wasn't speaking to Molly. "Let's think about how to help instead of worrying about how our *kaukau* can't do other people's karma for them."

"Wow," I said. "That's harsh. Thoughtful, yet harsh."

"You can stop catering our breakfast," Jade said. "Don't you think so, Timothy? I always end up eating Xavier's anyway."

"Fine," I said. "I'll refund the Festival."

"Why can't they eat breakfast here?" Ramona asked.

Alex said, "That beats me carting it down the street."

"Gosh, there's an idea," Jade said. "We don't need catering. Aren't Chaos House rules the same as at Fermat's Last House?"

"Fermat's Last what?" Alex said.

"I really have to go." I felt hot, my discomfort increasing with Jade both being kind and getting in my business.

I went upstairs to put on my teacher dress-for-success uniform. When I returned, they were all still at the table, debating how to help make this change work out, with Jade insisting that he and Timothy would do their part.

"Right, Timothy?" Jade punched his friend's shoulder to elicit a positive answer.

I didn't hear what the boyfriend said, given all the noise.

In the past, I'd struggled with enduring kindness from Jade. Until then, no one in my life (besides Chan-suk) had spontaneously offered kindness or even noticed when I needed it. I still don't know how to bear it.

Especially so soon after I'd been drinking hot coffee in a thin china cup to help my fingers forget what it felt like to guide a soft, worn shirt over that man's ribs.

—

On Monday afternoon in the middle of mural site work, Molly collided with Quinn, and two boxes of glass tiles scattered on the plaza. Apprehensive, the two approached Jade, but he offered that disarming smile which starts from the core of his being.

"Goodness, what an opportunity!" Jade exclaimed. "I promised that you'd work like Zen monks raking gravel. Find a third box and sort these. You can do it before today's session ends."

I blinked at that brief exchange since I too felt apprehensive at the sound of tiles cascading onto bricks. That mild, encouraging response wasn't what I'd expect from the Jade I'd assisted in years past. Back then, I'd been tolerated as an assistant because I made few mistakes. I'd observed back then that Jade didn't snap at other workers on site, but he'd take it out on physical objects. He wasn't the first genius I'd met at university who was intolerant of mundane talents. He hid his disdain unless someone's clumsiness or ignorance led to problems with a project.

Jade's mercurial nature coupled with his perfectionism had intrigued me when we first became friends. The only other person I've known who blew hot and cold was my brother Christopher. My mother, of course, was always angry. Jade was only rarely volcanic. Yet here we were, a decade later, and he smiled at a catastrophe just moments after he'd delivered a short sermon about how every moment counted in our race against the autumn frost.

At each mural work session, Jade expounds on aesthetic decisions and the cultural influences on the mural's design, which means that each day's work becomes a tiny Art Appreciation class. He has his own version of Socratic prompting to push kids' thinking. And he gives thoughtful answers to all questions asked. But Jade can charm his crew by eliciting brilliant insights and then send them back to happily gluing glass to a very uneven concrete wall. I was jealous. As part of getting my teaching credentials, I got a third master's degree in child development. I could seldom achieve what he did.

At the end of Monday's session, kids gathered around my car on the street above the mural wall, drinking chocolate milk and eating peanut butter sandwiches. I joined Jade on the street side of the wall. He'd taken off his site-mandatory long-sleeved shirt and draped it on the top of the wall. His t-shirt didn't reveal his anatomy since it was covered by the lump of bandage around his shoulder. He chomped on a peanut butter sandwich and chugged chocolate milk from the carton.

"Tell me, Sasha, what can I do better?"

I shrugged, thinking Jade was begging for compliments while I just wanted to go home and cook dinner. I offered what might border on being worthless advice. "The kids at the right couldn't hear your comments about Roman narrative mosaic styles. You should stand in the middle while teaching."

Jade chewed on his lower lip as he listened, then smiled and thanked me, as if what I'd said was worth a straw, after he'd had a dozen aspiring artists hanging on to his every word.

"Also, please allow me to say," I leaped into the personal, "that you handled the tile accident quite well. It helped everyone feel more comfortable."

He shifted his feet, didn't answer for a moment, then set down the sandwich and milk to rub his bare forearms. Where the sun had bleached the hairs white.

"A few years back," he said, "I was working a gig where I broke things too often. Nearly got into a fight. I was burning up with anger, with no good excuse. So I stopped. There's no use wasting energy that way."

"What were you angry about?"

"Goodness, that's a story."

I started to ask for the story, though it meant more intimate words than we'd shared this week.

He stood up, looking down Pioneer Street.

Xavier was coming up the street. Jade moved away. "I have a meeting for Xavier's production. See you tomorrow, Sasha."

I wandered home, at first pondering his lecture on Roman narrative mosaic styles. I wasn't hung up on the aesthetics and techniques, but on the pictures Jade passed around. The bottom of each picture identified the archeological dig where he'd worked on a restoration. Turkey, Cordoba, Cyprus, Valencia, Tudela, the English Cotswold Hills. A partial travelogue of where he'd been since we'd started out in 1974 to become Wandering Scholars, with Ashland as our first stop.

—

Years ago—too many stray thoughts start that way—when I'd just finished my PhD course work and was beginning my dissertation, Jade and I sat at Fermat's kitchen table, talking past midnight, which we often did. I remember it being April, with Seattle rain pelting on the corrugated fiberglass porch roof. Jade was sorting a collection of ceramic discs he'd made for a new project. The click matched the sound of the rain, at least in my memory.

He said, "My first ceramics prof at the UW still serves as a mentor. I seek to emulate her."

My job that rainy night was to place sorted discs into small cardboard boxes, so gently that they made no sound. I confessed my private dreams. "I intend to emulate my master in Hong Kong, Chan-suk. He set my life on its proper course."

Jade bit his lip, a sign of hesitation, which didn't happen often. "Um…that prof I call my mentor?"

"Who left the UW for a gig at another school?"

"She's on sabbatical this coming fall term. She got her school to ask me to take over her classes as a visiting artist."

A thousand feelings flooded me while the rain pounded. No, only one distinct feeling: *I'll be alone again.*

Then Jade said, "Want to come along? Though I should warn you, my mentor teaches in Ashland. Can you stand living near your family for three months?"

After I said yes, we swore then that we'd become Wandering Scholars, artists with no fixed abode, who'd pursue true scholarship and beauty wherever we found our next gig.

We both knew that my family was cuckoo—he'd heard plenty of stories. Yet neither of us felt a possibility of danger in being that close to the cuckoo's nest. As it turned out, I didn't wander or become more than a midnight scholar. I was instead sucked into another universe and swallowed whole.

Since then, Jade has created a great deal of beauty. I don't know what he's done about truth and justice out in the world. My focus has been like looking through the wrong end of the telescope. My world doesn't extend beyond Chaos House, my kids, and my friends. And the kids in Algebra II, Calculus, and remedial math.

28: It's Not Too Much

DINNER ON MONDAY WAS SOY sauce noodles with bean sprouts and the shredded chicken I'd prepped on Saturday. After dinner that night, Stephen dragged me into his room to talk.

"I closed today on my house out near Emigrant Lake. My ex is now off the title, and I don't owe her one more penny. She's moved out everything she wants. Thus ends that sad chapter."

I waited for him to open a conversation about the end of his marriage, but it was instead a conversation about the future.

He said, "I hope to move back into my house by mid-October. I just need to find workers to manage cleanup and repairs."

Typically, that'd be me, but I'd said yes to the full-time substitute gig. Stephen quickly moved on to more news. "You know the large mother-in-law apartment you helped remodel?"

"Yes. It turned out well, though your ex-mother-in-law never wanted to live there."

"I offered it to Valerie. I don't mean to poach your tenant, but it's better for Julio, don't you think?" Stephen rushed on before I got out an affirmative. "Val and Julio can ride into town with me in the morning. And one of the Festival bookkeepers lives nearby, so they can carpool home at night when I'm working at the café."

I'd known Stephen's exodus from Chaos House was imminent and, if I'd been paying more attention, I should have foreseen his invitation to Valerie, given how much time they'd been spending together. And he was right. Valerie's room at Chaos House was too small for a fast-growing four-year-old.

"I'm happy you got your house back at last. Congrats."

His ex-wife had been vengeful, in my opinion, given that she was the one who deserted him.

"Chez Margot had a good summer," Stephen said. "With this settled, I'll be on even keel financially by next summer. So…"

"Yes?"

"I think I can make an offer for your house when you leave for Hong Kong. I wasn't kidding last summer when I asked you about that possibility, because a bed-and-breakfast is the next business I should pursue. It's just that my finances have been a mess since it took so long to settle that…disruption."

"It'll be a cool thing if we can make it happen, Stephen."

After that, he was quickly off to Chez Margot for his night's tasks. Everything about Stephen has become quicker and lighter since he stopped carrying the weight of that quarrel with his ex.

I sat at the table. The kids were heads down in schoolwork. Alex passed his math homework across to me.

"In a minute, Alex. I have news. Chaos House is shifting members. Stephen and Valerie are moving to his house out at Emigrant Lake. Molly, Ramona, do you two want to flip to see who gets Valerie's room next month?"

"Molly can have it."

"Ramona can have it."

I had a quarter from my jeans pocket. "Heads it's Molly, tails it's Ramona. I'll help paint after Valerie moves out."

Molly won. She said thank you and resumed her homework. Which I found a tad disappointing.

While I reviewed Alex's math homework, Ramona and Molly passed me permission slips to sign. Molly wanted to transfer to a different English class, Ramona another History section.

For a reason I might never know, the girls still weren't talking and wanted to be in different classes. I signed the slips. "Let's discuss this after homework is done."

"Discuss what?" Molly tucked the signed slip in her pack.

"We just prefer different teachers," Ramona said.

Okay, I had no reason to enter into a drama where I have no role. So who knows why the twins aren't speaking to each other?

"What about Stephen's room?" Alex asked.

"It's staying open for now. A friend might need it."

I wanted to ask Gaye if she'd want to move back to Chaos House. Or would Becca follow Gaye to the house with the great sound studio? No, Becca had no known affinity with Gaye's rock-band housemates. And Gaye had breakfast here Saturday morning, which seemed meaningful.

How did breakfast end up being the touchstone between me and so many people? What about my astrology or karma or fate came to be closely associated with hens' eggs and wheat toast?

—

Alex again presented his math homework. I studied the work-sheet. "It doesn't look like you need help, Alex. Is there anything you don't understand in this?"

"No, Uncle Rik. I'm fine. Thanks for your help Sunday."

Alex had not sought more advice from me about Claudia. I believed his problem was only Claudia, not any soulful struggle over what it meant if a boy kissed him. Should I reach out?

The Heavenly Immortals, listening in, chose to interfere.

The phone rang. It was Claudia calling from London.

She demanded Alex be put on the phone.

The connection wasn't the best and Alex didn't have the same inclination for privacy as, for example, Molly. So we were treated to a one-way conversation shouted in the middle of the kitchen, with Felix the Clock wagging its tail in judgment.

He sounded happy to speak with her, asking where she was and if she was okay. He listened to what might have been questions or admonishment, then took command of the conversation. Whatever Claudia might have asked, it popped the bubble of enthusiasm he'd shown over the past several days.

"The counselor says I can graduate this year if I pass math. Uncle Rik has been helping and I aced the first quiz. I actually like it, since he showed me how music is just math with sound."

He listened for thirty seconds.

"Mom, I'm not playing in the garage all the time. I got into band class here, so I play third period every day. And I can't play music after school because I'm working on a civic art project. It's the biggest thing that's ever happened to me."

He was answering a likely question. "It's at the Shakespeare Festival. We're working on a mural of *King Lear.* It's huge. The design is a combination of Roman narrative mosaic style and Byzantine floor mosaics. But—"

He listened again. Then: "We get credit for it. The artist is pretty famous. And Uncle Rik is the school's chaperone. It's not like—" He held the phone away from his ear. We could only hear the anger. "Mother, the artist is Jade Solberg. It's a huge opportunity for us. He's critiquing our portfolios and writing recommendations for our college applications. And—"

He winced. I could hear her shouting, but not the words.

The phone connection is bad, Mother. I'm hanging up."

He sat back down on the bench, his homework spread in front of him. He folded his hands, his expression closed.

Ramona asked, "Do you get to stay here after she comes back from Europe?"

He shook his head.

"Tell us what she said," Molly insisted. "I cannot stand not knowing. She was yelling at you, wasn't she?"

He nodded. "She shrieked Jade's name, like five times, as if we're working with Fidel Castro or Roman Polanski or...I dunno. But she flipped."

"She said more than his name," Molly prompted. I wished she'd leave Alex alone. He wasn't just folding his hands. He was wringing them in agitation.

"She said," Alex cleared his throat, "'Is Rik Eliot trying to resurrect Christmas?' She wants to drag me back to Berkeley as soon as she gets home."

Just...just...Why, Claudia? And why now?

I said, "Let's talk." I dragged him out to the back porch, where both the washer and the dryer were running.

"What does she mean, Uncle Rik? About Christmas?"

"When Wendy left Ramona and Molly with me, she and Claudia had a big fight. They said terrible things to each other."

"What did that have to do with you?"

"Uh, nothing. But I didn't stop them when they started calling names. You don't remember that, do you?"

"No. But why did she go off her nut about Jade?"

"I guess because I knew him at the UW." I tried not to lie. "When people get upset, they say things that don't make sense."

"Will I have to leave Ashland?"

"I don't think so. Nick, our attorney, has a conference call with Claudia's attorney tomorrow. We'll know more then."

"Will she be on the call, too?" Alex still wrenched his hands, which I found to be heartbreaking.

"No, it's just lawyers. But I have to ask you about what Nick can say on your behalf."

"I don't want to go back to Berkeley. I like it here."

"I can see that. I have to ask..." I wanted to broach this carefully. "Nick is partnering with an advocate in California, an attorney he knows. They'll file for me to become your guardian."

"That would be so good." He unclenched his hands.

"The advocate can make the best case if abuse is involved."

"That's dumb. Claudia has never hit me. Ever. She doesn't believe in it."

I rubbed at my nose. The soap powder in the air was getting to me. No, Claudia's mischief was getting to me.

"There's another kind of abuse," I said. "Nick wants to know whether you want to claim emotional abuse. Like how she has harassed and yelled at you for being gay."

"When she gets upset, she just doesn't know what to do." He held his hands up, as if pleading for her.

I coughed to cover the huge breath I took. I wanted to beg him: *Please don't defend what she said to you.*

"When Claudia called last week," I said, "she yelled at you and wanted to send you to conversion therapy. The advocate can use that to claim emotional abuse."

I was about to say: *Please don't let anyone hurt you.* But I paused on a wish: if only someone had told me that long ago.

"That'd hurt her feelings." Alex was so sincere I wanted to fold him in my arms, shelter him from any harm.

"We'll do everything possible to keep from hurting her feelings. But she hurt your feelings, Alex. This is one way we can help you defend yourself."

I made myself stop talking. I didn't want to trip him into saying more than he wanted to.

"Just have the attorneys tell her that I'm not gay," Alex said, "so she'll cool down. She'd rather do her author tours than supervise my homework."

"That's really what you want?"

"I just want to play music. Do art. And graduate."

At last I had the opening I wanted. "Okay. You know I'm gay?" He nodded. I continued. "I had a teacher in high school who helped me understand how to know you're gay."

Chang-suk had explained that you know you're gay because of who you fall in love with. He was wise enough to see that I was in love with Kai, and that it didn't go both ways.

"Yeah, I'm sure I'm not gay," Alex said.

"How do you know?" I asked. What a let-down, after how pent up I'd been about having this conversation.

"Jade said he learned from a roommate that you know because of who you fall in love with. So that means I'm not gay. It felt kinda nice to be kissed, but I didn't even kiss him back."

I lost the thread I thought we were following. "Jade told you?" *Jade repeated Chan-suk's words?* "When was this?"

"We were working on the scaffold together on Sunday afternoon. I asked him if I could use the garage for music sometimes. He didn't know I played, and then he asked about my art, so I showed him some recent drawings."

Alex pointed to a new sketchbook I'd seen him with, but only just then noticed it was the same kind that Jade carries.

"While he looked at my drawings, Jade asked what else was going on with me, so I told him about Claudia breathing dragon fire. I asked if he thought I was gay. That's when he told me what his roommate said."

"Alex." A conflagration ignited in the organs behind my breastbone. I modulated my voice and tossed metaphorical water on the flames. "You cannot ask an older man that you just met whether you're gay. It's…not prudent."

There must be another word. I couldn't find it.

"I've known Jade for a week. He's a good guy. He listens. It's not like I asked some old creep in Haight-Ashbury if I'm gay. And Jade's not even gay."

Yeah, he is. But it's not my place to say so.

"Then why ask Jade if you're gay?"

"He knows things. And he's easy to talk to."

Okay. *But you could have asked me.* I clamped my lips on those words. Was I jealous?

"Oh! Ooh!" He jerked as if he just realized something. "You think I should have asked you. Do *you* think I'm gay?"

"No, I don't. But I wish you trusted me to ask."

"Uncle Rik, I didn't want you to worry about me. You have to worry about Claudia and Grandma and everything else."

"I understand." No, I don't, and I've spent all week worrying. "We'll talk about this again after Nick and the advocate in California speak with Claudia's lawyer."

I headed back to the kitchen. I desperately needed—what? A bucket of cold water to stick my head in?

"Uncle Rik." Alex called me back. "I know you worry about it. I'm sorry it's happening."

"Nick and I have it handled. You shouldn't worry."

"I mean about your tree frog friend." He pointed to the shelf that held detergent and bleach. "He's back."

—

While the kids finished their homework at one end of the table, I made tea and reworked my master daily list:

5:30 Run (any weather) and shower
7:00 Breakfast
7:30 Kids and me out the door
8:00–3:00 Math classes
3:15 Mural site
6:00 Math papers to Sally
6:30 Dinner; homework/tutoring
8:00 Sit with Ruby
8:30 House chores; prep next day's snacks + dinner
9:30 Translation work
11:00 Chez Margot (twice a week?)

While I finished my list (crossing off Chez Margot as long as Timothy is in Ashland), Alex and Ramona were talking.

"After we finished work at the site today," Alex said, "I asked Jade for a meeting to show him my portfolio."

My private alarm: I didn't know Alex had a portfolio. I'd only ever seen his cartoon sketchbook.

"Can I come, just to listen?" Ramona asked. "I want to ask for a review, but I'm nervous about what he'll say."

Ramona had insisted that she'd major in sociology or psychology. She just wanted to try both before deciding. Visual arts? Never once on her list. I sipped my tea far too soon, burning my lips. Am I not informed? Have I been too contented that the twins never caused trouble after their freshman year?

The Heavenly Immortals might be nudging the oracle bones to a simple answer: *Yes. Not in control of one thing. Anywhere.*

"Yeah, sure you can." Alex was enthusiastic. "But your work is so good, Ramona. Are you afraid of what Jade might say?"

"When is your meeting?" Ramona didn't answer the question about fear.

"That's just it. Given Jade's schedule, I didn't see how he'd have time." Alex then recited Jade's daily schedule. "Each morning, he's working in the ceramics studio or the garage."

I know that because I hear Jade down there while I'm doing my own chores or sitting with Ruby. I haven't, however, received chiding notes from my Disputatious Neighbor about Jade's noise in the garage. In fact, I'd encountered those two chatting on the street three times now.

Alex said, "Then he's at the college until our mural work starts in the afternoon. After we finish the site work, he has planning meetings at the Festival."

"How come you know Jade's schedule?" Ramona asked. "It's one of Rik's Rules. Don't be nosy about the tenants."

I should heed my own warnings.

Alex said, "I asked when I could use the garage for rehearsal. Quinn and I now have it Saturday and Sunday mornings, plus evenings till nine o'clock if there's no homework. Jade says he'll look at my portfolio before site work Saturday afternoon."

Which meant, given my new schedule, that I'd see Jade only at breakfast (with Timothy) and while chaperoning at the mural site. I was relieved for a moment, then remembered that Inez had signed me up as the go-fer for the raku kiln. But Jade seemed fully involved with the mural work and hadn't yet asked for assistance. Perhaps I wouldn't be needed for that task until Jade's college students needed it after fall term started.

I left the kids to their homework while I reviewed Sally's detailed notes for the next day's classwork. That task was interrupted when I looked out the window. The lone streetlight revealed that the garbage bin had been knocked over after I'd set it out for tomorrow's trash pickup.

If I didn't rectify that immediately, my Disputatious Neighbor would soon be taping a note to the back screen door.

—

It was after twilight when I came out of the house, snapping on kitchen gloves because I'm not a fan of touching garbage. I found Timothy already stooping to pick up trash and stuff it back into the garbage bin.

"Thanks, Timothy." I bent to grab trash that had found its way closest to my Disputatious Neighbor's property. "It's kind of you to help. But let me do the messy parts."

"We saw a car pass, and then the trash went flying." He retrieved a plastic bag filled with bathroom trash, passing by a disintegrating mound of kitchen garbage that was escaping its newspaper wrapper. "Jade thinks it was teenagers with a baseball bat. He's making cocoa, so he sent me out to help."

"You'd think garbage bashing would be a weekend amusement." I fetched up the dilapidated kitchen leavings. "I thought you'd be at the Festival tonight. Are you missing a seminar?"

"Jade said I should take the night off." He heaved into the bin a paper bag of three-hole–punched college-rule notepaper, castoffs from the kids' Trapper Keepers. "Xavier and I had a tiff this afternoon. I left when he started yelling at me."

"Best wait till he forgets," I said. "Xavier has a short memory. Unless he holds a grudge. Then he'll never forget."

Timothy didn't laugh. "I could not endure this without Jade."

"Endure what?" Not my business. I shouldn't ask. I'm not innately nosy like Becca is.

Timothy sighed. He'd picked up the last of non-filthy trash, so he brushed off his hands, taking care not to touch his clothes. "Through this nightmare of workshops and plays and meeting actors. Xavier is…"

"A dick," I said.

Timothy chuckled ruefully. "I was going to say a dictator."

"But Jade helps?" I know better than to ask. I should be back in the house, asking about my kids' artistic goals, since I'd failed to be aware of their hearts' desires.

"When I complain, Jade says I'm stronger than Xavier. That Xavier's so hard on me because he knows I have a grander future than he can hope for. Does that sound like I'm bragging?"

"It sounds like Jade is a good friend."

"Yes, thank heaven. I've never felt like I needed a friend. I hope…" He'd stepped onto the stoop of the middle cottage. I thought our tête-à-tête had ended, but he turned back. "I hope we're still friends a decade from now. Like you and Jade are."

After Timothy left, I settled the refilled garbage bin as far from the road as possible.

Jade came up behind me, so silent it startled me.

He was barefoot and still limping from Sunday's injury. "Sasha, can Timothy hang out at Chaos House if he needs to?" I could be more surprised, though I'm not sure how. I took too long to answer, so Jade said more. "Xavier is a problem. You can guess how. Becca told me about your adventure with him."

Freaking Becca. *Dear friend, can you never keep quiet?*

Yet I nodded, "Of course he can. Whenever he wants. I am familiar with Xavier's modes of aggression."

"I swear he's a sociopath." Jade pounded a fist into his other palm. "I think Timothy should ask his agent to get him out of this arrangement. But he's too inclined to do what his agent wants."

"Has Timothy complained to the Festival administration?"

"He can't bring himself to rat out an elder who did him a favor by inviting him here."

"So Xavier gets away with his bullshit."

"Timothy hasn't yet learned about how power can be used for evil." Jade grimaced. "He has learned that he has no affinity for either Shakespeare or live theatre. What do you think?"

"I think Timothy is right." I spoke as freely as I felt able at the moment. "He says he's lucky to have you as a friend."

"He has a kind soul. Thanks, Sasha. Good night." Jade went back to his cottage. To keep the cocoa from scalding?

Meanwhile, I was about to croak, like my back-porch tree frog. The gossiping Heavenly Immortals have decided that I must improve the cultivation of my yang soul. The rational parts of my being know I should be content with the life I have now, not hankering after more.

After all, I wrote four hundred scholarly pages to describe pop culture manifestations of pair-bonded friendships. I'd learned from ancient poets and scholars that such a special connection happens once in a lifetime. And it can be lost on one bad night, not to be found again.

29: A Specially Bad Christmas

"ALL QUIET ON THE WESTERN front, boss." Howard closed Ruby's door on Monday night. "Our girl was restless at bedtime. I coaxed her into swallowing a Valium and we watched *Happy Days* till she left for the Land of Nod. I betcha Danielle gets to sleep all night."

We said good night. I turned on the kettle, made lapsang souchong tea, and carried it upstairs.

My room still held the day's heat, so I opened the window to let in cool air, then stripped off my jeans and shirt. But instead of putting on my writing robe—signaling the beginning of my night's work—I sat in the desk chair and let the breeze from the Watershed waft over me. Two piles of papers lay on either side of the desk: the messier one was the engineering translation due by the first of October; the neat pile was the printout of my dissertation. At times like this, when I haven't slept the night before and too much has filled the day, I want simple work. I set a yellow pad alongside the summary of my dissertation and drew a grid, to sort the kinds of queries I could expect when I defended it, with columns for the basic types of committee members, sinologists versus comparative lit professors:

> Why this topic and why now?
>
> Explain your methodology in detail.
>
> Explain the concept of pair bonding and how you and other scholars have identified that theme in T'ang era poetry and later popular novels.

My pencil tore the paper before I filled in the second square. I couldn't stop replaying Claudia's angry phone voice.

Is that rat Rik Eliot trying to resurrect Christmas?

Jade Solberg! Jade Solberg!

After only a week in town, Jade had injected his unique chaos into our lives without trying. Without even knowing about it.

Okay, Claudia. Let's make it about Christmas. I folded over the page with my dissertation grid and started a list. I wrote the actors' names in block letters with prompts for the key players:

RUBY: Early onset dementia.

WENDY: Falling to pieces.

CLAUDIA: Shock; feigned indignation.

RIK: Anxious to leave; overflowing worry.

THE INNOCENTS: Alex, Molly, Ramona, Jade.

Friends retell their distinctive memories of family Christmases—the decorations, special food, games, and gifts. I have vague memories of my toddler self and Christmas when we first lived in Ashland. In Hong Kong, my mother insisted we observe local customs, so instead of Christmas we celebrated the Spring Festival, which my mother called Chinese New Year since she never learned more than ten words besides hello and thank you. Our only holiday gifts were red envelopes; the only holiday foods (prepared by the cook) were longevity noodles for happiness and dumplings for luck. The only sweets were *ba bao zhou* and *song gao*—eight treasure rice and sponge rice cake.

I am aware that many people have endured bad family holidays, especially at Christmas. The one time my family pulled it together as adults to celebrate, we created everlasting memories, as if we'd ordered a custom-made Christmas that'd be forever designated as *Specially Bad.*

Just days ago—the last time Ruby misremembered our Bad Christmas—we were watching a rerun of *Three's Company,* which has a small cast so she tries to guess what's happening. When it proved to be a Christmas episode, I rose to switch channels, but she insisted. Five minutes into the show, Ruby was laughing along with the laugh track. Then, inevitably, she shook her head sadly, the tell-tale beginning of her trajectory into mistaken memories.

> Ruby: Didn't we treat him kindly? But that penniless farm boy knew nothing about art or aesthetics.
>
> Me: I don't know, Mother. Want to watch *Happy Days?*
>
> Ruby: He had a hold over our Ricky that I had to break. Ricky's so sensitive. How could he ever make it through college without you, Chris?
>
> Me: I did my best, Mother.
>
> Ruby: That rent-boy keeps leading Ricky astray. Can't you stop it, Chris?

I do not know why Ruby repeats the same ill-chosen term as Xavier. She chose it eight years ago and it still bubbles up, always in a meaningless but cruel way. And she resurrects a version of Christopher I never knew. The original ran with a crowd who picked on the oddballs in the lower grades. He never bullied me, just let his friends do it. At the Bad Christmas, he couldn't stop anything. He'd been dead for two years.

Although Jade declares that we're still friends, we cannot overcome what fell out from that disaster. A chasm opened that cannot be crossed in this universe.

On December 24, 1974, Jade and I packed to leave Ashland, having just finished the first stop on our Wandering Scholars journey. That fall term we'd been living in one of my grandfather's spa cottages while Jade taught at the local college. We were bound for Boston, where Jade had a visiting-artist gig and I'd spend the winter finishing my dissertation. Come Christmas morning, we'd climb into my Datsun and drive down Interstate 5 to Sacramento, then over to I-80 and across the continent. Come spring, Jade had a Fulbright fellowship in Turkey that'd take us across the ocean. Our Christmas Eve plan: eat Liberty Caps as our farewell to the West Coast, likely for years to come.

Looking back, I have to say, we were so full of ourselves even a casual observer might laugh.

The day began with a deep freeze, frost thick enough to make you think of snow. We'd stayed in bed under a comforter, listening to music and drinking cocoa, until we finally bundled into sweaters to finish packing.

Then as a big surprise at midday, all my relatives arrived at Chaos House. Wendy came with her twins and boyfriend in a 1968 Pontiac GTO with New Mexico plates, the car's paint badly worn by desert winds. Claudia and Alex drove up from Berkeley in her shiny new gold Accord. And Ruby arrived in a taxi that bore a sign on the side window: *Medford Airport $5.*

> Wendy: What a happy surprise, Ricky. Thank god you're here. Who's your friend?
>
> Claudia: I'm happy to finally meet you, Rik. It's so good that Alex and the twins have this chance for formative holiday memories with family.
>
> Ruby: Is your friend a boy or a girl, Ricky? And why is your hair so long? Can't you wear decent trousers?

Yeah, the Summer of Love was years in the past by 1974, yet it's no surprise that Ruby reached for the easiest insult. It brought back old times, the not-good-old-days, enduring life as a young teenager with her breathing down my neck.

All three women are roughly alike in many ways: taller than average, wiry, rattling with nervous energy, yet each with her own brand of snark. Wendy looked frazzled, her hair a sunburned snaggle. She twitched like a speed freak and was thinner than she should be, all of which I attributed at first to the long road trip from New Mexico. Claudia, groomed and poised in casual silks and an expensive haircut, tended to pace while smoking black-and-gold Sobranie cigarettes.

Ruby was gaunt and tanned, having been in Palm Springs the entire four months that Jade and I had spent in Ashland. She'd dyed her hair a too-intense shade of red and thrummed like a hummingbird. If such birds chain-smoked Virginia Slims.

We are good boys, so Jade and I unloaded their cars, then carried everyone's luggage and Claudia's hoard of Christmas presents into Chaos House, where I tripped over a pile of mail that had been pushed through the door slot. The house, locked up for months, was freezing inside. For at least three hours, the conversation focused on the internal temperature, though you could actually see your breath indoors only for the first hour.

After sending me to search in the attic, Ruby set up an aluminum tree with shiny blue ornaments, resisting the kids' offers to help: "You cannot possibly do it without making a mess like you always do."

Jade and I walked uptown to get presents, taking the three kids with us, which proved fun even though we began as strangers with each other. Alex was eight and the twins nine that year, full of energy once you drew them out of shyness. And yes, we ignored Claudia's repeated admonishments about not having sweets before dinner. Jade and I took turns sitting at the drugstore's old-fashioned soda counter while the other raided the store's meager gift options. We felt compelled to repair the kids' missing experiences, since they hadn't ever tasted a chocolate malt or cherry phosphate soda.

When we returned to the house, I came in the front door first, just as Claudia was saying, "Rik couldn't even bother to come to Chris's memorial service, yet here he is—"

I stood in the doorway, blocking the others from coming in, and folded my arms. Since I'd scarcely talked to anyone there for years, I had only one grudge: "I was absent because no one told me Chris had died for a full month after the service."

Hence, others might assert that it was I who first harshed everyone's mellow. Meanwhile Jade was Mr. Nice Guy, drawing everyone out to talk about what they'd been doing, what they planned in the coming year. No one asked about our plans.

Wendy was headed for Tunisia to teach English at a university, traveling with a guy she'd met at a residential writing program in Taos (or was it Santa Fe?). He was two inches shorter than Wendy, with auburn hair and pointed ears, like a fox. He said *Hola!* instead of hello, then was intensely silent that day and quickly disappeared from Wendy's story. Now I can't remember his name. Zane? Shane? Shawn? Who knows.

For our holiday dinner, Wendy made boxed macaroni and cheese with frozen peas, since she'd turned vegetarian and that's all she knew how to cook. As the evening began, she rhapsodized about Tunisia.

> Wendy: I just cannot wait to get there. A secure two-year contract. A room of my own.
>
> Claudia: Do you imagine you're Virginia Woolf?

Claudia was provokingly unkind, seeking to shove herself in a niche above Wendy. Yet Wendy, exuberant about the future and unable to stop talking, waved away all of Claudia's swipes. Both women were writers, one focused on deeply word-smithed, unstructured short stories for literary journals, the other on counterculture genre novels sold from wire racks in grocery stores.

Wendy said, "I shall have what Mrs. Woolf wanted. My stipend includes meals at the refectory. It'll be like Bread Loaf Writers' Conference without the lunch baskets."

"Refectory?" Ruby huffed in disgust. "I read the brochure you sent about that place. They long to be British. You'll be frozen out of their expat cliques for being a Yankee."

"I'm always excluded from cliques," Wendy said cheerily. "I have two books on contract and no time for fraternizing."

Ruby said, "No one will invite a dilapidated strumpet like you to sundown cocktails."

One of the twins coughed. Then Alex coughed.

"Don't give us your disease!" Wendy shook a finger at the kids. "Go play in the back bedroom."

"It's too cold back there," Alex said.

Wendy jerked her thumb toward the back of the house. "It'd be just my luck, not getting through customs because I'm contagious with some kindergarten disease."

Jade and I followed the kids to the back bedroom, where we ransacked the closet for old games. But it was freezing, so we returned to a corner of the living room ten minutes later. Wendy didn't notice, being busy arguing with Ruby, while Claudia occasionally put in her oar to raise her raft above them.

The biggest argument began when Ruby lit a cigarette, leaned back to blow smoke like a dragon, and said, "Take your kids with you. I don't want to be responsible."

"What?" Wendy jumped up in alarmed surprise, greater than my surprise at the idea of Wendy leaving her kids. "Mother, you insisted they stay in Ashland. And you won't be responsible. Mimi is coming in the morning."

"I don't want that Mexican woman living in this house again, with her stinking food." No one can be as haughty and foul as Ruby when she's doing it on purpose. "And I already have a splitting headache from all their noise."

"Mimi isn't Mexican. You said they should stay with you. Didn't she, Zane?"

"Si." Zane said it without a trace of any kind of Spanish accent. He didn't look up from staring at the blue-and-silver tree and fiddling with a piece of Silly Putty.

I telegraphed my top thought to Jade: *They are all crazy.*

Jade nodded, having heard stories of my family life in Hong Kong. And I squirmed, embarrassed about Ruby's nastiness, but quickly more disturbed at the notion of the twins living with Ruby. And I had to resist putting my hands over my own ears, hearing Wendy repeatedly insist that it was impossible for the kids to travel with her.

Jade lured the kids into a corner of the living room to play a song-and-clapping game. As their noise rose, Wendy followed Ruby into the kitchen, pleading that Ruby had asked for the kids to stay in Ashland.

"You knew from the beginning, Mother, that the school does not accommodate foreign faculty with families."

Ruby folded her arms. "You have never once considered my needs. You always insist on destroying the fabric of my life. You ruined those girls and now you're running away."

"I'm only traveling for a spell, like our father did," Wendy said. "We just sucked it up then. The girls will have Mimi, who they love. We only had you."

"Your father didn't travel for work, you silly girl." Ruby clutched herself, red-lacquered nails digging into her white satin blouse. "He deserted his children one step at a time. Same as you."

I should have gone over to the corner with Jade and the kids, because the sound of Ruby and Wendy resurrected the fear and trepidation I'd escaped when I left for the UW. Their litany:

> Wendy: I am a successful writer. You, Mother, will never publish again.
>
> Ruby: You are a talentless harridan and a bad mother. You will not push those brats off on me.
>
> Wendy: You are a mean, judgmental witch.
>
> Ruby: You prove my point, being so nasty in front of your own children.

When Wendy called us to the table for dinner, Jade brushed close by me and murmured words from a sane reality: *We're soon off to be Wandering Scholars.*

Later, after dinner, I sat by Jade on the sofa while the others remained at the table. "Are you okay?" I asked.

"Of course. I'm a stranger here and don't even speak the local language. How are you, Sasha?"

"I'm fine, but I'm worried about the twins."

"Yes, and I worry about your sister. Wendy seems to be on the verge of her nineteenth nervous breakdown."

I drew a breath with a hiss. Yes, why hadn't I seen that? Ruby and Claudia said mean things about Wendy's frantic arguments. I was at that time ten years gone from my family's insanity. For the first time, it looked dangerous, and I had no clue what to do for my sister.

Then Ruby called, "Come to my room, Ricky. I have something to show you."

—

Ruby lit a long, thin cigarette and blew twin streams of smoke, like a dragon, like she used to do when I was in trouble. She didn't bother to close the door, just handed me an envelope, postmarked three weeks earlier. It held a letter from an attorney:

> As directed by Ruby Eliot, the trust's administrator, the fund for Aldrik Alexander Eliot has been revoked due to noncompliance with terms of the trust. The remaining funds have been deposited in the administrator's account.

Just like she'd threatened Wendy for years.

"But I am in school, Mother."

My tongue went numb; my mind raced. I'd been paying in-state tuition at a state school and lived so frugally that the trust had at least ten thousand dollars left—for my life as a Wandering Scholar. To be wholly mine when I turned twenty-five in June.

Ruby breathed smoke. "My father left funds for you children to become educated, to be successful." She stood, arms folded like she always did while scolding. "You are not in school, which the trust requires."

"I have several degrees. And I am in school." *I am succeeding.*

"No, I know you've been living like a damned hippie in one of Father's abandoned shacks."

"I'm writing my dissertation."

That didn't register with her. "I heard all about what you've been up to from the neighbor who watches the house for me. So I called my lawyer to put a stop to it."

In five months I'd turn twenty-five, when that fund was to become freely mine. But the letter she handed me meant I had no money to cover rent or the tuition for my 800-level dissertation work—or for my plan as a Wandering Scholar. And I'm not saying it like a whiny child: *My mother took my trust fund.* With that fund, I'd enjoyed ten years as a perpetual student, never having to write home for money. Better than most people ever get.

I cringe again to admit that I've never taken up any gauntlet my mother threw down. I'd learned years ago that it's useless to fight her. I have no good excuse for *not* quarreling, yet I just stood there, as if I'd turned to stone, crunching that letter, documented proof that my mother had abandoned me.

"You can thank me," Ruby said as she left her bedroom, "for saving you from being exploited by that rent-boy you're keeping. Your grandfather is turning over in his grave in disgust."

When I came out of Ruby's room, I paused at the archway into the living room, desperate to make my brain work. Jade, who'd been playing Old Maid with the kids at one end of the dinner table, looked up as if startled, then concerned, though he couldn't have heard what had just happened.

Me, I sank too quickly into a too-familiar sense of worthlessness when I should have gone to Jade, either to tell him about what just happened or to seek comfort. The loss of income would affect us both. What to say? *I can get a job as a fry cook in Boston, but I can't afford to go to Anatolia with you.*

However, my family proceeded to orchestrate a series of dramatic catastrophes such that I never had a chance to tell Jade I was now stone broke.

"Can we open presents, please?" Alex called. "Uncle Ricky came back."

"After dessert." Claudia repeated that all evening, as if Christmas treats must be doled out like chastisement.

Wendy went to get the cookies promised as dessert. I followed her into the kitchen, closing the door to the living room—back when a wall separated the two rooms.

Now entirely attuned to my mother's punishing ways, I said, "I'm sorry Ruby is trying to ruin things, Wendy. Are you okay?"

"No, I am not. I haven't been okay for months." She batted my hand away from her shoulder. "Listen, *sailou*." She only calls me *little brother* when she thinks I'm being a nitwit. "I'm being stalked. Have been for years. The kids are not safe with me."

"What? Who?" The idea was then far outside the realm of my experience."

"A guy I met years ago. He keeps finding me. That's why I need to leave the country."

"Have you talked to the police?"

"Repeatedly. Nothing has stopped him from finding me."

"But the kids—"

"They'll only be safe away from me. But listen, do not tell Ruby. She'll only blame me for my bad luck and jeopardy."

"Ruby cannot be trusted to take care of the girls."

"She won't. Never has. Mimi became their nanny when they were born. I have put two years' salary for Mimi and living costs in Ruby's checking account."

"This stalker is why you took a job that doesn't allow kids?"

"Ricky, I am fucking falling apart. This stalker is driving me out of my mind. I don't know if it's even possible to ever be sane."

"But you can't let Ruby—"

"Ruby? She wants to see me fall apart. That's why she asked for the kids to come here and now wants to fuck me over." She took a breath. "I have never been a decent mother. The girls love Mimi more than me. They'll be happy I'm gone."

"I don't believe that." I didn't believe it, but I was also relieved that a responsible person would care for the twins—not Ruby, who hated her own children, as I'd known for years.

Wendy put a hand on my arm, as if to console me, which seemed backward. "It's best for the girls. I hated Ruby for dragging us to fucking Hong Kong. Those posh Brit bitches at school made me miserable. I spent ten years with no friends, wishing every day that we'd go back to Ashland. The twins are better off with Mimi. It's only two years."

I'd also spent ten years at that posh British school, only I'd wished that my *mother* would do as she threatened and go back to the States—but leave me in Hong Kong.

So, on my last night in Ashland, was I supposed to beg my sister not to leave her kids? Or listen to her claim that she was in dire jeopardy and was losing her marbles? How could I help, since I'd just learned that I had nothing with which to help myself, much less anyone else?

—

Because Wendy and I talked for too long in the kitchen, Ruby called loudly from the living room, "Ricky, come here and tell me why you can't do better than this rent-boy. You were raised in a better class of people than this hippie cowhand you brought to dinner."

I came back to the living room, slamming open the kitchen door, choking on rage and dismay. I glanced at Jade, who stayed busying playing cards with the kids, as if he hadn't heard Ruby. Before I formed any words, Wendy banged the kitchen door into my back, carrying a Blue Willow plate with a tower of Oreo cookies and Keebler wafers.

"Do not use that word, Mother," Wendy said. "So what if Ricky pays Jade's rent?"

The room was filled with everyone's mistaken suppositions. I cringe now, since I only managed to say, "It's just roommate math. I pay rent. Jade buys our food." Then I on the living room sofa and remained silent.

I'd never come out to my mother, knowing it'd be a colossal waste of energy and emotion. So why…no, how had Ruby come to settle her vituperative homophobia on Jade? He has nice manners and no demonstrable gay affect. In fact, it took me a year to dare to make a move on him, having assumed he was straight. In hindsight, I know she chose Jade as her punching dummy though it was actually me she reviled.

While I burned inside and remained silent, Wendy set down her plate of cookies on the table and shook a finger at Ruby.

"Try not being a royal bitch for five minutes, Ruby. What joy do you get out of being mean to Ricky?"

"It's between Ricky and me." Ruby had her back to me, her shoulder blades sharp as demon wings under her white satin blouse. She'd just kicked apart my life, and now she said, "Trust me. I know what's best for the boy."

"Ha! Ricky's a grown man. He can have any damn boyfriend he wants. Don't you agree, Claudia?"

Why-oh-why did my sister think Claudia ally was an ally? All evening, Claudia had less than subtly implied that Wendy was a bad mother. At the moment when Wendy prompted her, Claudia was again chiding Alex for being too eager to open his presents.

Claudia jabbed a stern finger. "Wendy Eliot, watch your language. This is a night for children. Can you at least try to be a decent person just this once?"

"Oh, blow it out your butt, Claudia." Wendy laughed. "I'm defending Ricky's right to suck cock, which is no one's business but his. If you'd let Chris suck cock, maybe he wouldn't have joined the army, so he'd still be alive."

"You damned miserable bitch!" the anti-profanity Claudia shouted. "Christopher was not gay."

"He married you to deny it, but that failed. And you married a boy you hardly knew just to get control of your trust fund. Chris regretted it immediately."

"That's a foul lie." Claudia's voice broke.

Wendy raised her hands in false surrender. "I'm merely repeating what Chris told me."

This was a surprise to me—about Christopher, I mean, not about those two women being nasty and jabbing scolding fingers at each other. I hadn't seen my brother since I was fifteen, and…

Ah, Heavenly Immortals! That's it, isn't it? That's what broke Claudia. Now, eight years later, she has panicked about the possible resurrection of Wendy's claim that Christopher was gay. Alex is correct: we must tread lightly, to avoid hurting Claudia's feelings. She could not accept Wendy's smug claim then, and it's led to her current panic over Alex.

Jade left the kids playing Go Fish in the corner and sat on the sofa beside me. I had not before that moment longed so strongly for comfort from him. I slipped down onto the floor and leaned against his knees, the best I could achieve then, where it wasn't possible to crawl into his arms. He put his hand on my shoulder, as if to pull me closer, though it wasn't possible with my spine pressed hard against his fibula. I felt his pulse in the tips of the fingers gripping my clavicle, his tension amplifying my own.

Ruby revved her engines to attack me again. "There's a very pretty girl who lives near the end of Water Street. You should ask her out, Ricky."

The women at the end of Water Street were—and still are—members of the lesbian collective who'd tuned up my Datsun for our road trip. They'd replaced my transmission in exchange for the cost of parts plus me repairing aged gutters and removing a wasp's nest. They are a self-sufficient bunch, but all dislike tall ladders, so I had a talent to trade.

Jade murmured, "They like to hurt you, Sasha. Let's give the kids their presents and go."

Before I could answer, the squabbles escalated to shouts. Claudia packed Alex into the back of her car with his unopened Christmas presents and sped out of Ashland.

Ruby said, "Now see what you've done, Wendy? You are such a witless fool."

"Stop with the insults, *Mother.* You asked for the girls to stay here. Mimi will come. The girls *will* stay here."

Wendy said *mother* like it was a pejorative. She grabbed her bag and stormed out of the house with Zane trailing. The girls cried, given the massively bad vibes, though they'd come to Ashland knowing their mother would leave.

I motioned for Jade to distract the twins. I followed Wendy out the door.

"The girls need you, Wendy" I called from the front porch. "You cannot leave them with Ruby."

Wendy whirled, her eyes wild, her hand waving over her head. "Because our mother is a witch? You and I lived with it for years. Mimi will be here to care for them—something you and I never had. They can survive Ashland for a few months."

"You said two years. You *cannot* leave them with Ruby."

"Then you take them, Ricky. I am broken. I can't sleep. My brain is full of mush. And you saw it today. I am a bad mother."

"No, stop and—"

She got into the GTO, Zane in the driver's seat. Before she closed the door, Wendy said, "I know you saw it, little brother. You frown when I yell at them. I'm turning into Ruby. It's not safe for them to be with me, even if I weren't being stalked."

"I can't take them, Wendy. What are you thinking?"

"Why can't you? Oh, yeah. Ricky gets to leave and stay gone. You're all grown up now, Ricky. You can save them from Ruby. And you have a boyfriend who's nice to them. Not like this guy."

That guy, sitting in the driver's seat, didn't react.

"Go!" she commanded Zane, then slammed the car door before I could say more.

When I returned to the house, Ruby didn't mention Wendy or Claudia. Instead, she said, "I have a terrible headache, Ricky. Please help me."

"How can I help, Mother?" I wiped all possible emotion from my voice. Couldn't stop it from ripping up my insides.

"Take me to the hospital, Ricky."

Jade glanced at me. "Leave the kids here. We'll be fine."

"I guess—" The Heavenly Immortals know, I'm still humiliated by how I was indecisive and stupid that night.

"You will not leave those innocent children with your vile rent-boy, Aldrik Eliot."

The twins cowered against Jade in the shadows, their eyes black pools of despair. Or maybe I'm projecting. It's likely they didn't understand her words, but the pitch of Ruby's voice must have penetrated their bones.

"They can come along then," Jade said. "Molly, Ramona, get your coats. It's cold outside."

I was getting Ruby into her coat, her voice setting a vibration in my ears that made it impossible to hear words. Outside, I got her into the front seat and her seat belt fastened. Jade got the kids into the back seat. And I think he was getting in with them. I feel like he was.

But Ruby said, "I will not ride with that perverse creature. Call an ambulance for me."

"That's okay, Mrs. Eliot. I won't come along." Jade stood outside the still-open rear door. "Catch you in the morning, Sasha. Good night, Mrs. Eliot. Thank you for having me to dinner. I hope you feel better soon."

I wished I could follow him, but no.

This sounds like a Shakespearean tragedy. Yet the tragic part didn't come until we finished the Tennessee Williams audition and concluded the first live-action *General Hospital* episode.

After Wendy and Claudia went off in huff, and Jade walked away, I drove Ruby to the ER, the girls sobbing quietly in the back seat. I harried Ruby through the door marked Emergency, then scooped up Molly to carry while Ramona hung onto my jacket. The two sat with me in the dimly lit waiting area and played tic-tac-toe and I-spy word games until the on-call doctor insisted Ruby stay for observation.

After a half-dozen such incidents in the following weeks and months, I came to be on a first-name basis with the EMTs. For a few months I felt guilty about not noticing that Ruby was ill when she arrived from the airport, that she wasn't just being the monster I'd always known. But I gave up on guilt. It just is what it is, what it was always going to be.

30: After the Feast

CHRISTMAS 1974, IT WAS FOUR in the morning when I left Ruby at the hospital and brought the girls back to Chaos House. The light was on in Lazarus Cottage, and Jade's shadow moved behind the curtains.

I carried Molly and gently shepherded Ramona into Ruby's house. One might think they'd be ready to crash, but they asked for cocoa. It was cold inside, but I didn't know where the furnace controls were. I dragged a pair of afghans from the sofa to wrap them up, then gave them bowls of Cap'n Crunch cereal to eat while I made cocoa. I scrambled in the cupboards, vaguely remembering where marshmallows were stored when I'd lived in Grandfather's house ten years earlier.

"Can we open our presents?" Molly asked, while my spoon scraped at the metal bottom of the cocoa pan.

Jade leaned on the door frame, holding the presents we'd chosen for the girls. He set them on the table. "Shall I get the rest?"

The girls were almost happy at the idea.

It's ridiculous that I can recall the girls' Christmas presents amid what happened. Rock 'Em Sock 'Em Robots. A Magic 8 Ball. Two Spirographs. A Crayola workshop kit. Twister, Which Witch, and Sorry games. Doctor and nurse kits.

They squabbled over who was the doctor and who'd be the nurse. Jade suggested they trade off each week.

"If you start today, you can trade off every Wednesday morning at breakfast. Here." Jade held out a dime. "Flip a coin to see who gets which kit first. Molly, you call heads or tails."

I coaxed the girls into bed, which was a couple of blankets that made up the pallet they shared in a first-floor bedroom. They carefully arranged their new toys around them.

"Mimi will come in the morning," Ramona said. "She'll know what to do."

"Will you still be here when it's morning, Uncle Rik?" Molly asked, her voice full of hope.

An intense yet warm sensation fizzed inside my chest. We'd met for the first time the day before, and Molly was asking this as her first concern—and not when Wendy would return.

"Of course. I won't leave until Mimi comes and everything is all set."

"And Jade, too?" Ramona asked.

"Of course he'll stay if Uncle Rik does," Molly said. "Wendy says they're like Bert and Ernie. They stay together."

I left the girls, hoping they'd go to sleep. In the kitchen, Jade was pouring the last of the Cap'n Crunch into a clean bowl, then adding milk. The last of the milk.

I sat at the table, exhausted to the core. "I cannot express how sorry I am about what Ruby said to you."

"You warned me about her. And I wasn't hurt. I'm sorry she hurt you." He had his pocket sketchbook out on the table to draw the teapot and Blue Willow china cup left from supper.

"I'm used to it, but I let Ruby insult you. I feel like a prick for letting it happen."

"Forget it. The Cap'n Crunch is gone," he said, "but there's Lucky Charms. I'll get milk from our cottage."

"No, I cleaned out the fridge. Because we were going to leave this morning."

"I guess we'll have to wait until tomorrow."

I shook my head. It hurts now to think of that gesture of denial. I can't remember if it hurt then. "If we don't leave today, we can't be sure to get there in time for your first workshop. That's December 30, right?"

We both knew the date. We'd made all our travel plans around getting him to that visiting-artist gig.

We wouldn't know it for a few weeks, but we were calmly breaking up over empty cartons of milk and multi-colored too-sweet cereal. How could we know? We'd never talked about it or made promises to each other. When we came to Ashland for Jade's teaching gig, we'd made a series of decisions without thinking more than a few months ahead. Our mutual goal, our only goal, had been to venture forth as Wandering Scholars.

Unlike the other adults in my family, Jade and I were being caring, reasonable, and kind, yet we were breaking up while Jade washed his cereal bowl and I tried to guess where it might be possible to get milk on Christmas Day.

"You'd better fly," I said.

Jade said, "Do you suppose today is a good day to find a seat? I have to fly to San Francisco and then Boston, right?"

"I think there's also a Portland-to-Boston flight." I pointed to the wall phone. "United flies from Medford."

He finished the last of his cereal, then leaned against the doorway between the kitchen and living room while he looked up United's number in the phone book.

I'm always the person who needs to take action, to do something. I made tea. Coffee seemed too difficult.

After he hung up from the airline, Jade didn't ask how long it'd be until I came to Boston. Rather, I said it: "I don't know how to find Wendy. She so desperate to leave the girls here, she said I should take them."

"Yeah, your mom can't take care of them," Jade said. A statement, not a question.

"I don't think Ruby can take care of herself. I'll call Claudia, after she's had a chance to drive back to Berkeley. Maybe she knows where Wendy will be in Tunisia." Though Claudia had scorned Wendy's notions about her new gig. *"Teaching in Tunisia, of all places, won't boost the reputation for a paperback writer like you."*

"I pretty sure Claudia won't help you," Jade said. "These people? Your family? They don't care about you."

"I have to do whatever Molly and Ramona need."

"I agree," Jade said. "There's no other choice."

I made promises then, that I'd write to Jade as soon as Mimi came to take over the girls' care. Jade promised to call from Boston.

"Call collect," I said.

Two hours later, a taxi came. We said goodbye. No, we both said, "See you later." Parting isn't particularly painful when you believe it's temporary. At that moment, I mostly regretted losing out on the imagined joy of a cross-country road trip with Jade.

—

The few times I've told this story—to Nick, when he helped me become the girls' guardian; to my doctor friend Michael—I rather shamefully made it sound like Wendy's panicked choices forced me to withdraw from Wandering Scholars 101, that I walked into an Eliot family ambush and let the crazy trap me.

In truth, I chose at every turn to stay with the twins, and I have never regretted for one heartbeat that I embraced caring for them. There was, as Jade had said, no other choice. And there was never a good reason to resent Jade for inhabiting another, freer world—where there's no doorway through which I might join him.

However, it all might have been much easier if the promised nanny, Mimi, had appeared that morning. I had no information with which to find her. When I visited Ruby at the hospital, she vowed to have never known anyone named Mimi.

So we began the new adventure with no Mimi and no money. My mother's bank account was virtually empty. On the day after Christmas, I complicated the no-money situation with my first decision, to use my credit card at the Medford J.C. Penney's, although the card was no longer covered by my trust fund. Again, there was no other solution. I'd made a list: warm clothes, coats, underwear, pajamas. Shoes and snow boots. Hairbrushes, hair ties, nail clippers, nail brushes. Towels, shampoo, and washcloths.

Also—and I know how bourgeois this sounds—they needed real beds with sheets and comforters and pillows. I've never slept on the floor in my life. Even Lazarus Cottage, as ramshackle as it was then, had a proper bed. The girls could *not* sleep on the floor in a ridiculously cold mansion that held almost no furniture.

At the store, I had to ask a clerk for help. First, I didn't know girls need undershirts or even what such garments look like. Second, I was thinking of what kids wore on Disney movie posters. The twins were thinking of what might make them most invisible at school. I'd already found that they could barely read or add. Didn't know how to play any games or sports. Still had a secret shared language, like toddlers. Yet they knew it was important to be invisible. That's how, later, I recognized they'd truly progressed: they began dressing with individual styles.

By Friday, my card was declined when I bought groceries. Somehow, I got a new credit card at my mother's local bank and used it to pay off my canceled card. Thus began life with nagging debt. It took two years to pay off my first unavoidable debts. Meanwhile, I learned how to apply for food stamps. In 1975, the federal poverty line was $5,500 for a family of four; my income was zero. The rise happened quite gradually.

I enrolled the girls in school, making sure they were in the same class since they needed each other. I structured my days so they had breakfast and sack lunches, then took them to school. After school, I picked them up, making sure I had their homework assignments in hand and escorting them across the playground, since it took the entire first year to rid them of whatever taint led other kids to bully them. And we had bi-weekly meetings with a family therapist, further burdening that life-salvaging credit card.

I'm the only person who watched their transition and so can laugh when comparing those timid little girls from January 1975 with the assured—um, brazen—young women who help run Chaos House and maintain an honor-roll grade average.

—

The Chan family celebrates an annual day of familial remembrance. My family doesn't have much to remember, but I've tried to make each Christmas a decent family celebration. We bake, make delicious food, open presents. They call their mother on the phone. But for me, it's the worst day of familial remembrance, a reminder that my adult family doesn't respect me, and that I'm not out seeing the world as a Wandering Scholar alongside the spiritual brother whom the Immortals sent to the earthly realm to be the one who knows me.

After that Bad Christmas, I missed any phone calls Jade might have made. I did write to him. I knew his Boston address because I'd prepaid the deposit and first and last months' rent—with my trust-fund–dependent credit card. I sent a postcard to that address:

> *I cannot get to Boston yet. Ruby is still in the hospital. Mimi never came. Wendy cannot come back.*

Then it was *cannot*. Later, she would not. Neither assertion Wendy made mattered in terms of what I had to do. The girls needed attention. Lots of attention. In the first two weeks, I'd seen all the problems. Reading and math aside, they needed a rigidly regular schedule and constant reassurance. And family therapy, which I am still certain that abandoned children need.

When I heard from Wendy, it was a collect call from Tunis.

"Hi, Wendy. I'll get the girls so you can talk."

"No, don't. Listen, Ricky, I'm in hospital. It's all nuns and everything is in French. They say I had influenza, then I got pneumonia and lost my position."

"Good lord, Wendy. When are you coming home?"

"I can't. The university is making me pay back the airfare and expenses they spent to bring me here." Wendy stammered about her impossible life. She'd been falling apart before getting sick. "Then I went totally off my bean."

I said, "I've got this, Wendy. Don't worry. Just get well. I'll get money together for your airfare."

Somehow.

That night I wrote to Jade, explaining that I wasn't coming to Boston. And couldn't join him on his Fulbright come spring. I used words I'd never spoken in our conversations. Priorities. Moral responsibility as a son, a brother, an uncle.

In March, Claudia called. I said hello, expecting to learn she'd made progress on getting Wendy back in the U.S. But no. She refused to give or lend money to Wendy. Instead, Claudia said she'd seen Jade in Boston while on her recent author's tour.

"He's such a nice guy. When I told him you were doing well and had taken the twins' welfare in hand, he said he always knew you had that kind of strength in your soul. He said he's proud to have known you."

Later in March, a card came in the mail, sent to what had been our cottage, the one with the *Lazarus* mural:

> *Que sera. Live well. I know you will get what you most desire. That's who you are.*

My last postcard, filled with apologies, came back, addressee unknown. We didn't speak again. We'd broken up.

The resulting chaos—and the broken pieces of me and what I wanted, of what we'd planned—lay around me for months, as if a chaos monster had come to shatter the porcelain slip of the future we'd been working on together. The final scene of the Bad Christmas story is a coda, a fade-out scene, repeating the symphonic theme of grief: Man cries alone in the attic for months, at first without and then with meds to improve serotonin uptake.

Jade went his way as a successful itinerant artist and teacher. I went the way I had to go. And I wholly and purely do not know what either of us could have done differently. At least now, in September 1983, Jade has declared that we are still friends. At the mural site, I'm once again his acolyte.

Here, in my private attic, I retain a sense of deep shame that I didn't protect either Wendy or Jade from Ruby's venom on that Bad Christmas night. Ruby had heaped devastating wounds on Wendy for years. Jade claimed that Ruby hadn't hurt him, but the fallout of years of poison in my family had destroyed the bonds I'd imagined as existing then between Jade and me.

Rather than Ruby or Wendy causing the rift, it was the Immortals rolling knuckle bones as dice, then choosing me to serve others who couldn't take care of themselves. That dice roll did not match up with what Jade needed as the artist he was born to be.

And Wendy? She got a penicillin-resistant staph infection and remained in the hospital in Tunis. When she was finally released, she followed some guy she'd met to Barcelona, where she joined an American expat community. By then it was July, and the girls were on summer vacation.

"Wendy, I'm getting money together," I said over another collect international phone call, "so you can come back to the U.S. And back to Ashland."

"I won't come as long as Ruby is on this earth."

That's when *cannot come home* became *will not come home,* even after Wendy learned we never found Mimi. I never bugged her with details since she was so frail and tenuous. I didn't see what good it would do for Wendy to learn that Ruby had spent the girls' maintenance and nanny salary (along with my trust fund) on who the hell knows what.

—

I labored through the first two years as the twins' guardian, learning to perform my familial duties, all while frightened to the bone that I'd never touch him again. After those first two years, I'd lived long enough to settle down and just be sad when the background music leads me in that direction.

I cannot indulge that old grief now. I heard Chan-suk's voice explicating: *Your familial duty is about ethics. Respect. Good conduct. Dissuading your family members from moral unrighteousness.*

Hence, I make sure Ruby is cared for. And every day, I do the work to protect three kids who must never find themselves in the Eliot family cuckoo's nest. I continue to regret that I haven't found a way to help Wendy—from the heart, not out of duty. But my sister refuses every gesture.

For my own wellbeing, I must exert the mental discipline to stop the time-wasting agitation I'd indulged for the past week. The parts of me that aren't teaching and doing chores need to be either working with Nick to protect Alex or preparing to defend my dissertation. I must immerse myself in deep review of my text and in re-examining all the criticism provided on previous drafts. I've resolved all critical comments, but I suspect that many of my dissertation committee members have never read more than the introduction, plus the references and index to see if any of their own publications are cited.

Any parts of me that cannot contribute to that work must be put in suspended animation and hung on a wall for the Heavenly Immortals to admire. The ghosts haunting me are not real. My thesis defense is a real thing, with a real date: October 21.

I set out the cover page and studied it again for the slightest typo. Then I turned to the first page of the synopsis. A typewritten sheet fell to the floor—the written note to Kevin when I'd asked him to read the synopsis and critique its scholarly language.

—

A SYNOPSIS:
Pair-bonded Friendship Motifs in
Cantonese Popular Culture, 1950 to 1970

> These are stories of the grace and complex gestures [1] of men who literally give up their lives to the person who best understands them. [2]
>
> — Rik Eliot [3]

[1] This synopsis is provided for an audience of twelve people, just two of whom care about the topic, the rest of whom are performing due diligence as academic gatekeepers guarding the path to liberal arts doctoral degrees. Any stray readers may choose to skim the first paragraphs and then scroll to the conclusion.

[2] At this writing, the author has no expectation that such a person as the one who best understands him will ever read this. In an imaginary world that exists only in wuxia stories, if he did happen to read it, he'd skip to the conclusion.

[3] Those who've written a thesis can perceive the turmoil, self-doubt, and obsessive thinking that has gone into this project, from the original proposal to the tenth tedious revision in response to other scholars' soul-killing criticism.

PART II:
Midnight Sighs

October 1983

The journey of a thousand miles
begins at Chaos House.
— Ramona Eliot

31: News of the Day

MID-OCTOBER, IT'S BARELY DAWN and still cool when I get home from my run. I run above the fog line and on the upper streets where streetlamps reveal most of the potholes I want to avoid.

I cool down from my run by walking along Water Street, past the cottages, noting how few birds remain after summer. The flying-south business has robbed the neighborhood of towhees and cedar waxwings. Our dark-eyed juncos still visit the backyard feeders. We have robins, who are out at dawn getting the early-bird worms, but they say these are snowbirds, down from Alaska. One solitary mourning dove calls from the woodland by the creek. It might also be from Alaska but it hasn't found locals to keep company with. There's only me hearing that lonely sound.

The sparse mercury-vapor lamplights on Water Street blinked, having not yet made up their minds whether it's daytime. Under that flickering light, just past Chaos House, Lieutenant Colonel J.J. Smith (retd) patrolled the street, hands behind his back. He bent to pick up something in the gravel across from his house, pinching it between two fingers. Something small, like a cigarette butt. Hoo boy, I'd best plan on another scolding note. Yet I remain the friendliest neighbor on Water Street.

"Good morning, Mr. Smith." I raised my hand in greeting just as I reached my own driveway. That motion and my hail must have trespassed on the standards my favorite scrub jay seeks to uphold. It dived for my head.

I waved it away. It flew into the half-bare branches of the white oak next door and *cawed* at me, rather than writing a scolding note.

J.J. Smith, pausing by Jade's mustard-yellow crummy, had his hands on his hips, studying me like he must have surveyed his troops when he served. He didn't return my wave.

I pointed to the crummy. "I talked to the owner, as you requested. He's careful to park elsewhere when there's a space."

He waved that off. "Mr. Solberg talked to me about it. I know he's doing the best he can. And he assures me that he'll be gone by the end of the month. Two more weeks?"

"Uh, I don't know." Jade hadn't said anything about leaving. The Festival arrangement ended soon, but Jade would be in Ashland until Inez Saint returned from Italy.

"He said you don't have space for him. I warned him not to expect *anything* from you."

He could have just slapped me in the face.

"Why would you say such a thing, sir?"

"Isn't that like you? Setting him up and then pushing him away, yet again?" He shook his head grimly. "So selfish."

"What evils have I done, Mr. Smith? Why must you continually accuse me of bad actions? I am a considerate person."

"Considerate? Ha! You forced that boy out of your house. Broke his heart. And on Christmas Eve, too."

What the ever-loving...how...why is he in my business? I didn't mean to answer, but the words burst out.

"That isn't what happened, sir. You weren't there."

"But I was." He was actually shaking a finger at me. "That boy stumbled out of your house crying, ran right into me, not looking where he was going. I took him in and gave him coffee. I told him that's what rich kids do. They have a good time with you, then go home when their family calls. I saw it a hundred times among men under my command. It hit me once too, right when I was coming out of West Point. There's a wall between them that have, like you, and those of us who only yearn."

"I am not rich."

A thousand words could be screamed in reply to his stern sermon, yet I picked that witless defense. Otherwise, he was right. I had let my family insult Jade and done nothing about it.

"Just look at you," my neighbor scoffed. "It's hard to believe he came back to Ashland. Such foolishness."

He spun on his heel and marched away.

Which roused the scrub jay that dives only at me.

—

During my prep period on that second Friday in October, I used the faculty lounge phone to call Nick to discuss Alex's problems.

When the door of the faculty lounge opened, clouds of smoke billowed into the hall behind the dozen departing teachers. I entered, inhaling twenty years' accumulation of stale cigarette smoke, and instantly flashed to Grandfather puffing one of his Chesterfield Kings and exhaling the smoke over my four-year-old head while he admonished me about...I can't remember what. I only recall the smoke and the wagging finger. Ruby wagged her finger in the same way, but she'd smoked Virginia Slims up until she set the bedclothes on fire and we took them away from her.

"Claudia's lawyers don't have a response from her on anything." Nick sneezed. He'd caught the citywide head cold.

"Maybe that's just as well," I said. "She's now away on an East Coast author's tour. She also hasn't called Alex. A good sign?"

Beyond the stench of faculty-lounge cigarette smoke, someone had spilled coffee on the hot plate, leaving an acrid odor

Nick said, "I faxed her attorney all the materials you gathered. It's more than they requested. I think it will help."

The requests from Claudia's attorney had me gathering progress reports and attendance records from Alex's teachers (and from Jade for the civic project), plus details from the vice principal documenting the academic strength of Ashland High and the rigor of Alex's specific classes. What a lot of work Claudia's panicky tantrum created for other people.

"I'll keep my fingers crossed." I've gotten so good at being upbeat around the kids that I pretty much believe my own bullshit. Plus, Nick often said we'd be able to protect Alex.

"The best time slot I've managed for a telephone conference," Nick said, "is Monday morning at seven thirty. I hope that'll work for you."

"Yes, I'll make it work."

"I'll drop by your house this weekend with details for how to dial into the call."

"Take care of your cold, Nick."

By the time I hung up, I was ready to cough up a lung from inhaling old faculty-lounge smoke. My clothes needed to go into the wash as soon as I got home. And I'd best hang my teacher's blazer on the back porch until it smells like laundry powder instead of cigarette smoke.

I had just enough time left in my break period to arrange with Jacqueline, the vice principal, for a proctor to take my first two classes on Monday while I dialed into that call with the attorneys. Jacqueline said she'd take the classes, since I'd already copied the worksheets for those periods, along with a cheat-sheet for the proctor to answer questions.

"Have a good weekend," she said. "Get some rest. You've been looking a bit frazzled."

—

At two thirty on that Friday, I did as I have every weekday afternoon for the past month. When the last bell rings, I slip into my booth like Superman—that is, into the faculty men's restroom—and change into mural-manning chaperone clothes. Jeans, my most worn button-down shirt, old running shoes. It isn't yet cool enough to need a jacket, but I've been stuffing an old sweatshirt in my duffel. Anyone who knows me could guess how carefully I hang my blazer in my car before jetting up to the mural site.

That five-minute drive is a slice of the modest moments of solitude I get beyond my morning run, the shower, and the hour before bed when I work on my dissertation review and commercial Cantonese–English translations.

I will not complain. It's all going well.

Alex is passing his math class with a B. The girls had their usual positive six-weeks' progress reports. All three registered to take their SAT exams on October 21, the same Saturday when I must be in Seattle for my dissertation defense. It's a week away, and I have my MFR–SEA plane ticket pinned on my wall like a PTA raffle ticket, waiting to see if I'm a winner.

I'm not negligent. Rather, I'm confident the results of their SAT exams will be the same if I'm here or if I fly to Seattle the night before. Becca and Gaye volunteered to make sure they're fed and get there on time with #2 pencils. The girls talked Alex out of SAT practice tests, insisting that cramming is a capitalist fallacy (Molly's view) or a superstition (Ramona's). Me, I spend my private night hours cramming for my defense. It's not that I chose superstition. I don't trust anyone with my future but me.

Chaos House had settled into the rhythm of the season. The kids took over breakfast prep. I faithfully run at five thirty and return in time to say thank you when one of them pours a cup of coffee for me.

Overall, my full-time substitute gig didn't tip anyone out of balance. I can't give Mrs. Adams a midday break for her lunch, so I upped her daily pay. She hasn't reported that Ruby noticed my midday absence. I do see Ruby before breakfast and after dinner when Howard takes his break.

In only two weeks, the mural project will be done, and boy-oh-boy, do I long for that opening in my afternoon. The end date is now so sure that Jade allows the Festival PR people to film our work sessions whenever the daylight is good. Becca says the PR people are bugging Jade about how he appears on camera, since the expensive haircut he came to town with has turned scruffy. I'm betting he's too busy to care.

They've interviewed several kids on camera, including Molly, but not Ramona. Likely, Molly was chosen because quite recently she'd taken to wearing Oregon woodsy-girl jeans and flannel shirts. And her hair hangs in braids. In a fake-joking way, Ramona frequently deplores those choices as arising from the influence of Molly's boyfriend who, as it turns out, is Zooey's brother Zachary. He graduated last year, but isn't covered under Rik's Rule about college boys, because he didn't go to college. He works the graveyard shift packing pears in gift boxes at Harry & David, which I'm not critical of.

The twins are speaking to each other again. Alex told me that their rift was because of Zachary, and I'd cautioned him not to bear tales and not to get pulled into their drama. So I know nothing more. However, Zachary appears at the Chaos House dinner table a couple of times a week, then he's gone when homework begins. He never says more to me than hello or, more rarely, thank you. (That, I'm critical of.)

I'd guessed during their junior year that both girls had been in love. Ramona first, at Christmas time; then during spring break, Molly spent a great deal of time whispering over the kitchen phone. Neither girl said anything to me. My suspicions came from overhearing copious weeping and the rejection of murmured comforts from the other sister. That doesn't say anything good about me, that I associate being in love with copious weeping.

During the twins' rift, Ramona had chopped her bangs and deepened her retro-beatnik style, which is likely why she wasn't interviewed on camera by the Festival crew, though a non-biased observer should notice that Ramona is the most articulate among the mural crew.

My math classes incite joy daily, especially the two remedial periods. I bring a sack lunch and eat in my classroom, where anyone who needs help can meet with me. It'd be false modesty not to say that I'm a good teacher. My friends shake their heads whenever I declare what a good day I've had in the classroom.

I spent all of the one school holiday, Columbus Day, installing Nick's south-facing windows. It threatened at first to be a debacle but then wasn't. I'd hired Dharma from the Oak Street collective to help, since it is definitely a two-person job. We were in the middle of lifting the left-most of three windows when Jade walked by and watched for a minute. Then he insisted on helping: "You clearly need a third pair of hands." So I spent six hours giving Dharma and Jade detailed instructions every five minutes on what position to take and what to do. In the end, Dharma and Jade pulled me in for a circle of high-fives over a job well done. It was one of the least fraught days I've spent with Jade and set me on an even keel.

Currently, my main trepidation is fear of catching a head cold. After the Columbus Day holiday, half the school returned with head colds that spread among the teachers. I'm paranoid about it because a cold leads to bronchitis, and I can't afford to take even one day off teaching.

I used most of my first full-time paycheck to pay the dentist in the post-modern hut-like office on Siskiyou Boulevard. Both girls needed checkups, and Molly had her wisdom teeth extracted. In an effort to take care of myself, I'd also gotten new running shoes with that first paycheck.

Besides my running routine, I invented another good habit, which is to repeat a mantra: *It's a good thing we're still friends.* In fact, I've come to believe it. That was made easy because, as I'd foreseen, Jade and I seldom see each other in the course of the day, only at the mural site and at breakfast. I now hear Alex and Quinn in the garage more often than I hear Jade, since teaching Inez's classes at the college eats a lot of his time. He has not yet asked for my assistance in Inez's studio.

The other benefit of that mantra: I no longer walk around playing my own privately crowned drama queen, secretly cheesed off about Timothy being both beautiful and nice. Hence, I'm genuinely friendly, even kind, when Timothy comes to breakfast. I don't know where else I'd see either of them, since I have no time to hang out at Chez Margot.

Which also means that I've missed time with Stephen. There's been a gaping hole at the Chaos House table ever since Stephen, Valerie, and Julio moved to his house near Emigrant Lake. We run into each other on the Plaza behind Chez Margot. I ask after Valerie and Julio, Stephen asks about the twins and Alex. We comment on the weather and remark on the mural's progress. Now that he's recovered from the cataclysm of his divorce, Stephen is expansive like he was when we first met.

"Come to my house on Saturday for brunch," he said at our last encounter. "Valerie keeps asking how you're doing. And bring Alex. Julio would die for the chance at a good spin in the yard."

"Thanks. Another Saturday? I can't get away until we're done." I poked a thumb over my shoulder to indicate the mural, which has gobbled time since school started.

Seeing Stephen cheered me, until I walked far enough away to regret that I can't keep my good friends close if they aren't living in my house. I know it's a character flaw. But I have lots more flaws like that, none of which seem to mend themselves.

During my last period on Friday (remedial math), it was a challenge to command kids' attention. Once the bell rang, it freed us all. I headed for the mural site. After that afternoon's mural work, I owed nothing more to anyone besides dropping math quizzes at Sally's house so she could amuse herself with them. Then I'd fix Friday's dinner and be free.

At the site, Jade asked if he'd see me at Chez Margot that night. I begged off, wanting to go to bed early and sleep in the next morning before taking a run in my new shoes.

32: A Book in the Mail

SATURDAY MORNING, I DID MANAGE to sleep in for the first time in weeks. Just before nine o'clock, I came downstairs ready for a run. The kitchen was empty. Ramona had left instructions for people to find breakfast in the refrigerator. Me, I ate one of Ramona's protein bars and drank water. I was set to leave through the back when someone rapped on the front door.

It was Dharma from the women's collective down the street. She wanted permission to post a sign in the yard, protesting the expansion of the pheasant farm at the end of Oak Street. I agreed.

Then the mailman came. He mounted the steps to the house instead of leaving mail in the mailbox. He handed me a postcard and also asked me to sign for an international package. "It's from Hong Kong."

I felt a tingle of joy. These come four times a year from Kai, delivering a collection of comics, pirated paperbacks, and bootleg cassettes and VHS tapes.

The postcard was from Italy. Frankie had good news:

> As it turns out, you can have everything you want. That is, I have everything I want, and if that's true for me, then it can be true for you. But I wish you'd find it without leaving Ashland. I already miss you, *mio caro amico.*
>
> Can I hire you to move my stuff to Inez's house? That's where I'll be living when we come back from Italy in the spring. It's all packed up in storage at my old place.

That's the best news the U.S. Post Office has delivered since the letter from Cheung Bai Shing invited me to interview. It left me warm and gooey inside. I taped it on the refrigerator so Becca and Gaye would see it.

Bolstered by my friend's good news, I picked up the package from Hong Kong. It was slim. The international shipping notice on the outside declared a book. It was from Chan-suk, not Kai. I opened it with a satisfied smile, thinking this might be his response to having received the package with my final dissertation, a good result from our years together as student and master.

Inside the package was a cheap paperback edition of a scholarly text, the sort of package that Chan-suk sends once or twice a year to help my research. The cover was deep red, called oxblood on Jade's color chart, with a forest green panel displaying the title in Times Roman capitals: *Friendship in Popular Cantonese Stories: A Treatise.* The author's name was anglicized: James Wang.

Fine. I couldn't hope to have an entirely unique dissertation topic, especially since I'd taken almost ten years to write it. The topic didn't have to be entirely unique. The crucial question: must I revise my manuscript to include a reference and analysis in the end note? Could I simply acknowledge this text in the bibliography of source material?

I opened the book to the back to check the references, thinking my published papers would be cited. My name wasn't there. I flipped to the front. My fingers, rough from mixing cement, rasped over the toothy, cheap paper.

This was my text. That is, the English language part. Absent: the Cantonese ideograms painstakingly copied from the original texts, plus the chapter that discusses the challenges in translating written Cantonese to English. It was my draft from twenty months ago, before two rounds of deep emendations and corrections I'd made based on my old master's critique.

Fine. With every draft of my dissertation, I'd sent myself a postmarked copy and left it sealed as proof that I own the copyright of that draft. It would be easy to refute this theft.

I flipped to the copyright page, which cited James Wang. I didn't recognize the publisher, either from my research into Cantonese sources for popular stories or from scholarly texts Chan-suk had shared with me. However, the copyright and publishing dates were three years before I'd sent that draft version to my old master. The postmark date of my preserved copy would do me no good. I have no way to prove that I am the true author.

At the back of the book was a folded letter, ink on rice paper. The letter, dated from the week after I'd sent my uncle my last draft, was in the most formal Cantonese. He usually calls me Siu-Suiki (Ricky in Chinese—and endearing only from Chan-suk). But he addressed me this time as "Teacher Eliot."

> Eliot-lóuhsī, my second son~
>
> This morning I found this in the window of a bookstore near our home. I sit here pondering how this could happen. But do you remember last winter when I wrote that thieves entered our house while we were visiting Kai and his beautiful wife? They took precious books from my library and art from my study. They must have also taken an older draft of your text. I didn't know it until this morning. Now, my heart is bruised and wounded, unable to be repaired.
>
> I send you my deepest love, as if you were my true son. I have nothing I can give to repair this, though I have always desired to give you the world.

My dear uncle had signed his message with formal characters, not our usual warm exchange of names. The two characters after his name had a simple English translation: *Grief.*

How long did I stand at the open front door, making rational assessments about the cheap paperback I still held in my hands?

Was it so long that the sun's rays changed directions? Hours? Days? I felt caught, like an animal in a trap, not yet hurting. It wouldn't hurt if I didn't try to escape.

The twins came down stairs, treading heavily.

> Molly: You could talk to me about it instead of just being a bitch.
>
> Ramona: Why do I need to say one word? Did he suck your brain out?
>
> Molly: Don't be vile.

The wild animal within me stirred, sought escape. I dropped the book on the nearby table and banged the door closed behind me as I leapt down the front steps and ran out to the street. That damned scrub jay *cawked* but missed when it dived for my head. I was moving fast.

Instead of heading up into the Watershed, I ran east down Water Street.

"Sasha!"

Jade Solberg's voice called from the steps of Inez's studio. Of all the times in the universe, his summons came just as the abyss opened in front of me.

I determined not to respond, yet one ungovernable hand rose to wave.

—

At Helman Street, where Water Street ends, my friend Dharma called my name, waving from their front garden. My arm waved automatically in return, as if I were a normal human. I ran down Oak Street toward Bear Creek. Past Sleepy Hollow Road. Where Oak Street crossed Bear Creek, I turned onto Eagle Mill Road, followed it under I-5, then ran up Mountain Avenue as far as a road existed, beyond where people live in aging trailers and camper vans, up past someone's illicit yurt.

Why catalog streets petering out in the rugged golden foothills? Why catalog anything ever again? Someone will just steal the effort, publish it as their own.

I stumbled where the track had become impossibly rutted. No one had taken a road grader up here in years. Instead of pausing and resting, I turned back, counting my breaths in and out while still running. That brutal rush of adrenalin had taken me a good distance but was wearing itself out.

When I turned around—I had to spin three times to come back into my body and see where I was—I came down Mountain Avenue on the ragged remains of that rush, forcing best practices for running on a steep incline, letting gravity pull me down, using my core and arms for balance, never looking at my feet.

No use getting injured out of recklessness. Other people, total strangers, had already caused me the greatest possible injury.

Then my mental faculties re-engaged. I began a new list. As soon as memory and reason were again mine to control, I recalled what I knew about this predicament. A similar catastrophe befell a Comparative Lit candidate during my first year as a liberal arts PhD student, trying to get my 500-level classwork done. That crisis became legendary among the baby PhD people. Details were a jumble in my memory, but I knew what had to begin right now:

> File for a U.S. copyright.
>
> Protest the Hong Kong copyright.
> (I'll need Nick to help find the proper attorney. My minimal knowledge: Hong Kong copyright law is the same as British law. No idea what that will cost.)
>
> Present a portfolio to my advisory committee that attests my ownership.
> (Can I convert the Saturday defense date to an attestation hearing? If not, I need a refund for that Medford–Seattle plane ticket.)

Submit Chan-suk's letter as the initial proof.
(I'll need a notarized statement from my uncle that affirms he's seen every draft since 1975.)

Write an endnote for my manuscript.
(I'll acknowledge its existence but deny the validity of that cheap oxblood paperback.)

I calculated the hours required for all those tasks. My afternoons will open up next week, after the mural is done. So this is all doable, even while teaching full time.

Mountain Avenue finally took me to B Street, where I turned toward Chaos House, ready to climb up to my garret and begin the work. I came into the house through the front door without cooling down from the run. I kicked off my new, now dirty shoes, which didn't yet have a place on the rack by the door. I peeled off my socks and only then noticed that I should have applied prophylactic Band-Aids. I had new-shoe blisters. One had burst.

I went to the kitchen, my sweaty feet making squishing noises on the wood floor, and drank two tall glasses of tap water. After rubbing my sweaty fingers on my damp, dusty shorts, I called Dr. Randolph.

After briefly apologizing for interrupting his weekend, I began my story. While I talked, I wiped sweat from my forehead and neck with a dish towel. The sweat was left from my panicky run, not from nervousness while describing my problem and proposed solution.

Dr. Randolph listened patiently, asking a couple of questions when I talked too rapidly to be understood. After I finished citing every detail I'd thought of while coming down Mountain Avenue, I stopped.

"Is that all I need to consider, Dr. Randolph? What else?"

He drew a breath. I stopped breathing. I swear I could hear the sweat running down my spine.

"That's a pretty comprehensive list of actions, Rik."

"What else? I'm ready to start right now."

"Rik..." He paused, which was killing me. "I worry that you don't have time. The work you'd have to do to plead for an extension would fill every hour between now and the nineteenth of December. In thirty years, I've seen only one candidate convince the university to extend the ten-year requirement."

"Oh. Yes. I see."

"Even with the best attorney, it will take months to find and pursue the person who stole your copyright."

"I..." The crevasse in the earth's crust gaped again, as it had when I opened Chan-suk's letter.

"But I don't want to discourage you from trying. Because I know how hard you've worked." Dr. Randolph went on when I left only dead air. "I just want to warn you that, with so little ramp available to you before December, you will be undertaking an enormous task, with no guarantee of success."

"I understand." I felt very small and helpless. "I'll retract my dissertation."

Silence. Then he said, "I'll have my assistant notify your committee members."

"Thank you." I made sure to breathe well enough that my voice sounded adult. "I'll call each of them to thank them personally for their time. I am grateful for the time and guidance you've given me."

I sounded like I was alive yet couldn't find the wherewithal to be proud of what I was managing to say.

Dr. Randolph said, "I'm so sorry, Rik. But what I don't..." He coughed. "What I don't understand is..."

I held my breath. Was he about to offer me one last way out?

"I don't understand why you told me about it."

"What?" This time my voice cracked.

"No one on your committee, including me, could possibly be aware of a shoddy text floating around Hong Kong bookshops.

If you weren't so honest, you could have finished your defense, taken your PhD, and then spent the next year legally attacking your pirate. Why did you decide to be so honest?"

Music came up from the garage. Alex and Quinn were using their Saturday rehearsal time. I tried to hear what the song was. Something I'd heard all summer. Ah. 'Depression.' Black Flag. Two guitars. No drums.

"I have kids," I said. "I teach high school. I must be honest."

Even if that notion had occurred to me, I'd have declined. I cannot imagine lying to create an advantage for myself. And the terror of being found out would pursue me like an evil thundering heart in an Edgar Allan Poe story.

It only occurred to me then that colleagues of Cheung Bai Shing, my master's brother-in-law, could encounter that fictitious text in Hong Kong bookstores. I'd have to write to him too.

"It's refreshing that honesty is your knee-jerk reaction." A voice called behind Dr. Randolph. He said, "I'm afraid I have to go. The deadline for withdrawing from classes is this coming Monday. I think you can still get most of your tuition fees back, though I'm not positive. Contact my assistant and schedule a time when we can talk more next week. I owe you a dose of career counseling, at the very least."

We finished a series of thank-yous and goodbyes. I hung up wondering what more Dr. Randolph and I could find to talk about. Rake over the burning bones of my dead dissertation?

—

I needed to go write the letter to Chan-suk, the very first and most important chore. But how could I bear to sit in my study? It had been my private place of solace while writing my dissertation. While repairing everything that broke after that Bad Christmas.

Instead, I slipped my running shoes on bare feet, cursed the blisters, and took the narrow walkway along the hedge to the backyard. I walked down to the creek and kept walking farther east, crossing my neighbor's boundary, down near where the creek flows through a large culvert, bridged by Van Ness Avenue. A fallen tree lay there, partly hacked up where it fell, forming a rough bench just above the creek.

I sat, listening to the rushing water as it smoothed stones in the creek bed. I intended to be still, but my right knee jittered, so my shoe raised small clouds in the silt, which settled in the crevasses and folds around the new, bright-white shoelaces. A downy woodpecker tapped incessantly on a black oak. A winter robin kicked about in the leaf litter.

I'm not sure how long it was until an actual thought entered my consciousness. I was thirsty. But not enough to rise and do anything about it. Although gallons of water flowed past me, I couldn't conceive of drinking from the creek anywhere except far up into the Watershed. What I needed most was the sight and sound of the flowing creek washing over a broken and bruised part of the universe.

I continued to study how time and water had washed the banks of the creek this way and that, how some vegetation had crept close to the stream, then had most of its soil washed away, yet clung to the bank as if by root hairs alone.

I seized a crooked stick the creek had abandoned at its high-water point last spring. I scratched at the silt a stick's length from where it had been undisturbed by humans or animals, baked in the summer sun. When the stick broke the crust to bits, I drew ideograms in the loosened silt.

The same characters Chan-suk wrote after his signature.

Grief.

Distress.

As an adjective: Sorrowful.

In a compound ideogram: Woeful.

Wasn't this the kind of situation when normal people wept bitter tears? Or cried their eyes out, like I had in years past? I'd lost a dream before, and I'd grieved through several seasons. I could feel loss choking up my throat, but I couldn't find tears. Was October still too hot? Dried up all possible tears?

I wiped away the two characters, then drew them in the silt again. My knuckles were white from holding the stick far tighter than I'd ever held a brush when drawing ideograms.

"Sasha, what's wrong?"

My log bench trembled when another body sat down. Long legs stretch out near my ideograms.

I turned to answer. Couldn't bring a face into focus. Couldn't produce sound over the knot choking my throat.

"You look terrible, my friend. Like death warmed over."

Death. Of a dream. My modest thought-child had died, after being nurtured in my third-floor garret over solitary nights.

"I…I had bad news. The death of…"

"Goodness. I didn't mean to…ugh, wrong time to joke. I am so sorry."

I couldn't emerge from the rushing waters that flowed over me. I could scarcely hear his voice over the tumble of the creek that sought to sooth my stony surface.

"It's just gone now. Woe. Woe."

That's close to what I said before I heard that I spoke in Cantonese, crying out like a mourner on Hong Kong streets.

"Can I do anything for you?" Jade's voice sounded in the same tonal range as the rushing creek.

"No. I just want a bit of solitude."

"Of course. Sorry to intrude. I'll find you tomorrow, Sasha."

I'd gripped my stick so tightly my hands were numb. The dragon crystals, silent for weeks, ground against each other like broken glass as I watched Jade, who'd tried to comfort me, move away with that panther-like pace he had.

He and his shadow were soon lost in the veil of brush and tree branches along Ashland Creek.

33: Melancholia

I AM SO EXPERT AT HOUSEHOLD shopping that I executed my Saturday tasks without being aware I'd done so until I'd put everything away and finished arranging the after-school snacks. I chaperoned the required number of Saturday hours at the mural site. Nothing unusual happened, except I forgot to put on sunscreen, so my face felt stiff for the rest of the day. Jade didn't raise the need to speak with me again, being quite busy with his crew. In fact, I didn't notice if he ever looked my way.

For dinner, I made Sichuan-style pork dumplings with the last of the wonton wrappers Gaye had brought back from San Francisco. For the soup, I added bok choy and reconstituted dried shiitake mushrooms, which I'd found at the co-op. I didn't eat much, but the crew of kids who were at the table that night made rapid business of it.

All the denizens of Chaos House, except Ruby and Howard, deserted the place after dinner. I braced myself to go over to Lazarus Cottage, since Jade had sought me out twice that morning and I had yet to respond.

But no one was home in the cottages.

At my house, I read to Ruby until she fell asleep, but I don't remember what I read. While futzing around in the kitchen, I was still trying to calm the rapid vibration in my chest, to turn it back into an ordinary heartbeat. I tussled with the notion of a fair and just universe, given that my dissertation work had relied upon a host of cultural material for which the copyrights were either unknown or highly suspect: pirated cinema sent in packages from

Kai; bookstore discoveries of titles whose provenances could not be proven; the many facsimiles that Chan-suk had gleaned from university libraries in Hong Kong.

At least I avoided rambunctious worries about Claudia and Alex since I was too involved with my own woes.

At nine o'clock, I decided to begin my translation work early and made great progress on what an industrial engineer needs to know when doing business in Hong Kong. But thirty minutes in, I flipped a page in the dictionary, typed two words, and felt desperate weeping about to sweep me away. Nothing about the Cantonese-to-English translation of principles of etiquette for a business meeting should invoke that kind of human emotion.

I paused my work, fingering a ceramic memento from Seattle, a test pattern for a mural Jade proposed but never built. It was Roman narrative style: the face of a wide-eyed young man with laurels in his hair made of glass beads baked onto a ceramic base. Now it was probably too valuable to be used as a coaster, though that was the only use I'd found for it.

When I stood to move the memento to the other side of the room, I heard that I'd been playing music I shouldn't. This time it was the Rolling Stones, 'Paint It Black.' I shouldn't allow such music to cast ominous shadows in the empty spaces of my mind.

I'd learned better years ago, when I was seeking a confirming diagnosis from a local doctor to support placing Ruby's affairs under guardianship. That had proved to be a life-changing meeting. The physician, Dr. Michael Lyle, later became a good friend. In that first meeting, he began slowly.

"You understand now, Mr. Eliot, why I thought it best that we speak privately after I finished examining your mother?"

"Yes. I asked a friend to stay with her so I could come to this meeting alone. Can you please call me Rik?"

"Of course. I've already sent her physician my concurrence with his diagnosis."

"What will that mean?"

"He'll advise that she no longer drive, that she needs in-home care. And that she must have a guardian. She's not capable of managing her finances and other concerns. Will that be you?"

"Yes, though she'll hate it. If she remembers. Her doctor was cautious about making predictions. Do you agree?"

"We don't yet know how to predict progression. The varieties of dementia have different causes and show different behaviors, with varying rates of deterioration."

"I learned that much at the library."

"Her physician might be better able to speculate on the future when he sees her again in six months. Did he give you references for resources?"

"Yes. I've found home health aides. My attorney is already working on guardianship."

"Is the expense daunting?"

"No, Nick's a friend. He already helped me gain guardianship for my two nieces."

"I meant the expenses for home health aides. Rik, you need help as soon as possible, given how your mother behaves, especially toward you."

"That was a bad day. Many days, my mother thinks I'm my dead brother Christopher and is happy to see me."

"Yet you are clearly exhausted."

"I didn't sleep well last night."

Dr. Lyle picked up my hand. He's the handsomest man I've met in Ashland. When he has summer color, he reminds me of Peter O'Toole in *Lawrence of Arabia.* He also has the most reassuring presence one can hope for. Since he moved to San Francisco, his practice has focused on treating traumatized adolescents. I'm absolutely sure the world is a better place for that.

He ran his fingers lightly over my scraped knuckles. "How did this happen?"

"I'm refurbishing cottages my mother owns, hoping for better renters than students. I raked my knuckles over roofing shingles."

"You should wear gloves. And I recommend Cornhuskers Lotion. It's a ridiculous name for a product, but you need it for rough work. And wear eye protection, not just sunglasses." He opened a desk drawer. "And wear this. The new formulations of sunscreen block more UV rays and last longer than whatever you are using." I felt the man's eyes on me. "You aren't using sunscreen. Or wearing gloves or eye protection. How old are you?"

"Twenty-five."

"You look haggard. You're too thin for your bone structure." He again ran his fingers over my knuckles. "If you weren't burning up in the sun, I suspect you'd have a complexion that many women would die for."

I tried to smile, as if that were humorous. I was finding Dr. Lyle's caring tone nearly unbearable.

"Does your mother have a partner to help? Your father?"

"No, he's out of the picture. There's only me."

"What's going on besides the difficulties of your mother's health? Money worries?"

"I almost have that under control. She lost her own money last year. It's just…"

"May I guess? Shake your head when I'm wrong. First, you don't sleep enough. Getting out of bed is nearly impossible."

"No, I have to get out of bed."

"Only for your mother's sake?"

"I'm also guardian for my sister's daughters. They're ten now. I have to get them to school in decent shape, supervise their homework, get them to bed on time."

"Then I'm not wrong about your lack of sleep? How much time do you spend crying? How often?"

I couldn't abide that gentle tone any longer. I squeezed my eyes shut. Water still leaked. I caught a teardrop with my tongue.

"You have depression," Dr. Lyle said.

"It's just because of all the work. I'll get better rest when I finish the cottages. And when there's help with my mother."

"Yet often depression doesn't rise from an external reason. Would you be amenable to medication? You have all these problems to solve for other people. I think you should consider help that's just for you."

I couldn't swallow and so couldn't speak. I nodded. Which was beyond weak.

"We'll try Elavil to start. Then see me every two weeks, so I can evaluate whether the medication is working."

"I can't afford it. Either the extra bills or time off from work."

"Let's do it at the end of the day on Fridays. I won't bill you for just a twenty-minute conversation."

"Why would you do that?"

He held up his hands. "You're far too busy helping others. I might be one of the few people in this town who can understand all that's being asked of you."

—

A month after meeting Dr. Lyle in 1975, I'd stopped crying every moment I spent alone, though not ceased completely. After three months, Dr. Lyle joined a practice in Berkeley. We still write to each other, usually only postcards. I stay at his house when I come to San Francisco for the Gay Freedom Day parade. And we enjoy at least one hike in the Siskiyous and a meal together when he's in Ashland to see the plays. In our current life, he's Michael and I'm Rik. His partner Gerard also treats me as a close friend.

Since then, I've learned to solve dips in mood without Elavil, which avoids the dry-mouth problem. To do so, I imagine a conversation with Michael, and then take his imaginary advice to make necessary changes.

Listen to different music. Read different kinds of books.

Change the hour and route for my daily run. Or ride a freaking bicycle instead.

Go to dinner with a friend I haven't seen for too long.

Get bedsheets in a new color.
(Not red or black. Those were catastrophic for my dreams.)

Treat food like medicine. More protein, less sugar.
(My mother complains when I make such changes, but the twins never have, because there's always the after-school snack cupboard.)

Michael Lyle also first told me about what people in San Francisco were calling the new gay cancer. He taught cautious behavior. We've all been through immense challenges since the beginning. For example, I am principally celibate.

However, here I was up in my study, playing music while translating texts, wearing only my writing robe, a soft breeze coming through the window. On this night, it wasn't until I had to find a tissue because my nose was running and my cheeks were wet, that I heard what music had been playing over and over.

I thought I'd lost—or discarded—that Seventies heartbreak mix tape...a soundtrack that begged the Immortals for relief:

'Ain't No Sunshine'
'Heart of Gold'
'Helpless'
'Just My Imagination'
'Knocking On Heaven's Door'

Then a string of songs recorded off *Blood on the Tracks,* because why not play the saddest songs in the world on repeat? I should have thrown that mix tape out the window long ago.

Have music publishers tried to restrict the creation of mix tapes just to prevent deep depression among the brokenhearted?

I couldn't take any depression-fighting actions at the moment except to pop that tape from the player and toss it into the bathroom trashcan. I sat down to work again. Then returned two minutes later, grabbed that cassette, and ripped out so many feet of tape, it'd take an hour with a Bic pen to rewind it.

I grabbed a cassette the twins brought back from their Berkeley odyssey. The first one—the Cure—didn't work, added to the tear-jag. I switched to an older cassette of the Clash.

I must remember to drink more water.

After receiving Saturday morning's mail, I must focus on the straight path through the darkness.

Else I'll be back to suffering dry mouth again.

The first therapist Michael referred me to listened closely when I said I knew by age eleven that my mother didn't love me and was...vituperous. That I'd learned to stay away, to be grateful that she ignored me, and to leave before she attacked. My brother Christopher received most of her scolding criticisms, until he left home. Then Ruby switched her ire to Wendy. But I insisted that it was boring to talk about my mother while paying by the hour, and I most needed help coping with the sudden change in my life's direction.

He watched me for so long, it became uncomfortable. He finally said, "I sense that you're grieving an enormous loss, greater than just a change in your professional direction. It's a death or a missing loved one. Do you want to talk about that?"

"No." I replied automatically. His words launched a terrible movie that often played in my head: Jade leaning on the arch by the Chaos kitchen while we were softly and kindly breaking up.

The therapist said, "You are clearly a visual person. I can help you ease that tendency to replay scenes of pain and loss."

I shook my head, stood as if to leave, then sat down instead of fleeing. I said, "No. If I don't see it anymore, I'll have nothing."

I'd been left holding nothing once before. After six months seeing Kai every day in Cambridge with his fiancée, I'd also lost mathematics as a principal spark in my life.

"I'd rather have grief than have nothing," I told the therapist. "Can we instead talk about the changes in my life's direction?"

The weekend after that session, I didn't have paying work. I tore down the wall between the Chaos kitchen and living room. It wasn't loadbearing and had always made both rooms feel small, though Chaos House itself is massive.

I tore down the archway Jade had been leaning against before he left Ashland. After I repaired the floor, added drywall patches, hung a faux beam, painted, and swept up the dust, I stepped back to see the result. Morning sunlight reached the living room, appropriately incorporating thin air as a memorial to the last moments of that Bad Christmas.

It didn't make me happy, but I stopped walking into a wall of grievous loss whenever I walked through that door. I felt free to get busy with what I needed to do to make what I could of the strange new world where I found myself.

34: Green Eyes

I WROTE MY LETTER TO CHAN-SUK, using the proper language and on the best paper, to reassure my dear uncle that he must not grieve, to absolve him of all responsibility. The other correspondence and phone calls could wait until Monday, there now being no hurry for one single thing.

My professional translation work progressed so slowly that night, I finally decided to go up to Chez Margot with hopes for a distracting conversation with Stephen and Kevin. When I came down through the Chaos kitchen, I found the porch light on and a slew of cups and plates on the backyard table. Even though it was night time, dark-eyed juncos gleaned the leavings. I stepped onto the back porch to retrieve the dishes. The scrub jay landed, chasing away the juncos. When I opened the back door, the jay cursed me, then rose up, beating its wings. The rippling creek was louder than usual. Or did I imagine it?

Timothy sat on the back steps of his cottage, talking with a woman. Then her voice pierced the night air.

"Gag me! He did *not* say that."

"I admit it," Timothy said. "I do *not* understand his art."

"What's to understand?" she said. "He's so yummy, he's like a work of art when he's just walking around."

Not a woman. A girl. I recognized the voice.

"Zooey, it's ten o'clock. Time to go home."

She jerked away from Timothy, stumbling to her feet.

"Mr. E? Is that you?"

"Yes. Go home now, please."

"Are you going to tell my parents?"

"No, Zooey, I won't. You are leaving right this minute."

"Fer sure, Mr. E. Bye-bye, Timothy. It's been, like, so bitchin' rapping with you."

Neither Timothy nor I spoke while her bootheels clacked along the path, echoing until the sound was lost in the distance.

"Are you out of your mind?" I spoke more sternly than I do with my own kids.

Timothy looked up at me, surprised. As if he had no idea what I said.

Yeah, because I'd said it in Cantonese. I began again, this time in English.

"Timothy, she's barely seventeen."

"She said she was nineteen."

"Yet she's dressed like a schoolgirl. She wears pink plastic barrettes." I didn't mask my freaked-out irritation. "How the heck did you end up with her? At your *house?*"

Timothy scratched his neck, as if annoyed. "She came to find Jade. To ask him to review her portfolio. She asked if I didn't think Jade was dreamy. Then we got to talking."

"Respectfully, you are a danger to yourself, Timothy."

"She was sincere. She really likes Jade."

"It's a schoolgirl crush. And you need better situational awareness." I tucked my hands up in my pits to keep from shaking him. "Ask your agent for a common-sense coach."

"It's not like I'm interested in her. I was only being polite. Anyone could make that mistake."

"Not someone who doesn't want to ruin his career. Or put Jade in danger."

"How could I put Jade in danger?"

"He's a teacher in charge of high school students. If her parents end up asking why she was here, what's your answer? 'We were just talking about how dreamy my gay friend is'?"

"But I wouldn't say that. I'm bi." He stood up, starting for his back door, then paused. "Do you think I'm bi?"

"It's not any of my business, so I don't think about it at all. I have to go. Good night."

I grabbed the dishes left out on the patio and headed inside. The next time Jade asked for advice about teaching, I'll warn him not to review portfolios at his house. Go to the library. Or go to…

Oh, this must be what J.J. Smith meant when he said Jade would be gone soon since he didn't have enough room. Space aside, Jade cannot be meeting privately to review kids' portfolios. Anyone with sense knows that.

May the Heavenly Immortals condescend to intercede when grown men are witless.

—

After hauling dishes into the kitchen, I took a longer route to walk uptown: east to Van Ness, then down Helman. I had to cross the wooden pedestrian walkway over Ashland Creek, the thump of my shoes echoing loudly. I'd set out for Chez Margot, not because I wanted to see all my friends—rather, I hoped they wouldn't be there. I wanted to talk to Kevin.

Kevin, a medieval scholar, is the only friend who'd understand where I ended up after reading my morning mail. Our earliest conversations had dwelt on our shared circumstance: All But Dissertation. One step away from finishing a PhD. We were scholars stranded in the same small town. He, however, has had better success at publishing in academic journals than I have. Last year, he published a monograph, "Medieval Dramatic Forms and Kabuki: A Comparison," which garnered him that consultant's gig with the Festival. The last article I published was "Cantonese and English Language Engineering Texts: A Translator's Guide." I was paid five hundred dollars plus five copies to share with my friends, followed by an offer to write "Kantonesische und deutsche Mathematiktexte: Ein Leitfaden für Übersetzer." However, my

German has rotted on the vine since I left my math program. I should resurrect my German skills this winter. It's not like I have to speak it aloud.

When I came in the door, stepping out of the chill October air, the garlic-and-butter warmth of Chez Margot embraced me. One couple remained from the last dinner seating, lingering over glasses of wine. No one from our usual crew was there.

His thick hair tied back in a new samurai headband, Kevin nodded hello when he saw me come in. He took down an Old-Fashioned glass and began mixing my usual weak-ass drink.

He set it down before me, then turned to sneeze three times. "Excuse me." He disappeared into the washroom, then emerged, wiping his hands dry, another victim of the October head cold.

"What's up?" Kevin said. "I thought you'd be out hearing music tonight."

"My dissertation was stolen. It's been published under someone else's name in Hong Kong."

Kevin set my drink on a coaster. "That simplifies things. Trust me on that."

"What?" My voice broke.

"Now you don't have to torture yourself silly while preparing for your defense. You're free, Rik."

I must have looked dull-witted.

He laughed. "C'mon, Rik. You came in here looking like your dog died. I'm consoling you."

"It feels just like some creature died. Surely, you can imagine. What if your dissertation were stolen from you?"

"I abandoned my dissertation last June." Kevin polished a glass and set it on the rack.

"You didn't tell me." It felt like a jab of betrayal, that he hadn't shared such news with me.

"That's because it was like giving up on a bad love affair."

"I don't know about that."

"It is though," Kevin said. "If you talk about your feelings with others, they'll think you're describing an abusive relationship. So I've kept it to myself."

"But that's why I came in tonight. To talk about heartbreak with you." I cogitated on Kevin's news. "And you've published new papers since June."

"Just enough to advance new gigs at the Festival. I hope this current gig proves my worth, so I can keep consulting while avoiding medieval academic scholars altogether."

"You don't want..." Want what he and I claimed to share when we first met? "To become a professor and researcher?"

"I prefer being a consultant, discussing technicalities with actors and directors, instead of dodging backbiting grad students in the common room. This consultancy lets me share what I know without worrying over my students' success. I didn't like all the worry as a TA. Giving up on the notion of a professor's life has been exactly like leaving an unsuitable lover."

"What...How..." What to ask?

"Shall I give you a shorthand version of the questions I pondered?" He began counting them on his fingers. "If I really cared, I'd have finished sooner."

"Uh..." I'd fought all day against accusing myself of that.

Kevin tapped another digit. "Did I truly need it for what I want to do next? Isn't your next goal to return to Hong Kong? You don't need a PhD for that."

"Yeah, but..." Was the perpetual writing of my dissertation tying me to the past? The last vestiges of my life as a professional student? "No, Kevin, it's..."

He persisted. "Did I cling to the ritual of the damned writing to avoid living my real life?"

"Stop freaking me out. You always say people at the bar only want you to feel sorry for them. I came for sympathy."

He nudged my glass closer, pushing at the edge of the coaster. "Drink your pretend drink. We haven't discussed it for ages, but I can guess your answers. However, it'd be rude of me to do that. You're still saying goodbye to your long-time paper lover. I'm here to tell you, Rik. Your dissertation was never your best boyfriend. Did that bastard really care about your needs and feelings?"

His familiar baritone struck hard. Hearing his words, my fake Old-Fashioned just wasn't palatable. When I first met Kevin, I had to work hard to listen to him. His resonant voice was too similar to Jade's. It took a while, learning not to turn my head whenever Kevin spoke. I unlearned that response because when he called me, he said, "Rik." Wrong name; wrong voice. I'd learned to listen closely to Kevin over years of discussing our writing and other aspirations. He's always insightful.

"Does this also mean," Kevin was polishing a glass, "that now there's no reason for you to run off to Hong Kong? I hope it means you'll stay here, where everyone wishes you'd stay."

I shook my head. "No, I haven't changed the master plan. I can always teach math without a PhD." I fiddled with my stupid Old-Fashioned glass. "I should go home and toss the pages one by one into Ashland Creek, so it all really floats away. Not just metaphorically."

"Nah. You can beat the pirates' game. Go publish monographs of your chapters, here in the U.S. and in Hong Kong. A poet-translator from my university advised me to do that. Get a U.S. copyright for each chapter."

That practical suggestion didn't penetrate. I still wanted to debate it all with Kevin. "But you just stopped doing the work. You didn't get it stolen from you. I was about to grab the golden ring. But you decided to…to…settle."

"I settled on not pursuing a PhD. It was like deciding not to pursue an unattainable and cruel lover. I know that's a proper metaphor since the last lover I pursued put himself in the Unrequited Penalty Box and refused to come out."

He topped my Old-Fashioned glass with Perrier.

"As you know, Rik."

That pointed jab made me blink several times. I believed that when Kevin moved into Chaos House, he'd just dumped the person he came to Ashland with.

"How did I miss that?"

"How did you miss that I gave up on my PhD, the biggest decision of my life? You missed it because I haven't talked about it with you or anyone else."

"No, that you quit being in love with someone who didn't love you back. I thought you chose to split from the guy you came to Ashland with, not the other way around."

Kevin leaned on the bar, his long, narrow torso intruding on my personal space. He traced the curve of my hand where I cradled my unsipped drink.

"You were there, Rik. Don't you remember sitting under that tarp with me watching storm waves at Brookings?"

"Of course, I remember that." He'd persuaded me to take a long weekend and camp near the ocean, riding behind him on his motorcycle through the redwoods. I remember feeling the micro-climate changes as the bike followed the highway's dips and curves along the Smith River. "I don't remember what we talked about."

"We didn't talk. We'd just spent two hours on the bike, your thighs wrapped around mine. But you showed no inclination to sit close and get warm, so we shivered and watched the ocean while it rained."

I did remember one moment, sitting under that rain tarp. I'd drifted back two years, when I'd driven Jade to the redwoods in my Datsun, because he'd never seen them. I was thinking that the redwoods would forever smell like Jade's bay rum aftershave.

Oh good heavens. I'd hurt someone and didn't know it.

Kevin wiped down the other end of the bar, which didn't need it. "Part of me knew it rationally before my irrational self sat shivering under that tarp. I saw then that there was no possibility you'd join my loner biker lifestyle. And I'd seen the problems that rose when my cousin married a woman with two kids. I am self-aware enough to know I'm not domestic. Don't you agree?"

Stunned, I failed to answer. Kevin kept talking.

"That moment of enlightenment launched two actions. First, I moved out of Chaos House. Then I practiced mental hygiene to forget about it."

"Mental hygiene." I repeated the words like a fool, given that such practices had kept me in motion for years.

"Which meant that I didn't have to leave town," Kevin said. "That's a good thing. I didn't want to chase myself out of a town I like because of unrequited love. It's such an adolescent condition."

Hard to answer when overwhelming shame chokes off air. I sipped my pathetic drink, which I couldn't swallow any better than I could swallow shame for being so unaware.

"I…I'm sorry, Kevin. I didn't know then. Or until now. That day I was caught up thinking of…"

Jade and the particular scent that trails after him. Bay rum in the redwoods.

"Oh good god!" Kevin cried. "While I was pining my heart out, you were sitting there in love with someone else!"

I must have looked stricken because Kevin burst out laughing, putting a hand over his mouth in a fake attempt to stifle it.

"C'mon, Rik! Why didn't you tell me? I thought you were just too polite to mention my crush. You're so adorably innocent, I could almost fall in love with you all over again."

"I am seriously shortsighted." And I prove it repeatedly.

"Yes. A good optometrist could prescribe spectacles."

"Why didn't you say that you…" oh lord "…liked me?"

"Because, trust me, that'd be a dim-witted thing to say to a guy when there's clearly no reason to hope. Who were you in love with back then?"

"It doesn't matter now, does it? Anyway, I am humbled."

"Don't be," he said. "It's long ago. Right now, I have a good chance with someone worth longing for. If I can beat out the competition." He glanced over my shoulder. The Chez Margot front door opened. Figures appeared in the mirror behind the bar. "So pay up and go home, Rik. I don't need two competitors."

I put the usual two dollars on the bar and rose.

To go out the front door, I had to pass Jade and Timothy. We all said good evening. Jade had his hand on Timothy's shoulder when they stepped aside to let me pass.

Well, oh well.

Best of luck to Kevin. I lost that chance a long while ago.

Kevin's existential slap upside my head took my mind off my dead dissertation. I stepped down onto the street, feeling chastened. No, feeling in need of severe chastisement. How could I have been so blind? All those nights practicing my own mental hygiene, battling the grief of unrequited love, I'd been busily fighting against feeling foolish, doltish, unworthy.

When, in fact, I *was* foolish, doltish, unworthy. And utterly self-involved to the exclusion of my friend's feelings.

"*Kaukau!* We found you!" Molly called.

Ramona ran up past her sister to grab my sleeve.

"Alex got busted. You have to save him."

35: The Eagle

MY AGING VICTORIAN MANSION HAS squeaky parquet floors and wind shrieking through closed windows. I spend every weekday in an institution where athletic shoes squeal on the linoleum floors like wailing banshees, the rooms are either too hot or too cold, and you are fortunate if the janitor takes less than a week to change out a blinking fluorescent tube in the ceiling array.

The police station? I'd never been in one until that night. It felt like the waiting room outside the ER at Ashland General Hospital. People spoke softly by the front desk. Indecipherable conversations seeped from behind closed doors. A metal chair scraped across the floor, the screech raising the little hairs on the back of my neck. Every movement in the room passed in slow motion until—bang!—a trio slammed through the front door, two cops who quarreled noisily with a third cop, and then they all disappeared behind a closing door, trailing a pungent odor of alcohol.

I stood before the front desk, nervous, feeling tortured.

"Do I have your name spelled correctly?" The desk sergeant had taken pains to have me repeat my name three times and then spell it twice.

"Yes. And it's the same legal name as the boy you are holding. We are both named for my grandfather."

I'd been careful all month not to disturb Nick after working hours, but I'd sent the twins to the payphone on the plaza with all the change from my pocket, to call Nick's house and answering service until they found him.

"And you're the boy's guardian? You don't look old enough to be more than his brother."

The sergeant had my driver's license in front of him on the desk. He could see my birthdate. And my name. He couldn't see me clenching and unclenching my hands at my sides.

"I am his guardian."

"But you have no proof of that." Not a question.

"I didn't walk out of my house thinking I'd need it. My attorney will be here shortly."

"You're the guardian. But you allowed that boy to roam after curfew." He sneered: his face blank, his voice laughed at me.

"No, never. It wasn't yet curfew when you picked him up." What I wanted most at that moment was not to feel helpless. The anger now boiling up was not useful. "Please explain again why you're holding him and why I cannot see him."

The desk officer said, "Malicious mischief in Lithia Park. And possession of a violent weapon."

"My Alex? You are mistaken. Highly, highly unlikely."

And boy, do I hope it's a mistake. Else, Monday's conference call with Claudia's attorneys will be a shitshow. Since afternoon, repeated waves of emotion wanted to join with roaring resentment to seize my core. Seriously, the Heavenly Immortals must stop dicking around in my business.

Nick arrived at last. He knew the right questions and asked to speak with the arresting officers, declaring that the story at the front desk was too lacking in detail to explain what sounded like unlawful custody of a minor.

The officer who appeared was near retirement age. And he seemed bored spitless.

"We had a 911 call from a residence on Granite Street about a commotion by the upper pond. Our car was nearby, and we responded within minutes. The commotion had ended, but we heard runners on the trails. When we shined our light on the menagerie, there was just one boy. We found the wire-cutters nearby, plus evidence of tampering on one of the cages. He couldn't answer us, except to state his name and to say he was on his way home. He had no ID other than his student body card."

"That's all the ID he has." I shouldn't interrupt but did, my fists still clenched. "He doesn't have a driver's license."

The officer didn't acknowledge my helpful addition. He continued. "Due to the weapon and obvious damage in the park, an arrest was deemed necessary."

They let Nick in to see Alex.

I was calmer once Nick arrived, but the anger and demons in my core held hands. I was left on the hard bench, where I catalogued the sounds, smells, and sights in the institutional foyer—and tried not to think what this might mean for the ongoing fracas with Claudia. I sank into chiding myself for cataloguing cop station details, since I'd just that morning vowed that the end of my dissertation was the end of my cataloging habits.

The second hand on the clock—identical to the clock in my classroom—traveled around a hundred times. Well, not quite. Nick returned with Alex in less than ten minutes. Alex limped. And looked more wretched than the night when Claudia had castigated him so unfairly.

Nick addressed the arresting officer and the desk sergeant. "You picked up a minor with obvious signs of physical injury and offered no medical treatment. You have no evidence that he participated in any crime. And the object you are calling a violent weapon is a common tool found in most every garage and which my client has never touched. I'm formally requesting that you release him to his guardian immediately. If this so-called crime goes before a judge, I will not present a friendly demeanor when I seek dismissal. Further—oh, shall I stop now? You know what to do."

Alex was free. Nick had one more demand. "Please return Mr. Eliot's ID. You have no reason to hold it."

The effing desk cop was still sneering when he slid my ID across his desk. My arm around Alex's shoulder, I walked out of the station, wanting to shelter him from any further assault. This wasn't a kid who needed anyone to coerce or yell at him.

—

On the deserted street outside the police station, the streetlights cast noirish shadows on the stone-and-concrete buildings. Downtown had never before seemed so ominous. Nick gave us a ride to Chaos House. Molly and Ramona had gone home after Nick answered their call. They were still awake, sitting in the silent, dark living room, and they rushed to embrace Alex and murmur their concern when they saw that he limped.

Nick told me to put the kettle on, modulating the voice he'd used with the cops. "Do you have any alcohol in the house? Knowing you, I fear the answer."

"There's brandy from flambéing the Christmas pudding."

It took me a moment to find where it had been shoved to the back of the highest shelf. Meanwhile, Nick made an icepack for the massive bruise on Alex's shin—the reason he hadn't run when others in the park did. I resisted asking about the bruise or why the twins began whispering "Sorry, sorry, so sorry" as soon as Alex came in the front door.

After the kettle whistled, loud enough to rouse half the underworld, Nick brought the twins mugs of mint tea. Alex and I got brandy, lemon, and honey in hot water. Nick poured himself a couple of sips of straight brandy in an old jelly jar.

Ramona frowned. "Aren't you supposed to set an example, Mr. Lawrence? Be law abiding and everything? Alex is a minor."

"Think of me," Nick said, "as your great-aunt offering a cordial to revive essential spirits in trying times." He sipped from the jelly jar. "It's not the first time I've dealt with that arresting officer. He has a hard-on for busting kids in the park. That's why,

I will bet, his car was so near the duck pond when that noise complaint was called in."

Alex said, "The cops kept harassing me about weed, even after I turned out my pockets."

Nick waved a finger. "You don't have to tell them anything except your name. Keep your hands in clear sight. Don't make sudden moves. You don't have to agree to be searched. Just say, 'Am I being arrested? If so, I want an attorney. If not, I want to leave now.'"

Molly and Ramona nodded as they listened to Nick.

Alex shook his head. "I'm never getting stopped by the cops again. That was enough."

"You should be so lucky," Nick said. "But I have questions. First, about that bruise. It must hurt like the dickens. Were you injured before the cops showed up?"

"Yes." Alex dipped his head, looking timid again, which I hadn't seen for a month. "Quinn and I were playing hacky sack by the duck pond and…I got kicked."

The pause was *not* so Alex could sip his weak still-too-hot toddy. The whole story lay in that pause.

"What about the wire-cutters?" Nick asked. "And the commotion that brought the cops? Why did people flee into the bushes? Why didn't you run too, Alex?"

"He couldn't run," Molly said.

Ramona said, "If I knew he couldn't run, I'd have stayed with him." She nudged Molly. I think I wasn't meant to see it.

Nick, the only person who could sip his drink since it wasn't steaming hot, tilted the jelly jar and watched the brandy run down the sides. "I want to know more about the wire-cutters."

The latest generation of Eliot kinder offered no answer.

"It's too obvious." Exhausted, I wanted everyone let off the hook. However, I resented that Alex had been left behind. "The cops interrupted a plan to release that pathetic eagle in the menagerie. I've wished I could do it every time I run past it."

Ramona nodded. Molly remained stone faced. Alex got busy giving himself a brandy-steam facial.

"And the bruise?" Nick prompted. "It looks like more than a hacky sack injury. Hacky sack is a sort of pacifist dexterity activity, not a full-contact body sport."

"Alex didn't want—" Ramona began.

Molly tossed a Medusa-like glare that stopped her twin from speaking.

"Which of you here," Nick asked, "was on the 'let's free the eagle' team? And who belonged with the hacky sack pacifists?"

All three kids bent their heads.

"That's not the question," I said. "The two questions are simple. Who kicked Alex? And who left him behind with the wire-cutters?" While I drank half my toddy, no one spoke. "I suppose there's no use asking those questions, because none of you will ever narc on your friends."

The three visually relaxed, but I wasn't done.

"Go to bed, all of you. I expect breakfast in the morning. And I expect to be reassured that you'll collaborate to gain complete respect for Alex from your so-called friends."

Ramona said, "Acquaintances, not friends."

Alex shook Nick's hand and thanked him before going to his basement studio. Nick and I were left alone at the Chaos table.

"They're so lucky to have you," Nick said, not for the first time since he'd begun using the law to intercede on my behalf. I, however, was still too shaken to accept accolades.

"You can't measure how scared I was while I waited for you. Both for Alex and for next Monday's call."

"Yeah." Nick accepted the depth of that statement. "And from what I can tell, Alex doesn't know how crucial Monday is for his future."

"He knows that this incident might become important." I'd seen how pale Alex was when he emerged from the back of the cop shop. And how it had taken all of that weak toddy to wash the fear from his eyes. "I'm not about to torture any of them with warnings. This isn't a problem he created."

"But the bruise?" Nick raised his brows. "Wouldn't you like to see a morsel of retribution for that?"

"Secretly, yeah. But I'd like to find ways to stop bullies without using physical violence. If only there were metaphysical weapons that could be applied."

Nick eyed me over his jelly jar. "I bet you were bullied."

"Yeah." Let me count the ways. "You?"

"No. I was one of the players who hung back, behind the bully. To my shame." He downed the last of the brandy. "Maybe that's why I chose a career that put me more on the side of justice."

—

Sunday morning, Quinn showed up for chocolate chip pancakes. Every House resident was present, so the kitchen bustled, and the Saturday night story had to be told and exclaimed over.

I sat at the far end of the table and drank coffee, listening. I had my own tragic story from Saturday, but it wasn't the kind that might hold interest for people at the Chaos kitchen table.

Then Jade and Timothy came in for breakfast. Jade gripped my shoulder when he sat on the bench beside me. "Sasha! Kevin said your dissertation was plagiarized. What will you do?"

That caught Becca's attention. She was sitting by me, which made it feel like she was in my face. "Plagiarized? Like, someone copied your work?"

"Worse." Time to practice telling this story. "A thief in Hong Kong published an earlier draft under a false copyright."

I reached across Timothy to pass the plate of pancakes to Jade. Timothy reached for it, caught himself, and put his hands in his lap. Molly slipped a plate of scrambled eggs and a protein bar in front of Timothy. We'd heard every Sunday for a month that Timothy doesn't eat pancakes.

"That's horrendous. What will you do?" Becca voiced outrage. I hadn't gotten that far. The grief from the day before had subsided into a sadness in my heart and lungs. Funny how an hour waiting on the police can numb one's response to an earlier tragedy.

"I withdrew my submission. I had to finish my PhD by mid-December. There isn't time to prove my dissertation is my original work. So, no PhD for me. Which also means I don't have a teaching job lined up for next year."

"*Kaukau!*" Molly cried. I didn't know the people at the other end of the table were listening. "But your defense!"

I shrugged. "I requested a refund on my ticket to Seattle. Tomorrow I'll get my tuition refunded. I'll be here Saturday for your SATs, so I can make waffles and cocoa for breakfast."

"But gosh, Sasha! You own the copyright!" Jade exclaimed. Gaye said something similar but without the minced oath that freezes my brain whenever I hear it coming out of Jade's mouth.

"Kevin thinks I should copyright it in the U.S. and publish chapters as monographs or separate books. And to just forget the PhD. I'm mostly convinced that he's right. I've already consulted with my advisor. We agreed that I should withdraw it."

That whole thing with Dr. Randolph saying I should have kept it to myself…no use repeating it. Ever.

"I can't imagine what you're feeling." Becca's vehement declaration sent a nice, warm feeling through my middle. She wrapped her arm around my shoulder. Then Jade reached around Timothy to grab the knob of my other shoulder, which sent a two-bell alarm from my middle down to my knees. I wanted to shrug them both off. The rattled, rasping crystals in my chest had to handle unfamiliar consolation. Although the Heavenly Immortals had cast me into the underworld, the people who know me best offered honest comfort. I can live with this.

After breakfast, when the adult boarders had left, Quinn produced an Atari console from his backpack, and Alex hooked it up to the TV in the living room. Yes, the kids have handheld games that they got last Christmas, but there's no console in the house. This had been a mutual decision. It's not like we're out in the country, where lack of a game console might be a deprivation. It's a social activity, and there's enough society here without introducing a game console. I host rehearsals in my garage and regularly feed a chunk of the neighborhood. Other adults can host a game arcade at their houses.

Quinn and Alex had previously invited me to play, but only because I always lose, no matter how much I'm coached. It's similar to school life in Hong Kong, where I wasn't good at sports with scores. Alex had complained last summer that my inadequacy was embarrassing: *You should be able to play. You're good at math!*

I can also type quite well. But the stress in a game undoes me.

"I'm pretty good at pinball," I said, recalling Saturdays at arcades with Kai.

"Were once good," Molly said. "Past tense. Not sure they have those anymore, even in Hong Kong."

"We'll find out when we get there," Ramona said.

Yes, we will. Whether or not I secured a job, we were still going to visit Hong Kong come spring.

After Saturday's travails, that Sunday morning felt good. *Caverns of War. Space Invaders. Yar's Revenge* is the one game where I make a decent showing. Any observer might notice that the kids enjoyed defeating me at every turn.

Ramona and Molly disappeared upstairs after an hour, which I took as more evidence that they were speaking to each other again. I felt a small portion of my residual tension dissipate. I needed fewer things to worry about, not more.

I got up to make lunch, promising people toasted cheese sandwiches and tomato soup, as if everyone besides me required my best comfort food. I'd flipped two griddles' worth of cheese sandwiches when someone knocked at the front door. Alex got up to answer.

It was Zachary Helman, Molly's steady boyfriend.

Alex sank back down on the sofa with his game controller. He'd left the door open but offered no invitation to enter.

Quinn got up and stood in front of the door, his arms crossed, his stance wide, a definite "None shall pass" posture, but without the humor the Black Knight provokes.

Being the tallest of any kids who frequent the house, Zachary called out over Quinn's head, "Can you tell Molly I'm here?"

I called up the stairs, as if I were the head resident of a dorm, "Molly, you have a visitor," then went to flip my batch of sandwiches before the edges turned black, which Ramona really dislikes, even if I scrape off the burned parts.

Quinn returned to the sofa, and neither he nor Alex looked up from their game.

The girls stomped downstairs in their outrageously expensive basketball shoes. Ramona came first so that Molly didn't appear until they reached the bottom of the stairs. Molly's hair, no longer in woodsy-girl braids, stood in a spiky brush cut dyed an unnatural black. She wore baggy jeans and a Social Distortion *Mommy's Little Monster* t-shirt that I'd never seen before.

Zachary raised his hand in greeting. Hesitant.

Molly also took an obstructing stance. "Why are you here?"

"We were going to hang today."

"I don't think so."

"I…I…" He shuffled, uncertain.

I flipped sandwiches onto plates and cut them into triangles.

"How dare you come to my house?" Molly is too small for her voice to be called a growl, but it was an animal-like snarl. "You know my creed. Honesty. Justice. Loyalty. You…you are…"

Molly fumed for a second.

Ramona finished the accusation. "A betrayer. Without honor among men."

Zachary stood there, not answering, faced with two Furies.

"Lunch is served!" I called, ladling tomato soup into bowls.

The game on the screen immediately blacked out. The kids headed for the kitchen table. Quinn shut the front door as he passed. Zachary didn't step back from the doorway fast enough, so Quinn shoved it closed with his shoulder.

I served up soup all around. "I like your hair, Molly. You have a perfectly shaped head for it."

Ramona said, "I agree. It's A-plus perfect."

Alex said, "If it was me, I'd worry that everyone would write me off as a punk wannabee."

"That's still your main problem," Molly said. "Stop worrying about what people think of you."

I delivered lunch for Ruby and her weekend caretaker. When I returned, the kids were nearly done with their sandwiches. I asked if anyone wanted to join me at the mural site for the afternoon. "I'm sure Jade will be working today."

"We're playing music," Alex said. "The garage is free."

Quinn nodded.

"I have a history project due," Ramona said.

"And I owe an English paper," Molly said, "since we don't have midterms in that class."

Gotta *love* administrative academic planning. Midterm tests and papers due the same week as SAT tests. If kids aren't anxious enough in everyday life, might was well crank it up artificially.

I went to the site, where I mixed cement and carried boxes of tiles on demand. Half the crew showed up that afternoon. My kids did come for the last couple of hours of good daylight.

Jade hadn't sought a conversation at breakfast and didn't seek to talk on the work site. In fact, Becca and the Festival's PR crew had him so busy with a photoshoot and filming an interview that he had little time to supervise his crew. The mural was supposed to be done at the end of the week. A celebratory event was planned for donors and community leaders. During the photoshoot, Jade appeared as the same person I'd known in Seattle, who didn't care how he appeared on camera, though he was polite when the Festival makeup artist stopped the filming to fix the shine on his face or to make his hair do something it didn't want to do.

Speaking of someone who didn't worry about what people think, Molly, in her new spiky hair and aggressive black t-shirt, was ignored by the filming crew. She didn't care. And since the film crew was avoiding her, I hung around her work area whenever I could, so the cameras didn't catch me either.

For dinner, I made stuffed buns, half with curried veggies and half with shredded beef. I'd made *tangzhong* slurry as the starter for buns after breakfast. I use less sugar than any buns we ate in Hong Kong, but sweet enough that the Hong Kong math freaks at Fermat's Last House ate their fill, though they always had to comment that their mothers' were better.

Alex made a salad, and Ramona made brownies. After dinner, we watched *Archie Bunker* while Molly made rude comments and we ate the brownies with frosting from a can. The kids went to their rooms to work on their term projects, and I finished my condoling letter to Chan-suk, plus a generously polite letter of gratitude to his brother-in-law to decline his assistance at the university.

I was thinking that we had to put a rough weekend to rest in decent style. Then Alex appeared.

"*Suksuk,* will you check my math homework? I'm not sure I got problem five right."

—

While I checked Alex's math homework (which had no errors), he flipped open his sketchbook and took up his pencil. It looked like the multi-page comic he'd worked on all summer.

"Did you start a new story?" I asked.

"A new chapter," he said. "I have a new sketchbook."

The same brand, I noticed for a second time, that Jade always carries. In my Adolescent Psych class, we discussed how teens imitate others' behaviors while seeking their own. Not my business.

"Whenever you feel it's ready," I said, "I'd like to see your art. If that's okay."

"It's just a comic. It's not, like, art."

"I beg to differ. Part of my dissertation is about old stories being told in new comics. I believe comics are in fact art."

"Really?" He tilted his head at that notion. "I started making up stories after I found an old comic that belonged to my dad. My story is called *Skate Monkey*. He carries a steel string from a guitar player he admires and uses it to play a magical chord."

"Did your dad save one of the *Journey to the West* comics?"

"Yes! You know it?"

"I have a complete collection up to 1980. Do you want them?"

Where did that impulse come from? Giving away my most cherished treasures?

"Choice!" He jumped up, knocking over my empty teacup. "Yes, I do!"

"The answers on your math handout are all fine. Next, we'll work on your self-confidence."

He nodded, still shining with excitement. "I couldn't concentrate tonight. Don't know what's wrong." He picked up the homework sheet. "Is it too much trouble to look at your comics now?"

"I will never stand in the way of an ambitious artist."

Halfway to the top floor, I heard what I'd just said.

Alex sat at my desk to choose which comics to carry away immediately. He gave me his sketchbook to look at. I sat on the chest that contains every draft of my dissertation and printouts of microfilm research papers.

In Alex's sketchbook, I saw that the Heavenly Immortals had decreed that the Monkey King must take up skateboarding.

36: The Middle Child

COME MONDAY MORNING, AFTER EVERYONE was out the door, I was so nervous I couldn't correctly dial the string of numbers for the conference call. It took four tries, so I was a minute late.

The first words I heard were from Claudia.

"As I've attested, Rik Eliot cannot be relied upon to perform his duties, most certainly not in a timely way."

"When—" I began, but Nick coughed twice, his signal to prevent me from manifesting ire. "Hello, Claudia. I hope you are well."

I greeted the two attorneys that I'd been warned would join the call. The only surprise was Claudia's live participation.

Nick spoke in the lawyer voice he'd used on Saturday night. "Let me repeat for Rik what has been said in the sixty seconds since we began the call. Claudia and Wendy intend to ask the courts to reject Alex's plea to be placed under Rik Eliot's guardianship. They also wish to repeal the guardianships Mr. Eliot holds for Ruby Eliot and for Wendy Eliot's twins, Molly and Ramona."

Wendy? I drew a breath. What the hell? How could my sister have turned against me?

Nick coughed twice, then continued. "You want the court to appoint a guardian ad litem. I suppose that is to evaluate the need to place Rik's mother in a care home and administer all financial and care arrangements."

I sucked in enough air to empty half the living room while I paced, the yellow phone at my ear. "That would undo all we've agreed on. My arrangements have worked well to ensure that Ruby is cared for and her funds protected. Why undo that?"

"Mrs. Eliot seeks—" Her attorney tried to speak, but Claudia interrupted. Her voice sounded rougher than usual. More cigarettes as well as more tension.

"I've spoken extensively with my sister-in-law Wendy, and we have agreed on two things."

"How is Wendy?" I can be pleasant under duress. I began practicing early in life. "Still at the Big Sur commune with the disciples of the Ascended Masters?"

Claudia didn't answer, just continued on with what must have been a prepared speech. "First, we don't agree with Rik Eliot's selfish plan to force Ruby into a warehouse for old people. We will be seeking a formal accounting of where Ruby's money has gone. And we intend to challenge all of Rik Eliot's actions as Ruby Eliot's legal guardian. He has been accountable to no one while making decisions for her."

Throughout Claudia's tirade, she referred to me solely in the third person. I wanted to be heard. "How exactly does that help Ruby? Neither you nor Wendy has been involved in her care for five minutes over the past eight years."

Nick coughed twice, so I stopped. He said, "I will interject here that Wendy and Claudia have been invited to discuss every crucial decision Mr. Eliot has made, though neither has any legal position with regard to Ruby Eliot's affairs. We have all correspondence about Ruby Eliot's care and annual financial accounting, which will show that social security is her only income."

I thought Nick was being paranoid when he'd sent all decisions on his letterhead to Claudia and Wendy via registered mail. But he'd prepared for this from the start.

"Okay, Claudia." I still sounded pleasant. "What's the second agreement you two enlightened beings have reached?"

"Wendy Eliot and I agree," her voice shifted one tone lower, "that Rik Eliot is not a fit person to have charge of our children. He doesn't even have a job."

"I teach full time, Claudia. That's a real job. And what does 'fit person' mean?" I struggled to keep any sting out of my voice, while feeling she'd just injected icy shards into my veins. Shards named Wendy. Who would never—

Claudia snarled in response. "Our children must not be exposed to the perverse elements of Rik Eliot's inclinations. We will ask the courts to return our children to our care."

Nick kept coughing, so I didn't answer while Claudia talked about my imagined inadequacies and her intended protective legal course. I foresaw my savings draining off into attorneys' fees. And a daily struggle to keep the kids out of the whole mess.

Her voice deepened. "We are petitioning the court to appoint a guardian ad litem to inspect the house where our children are living. Given that Rik Eliot himself calls it Chaos House, we expect to prove that Mr. Eliot has been derelict as a guardian."

"Your attorneys have documents proving Alex's wellbeing and current academic successes." Nick was coughing for my benefit, so I took a breath. "My grandfather named Chaos House after his bestselling book. You'd know that if you were actually—"

Someone knocked on the front door, which meant it was not—bless the Heavenly Immortals—my Disputatious Neighbor, since he only goes to the back door.

"Hold on, please."

I pressed the receiver against my thigh to muffle it while I answered the door.

—

"Hi, Sasha."

Unaccountable fear flooded through me.

"What's wrong?" My twisted greeting held the panic I'd hidden from Claudia. My hands shook with residual adrenalin.

Jade looked fine. He always looks fine.

"Yes. No. I might be catching the cold everyone has. Though I'm not sure yet."

"Is there a problem in the cottages?"

"Are you free? We need to talk—"

"Can it wait? I'm on a long-distance call." My voice broke into all the pieces Claudia had cracked loose. And I didn't, just then, give a flying frig-all about rent or who lives in the damned cottages. "I'm dealing with a family situation right now. Then I have classes to teach."

Jade could see right past me, into an empty house that held no visible sign of crisis.

"Uh, okay. Another time? Let me know."

"I don't know when. Breakfast tomorrow maybe?"

Dangling the yellow phone, I could scarcely clock the surprise on Jade's face as I closed the door on what felt like years of secretly hoping we could just talk. There was neither time nor space for it. One more thing I can't have.

I put the receiver to my ear as Claudia said, "After today, we will communicate only through our attorneys."

I listened to the click on her end, wondering if my brother Christopher had lived long enough to learn that his wife knew how to use the pointed toes of her high-heeled shoes to kick the life out of you, inflicting as much pain as possible. However, I'd lived with maternal unkindness. I will die and continue as a ghost haunting from the underworld before I let any of those kids experience even five minutes of maternal vituperation.

The many clicks of people hanging up on the call were followed by a dial tone. I banged the phone onto the receiver on the kitchen wall. It rang again immediately.

Nick didn't bother with hello. "They want to destroy everything you've achieved."

"Not 'they.' Just Claudia." I can't believe it's Wendy too.

"Whatever Claudia does, our strategy will protect Alex."

"Yes. Strategy." I was numb. My shaking right hand hung in the air, The left clutched the receiver, white knuckled.

"Chet says—"

"Who's Chet?"

"My old roommate," Nick said. "He's filing your petition for guardianship in California. He says it's common in these conflicts to prove the other party is an unfit parent."

"What the...no, Nick. Never. That's essentially saying, 'You are a bad person.' I won't do that." It's what Ruby yelled at Wendy, even when we lived in Hong Kong.

"I already told Chet you'd say that." Nick said more, but I couldn't follow.

So I interrupted.

"I don't think of myself as perverse." I wanted to cover my ears, because I kept hearing it while Nick was talking about...I don't know what.

"You're not, Rik. And we will officially warn her attorneys to keep such language out of all proceedings. Shall we discuss our strategy this afternoon? Are you okay until then?"

"Yeah. Have to go. I have a class in twenty minutes."

First, though, I dialed Wendy's number, which she'd given me only after a warning to call only in a dire emergency.

This was fucking dire.

I didn't know what I'd say besides *What the hell, Wendy?* I couldn't remember ever being so angry with her. I slipped into Cantonese dialect, chanting. *Even the Buddha is inflamed.*

It rang twenty times before I gave up.

Then I headed out the back door since I needed to get to class on time. But there was my nemesis, Willie Smith, one hand up to knock on the screen door, the other wrapped around the belly of his softly growling chihuahua.

—

The dog bared its teeth at me, a low rumble in its throat, though this was my porch. It's an old dog, so I could smell it without taking a step closer.

"Richard—"

"It's Rik. My name is Rik."

That flew past him, didn't cause a blink.

"I want you to be the first to know, Richard. I asked Ruby to marry me. And she has accepted, bless her kindly heart."

I'd be astonished, except at that moment I only saw Claudia's angry face in my imagination. Willie rushed on, with no sense that he was intruding.

"We think Thanksgiving will be the perfect day. We'll gather to praise the Almighty for this new blessing. Ruby and I think—"

"Stop, Willie. Mr. Smith. You cannot marry my mother."

"Now, I understand your feelings, Ricky, since you've had Ruby to yourself for so long. But she—"

"It's Rik. Not Ricky. I cannot let you do that."

"Ruby says you always have to get your own way. But she's entitled to live her own life and find her own happiness."

"She has severe dementia. And I am her legal guardian."

"I can relieve you of that burden. I'll be her guardian."

"No. I cannot allow it. I mean no unkindness, Willie. But it cannot be. You may continue to visit, to be her friend." And eat my food at lunchtime. "But you must cease this talk of marriage. I don't want you to upset her."

He abruptly turned away from me, but then sat at the patio table where he often ate lunch with Ruby. He folded his hands, resting them over his chihuahua, and began to recite aloud the Serenity Prayer, looking up every few words to see whether I watched. He repeated amen twice at the end.

I wanted to say more, like: she has no money; her last lover took all of hers *and* mine. But I didn't say it. Willie is too much of a sad sack to be scheming. Rather, he likely has the misfortune to believe in true love.

From the steps, I called back into the house.

"Mrs. Adams, please keep my mother inside today. It's too chilly, even with the afghan over her. Leave a message at the school office if you need my help."

I wanted to make a flourishing exit, but of course my old Datsun needed a tune-up, and it took a great deal of coaxing to get the engine to turn over so that I could, at last, escape to the riotous sanctuary of my third-period math class.

37: A Path Diverges

ON MY AFTERNOON PHONE CALL with Nick, I choked on aged tobacco smoke in the faculty lounge and listened to him repeat that we had all contingencies covered in our strategy. I could barely croak my sole question, given the ancient cigarette smoke curling down my throat.

"The perverse elements of my inclinations?"

"C'mon, Rik. If Claudia hires an investigator, there's no one in Ashland who'll offer up such fictitious slander. You're the most innocent guy in Jackson County. And her attorneys know I will counter with a defamation suit. Are you listening to me? Tell me that you understand not to worry."

"I understand."

Except there's an annoying and vengeful Festival director living in one of my guest cottages. Who knows what he'd say if anyone asked.

I still wanted to talk to Wendy, but I couldn't be calling Big Sur from the faculty lounge.

When I went to Monday afternoon's mural work, the wind blew harder and colder than we were used to. I kept glancing over my shoulder, foolishly checking for who might be assessing my perversity. Unlike Sunday's work session, Jade glanced my way every time he came into my line of sight.

After the mural work, there was no time for a brief run between dropping math papers at Sally's house and getting home in time for dinner. Instead, I kept repeating one reminder that hadn't made it onto this week's list: talk to the women's collective on

Oak Street to schedule a tune-up for my Datsun. Anything else that might be allowed to enter my thoughts would feel like a case of poison oak.

Dinner Monday night was fried noodles and Cantonese-style scrambled eggs. I made broccoli the way I usually do, with garlic and ginger. Ramona made lemon poppy seed muffins for dessert. We had four extra kids from the mural crew, and our guests again raised the issue of how much to cram for Saturday's SAT event. Ramona passionately pleaded that they required only rest and adequate nutrition. One of the kids complained about the geeky math tutor his mother had hired for SAT prep.

I'd been silent through dinner, but I tried to join in. "I must take umbrage at that. I was a geeky math tutor in college. I protest your prejudice against our kind."

Everyone laughed.

"You laugh." I pointed my chopsticks around the table. "All my geek-taught tutees scored above average on their SATs."

"When did you turn out to be cool, Mr. E?" Quinn asked.

"He never did," Molly said. "He's still a math teacher. And still geeky."

Ramona said, "A geek is a circus freak who bites the heads off chickens. Uncle Rik is a math freak who fries chicken in a wok."

"We are the only circus he has," Molly said.

When the phone rang, I answered immediately. It makes me jump every time it rings. The caller's voice was unmistakable.

"Hi. Just a second."

I walked from the kitchen to the far edge of the living room, stretching the coiled yellow cord, then opening the front door and stepping onto the porch, dragging the door mostly shut behind me. The brisk wind caught my hair, so it stood on end.

"Hi, Wendy. How are you? Hope you're well."

Animals bleated on the other side of the call. I shared that sense of wanting to complain.

Wendy was calling from her Big Sur collective, where the phone is in a barn that shelters goats in bad weather, plus a pair of horses, the collective's recreational vehicles.

"Um, hi, Ricky. Claudia told me you talked today."

"Talked? It was only Claudia ranting." I'd been building up a rant all day.

"Yeah," Wendy said. "I guessed she was upset. She talked a lot when she called me but didn't make much sense."

Though I couldn't tell whether we had a tinny connection or her voice was weak, I began the argument I hadn't had a chance to use on Claudia.

"Wendy, the girls turn eighteen in December. Don't waste money on an attorney who'll just mess things up for a few months."

"It's her attorney, not mine. Claudia keeps telling me that the twins would be safer here with me, learning to do chores and taking responsibility."

"Neither girl has expressed interest in chopping wood or carrying water." I spoke calmly while a Swiss clock in my head chirped *cuckoo!* "I cannot see them happily milking goats."

"Sheep too, for both wool and cheese. Our Enlightened Master says such chores strengthen the soul."

My soul cried: *Ew! Ick!*

My brain sought a rational track to run down but found only one thought: *Do not drag them into your bughouse commune.*

"Ricky, I told Claudia that you'd try to prove we're both unfit mothers and—"

"I never would!" Wait, I wanted to beg Wendy to be rational. I didn't need to defend myself.

Wendy ignored me. "So I told her that I'd better move in with her, to prove we have joined together to create the best environment for our growing children."

"Move in?" Had my sister gone completely batty?

"Yeah, and since it's getting fucking cold here in the fog, I said I should move in right away. I promised Claudia I'd be in Berkeley tomorrow with my baggage."

This call was like an unexpected dose of psychedelics. All my pent-up resentment deflated, popped like a bubble. Wendy was still Wendy. The world had not shifted so radically.

"Ricky, seriously." She laughed. The phone crackled. "She had to be in a pure panic to call me. Why would she think I'd help her be mean to you? What did you do to piss her off?"

"Alex showed up in Ashland, and I refused to send him back to Berkeley. Claudia wants to put him in military school to—"

"Scare him straight?"

"Yes. She also threatened conversion therapy."

"Hah! What a fool. What do you want, Ricky?"

"I want Alex to be safe. Claudia is so wound up, he's better off here than with her. For now at least."

"No, I mean, what do you want *me* to do? Do you want me to argue with her because you're too chicken? Like you were always too scared to argue with Ruby?" She *bawked* like a chicken.

I pressed the phone's mouthpiece against my forehead for a moment, so she couldn't hear the rasp of my breath. Of course she's right about Ruby, but not about Claudia. When I got it together, I said, "It's impossible to argue since Claudia is not in a reasonable frame of mind. Tell me what Claudia wants to do about Alex."

"She didn't mention Alex once." Wendy muffled the phone. Animal sounds and shouting voices intruded. "Claudia says you're a bad man who's queer as a clockwork orange, so it's dangerous for our kids to be with you."

I tugged on the phone cord, hoping it'd keep me anchored to a sane world.

Wendy was on a roll, however, not waiting for me. "I think she means queer like gay, not just weird. Though I suppose both are true about you, Ricky. But the part about being a bad man is definitely not true. I guess this is all my fault. Claudia panicked the first time I said that Chris was all clockwork and no orange, and that it's a mystery he married any woman, much less her. She didn't like it when I mentioned all that today."

"I've thought that might be the source of her panic about Alex. But her freak-out is not your fault."

"I'm not doing what Claudia wants. Did you think I would?"

"Uh, you mean she lied to me?"

"Do you know me at all? Or her? Of course she lied. But I don't understand. If she's all uptight about you being gay, why does she want to pull me in? I mean, she got so pissed off when I said Chris was queer. I mean, yeah, I should have kept my mouth shut then. But why try to recruit me into her bullshit now?"

"Anger can do weird things." The only explanation I had.

"Why does she think I'd ever be mad at you, Ricky? You saved the girls—and me—when I was royally fucked up. Even in Hong Kong, you covered for me when I came in late or skipped school."

"Yeah, but you're right about me being chicken. I was never brave enough to skip."

More shouts in the background. From the echoes, the phone must be in quite a large barn. Wendy's voice became wistful. "I wish I had you to cover for me now. I can trust you."

Where I stood out on the porch, the wind was chilling, given that I wore only a thin shirt. What I heard in Wendy's voice was pain and longing, like a song played on an antique instrument.

I changed the subject, back to what she'd said earlier. "Is it getting cold where you are, Wendy?"

"Yes. The Blessed Goddess knows I've been in a sweater and long-johns since the equinox." She sounded deeply sad. "It won't be warm again until summer. A long time from now."

"Wendy, our internal heating works here. It's not Mexico, but we aren't freezing in Pacific Ocean fog."

"Are you bragging, Ricky? That's just cruel."

"No, I'm tempting you."

"What?" Her voice cracked.

I had a sudden notion, like I'd experienced only with psychedelics. I knew what I should do.

"Come stay here until spring, Wendy. You can warm up. A two-room flat in the house just opened up."

Wendy remained silent for too long. I'd have to push while hoping it didn't recoil on me.

"It's big enough for you and Jophiel." Though I hoped that Jophiel, the reincarnation of an Ascended Master, might choose to stay in the chilly Big Sur back hills.

Wendy said, "We're on hiatus."

"You broke up?"

"That's not what hiatus means." She cleared her throat. "It means one person wants to break up but doesn't want to be yelled at for splitting."

Wendy's voice was filled with emotion that must be pain, which hurt me to hear, even over the phone.

I said, "All the more reason to come here, Wendy. It's hard to say 'good morning' each day when the person is right there."

Believe me. I know.

She sounded vague. "Given the rules here, I'm supposed to ask Dikshant, our Enlightened Master, for permission to be absent from the community."

Of all the names for a self-professed enlightened being to choose, why that one? And how had Wendy, the incarnation of Defiance, ended up in a situation where she had to ask permission from anyone about anything?

"Tell him your family needs you urgently. Then come where you'll be warm and comfortable." I took a big leap. "And you can tell Claudia exactly how you feel."

"Claudia can stick it up her…" She didn't finish.

"Also," I began reaching for more lures, feeling in my bones that she needed to be here, "there's a woman in Ashland who studied yoga under Desikachar in Madras. My friend Frankie sits with her and says she's a no-blame, positive-energy person who only asks as much as you feel capable of."

Take that, *Dick*-shan't. Ashland's yogini won't bully my sister.

"Madras, Oregon?"

"Madras, India." A portentous silence followed. I know better than to push her, but I did. "Do you need bus fare, Wendy? I can send you a cashier's check in the morning."

It took more coaxing. At last Wendy said yes, but that she didn't need bus fare. I'd hoped before now that I could help get Wendy somewhere better than a goat farm in the fog. This is that opportunity. The best possible action at the moment.

I said, "Good night, Wendy."

She said, "'Night, Ricky. I love you."

Just, wow.

Not what's ever said in my family.

This enormous rush of energy rose up in me, like a fighter's qi in a Hong Kong fight movie. I'd been buried under a cascade of events, and Claudia had delivered a violent blow that morning. But now, even in the tangle of Wendy's answers, I had a rational way forward. Claudia lied about having an ally—and attorneys on both sides had heard the provable falsehoods. I was even feeling optimistic that Nick wouldn't have to take depositions from everyone I know to prove I'm not a perverse piece of shit.

The only catch: I had to introduce the twins' karma-fraught mother into our everyday life, and without having consulted them. But the soonest Wendy might arrive in Ashland was next Monday, so I had plenty of time to explain everything.

—

While I talked with Wendy on the phone, the wind had picked up loose trash from the street outside the cottages. Papers drifted past Chaos House into my Disputatious Neighbor's driveway. I hung up the phone and went back outside to forestall a new conflict with the neighbor who refuses to be neighborly.

I'd gathered the blowing trash and stuffed it into the Chaos House bin, which I again firmly anchored along the farthest edge of the street. I glanced back up Water Street and noticed more paper trash stuck in the firethorn shrubs outside the cottages. I retrieved what the bushes had caught, stuffing some into my jeans pocket before my hands were too full.

When I passed Timothy's cottage on the way back to Chaos House, all the windows were open. Raised voices echoed out to the street. I'm not as good a person as I intend to be. I listened.

Timothy said, "Just forget it. Let's finish rehearsing this scene."

"How can you forget it? Are you blind?" It wasn't Jade or Xavier. It must be another actor from the Festival. "Ray Charles could see you need to report him. We all see him jumping down your throat every single day."

Timothy coughed. He'd caught the cold everyone in town had, including the actor he was rehearsing with. "My agent says I can't afford to alienate Xavier. He can help my career."

"Xavier isn't criticizing your acting," his friend said. "He's harassing you because you refused his advances. Which was brave of you. Does your agent understand that?"

"Yes. No." Timothy was silent. Then: "I didn't tell him."

"You need to tell him. Xavier is a predator," the insightful actor-friend said.

"I'm uncomfortable with saying that."

"If I can't convince you to report him to the Festival, will you listen to Jade?"

"He already tells me that every day. Like, 'Good morning, Timothy. Will you report Xavier to the Festival today?'"

"And he hasn't convinced you? You hang on Jade's every word whenever he's around," the friend said.

"This is so embarrassing," Timothy said. "Jade's cautions are embarrassing. He's being kind, but I don't want people to think I can't take care of myself. Especially Jade."

"Are you in love with him? Or is Jade in love with you?"

Timothy said, "I don't know. Maybe?" *Fercrissakes.* "He keeps saying, 'I'm so glad we're friends.'"

His insightful friend said, "That means Jade thinks *you're* in love with *him.* A guy says that when he doesn't want responsibility for your heartache."

The Immortals know it! Jade says that to me all the time.

"I've never been in love," Timothy said. "And my agent has warned me to be cautious. But I trust Jade and it feels good when he says we're friends."

"Oh good god. This is far more drama than you should allow in your life." The last I heard from Timothy's actor-friend: "Now, let's finish working on this scene."

I walked up the street to toss the last of the retrieved trash into the Chaos House bin.

It's wrong to eavesdrop. Yet my bad behavior left me with a skoosh of gratification. I don't want what I can't have. I also don't want someone else to get what I want, especially while living right down the street and eating breakfast at my table. I still don't know what's going on between Jade and Timothy, but neither does Timothy. That leaves me close enough to satisfied for now. I don't have time to fret about any other drama in the cottages.

38: The Flower Duet

AFTER TUESDAY'S SESSION AT THE mural site, the kids asked to use the car to run some errands. So I was walking home along Main Street when a rich baritone called my name.

"Rik!"

My friend Michael Lyle hailed me from the door of Chez Margot. It's curious how people magically pop up when you've been thinking of them.

"Michael!" We embraced on the steps of the café.

"Sorry to wake you from your reverie, my friend. I called your name twice."

Michael, the doctor who'd helped me when we were confirming a diagnosis for Ruby, has become one of my closest friends. He'd gotten involved with an older lover and followed him to San Francisco. We see each other a few times each year. He was last here in July with his partner, so I was surprised to see him now. But delighted, too.

"I'm waiting for Gerard to join me for dinner," Michael said. "We're only here until tomorrow morning. Come in and have a drink with me if you have the time."

I gestured to my mural work clothes—a denim shirt, black jeans splattered with cement, my raggediest tennis shoes.

"Come in." Michael tugged me by the elbow. "This is Ashland, not the Cliff House."

I did want to chat. Yet it took me a second to mentally check my list (yes, the kids would find the stew in the refrigerator when they got home) before I said, "I can stay for a few minutes."

He dragged me over to a table for four by the window, an ancient piece of glass Stephen refuses to replace, which contains so much lead that the window appears to be melting. This early on a Tuesday evening in October, only one other table held customers. Kevin was setting up drinks for a couple at the back bar. The café was redolent with the aroma of chateaubriand, butter, and garlic. Soft dinner music played, matching the glow of the wall sconces. I hadn't been aware of being chilly from the late afternoon air until the door closed and the café's comfort enfolded me. Yet when I sat down, I felt the chill through the window.

"What are you doing in town? The Festival season is over."

"Buying a house." Michael grinned, deeply happy.

"That's great news."

"Gerard has finally agreed that we should invest now if we intend to retire here. We're having dinner tonight with a real estate agent who promised to find the house of our dreams."

I was happy for him, though I remain baffled by the concept of retirement. "You and Gerard have bantered about retiring for a while now."

A flash outside the window drew Michael's attention. He pointed to the east, where the last gleam of light faded at the golden tip of Grizzly Peak. "I haven't seen exactly that light at dinner since we were here last April."

"When you talked me into an overnight backpacking trip with you and Gerard."

"I won't ever live that down." Michael laughed.

"You just wouldn't believe that the previous day's sunset wasn't a reliable weather indicator."

"Yeah, I kept saying, 'Red sky at night,' and insisting on my dreamy notion of sleeping under the stars."

"However," I poked him with my foot under the table, "I have amusing memories of the three of us shuffling positions all night to keep each other warm in my two-man tent."

"It was a hard lesson. And because of that, Gerard declared we aren't house hunting up in the Applegate Valley." He laughed at the outcome of our cold-night disaster. "He won't look any higher on the western hillside than Terrace or Granite Street."

"When is this retirement happening?"

"Gerard says five years. I'm not as sure. We'll use the house as a vacation home until then. Then we'll be fulltime neighbors. But whatever we find is sure to require work. Will you take on our home repair gigs?"

I smiled, then bit my lip. The music continued, quiet enough not to intrude, but it was getting under my skin.

"What? Wait, Rik, where did you just go? I saw your eyes flitter away. We won't be neighbors?"

"I am about to reach my financial goals for a long-planned return to Hong Kong. After the twins graduate in the spring, we'll be gone from Ashland."

"That's too bad for me, but good for you, Rik."

"Want to buy Chaos House come spring?"

"It's a bit big for us. And Gerard wants a view. And—oh, you're teasing." He touched my hand, appreciating the jest. "Well, then Rik, what are you up to in the meantime?"

"Being busy."

"Ah, hypercompetent. Your modus operandi."

I accepted Michael's tease with a modest wave. There are worse things than being super busy as a way to stay alive.

"I'm teaching math full time for a few months. And chaperoning a civic art project for a dozen high school seniors."

"All is going well then?"

"Mostly. There was a hitch last week with my dissertation."

I explained the theft and its consequences, telling the tale with humor, not letting that sensation rise, that the universe was about to crumble to pieces. The café's taped music was on repeat, but no one else noticed we were stuck in a soft, operatic loop.

"My friend Kevin helped calm me after the initial storm." I gestured to the bar where Kevin was doing bar-back tasks in advance of the evening's business. Kevin noticed me pointing, and so sent a glass of Perrier to our table with the waitress who was delivering Michael's sidecar. "He did a rather provocative job of convincing me that if I really cared about my dissertation, I'd have finished it long before now."

"Yet you had every good reason to take as long as you did," Michael said. "Your persistence through all of it has been heroic. I'm so sorry that precious work was taken from you. It would have been so much better if you'd had the choice to give it up."

He touched my hand in the way he did when we shared intimacies. I recognized the music: 'The Flower Duet' from *Lakmé*. My mother once had a 78-rpm record with songs from that opera which she played on nights when my father didn't come home.

"Look at you," I said, pleased that I didn't choke up while telling my story, "getting to the heart of things. Your special talent."

"I am sorry for your calamity. What ill fate!"

"Michael, I very much appreciate you saying that."

"You look healthy, though. Taking care of yourself, Rik? Along with everyone else?"

"Yes. It's just everyday life until spring comes." I was about to say more. The waitress came by to light the votive candle on the table, which gave me a moment to decide to skip any tale of Claudia's existential threats. (Nick insists he can take care of it.) And nothing need be said about how Jade's reappearance tore at the ligaments and tendons that kept my soul in place. (Nothing to be done about that. And Michael knows no more about Jade than any other friend I've met in Ashland.)

The candle's scent filled my nose, overwhelming the usual Chez Margot scents of the kitchen and well-oiled woodwork.

"The twins are well?" Michael tapped my hand. "This is a chance for you to brag."

"They're finishing their college applications. My nephew is also staying with us, which has been interesting."

And there was no use telling the eagle story or Alex's other challenges until a later season, when I could relate it with all the humor due such tales—that is, after time smooths the rough bits.

Michael said, "I assume your mother is still in this world, or you'd have said something. Is her care facility satisfactory?"

I began tracing whorls on the polished wood tabletop. "She's still in care at home, which is working well." I prepared to tell a tale about Ruby's boyfriend, but Michael grabbed my hand again.

So tightly, it hurt.

"Rik, no!" He looked stricken. Then he wrapped both of his hands around mine. "Didn't home care end long ago? She's surely too far gone on her journey."

Yes, I see Michael a few times a year, and no, I haven't mentioned Ruby in years. Because I knew he'd look at me like that.

I said, "She has good twenty-four–hour care." I didn't remind him that when we first knew each other, I'd explained to him why I wanted to avoid a nursing home solution. *More than an obligation, it's the foundation for cultivation of righteousness.*

I still hadn't cultivated righteousness, so I couldn't make a better claim than *we manage.*

"This is bad for you. Other people can indulge old-fashioned filial piety. But you don't owe it, Rik. You shouldn't attempt it."

Michael began massaging my hand in that tender way he has. I longed to be distracted from that comfort and began shuffling my feet over the floorboards of the café, feeling the gaps between the boards through my thin, worn Keds, the cheap ones I got three years ago at Blackbird in Medford.

Outside the window, the sky was descending into twilight, the last tip of golden rays now gone from Grizzly Peak to the east. In the evening light, Timothy had stopped beside Jade, speaking earnestly. Jade tipped his head, listening, while at the same time looking at me through the melting lead-glass window.

The crimson crystals behind my breastbone roused, began to rumble, making it hard to hear Michael.

"We talked about this years ago." While Michael was scolding me, out on the sidewalk Jade lifted his hand and rubbed his earlobe. "The kind of trauma your family has inflicted on you, over and over? It lives on in your body. It affects everything. Lovers, friendships, your sense of place in the world. Your health and well-being."

"I'm fine." If Jade would just look away.

"No, you're like a battle-shocked warrior taking grenade rounds over and over again." Michael lifted my hand and kissed it, like you kiss a child's scraped finger. "You've been braving it too long. You must stop."

"Yes, doctor."

"Don't laugh, Rik. I love you, my friend. I don't want to see you in pain."

I wanted to melt into the comfort of his healing caress, but his words pricked at my core, so that I also wanted my hand free. Yet Michael kept a firm hold. Being who he is, he must feel my unease, but he didn't notice Jade by the window, watching us.

I closed my eyes for a heartbeat's respite, saw myself like a stick caught between rock outcroppings while the creek flooded. I squeezed my eyes tight against the flood.

"Let me find you a good therapist," Michael was saying when I could hear him over the rapids rushing in my ear. "I can't help professionally since you and I are friends."

"The last therapist you found for me," I took back my hand and sipped at the Perrier, "advised that I stay out of intimate relationships for at least five years. Friendships only, he said, as if he were my AA sponsor. Otherwise, I'd be looking for a lover to provide the consolation my parents never did."

"And you took his advice, didn't you?"

"Yes." No, I didn't. I just hadn't met anyone worth being intimate with. But I didn't say that. I scuffed my Keds on the floor.

Michael smiled. "It's good advice, since anything else isn't fair to a partner." He spoke softly as he again stroked my hand.

Just as Timothy led Jade further down Main Street.

"Michael, please stop. I can manage my mother's care at home. And give me credit for being a rational creature. She's no longer causing me pain."

"Rik, please. Listen—"

Michael's partner Gerard came in at that moment, along with a well-preserved middle-aged woman whose perfectly coiffed hair declared her to be the real estate agent.

I was happy to see Gerard (not just because he interrupted an unwanted scolding). He and Michael are a matched salt-and-pepper set, though Gerard has the sunnier disposition. He grabbed me in a bear hug, then introduced me to their agent. I pleaded the need to be on my way. If I didn't get out of there, my smile might crack my face, like badly set cement.

Michael stood, reaching across the table to shake my hand in farewell. "I'll call you next week to finish our conversation."

I set off for home, wrapping my arms around my torso since I wasn't wearing a thick enough shirt to keep warm. Half of me vibrated with the rich pleasure of seeing good friends. The other half was tempted to stop off at the police station and report a hit-and-run attack by a kindly doctor with a Masters in Social Work, focused on traumatized children.

—

As I tramped through downtown, headed for Chaos House, my tired feet turned my thoughts to the basics. I should save these worn Keds for painting and house tasks. The soles are worn so thin, I'll end up wrecking my feet for running if I walk around the streets in them. My little toes were opening holes in the canvas sides of the shoes.

It lives on in your body.

I reached for any thought other than what Michael had just jammed into me while holding my hand, driving me near tears while Jade watched through the Chez Margot window.

I took a breath to shake off the discomfort Michael aroused. That breath rasped like a wheeze. My rationale—that I know my family's craziness well enough to protect myself—is incomplete.

My mother hurt me. I know it. Before she forgot me, I protected myself with physical distance. During my life as a professional student, I visited Ruby only twice.

That Specially Bad Christmas opened a divide within me, like a crevasse in a glacier. On one side, that old version of Rik was about to become a Wandering Scholar. Over here, modern-day Rik pastes reality together with lists and insists he doesn't resent fate. I force my attention away from inspecting the Bad Christmas story where those people, my own family, hurt me. On purpose. I had not done—have never done—one thing to deserve it. I'd only wanted to take off with Jade to be Wandering Scholars.

Yet on that bad night, I let them hurt my sister and hurt Jade, the one person who has never caused me pain. That's part of the wound still living in my body. I know it needs mending, but I don't believe Michael's therapist can help. It needs…what did that ceramics professor at the UW call it? Kintsugi. Golden joinery. The ancient art of repairing pottery with gold. How do I begin?

39: Duty

WHEN I DROPPED THE DAY'S math quizzes with Sally, she asked about two of her most challenging students. I offered a brief report, then begged to call later since I was late for dinner.

In the Chaos House kitchen, no one had discovered the pot of stew in the refrigerator. Instead, people had raided the snack cupboard. Since Valerie and Stephen had moved out, I'd expected only the kids at dinner, but on this night, Gaye and Becca were also making peanut butter and jelly sandwiches.

Alex called out, "Who else wants chocolate milk?"

Then a voice behind me said, "Can I join you tonight, Rik? Jade said I should ask."

I'd just seen Timothy on Main Street, but tonight must be an instance of his need for safe shelter, which Jade had asked me to accommodate.

"Please come in. Have you had dinner?" Since people had settled on PB&J, I scrambled to think what to offer a guy who's afraid of bread. "I'm making a salad, if you'll join me."

"Thank you." Timothy set his messenger bag near the door and took a place at the table, where he's been a regular at breakfast for the past month. "No croutons, please."

Fercrissakes.

Molly, unable to mind her own business, said, "We never have croutons. If you want crunch, it's got to be peanuts."

"Oh," Timothy said. "But aren't peanuts only for dessert? And baseball games?"

"Not in Hong Kong," Molly said, "which is a mysterious and wondrous world, not at all like our own world."

Timothy always looks too thin, but now he looked beleaguered. He needed more than shelter. He needed a toasted cheese sandwich and a bowl of soup.

For that matter, so did I. But first I made the salad and gave Timothy a bowl, with a bottle of rice vinegar for dressing.

Then I began making toasted cheese sandwiches. Alex and Gaye each asked for one as soon as the smell of buttered toast wafted to the table. After I set a plate of sandwiches on the table, I sat down beside Timothy to eat mine. I was halfway through my first toasted triangle when he reached for one. He glanced my way, but I was satisfied with the result of having prepared a temptation, so I looked the other way, secretly promising not to tell his agent that Timothy had eaten a piece of bread.

Ramona set out a plate of protein bars plus a dish of peanuts and a bottle of Hershey's chocolate sauce, which we all consider a reasonable weeknight dessert. Gaye and Becca adjourned to the living room and shared headphones to listen to a tape of the audio recording project they'd been working on, whispering comments to each other. The kids settled into homework. Normally, I'd begin reviewing Sally's lesson plans for the next day, seeking opportunities to insert my own mini-lessons. I rarely have to make substitutions for things I don't agree with.

But what to do with Timothy?

"Would you like tea?" I asked. "I have Darjeeling. And low-fat milk."

"If it's no trouble. Can I also join you at the table? I have my own homework."

Timothy fetched a script from his messenger bag. Ramona, of course, had an extra #2 pencil in her backpack to lend him.

What followed proved to be an amazingly peaceful half hour, given how rockily the evening had begun. I was again struck by the sense that, with the addition of Timothy, I'd taken responsibility for four adolescents. I had no sane reason to wish Timothy to perdition. However, for his own sake, I still wished him back in Los Angeles where he belongs.

Someone jiggled the front doorknob for entry and tried twice before knocking. The door isn't usually locked, but I'd thrown the latch when Timothy came in, thinking he sought safety.

I pushed the mechanism on the fifty-year-old doorknob, which sticks at the best of times, while whoever was at the door banged on the glass. The commotion drew everyone's attention, followed by audible gasps of surprise once I got the door open.

Wendy handed me a Scottish Terrier. She nodded to the duffle and rucksack she'd dropped on the porch, as if I were the bellboy.

"Hi, Ricky. I'm starved. So is Pandora. Is any dinner left?"

"Wendy! Hello. What a surprise." And I am screwed: I hadn't yet spoken to the girls about Wendy coming.

"Why? You told me to come." Wendy squinted at me. "You're teasing. That's just like you, Ricky."

The twins came over and greeted their mother. If they were surprised, they masked it. Which is about what I'd expect of them. Wendy didn't offer to embrace them, and they didn't reach out to her. Wendy did remark on Molly's newly punk hair.

"It suits you, sweetheart. Wish I had the balls to do that."

I got hung up on the notion of "sweetheart" applied to spiky Molly, who said, "Don't forget to take off your shoes, Wendy. This is the Siskiyou outpost of Hong Kong household customs."

Ramona relieved me of the dog. "Give me Pandora, *kaukau*. Before you start sneezing."

Alex said, "It's nice to see you, Aunt Wendy."

"You lovely boy. I'm happy to see you." She *was* happy. And she skipped any kind of you've-grown-so-tall comments.

"I'll fix you some supper, Wendy." I nodded toward the table. In the living room, Becca still held Gaye's hand but stared in surprise. "This Becca and Gaye. That's Timothy, who's staying in one of the cottages. Wendy is my sister."

Timothy stood, like the well-mannered boy he is, and held out his hand, murmuring a greeting.

"Hello, Timothy." Wendy smiled brightly, shaking his hand for too long, apparently mesmerized by his beauty.

Molly set out a bowl of water for Pandora. Ramona set out one of my grandmother's Blue Willow dishes and tore one of the cold cheese sandwiches into it.

"At last," Molly said, "we have a puppy."

Ramona said, "We can make Pandora a bed with that Smurf quilt Julio left."

They pointedly did not look at me. I'd have to answer to them later. I was overwhelmed at this moment, attempting to evaluate Wendy's state of being.

"I didn't expect to see you until next week, Wendy."

"Yeah, plans changed. They gave me a ride into town and community funds for bus fare. 'So long and don't forget to write' and all that." A deprecating hand gesture.

I endeavored to read between the scant lines of that answer: she'd been sent away; wasn't going back. A major rift had again opened in Wendy's life. My invitation came just as she'd needed to escape. She'd said as much, but I'd thought it was a joke.

Her delicate face was ashen with dark circles under her eyes—and not just from her bus trip north. She looked worn to the bone. She's only two years older than me but could be mistaken for much older. Her hair was fried to straw from the summer sun. Her hands were chapped and red, her knuckles too large, with several scraped raw. I diagnosed malnutrition and exhaustion. She needed a doctor.

Wendy's sleeve fell back when she drank the glass of water Alex gave her, revealing bruises on her forearm, the kind that look like fingerprints. I felt a crunch inside, but it wasn't my pestiferous crystals. My heart was breaking for my big sister.

—

Becca and Gaye escaped the house. Timothy moved from the table to take the space they'd deserted on the living room sofa. The girls were busy with Pandora. Alex carted Wendy's luggage to what was now her room, then sat at the table, pretending to do his homework.

While I toasted another sandwich and made a glass of chocolate milk, Wendy munched on a protein bar and ignored any questions that weren't about Pandora.

Howard came into the kitchen to make chamomile tea, part of his bedtime rituals for Ruby.

"Howdy, ma'am," he said when I introduced them. "Pleased to meet you. I'm getting Ruby into the mood for sleep, so it's best if you wait until tomorrow to see her."

It was a decent thing to say, but as soon as he'd gone back to Ruby's room, Wendy grabbed my arm.

"Do I have to see her?" She whispered, but I'm sure it was loud enough that the girls heard.

"No." I wanted to soothe her. "She doesn't know what's happening in the house. She won't know you're here."

"I can't." Her hands were shaking. She rubbed her bruises.

I recalled what Michael said at Chez Margot earlier: *The kind of trauma your family inflicted on you lives on in your body.* And Ruby had treated Wendy ten times worse than what I'd endured.

"C'mon, *jehje.*"

"Older sister? You haven't called me that since Hong Kong."

"Let me show you the room you can have."

I settled Wendy in Stephen's former room, which has a door to the backyard. She exclaimed, "How perfect for you, Pandora!" When she set her dog down, it sniffed in the corners, tail wagging.

I pulled Julio's abandoned Smurf blanket from the closet in the hall and folded it up to serve as a dog bed.

"Put it in the other corner, *sailou,*" Wendy called me *little brother* without shrieking it like she used to, "so there's no breeze from the door."

I complied, expecting that the dog slept with Wendy. Warmth ran through my core, hearing her call me little brother once more.

"I'm halfway through setting up the room for guest use," I said. "I put a new mattress cover on the bed and left fresh sheets and pillows." I pointed to the foot of the bed. "If you need a toothbrush, the medicine chest has one."

She shook her head. "I'm fine."

"Excuse me for a second." I went to retrieve the best quilt in the house (from my bed), plus towels for the bathroom. When I returned with the quilt, Wendy cradled the sheets as though she didn't know what to do. Likely a sign of fatigue from the long bus trip to Ashland.

"Let me help you make the bed."

"Are these brand-new sheets, Ricky?"

"No. I planned to fix up the room for you this weekend."

"They look new."

"Do not make fun of how I fold sheets. The twins insist I need therapy." As does my friend Michael.

I took the sheets from her and unfolded the bottom fitted sheet. She took the end opposite me.

"Don't we all?" she muttered. She pulled her corner in place.

"That's what my friend Michael says."

I offered a chicken-shit answer because I didn't know how to talk to her. We did, however, cooperate to get the bottom sheet smoothly in place.

"You're dying to ask, Ricky." She huffed a laugh. "I should play fair and tell you. I had to leave paradise. Master Dikshant," *ugh, cringe,* "assigned Jophiel to a new lover, a very young woman who's been Dikshant's bedmate."

"I can't imagine."

"No one else thought Dikshant was insulting me." Wendy pursed her lips. "And he denied he was insulting Jophiel."

"I thought Jophiel was a girl."

"No. He claims to be bi."

"Well, if it was me, I'd be furious." I had no experience with that kind of betrayal, but how could anyone feel anything other than rage?

"Yeah, I was mad," she said. "Mad enough to do worse than I did. I told everyone it was because Jophiel and Dikshant teamed up to hurt and insult me. But I was ready to leave."

Wendy bit her lower lip, which was chapped. I guess she was thinking about whatever had happened. I shook the top sheet free and spread it over the bed. She made no effort to tuck in the lower edge. Just as well. I like hospital corners done right. I tucked them the proper way.

"What do you think, Ricky? Dikshant says I cause turmoil because of my compulsive need to be in love. Do you agree? Can I blame all this on Ruby? I mean, why not?"

I couldn't. I wouldn't. But she wasn't waiting for an answer. Her voice pitched up to a sharper tone. "Then I yelled, 'You can suck my big toe.'" She tossed her head, laughing. "Not very creative, huh, Ricky? But then I thought I broke my toe kicking him in the gonads. I'm lucky though. It's better now."

"Wait…What?"

"I kicked Dikshant in the kneecap and then his crotch."

"You did not!"

"I did. I'm bigger than Dikshant." She grinned.

I said, "Privately, I've been calling him *Dick*-shan't."

"Good one." She laughed. "So your invitation was timely."

"But the collective gave you funds to travel?"

"Jophiel did. Out of guilt, most likely." She kept rubbing her damaged hands. "Though I bet he stole the money from me. The others only wanted me gone before the cops came."

"Cops?" No, I'd already done all the cop business I cared to for the year.

"Dikshant called the sheriff, saying he'd swear out a warrant on me for assault. His holy Enlightened Highness was so mad, he called the cops to say a woman whomped his ass. And these will fade." She rubbed the bruises on her forearms. "So I can't claim self-defense. I shouldn't, anyway, because I got the bruises from people pulling me off him."

She shook a pillow into a pillowcase, but she didn't have a good technique. I encased the other pillow more efficiently.

Wendy said, "When he called the sheriff, I decided to take his dog with me. There's no way someone like that should be keeping an innocent animal." She shook her finger, scolding an imagined Dikshant.

"That scraped finger," I pointed, "looks infected."

"I think someone bit me. It was chaotic." She laughed ruefully. "I've been living in chaos, and now I'm at Chaos House pleading gimme shelter." She began softly singing the song.

From the tiny bathroom, I retrieved the too-basic first-aid kit I'd stocked in the medicine cabinet. I sat by Wendy on the bed and applied Neosporin and a Band-Aid.

"You should see a doctor, *jehje*."

I explained alternative medicine options in town, but Wendy wasn't listening.

"*Jehje* again? You can be so freaking hilarious, Ricky. What do you call our mother?"

"Ruby."

She laughed. "Should I buck up and see her tomorrow?"

"You can. But it's highly unlikely Ruby will recognize you."

"Won't recognize me? How delightful."

"She doesn't recognize me. And since we're strangers, she's usually polite. Sometimes she's sweet."

"Then her first words to me won't be as evil as her last? I rather resent how Ruby fucked up my life, even before I asked her to introduce me to her agent. She hated me for asking, since she hadn't sold a book since 1959."

I said, "She hated all of us. For no reason."

"Brilliant deduction, Mr. Peabody, said his orphan child Sherman. Let me check the Wayback Machine. Ah, you got off easier than me by running off to Seattle and not being a writer."

"Yeah, I remember her telling Grandfather that we ruined her ability to write."

"She was never good at it. No need to blame us. But you? You left me alone when Ruby wanted to kill me." She sounded suddenly like a betrayed little girl. "But that was a long time ago."

Pandora jumped up onto Wendy's lap and stole her attention. Everything indicated that she and her dog were exhausted, so when I heard a knock on the front door, it didn't feel like desertion to say good night and leave Wendy and Pandora alone. By the time I got to the common area, Alex had answered the door.

Jade came in, kicking off his shoes and greeting everyone like he did at breakfast every day, then sat on the sofa beside Timothy. I tried to say hi like a normal person, but just wheezed. My chest closed up, like I was in a vise, Jade squeezing on one side, Wendy on the other, neither of them aware of pressing on my core being.

However, Timothy showed amazing thoughtfulness, saying, "Rik has company," and so they were soon gone.

That left just the kids, who may or may not have managed to do any homework.

"Clean up when you're done," I said. "Wendy is too tired to talk, and I have work to do."

I was taking advantage of our baseline family agreement. That is, I don't press them and they don't press me at difficult moments. Whatever needs to be said can be said later.

Fleeing upstairs, I intended to work on the easiest translation project at hand. That proved to be a worthless endeavor. Instead, I stared out the window. The wind had picked up again, shaking the trees. Beyond, the stars shone.

I'd set out to offer Wendy kindness but had taken on more than I thought. Still, I'd wanted to offer her an open hand for years, and this was my best opportunity. I will do all that's possible to ensure that everyone under my care has what they need to thrive.

As for healing my inner core, where Michael says my old trauma lives? It's up here in my third-floor garret, listening to music and wanting a man—a very specific man—that I can't have. The only action I can undertake right now is to find the bottle of antihistamine. Pandora's dander tickled my allergic nose.

Then the door to my room sprang open, banging against the dresser. The Roman narrative coaster from our UW days crashed off the box where I'd propped it and tumbled to the floor. The tape player warbled, lost its place for two seconds, then resumed playing 'Straight to Hell' from *Combat Rock.*

The three under-age Chaos House residents stood at my door.

40: Dragons, East and West

"WHAT THE HELL, UNCLE RIK? Why is Wendy here?"

Molly stood with her arms crossed, fuming. Ramona said, "Did you make some kind of deal with her?"

They were shouting over the music (I think that's why they shouted), so I clicked off the tape player.

I hoped to sound reasonable. "I planned to discuss it with you after your SAT exams, but she came earlier than I expected."

"Why is she here?" Molly never whines; her voice broke.

After a month of protecting them as intensely as I could, I explained. "Claudia is filing suit to get Alex back in her house. She asked Wendy to join her in claiming I'm not a fit guardian for Ruby or you." They looked suitably shocked. I skipped the part that shocked me, the accusation about my perverse inclinations. "When I talked to Wendy, I found out she isn't joining Claudia's BS. But she needs temporary shelter. So I asked her to come here."

Ramona towered over me. "You've been worrying about all this and didn't tell us?"

Alex uncrossed his arms, then crossed them again, as angry as I've ever seen him. "You're letting my mother do this to you when her problem is with me? That is totally unfair, Uncle Rik."

Molly said, "I told you, Alex. You have to solve this on your own. You'll have to hide out. Just suck it up about missing school."

He shook his head. "Quinn and I have figured out how I can both go to school *and* run away."

"Wait." I held up a hand to stop this conversation.

They ignored me.

Molly said, "Zachary ran away when he was sixteen and—"

"Zachary?" Ramona interrupted, spitting the name with disgust. "What life lesson do you suggest we learn from him?"

I'd forgotten about Zachary after they'd basically thrown him out of the house last Sunday. I'd recognized then that the twins' rift had disappeared with him.

"Pretend this story is about a stranger," Molly said. "The cops told his mom they couldn't do anything about it. There are too many teenage runaways to track. Unless it's a kidnapping, they leave it to the parents and don't get involved at all."

"Then how'd his parents get him back?" Alex asked.

Ramona still had her arms crossed, her head turned away out of antipathy for Zachary.

Molly said, "His folks called all his friends' parents, so no one would let him stay at their house. He went back home when it was too hard to find a place to sleep. But," she pointed heavenward, declaring a victory point, "*your* guardian won't call your friends' parents to find you, Alex."

"I most certainly will." I gently tucked her hand back to her side. "There will be no running away. It's Rik's new rule."

"But it's perfect," Molly said. "Alex won't be around for the courts to assess anything. And the cops won't look for him. So he can just live his life."

"This is preposterous." I made sweeping motions, indicating they should leave. "Nick and I have a strategy to address Claudia's ridiculous legal motions. Wendy is here, and safe. You just...go to school and keep your heads down."

"No, we are called upon to help you worry, *kaukau*." Ramona folded her hands prayerfully, one fist over the other like a monk in a kung fu movie.

Help you. That broke my heart into more pieces.

"If you guys want to worry," I managed to croak the words out, "then worry about the SAT on Saturday. Worry about helping

Jade finish the mural by Friday. Worry that you're staying up too late. You'll end up catching the Ashland head cold."

Alex persisted. "I should fight Claudia, not you, Uncle Rik."

I wasn't physically big enough to move any of them out of my room if they refused to go, except maybe Molly. All I possessed were words. And I had to, sort of, lie.

"I am your guardian. So I am the vigilant celestial dragon in Chinese legends. I am power, strength, and good fortune."

Ramona and Alex blinked. Both stepped back.

"I know dragons." Molly pursed her lips, shook her head. She'd done a tenth-grade project on the history of dragons in Asia and Europe. "Claudia is a western dragon. She breathes fire and searches for gold. We are eastern dragons. In your valiant fight, you need us."

"You," I waved my hand toward the door, "need to go to bed, then get up and go to school and do your best."

"Why can't we help?" Molly persisted.

After too long a night, I accidentally told the truth. "Because it hurts my heart that you don't believe I can take care of you."

Molly blinked, then she too stepped back.

"But Claudia…" Alex began.

"Claudia feels hurt," I said. "She hasn't found a way to deal with her pain."

"She caused it," Alex said. Rightfully so.

"Still," I said, "we have to do what we can to heal the rift. That just means doing your current job. And what is that?"

"To go to bed and get up in the morning and go to school," Ramona said. "And do our best."

"Fine," Molly said. "But it was a dirty trick, treating us like little kids who can't handle the big, bad world."

"Just pretend to let me do that until you're eighteen," I said. "I'm sentimental."

"Why did Wendy bring Pandora?" Ramona said.

"You'll be coughing all day and all night," Molly said, "Or you'll end up with an asthma attack and scare the hell out of us."

"I didn't know about Pandora. And Wendy won't stay here forever." Though I wasn't sure that was true. "I'll take antihistamines. Help make sure the dog doesn't get into my bedroom."

They shook their heads in unison, still disappointed in me.

"What*ever*." The girls managed to say it in chorus, two notes in the key of C, the mantra of adolescents' disdain.

"I believe I'm doing the right thing," I said. Protecting yet one more Eliot family member wasn't an overwhelming chore. "Pandora won't be a problem. But please give it a bath the first chance you get."

"Pandora is a girl. A her," Ramona said, "not an it."

—

Ramona and Alex left. I heard them on the stairs. Ramona's door clicked shut.

Molly still stood at my door, but her fierce defiance was gone. Her arms weren't clenched. She rubbed on the floor with her stocking foot, about to say something. She bent to pick up that narrative Roman mosaic disk, replacing it on my shelf. I waited.

"Um, about Wendy," she said, "We were just surprised. It was like two worlds colliding. And you've been so uptight lately, it's almost scary. That's why we came here."

"I understand. You want to know what's going on."

"Uh, yes. But also, no, Uncle Rik. You also need to know more about what's going on."

"It's pretty late at night for a serious talk."

"It'll only take a moment," she said. "Ramona and I have been seeing Wendy whenever we visit Alex in Berkeley. We eat lunch and go to a museum. Or take a long walk in Golden Gate Park."

"Oh. When did this start?" Plus a thousand more questions.

"The summer before sophomore year. Wendy called us at Alex's house and asked to meet. She wanted to get to know us."

"And you also got to know her. That's good." I silently pondered that trip to Berkeley, which ended when they'd met me at SFO Departures and helped insult Xavier.

"We knew a lot about her," Molly said, "because you never hid anything. Like, about where she was and what she was doing. But now we understand a whole lot better. She's funny, and she's nice. She's easy to be around."

"Yeah, she's funny," I said. "That's always been true. And she tries to be kind."

"Too bad Claudia doesn't try." Molly laughed, but quickly sobered. "Wendy says Ruby abused you. All three of you."

"Only with her tongue. Ruby never hurt us physically."

"Still, a lot of things made sense after Wendy told us about that. I'm sorry it happened to you, *kaukau*. And to Wendy."

"Don't think too much on it. It was a long time ago."

"That's what Wendy said."

"You can ask me about it if you feel you need to know more. But not tonight."

"Wendy said you tried to protect us by keeping it secret. About Ruby, I mean." She had a steady bead on me right then, shaking her head when I started to answer. "We shouldn't have kept that secret from you. But now, I'd better confess more. Those presents we bring back from Berkeley? Like the shoes and the leather coats? They're from Wendy, not Claudia." She looked for my reaction but wasn't waiting for me to answer her. "Claudia only gives us sweater sets, which we can't wear without humiliating ourselves."

They weren't expensive presents, but I'm sure Wendy never earns much above the poverty line. Ever since she came back to the U.S., she's lived in a series of chicken-shack communes. So, while not expensive gifts, those presents must have stretched her.

"Why didn't you tell me?"

I meant: *Why didn't you trust me to know?* But at the moment, this wasn't about me.

"Wendy asked us not to in case it made you unhappy. Alex helped us meet with her, so even Claudia doesn't know about it."

"I'm not unhappy at all. I'm relieved. I do wish you'd told me." I was fighting down my feelings, saving them for later, so I could just attend to what Molly needed.

"It's..." She shrugged, as if throwing off a burden. "It's something that's just ours. Private and special. Our afternoons together belong only to Ramona and me. And Wendy."

I rubbed my nose. I could blame Pandora, but it wasn't dander that was getting to me.

"It's sort of like," Molly paused, "how you never tell us about your love affairs."

"But I don't have love affairs."

"Oh I'm sorry," she said. "I shouldn't have used the word love. Crushes, maybe?"

"Yeah, I don't have those either," I said. True: the last one was ten years ago.

"When Claudia called Alex the last time, wasn't she screaming Jade's name?" Molly wasn't waiting for an answer. "Ramona thinks Jade is the dude who gave us our Christmas presents when we came to live with you. Is that right?"

"Yes. We were both in Ashland then."

"We like him—and not just because of the mural and all. Do you like him?"

"We're friends from a long time ago."

Molly nodded. "Then you know what I'm trying to say. It's just uncomfortable that our separate worlds are colliding. But now that you know about us meeting, it'll be fine that Wendy is here. Especially since she needs a safe place to be. That's what Chaos House is supposed to be, isn't it? A safe place?"

"Yeah, it is. But go to bed now, Molly. We'll talk again."

"Okay. I'm sorry if we hurt your feelings. But I'm not sorry about meeting with Wendy and getting to know her."

"You did a brave thing. You should be proud of doing that kind of karma on your own."

"It was only hard the first time we met."

I wanted to hug her, but she was hugging herself, her shoulders arched up. I just said, "You did good. I'm proud of you."

Molly rolled her eyes, but in a good way.

When she went out, she didn't close the door.

It could be said that the house was quiet, yet it felt like I was sitting atop a great sleeping beast, as if the house breathed, along with all my family sleeping in it.

I needed to sleep, but each time I dozed off, I jerked awake. There'd been too much that day. Michael upbraiding me. Or warning me? Wendy showing up too soon, in an unexpectedly rough state. Alex's runaway strategy. Molly's confession. Jade appearing, weaving in and out of the day, focused on keeping Timothy safe.

It's good I don't believe there are Heavenly Immortals. Or saints. Or bodhisattvas. Else I'd be on my knees with incense and burnt offerings and indulgences in hand, begging for an enlightened way through all this. However, I can do it without divine intervention. I am, after all, the landlord of Chaos House.

41: Secret Knowledge

WEDNESDAY MORNING AT BREAKFAST, JADE hadn't caught the local head cold, but his face and posture showed huge stress, greater than before his MFA exhibition. His voice was dull.

"The radio forecast frost across Jackson County. We can't finish if it's freezing. The face work is too delicate."

Although Timothy seemed unaffected by Jade's distress, Becca and the kids shared his worry. Becca said, "What will we do if you can't finish? The mural presentation event is Saturday afternoon. We invited the press and everyone who matters."

Molly said, "Is 'everyone who matters' only the people who gave you money? Or can we invite our friends?"

"Yeah," Ramona said. "Our friends haven't seen our work the entire time we've been slaving away."

Alex said, "We aren't slaves. We volunteered. And get credit."

Jade, however, was listening to Becca, who proposed gathering people to work that day and to work as late as possible.

"The Festival has Klieg lights," Becca said. "Our crews typically work late before opening night. We can ask everyone who worked that Sunday, plus people from our scenery crews."

Becca and Jade began calling people.

"Can we work late?" Alex asked me.

I agreed. "If you don't have homework."

We were leaving for school when Jade caught me. The others went on ahead.

"Can you be there tonight?" He was still distressed. "If we invite a bunch of new people to work, it will just be chaos."

I'd guessed the same problem. "This isn't a teaching moment. It's a team crisis. Make sure Becca only asks people who've worked under art directors."

He nodded, though still biting his lip, not de-stressed. "I can always count on you, Sasha."

Dammit, now I was stressed. We did not have an agreement that he could count on me.

"Uh, I have to go," I said. "Don't be so anxious. There might be morning frost for a couple of days, but it'll be warm enough later in the day to work. And the Festival can hold its event with a few tiles still in boxes."

He nodded but wasn't mollified.

I said, "Jade, I promise you, it's going to be okay."

Wendy appeared just then, of course.

"Hi, Timothy," she said. "What's going on?"

She didn't recognize Jade. Then again, she'd met him only on that Bad Christmas. When she'd been in extreme duress.

Pandora barked. Wendy put the dog down by the bowl of scrambled eggs the twins had set out.

"Here, Wendy." I took five dollars from my wallet. "Get some dogfood. You'll find everything you need to eat in the cupboards and the refrigerator."

She took the money without looking, and then said again to Timothy, "What's going on?"

"Beats me," he said. "I usually ask Becca. She always knows what's happening."

My day's work was calling me. I introduced Wendy to Mrs. Adams, shooed the kids out the door, and then left the rest of Chaos House to figure out their problems. I ran the day's lesson plans through my head on the walk to school, shutting out most everything else that wanted to find a place in my brain.

I can always count on you, Sasha.

—

The student crew worked its usual hours after school. Besides my kids, Quinn was the only one who obtained permission to work into the evening hours.

Stephen showed up with café food: Croque Monsieur sandwiches, which Alex and Quinn called toasted cheese. Jade was more worried about frost than sparrows, so the kids ate on site and helped advise the guest workers about what needed to be done next. Jade was so busy teaching and admonishing that his voice was hoarse, but that didn't stop him from talking; he just had to get close to whoever he was speaking to.

We had Becca, Timothy, and Stephen. Kevin called the new bartender to take his shift, so he came out to work too. Two guys and one woman from the Festival scenery workshop came. We worked until nine o'clock, when I insisted the kids go home. The others debated whether to keep working when we took off.

It wasn't freezing. In fact, the temperature couldn't be below forty-five degrees. But I'd pulled off my work gloves, and my fingers were cold by the time we walked home.

As soon as I came in the door, I phoned Quinn's mother, thanking her for letting him participate, offering to feed him dinner, and (the two boys were silently pleading beside me) suggesting that he stay the night. "I'll make sure everyone finishes their homework."

I hadn't hung up before Alex and Quinn were raiding the refrigerator to get dinner ready—just the stew I'd planned for the previous night. I had biscuit dough in the refrigerator and started a pan to bake. It wasn't unusual to have a complicated evening on a school night. And there were only three more days of site work. Then there'd be less chaos.

Neither Timothy nor Becca appeared for dinner. Stephen was probably feeding the late-hour work crew. Wendy joined us to eat dinner, then disappeared into her room, leaving Pandora with the girls while they cleaned the kitchen. Quinn and Alex went to the basement, it being too late to play music in the garage.

I dawdled over a cup of tea, considering what to prep for the next night's dinner, then decided to set the emergency pan of lasagna from the freezer to thaw in the refrigerator. With only a slight hope of doing more that night, I added hot water to my tea, cupping my hands around the heat.

I glanced out the back door to see a small mountain of laundry by the washing machine on the porch. Since that wasn't an allowed household habit, I guessed it to be Mount Wendy.

I flipped on the back porch light and began to sort. A load in the dryer needed to come into the house, so the wet load in the machine could go into the dryer. Then I stuffed another load in the washer. A sweatshirt and three pairs of jeans. I found a fourth pair of jeans in the construction-clothes-only hamper, left after I'd been out picking up garbage. I pulled everything out of its pockets and added that pair to the load.

Sneezing from laundry powder, I went back inside just as the girls went out to take Pandora for a last walk in the yard.

"Turn off the outside lights when you're done. Then go to bed. It's almost eleven o'clock."

"Sure, Uncle Rik," Molly said. "We finished in the kitchen."

Ramona said, "There's hot water for you to make fresh tea."

It beats me why I still offer obvious admonishments to those two. They're fully capable of choosing the right action.

In the kitchen, I bent to drop the scraps from my jeans pocket into the kitchen trashcan, but noticed one was a drawing, obviously one of Jade's. I pulled the crumpled paper smooth. It was a drawing for the Lear mural. When the kettle whistled, I poured hot water over an Earl Grey tea bag and sat at the kitchen table to study the picture. Black ink and oil crayons, the colors smeared where the paper had been crushed.

Like the mural, the landscape resembled a scholarly painting from the Song dynasty. The stark figures were like Daoist cultivators from an earlier dynasty, the Lear figure resembling a philosopher from an ancient painting, with long hair and wispy beard.

The two daughters, Goneril and Reagan, stood on the far left like in the mural, farther back in perspective from the Lear figure cradling Cordelia. Lear commanded the drawing, standing in the foreground but slightly to the right, positioned similar to Lazarus on the cottage wall. Unlike the mural, these figures had vivid, lifelike faces. Shocking faces.

The two daughters were Claudia and Wendy.

So Jade had recognized Wendy at breakfast, though I don't think she'd known him.

Cordelia's face was hidden in Lear's robe, but the grieving Lear was Ruby, the way she'd appeared eight years ago, before her illness cruelly destroyed her face and frame. A thin, straggly beard had been scratched in ink.

Unlike the mural, there weren't other lords or unruly knights and horses in the scene. As I studied the Lear figure, I thought I might be the cradled figure. Then I unfolded the last edge of the crumpled wad. The figure at the bottom was Edgar, the banished and disowned son who roamed the wilds in the guise of a madman called Tom o'Bedlam.

Edgar's tortured face was mine.

I stared intently enough to sear the image onto my brain, the blue and red and gray colors flashing across my lids when I closed my eyes. The person who made this drawing rents a house and garage from me. Keeps saying we're still friends. Eats at my table. And this is how he sees me? This is far beyond the chaos I predicted when he first arrived in town. How am I supposed to say good morning each day and see him smile while I know that he thinks I am a tortured but false Tom o'Bedlam? I feel...

Betrayed?

No. Seen. Exposed, though I've done everything to hide my ever-present grief, since I can't seem to just get over it.

When the girls banged open the back door and came in with Pandora, I was still trying to see what to do, but so far saw only an empty landscape and that flashing image. I have to decide how to…if I *can* live beside him every day. I crumpled the drawing into a tight ball and dropped it into the kitchen trash.

Wendy came in, cooing baby-talk at her dog. "Did the girls take you for a walk, Pan-Pan? Do you want some supper?"

Ramona said, "We already fed her."

Not listening, Wendy poured dry dog food into a metal bowl that sat right by where Pandora had her face in the water bowl. The noise startled the dog.

Pandora bolted through the open kitchen door and jumped up on the back porch screen, which tore under her slight weight, and she was gone into the night.

"I'll get her." Molly started for the door.

"No, I will." I had to move. This was the best option. "You both should be in bed."

Molly said, "Wendy, stand at the door and call her."

"Why?" my super-smart sister asked. "Ricky is looking."

"She doesn't know Uncle Rik," Molly said, hands on her hips. "She'll get lost if you don't call her."

I went out into the night, whistling the way people whistle for their dogs. At the edge of the wilderness, I called for Pandora.

From the back porch, Molly said, "Let Wendy call her. You'll just confuse her."

This arrangement with Wendy is a solution, not new, unmanageable chaos. If I keep telling myself that, I'll believe it. At least I know that, despite having notions about how fucked up I am, Wendy doesn't pity me.

—

While I searched for Wendy's dog in the undergrowth above the creek, Ramona came out onto the back steps, shaking the metal bowl of dog food. Wendy repeatedly called Pandora's name over near the hedge, so I'll have yet another note from my Disputatious Neighbor come morning.

I headed out from Chaos House straight into the narrow strip of woodlands by the creek, winding west through the undergrowth to below the cottages, thinking I heard the dog in those bushes. Loud voices echoed down from one of the guest-cottage patios to where I was whistling for Pandora.

"You're being such a little bitch. You'll fucking get me fired!" Xavier shouted.

He sounded hoarse, so it took me a second to understand what he said. A warm feeling flowed through me. I was a bad person to again be eavesdropping, but Xavier being fired sounded like good news. That warmth disappeared into my own cold anger: the twins did not need to hear vile male rage.

Another hoarse voice. "You asked for it, Xavier." The noise came from the patio in back of Timothy's cottage, the one closest to Chaos House. But it wasn't Timothy shouting. "I warned you more than once."

Jade, then.

"You went to the Guild, you bastard!" Xavier was ranting. "How dare you! My attorney won't let this stand."

"Just go away, Xavier." That was Timothy, coughing. "Leave me alone."

"You're trying to destroy my life. I will seek retribution!" Xavier shouted.

I started up from the creek, ready to demand quiet, taking the longest strides possible, with only a porch light to guide me up to the cottages.

Timothy spoke. "A gun, Xavier? Seriously?"

No! Adrenalin jangled in my hands. My heartbeat thundered. I picked up my pace, tripping over manzanita and Oregon grape. Why was Timothy not shouting?

"Is that even real?" Jade asked, his hoarse voice full of scorn. "You got it out of props, didn't you?"

I shouted, much louder than before. "Molly, Ramona! Get in the house!" I shook my hands to break up the jangle of fight chemicals running through me.

Then Pandora bolted for the open door—the wrong open door. Leaping across the Lazarus Cottage patio, she ran up to Xavier. She reared back and growled, baring her teeth.

"Scat, you rat!" Xavier kicked at her.

He missed, his backside hitting the concrete patio. Which took an edge off my fear. Pandora leapt away with a yelp.

Molly ran up close to Xavier, who was trying to leverage himself up from the concrete. She scooped up the dog. "You kicked Pandora? You beast." She stomped, barely missing Xavier's hand.

I revived my fear: *Where's the gun, Xavier?*

Wendy called from the Chaos House porch. "Who's hurting Pandora? Stop him, Ricky."

When I reached Timothy's patio, I looked for Xavier's gun. Timothy beat me to it, picking it up like it was foul trash, holding it at arm's length between two fingers. He said, "It's not real."

"Chekhov's cowboy cap gun?" Jade laughed. "What the fuck, Xavier? What are you thinking?"

So, Mr. Oh-Gosh fell into his old language under tension.

I called again. "Wendy. Ramona. Molly. Go back in the house. Take the dog inside."

"We want to—" Wendy started.

"Inside now! All of you!" I shouted. "Don't argue."

Blessedly, the Chaos House back door closed.

Jade's raspy voice drifted into the backyard. "We're leaving, Timothy. Come away with me." A door banged shut.

A good solution. If anyone could help Timothy in crisis, it was Jade, who Timothy trusts. I had no idea how to deal with that much drama. Do you offer tea if someone's been threatened with a gun? Excedrin? A splash of leftover Christmas brandy?

"Get on! We're going now!" That shout out on Oak Street carried to Timothy's patio. Then a motorcycle kicked alive with a single *braaap* and sped away, its *ring-ding* engine noise fading into the night.

Kevin? Not Jade? What the hell? Kevin left with Timothy?

Behind me, Jade's voice rumbled. "What's going on? I was working in the garage and heard shouting."

Timothy left with Kevin.

And Jade once more appears when chaos is all around me.

Yet, unexpectedly, I felt secure: *This man has my back.*

Xavier, still getting to his feet, brushed off his trousers, not looking at Jade or me. Jade stepped up beside me.

"It's not a real gun," Xavier said. "Why all this alarm?"

"*Sau pei la!*" I told Xavier to shut up, jabbing my finger at him.

He only blinked. I'd spoke in Cantonese. I pulled it together, becoming stern and unyielding. In English.

"Mr. Torres, for some hare-brained reason, you brandished a gun on my property."

"What the fuck?" the actual Jade exclaimed. "There are kids here. What the hell were you thinking, Xavier?"

"The child here," Xavier roused indignation, "was Timothy Bonham-Day, who is a despicable cock tease."

"I don't think so," Jade said. "And you don't point guns at people who choose not to be mauled and harassed by you."

Xavier, in the thin light drifting from the cottages, pouted.

Jade said, "Are you utterly unhinged, Xavier?" but didn't get an answer.

"Under house rules," I said, "you are barred from these premises, Mr. Torres."

"You can't do that!"

"I can. Gather what you need for the night. I'll send the rest of your luggage to the Festival offices in the morning."

"It wasn't a real gun." Xavier sulked. And coughed. If he gave me the cold stalking people in town, that'd be a second disaster.

"Which is the only reason I didn't call the police," I said. "I'll relieve you of the key now." I held out my hand, ignoring Jade, who hung around to watch the famous director take his final bow. "The Bard's Inn is closest, just up on Main Street. Next closest hotel is the Mark Antony."

I walked into the cottage behind Xavier. Jade was still following me. I reached past him to flick the deadbolt shut.

Xavier complained while he packed a bag. I made shooing motions to get him out the front door. Then I locked that door and stood on the cottage porch with Jade while Xavier hiked down Water Street.

My least favorite tenant wasn't out of hearing when Molly's voice from Chao House followed him down the street.

"Fuck all of that, Xavier!"

Which made me laugh.

Or maybe it was the relief after the tension of danger and a ridiculous situation dissipated. Come morning, I'd receive a strongly worded note from my Disputatious Neighbor for all the shouting and commotion. However, I wasn't about to upbraid Molly for shouting my thoughts at Xavier.

Jade again said, "What's going on?"

"The last part," I said, "was one of the most enjoyable five minutes this year. In the first part, Xavier scared the bejeezus out of me, since the kids were in the yard. In the middle, Kevin took Timothy away."

Jade listened to my recap, nodding. "We've been in town for forty-six days. Kevin is the best thing that's happened to Timothy so far. Don't you think so?"

"Maybe?" I'd had no idea about that until a few minutes earlier. "Kevin's ten years older. But Gerard is ten years older than my friend Michael, and that seems to work."

"Want to come inside and talk, Sasha? I have tea."

He smiled. I blinked. That drawing of Tom o'Bedlam flashed behind my eyes.

"*Kaukau?*" Ramona stood at the Chaos House front door. "Ruby is having a nightmare. It's freaking Wendy out."

"Thanks. I'm coming." Stepping away from Jade, I said, "Perhaps another time?" I waved good night and went inside to perform the next episode of familial duty, though still shaking off the adrenalin rushing through me.

The only fight or flight left to act on: what do I do about the remaining tenant in the cottages?

I couldn't think about that, since I had to quickly explain the drama from the cottages to the three women in the living room while on my way to relieve Danielle and coax Ruby out of a frightening nightmare.

42: No Waiting Period

AT BREAKFAST ON THURSDAY MORNING, the twins fed the dog and went out the broken screen door to walk her in the yard on a leash. Becca, Gaye, and Jade sat at the table just as Alex and Quinn emerged noisily from the basement.

Becca asked, "Where's Timothy?"

Molly led retelling the previous night's adventure.

"What the hell?" Becca said. "What was Xavier thinking?"

"We asked," I said, "but he didn't have even a thin excuse."

"I hope he's laughed out of town," Gaye said.

"Timothy and Xavier have both left the cottages, though for different reasons." I added, "Wendy can live in Xavier's former cottage. I'll fence the yard for Pandora this weekend."

Gaye said, "I saw that Timothy was hot for Kevin but I didn't know it went both ways."

Becca said, "I'll send people from the office to get Xavier's things. And I suppose I'd better wear my sternest administrator clothes today if we're going to be firing a director."

So, a typical Chaos meal, despite the waving of a prop gun the night before.

Alex turned on the radio. Jade asked him to find the weather report, which promised snow in the mountains, but still no frost in the valley.

Molly said, "Is Ashland in the mountains or the valley?"

"Will it be too cold to work on the mural this afternoon?" Alex asked, a plea, as if the weather challenge were personal.

"We'll have to see." Jade's eyes flashed my way again.

I said, "I should not have made that promise yesterday."

"I appreciated your promise," Jade said, "but I know you aren't the god of weather."

"No, he's just a celestial dragon." Molly at least covered her mouth while she laughed.

Wendy appeared, sleepily seeking coffee, then asked me if she could borrow my car. "To take care of business."

I agreed, not seeking specifics. The kids had to put up with me insisting they take heavy coats. I followed them out the door, leaving Jade, Becca, and Gaye to finish the breakfast dishes. Which was only weird because it wasn't weird anymore. Outside, the sun had supposedly risen, but the skies remained dark.

At school, the persistent thick clouds put the idea of snow in everyone's mind. Each of my math classes discussed the possible thrill of missing Friday's quiz if school closed for snow. The same script ran in each class:

> Me: It doesn't snow here in October.
>
> Student #1: Why can't it snow? Last year it snowed on the first of May.
>
> Student #2: I already had a sunburn from hanging out at Emigrant Lake.
>
> Student #3: Don't try to kill our hope, Mr. E. It's cruel.

Fifteen minutes before the end of fifth period, my remedial math class began a game in pairs, solving problems in tic-tac-toe squares. I'd simplified the game after learning that kids in remedial math typically cannot hold complicated game rules in mind. The way the game is played in my classes, every player wins points, represented by M&Ms as if they were Go stones, except edible. People lose only if they refuse to participate, which happened just once, the first time I taught the game.

I enjoyed watching them tussle over answers, pleased that these kids were getting it while noisily happy to be playing.

Fifteen minutes before the bell, a student aide knocked on the classroom door, then entered. "Mr. Eliot, there's a call for you in the attendance office."

Everyone in the room saw my alarm. It had to be a crisis since the secretary seldom pulls a teacher out of class. Usually she just sends a message for the teacher to call back when free.

"Okay, class. Do me a big favor and don't start a riot. I'll be back in a flash."

In the office, the secretary glanced up with her most severe expression, eyebrows halfway to her hairline, the creases at her mouth turned down. She pointed to the phone.

"The woman says she's your sister."

In the office, I took the phone, then turned my back, seeking privacy while certain that the secretary listens to every call, whether student or teacher.

"Wendy? What's wrong?"

"Ruby's gone." She choked. Crying?

"Mrs. Adams knows where she is. It must be Ruby's day for lunch at senior daycare."

"Mrs. Adams had to go to the drugstore and left me here. When that guy, her friend, came to visit, I took Pandora out to go pee, but she ran down by the creek and didn't come when I called. When I came back inside, they were both gone. Mrs. Adams is going to kill me."

"Call the police. I'll be home in ten minutes." It'd take fifteen minutes since I'd walked to work that morning. No, I'd run home, even in teacher shoes.

"You know I can't call the police!" Wendy hung up.

For the second time that week, I begged Jacqueline to proctor for me. "Before you dismiss this class, make them vote on how to divide the dish of sixty M&Ms so they each get the same number. They know to vote until they have a unanimous answer, but please make them vote till they get the correct answer. Here are the papers for the math game my last class expects to play today."

By the time I ran home, I was hyperventilating and 75 percent of the way to an asthma attack.

Mrs. Adams met me at the door. "This is all my fault."

"No, it's not. Don't think that."

"I wanted to call the police, but your sister insisted I don't."

Wendy yelled from her room, "Do not call the police!"

It sounded like the fearful cries from Ruby's nightmares.

"Tell me what happened." I called Mrs. Adams's attention away from Wendy's shout.

Mrs. Adams said, "Ruby was upset all morning. I wanted to give her a Valium, but the bottle was empty. I'm sorry, Mr. Eliot. I must not have given you a list last Friday. So it's my fault."

Taking Mrs. Adams by the hand, I offered comfort while repressing my own panic. I kept shaking my head at her professed guilt. I had not checked Ruby's meds on Friday. So: my fault.

"It only takes twenty minutes to drive to the Rexall and back," Mrs. Adams said. "Ruby wore herself out and fell asleep. Wendy said she'd sit with her. But I should have waited for Howard."

"It's definitely not your fault. It's Willie Smith's. How did he manage to take Ruby away?"

"Somehow he got her into the car without assistance."

I picked up the phone and dialed the police. "What kind of car is he driving?"

"Yours, Mr. Eliot. The Datsun."

Of course. Now I can't chase after them.

Wendy came into the living room, her face ash white. "This is my fault. But if you call the cops, I'll get arrested."

"No, you won't. And this isn't your fault."

"But Dikshant's warrant in California!"

"This is Oregon. The cops are *not* looking for you." I held up my hand for silence. An officer had answered my call.

"Ashland City Police."

"This is Rik Eliot. I live just over on Water Street." I shared the address while hoping that last Saturday night with Alex was forgotten. "My infirm mother has severe dementia. A neighbor snatched her from home."

He asked questions. I answered, guessing the situation.

"The man, Willie Smith, lives next door, and he took my car. I'm sure they're headed up the Green Springs Highway. He has a notion that he wants to marry my mother, so I suspect he's headed to Winnemucca."

Fleeing like Romeo and Juliet to the nearest state where there's no waiting period.

Blah, blah, blah is about what I heard on the other end of the line. I said, "She has severe health issues. They are traveling in my white Datsun." After I recited the license plate number, the desk officer said he'd notify the state police and send a city officer over for more details.

When I hung up, Jade was standing inside my front door.

"I was working in the garage," he said, "but heard Wendy shouting about the police. What's wrong? Can I help?"

All week, he shows up in the middle of everything. It splits me in two, dividing my feelings between two crises, the one right in front of me, and Jade. No, wait. Jade isn't a crisis. I repeat my mantra: *It's a good thing we're still friends.* And again I repress the image of Tom o'Bedlam.

That effing drawing might make me crazy, if it wasn't Jade who first made me crazy by rising from the dead like Lazarus and walking around amid the chaotic pieces of my life.

"Not now, Jade. You can't possibly—"

"Howdy, boss. Hey, Jade, how's it going?" Howard stood at the front door, a little early for his caretaker shift, tapping Jade's shoulder to let him inside. "What's up, boss? Surprised to see you here at this time of day."

Is Jade friends with everyone in Ashland?

With Mrs. Adams's help, and Jade listening, I told Howard about Willie fleeing with Ruby. Then I begged Mrs. Adams to go home. "I'll call you as soon as I have news." She was reluctant, but finally departed.

Howard said goodbye to Mrs. Adams, closed the door, and shook his head. "That sucker Willie told me he was at AA every day. AA, my ass. If that joker goes to meetings, it's for free coffee and cookies. Whadda we do now, boss?"

"Let's go find them." I wanted to do that so badly, I was about to run down the street.

"Good idea," Jade said. Still there, dammit.

"Can we take your car, Howard?"

"No can do, boss. I rode the bus in from Phoenix. Mine needs a tune-up in the worst way."

Which mine needed too. My heart thumped again. Could the Datsun make it over the mountains? Would the fleeing pair end up stranded in the cold?

"Rats. Can you please make cocoa for Wendy? She's upset."

"Roger wilco, boss."

Wendy was in Ruby's room, sitting on the empty bed with Ruby's quilt pulled over her shoulders. She said dully, "I was right here when he took her! It's my fault."

I sat down and wrapped her in both arms, gently rocking her. While trying to get my heart to beat in a normal way.

"It's okay to cry," I said. "I'm upset too."

"No. Crying is useless. It weakens your chakras. Leaves you dehydrated."

"But you're upset. I can see that."

"Jophiel says I'm a tragedy magnet. It's like I can't walk in the world without fucking things up."

"I don't think that's true."

"Isn't this the last straw, Ricky? You take care of Ruby when no one else will, then I come along and fuck it up. Now you'll throw me out, just like everyone else has."

"I don't blame you, Wendy. And I will never throw you out. We just have to do all we can to make sure Ruby is safe."

"Like she never did for us." Wendy rocked a bit in my arms, then sat up. "Ruby didn't know me."

"I warned you."

"She called me Xiong An."

That was our housekeeper in Hong Kong, barely five feet tall, from a Taiwanese Hakka family. Wendy is as tall as I am.

"How could she dare forget me?" Furious, Wendy wrenched the quilt tightly around her.

"*Jehje.*" I called her *sister* to get her attention. "Ruby has forgotten all she ever knew. She's insisted I'm Chris for six years."

"That's different."

Before I could ask how it was different, Howard knocked on the door. "The police are here, boss."

After he closed the door, Wendy jumped up. "I have to hide."

Instead of trying to argue with her, I said, "Go up to my room. It's going to be okay. I promise."

It's what I'd promised the kids about Claudia. It's what I'd promised Jade about the pending frost. The Heavenly Immortals know I have no right to make those promises.

Wendy scooped up Pandora and fled up the back stairs.

So if I ever regain the solace of my room, I'll have to swallow antihistamines and then wash every single thing.

—

Jade sat on the living room sofa with Howard, who explained to the two officers about Ruby's medical requirements.

"None of her meds are gone," Howard said, "Only her coat and a few clothes are missing."

I offered her picture, taken last Christmas with the girls. Her Medicare ID. Confirmed that Willie Smith did not have permission to take Ruby or use my car. Willie's address.

"It's just next door," I said. "He lives with his brother."

The two patrolmen were ready to go too quickly. At least, that's how I felt.

"What can I do?" I asked when they were halfway out the front door. "I want to help search."

"I don't advise that, Mr. Eliot. Especially since the weather is about to turn. Leave it to the state patrol. They're professionals."

Howard closed the door on them. "We'd better go look, boss. You ready? Can you borrow a car?"

I already had the phone in hand, dialing Stephen.

But no, his car was in the shop.

"We have to go to Medford to rent a car," I said.

"We can use my crummy." Jade was still there.

I folded my arms, the way one indicates refusal. Bringing Jade into Ruby's crisis felt wrong. I offered my best plea to avoid his involvement. "You have mural work."

"I can always count on you, Sasha." *Not that again!* "Let's have one time when you can count on me."

Jade took the phone from me and called the school, asking for an announcement that mural work was canceled for the day. Then he called the Festival and announced the same cancellation. He listened for a moment, then said, "You'll just have to reschedule all interviews for Saturday. Please."

"But…" I wanted to stop him. "You have to finish the mural. It's too important. And Becca says the advance PR is crucial."

"Until it isn't," Jade said. "We need to do this right now."

"He's got that right, boss." Howard asked me to make a thermos of coffee and grab food while he collected Ruby's medication, more of her clothes, and a couple of blankets. He shook his head sadly. "Asshole didn't even take her slippers."

Jade said, "We need warm clothes too. The crummy's heater overworks until it doesn't work at all. It's not predictable."

While I was in the kitchen making coffee, Jade dashed to his cottage to change into jeans, boots, and a worn sheepskin jacket. Howard asked if I had an extra sweatshirt for him, though he's a head taller and much wider than me.

"I've got one for you." Jade darted out again.

When I went upstairs to change, I had to coax Wendy out of my room, telling her what Howard and I planned.

"I should come too," she said. "Since this is my fault."

You can't argue in a crisis. Or listen to dumb stuff people say when they're upset. I used what I'd always do with the girls: calm explanations.

"No, you should stay here. Pandora wouldn't like it." I pointed to the Scottie in her arms. "The crummy is too noisy. And the kids need someone to stay with them."

Actually, the reverse: Wendy needed the kids to stay with her, though they couldn't be asked to take that responsibility. After I sent Wendy downstairs ("Howard made cocoa for you"), I called Becca at her office.

It took half a minute to explain the crisis before I made my request. "Becca, I can't leave Wendy and the kids here alone. She's pretty upset about what's happened."

Becca hesitated. "I can be there in thirty minutes."

"You don't want to do it." I heard it in her voice.

"Yeah, but I'm like you. I don't see a choice. However, it'll take me that whole thirty minutes to find a few drops of the milk of human kindness within me. I don't hold Wendy in esteem for all she's put you through."

"No, she's had a hard time and needs help. While you're here tonight, see if you can talk her into going to a doctor. I think she's been abused."

"Saint Christopher on a goat!" Becca said. "What else?"

"Maybe a lot? Ask the kids to spend the night with friends. If they stay home, there's lasagna in the refrigerator for dinner."

"Is it possible for you to stop worrying about everyone else? Let me take a turn."

Howard called. "Ready to go, boss?"

"I'll phone if we find Ruby," I said to Becca. "Or if we decide to head back tonight."

"Wait!" Becca shouted before I could hang up. "If your car's stolen, how can you chase after Ruby? Who's with you?"

"Howard. He can help calm Ruby when we find her."

"Yikes! His old beater of a pickup must be a dozen years old. And he is the worst driver in Jackson County."

"Jade's driving." I wasn't sure exactly when I'd agreed to that. "In his crummy."

"That's good." Her tone totally changed; she became her bright self. "Tell Jade to be careful on the Green Springs. It's a twisty road, even if it doesn't snow."

"Sure."

"And tell him this might be his chance."

I was saying *what!* when Becca hung up. Howard was calling me. I came downstairs with gloves, stocking cap, and my warmest coat, now stuck on a new mystery: *This might be his chance?*

—

Out on the street, the two officers were departing from my Disputatious Neighbor's house.

"Let's go." Howard nudged my shoulder.

I stood stock still in the road, staring at Lt. Col. J.J. Smith, who watched the cops leave from his gate. Without answering Howard, I went to ask my neighbor what he'd told the police.

"Mr. Smith," I've never called him Colonel and wasn't about to start, "did you know about this?"

"I just learned it." He glanced over me, as if assessing something, then rolled his eyes. He hooked his thumbs in the armholes of his navy-blue sweater vest. "I didn't know Willie had met any of you folks."

"Your brother has been visiting my mother every day since he moved here."

"He's only my half-brother. And I don't keep track of him. He and I have little to say to each other."

"What did you tell the police?" I was begging, speaking as respectfully and calmly as I always do when we encountered each other. "Are they headed to Winnemucca?"

His eyes widened. "Whyever would Willie go to Nevada?"

"He asked to marry my mother. Nevada is the closest place to go that doesn't have a waiting period."

"Marry your mother? Don't make me laugh. He's got one foot in the grave."

"My mother is ill. Your brother has put her in jeopardy."

"Maybe it will work out better for my brother than the last time a man needed something from you."

He could have just kicked me in the gut.

I wheezed. Could find no answer.

"Boss." Howard called. Twice. My Disputatious Neighbor, who hated me deep in his heart—I guess for Jade's sake—was headed into his house, not glancing back at me.

"Green Springs or bust!" Howard called.

Jade was warming up the crummy and studying a map. "Do we take Green Springs or Highway 66 like the map says?"

"They're the same." Howard's laugh thundered over the crummy's thrumming engine.

"Get in and buckle up, Sasha."

The crummy's lap belts had been bolted onto the floor, likely retrofitted in the late 1960s, both pieces oily and gritty.

Howard got in the back behind Jade. "Ondalay, pardner."

43: Green Springs: A Quest

AFTER WE PASSED EMIGRANT LAKE and began climbing up Green Springs Highway, light flakes drifted from the slate gray sky.

The crummy threatened to shake the tendons loose from our bones. It smelled like a deserted barn or a woodshop shut up too long: rust, old dirt, overbaked vinyl seat covers. Though Oregon doesn't salt its roads in winter, the pavement showed through rusted-out gaps in the crummy's floor, with road noise coming loudly through. Other gaps in the floor had been pasted over with a generation's worth of smashed cardboard beer cases and fast-food takeout bags.

Howard said, "This is like a bodice-ripper romance, where the fated couple flees through the snow to Gretna Green, pursued by an angry lord whipping his horses down the road."

"You read bodice rippers?" Jade asked, checking Howard in the rearview mirror.

"I'm omnivorous," he said. "Westerns, thrillers, mysteries, sci-fi. Romances can be pretty humorous."

"In the far future," I said, "today will be a humorous story."

"It already kinda is," Howard said. "Three guys in a crummy chasing after eloping lovers? You're the angry lord of the manor, and Jade and me are the faithful retainers."

"I'm not angry." I'd had several moments to adjust my internal turmoil once the highway began climbing into the mountains. "Just afraid for Ruby. And annoyed. I was too distracted on Monday when Willie said he wanted to marry her. I should have asked Nick to get a no-contact order."

"Who's Nick?" Howard asked.

"Nick Lawrence, my attorney."

"That jock guy at Chez Margot is a lawyer?" Jade asked.

"He's good at divorce and guardianships if you need it."

Jade glanced at me, then back at the road. "You're never at Chez Margot when I go there."

Yes, I'd struck it from the list of weekly activities when I began teaching full time. Though my real reason for avoiding the place—Timothy and Jade together—had proved spurious. Would I know better what was going on if I left the house for more than school, the mural site, and a run?

Howard said, "Where d'you suppose Gretna Green is? It must be the Reno of Britain."

"It's just over the English border in Scotland," I said.

"Winnemucca then," Howard said. "How do you know about Gretna Green, boss?"

"Accumulated miscellanea. I've got lots." *Pride and Prejudice,* Remedial Liberal Arts 501, Fall Term 1971.

A few miles above Emigrant Lake, where the highway begins to twist, Howard called from his seat behind the driver. "Hey, boss, don't be swiveling your head. You watch the right. I got the left side covered."

I focused straight ahead and to my right, repeatedly hallucinating a Datsun 510, as if I were riding in through a spooky folktale landscape where ghosts of fallen armies moved in the trees. All of them riding in white Datsuns.

Oregon Highway 66 is not the jazzy route that the hip TV guys cruised in their Corvette. It's a narrow passage between Ashland and Klamath Falls that mostly follows an old wagon trail—the kind where they had to tie wagons to trees to leverage their way down steep slopes. The Pacific Crest Trail crosses it near Milepost 15, where we left the Siskiyous and entered the Cascades.

On the right side, which I was responsible for, I studied the ditches cut along the hillsides and the slopes that dropped down the mountain sides, so steep I felt physically uneasy. This highway features way too many hairpin curves and often the edge has no shoulder and no guardrail—or no guardrail that isn't crumpled and decorated with plastic flowers memorializing a poor soul who'd missed his last turn in this lifetime. Farm tracks perpendicular to the highway, with no signposts, plunge down into the narrow valleys where homesteaders have been subsistence farming since white emigrants came a hundred years ago.

My fears for Ruby dampened any enjoyment of the ethereal beauty of the rising landscape. Plus, the vista along the highway wasn't as grand as it is on a clear day. The cloud cover was too thick to see either Mt. Ashland or Pilot Rock. But no matter. My eyes wanted to see a white Datsun 510.

I did not feel a child's joy when serious snow began falling.

Howard tapped Jade's shoulder again. "Do we have music, compadre?"

"An eight-track player. But Canned Heat is the only tape."

"Let's have that," Howard said, "while we keep a lookout and enjoy the falling snow."

Then boogie rock competed with the crummy's roaring engine and the road noise rumbling through the ravaged floor.

This crummy was built to carry twelve people up rutted logging roads. Crummies must come out of the factory already old. Has anyone ever seen a new crummy? I worked on a tree-planting crew in summer 1975, and our crummy must have first hauled railroad crews in the last century. Jade's rented crummy might be that same one that hauled our hoedad crew up narrow mountain road to hack seedling trees into steep clearcuts through all the available daylight hours. Likely that Canned Heat tape played, too. Though I don't remember it thumping on my last nerve.

The month I worked as a hoedad, we were paid by the tree (I wasn't part of a reforestation cooperative), and the crew I joined wasn't a collection of enlightened hippies. So I was harassed along with the three women on the crew. It's the hardest physical work I've ever done, and I was voted the most likely to slide fifty feet down the hill through logging slag at least once a day. What a relief when Stephen hired me to gut the greasy spoon that became Chez Margot.

Jade's crummy, an International Harvester Travelall from the Sixties, had been repainted school-bus yellow a few years ago, but without first patching the rust patches. A case of 30-weight Pennzoil sat in the back, two empty cans in a paper grocery bag. Whenever Howard commented about freezing from the breeze through the floor, Jade cranked up the heat, until we were overpowered by the smell of burning oil. Then it was back to freezing with the crummy's natural air conditioning.

While I watched the highway for a Datsun, either ahead of us in the turns or alongside the road, I kept thinking about crummies and hoedads because I couldn't bear what wanted to eat all my headspace: that today's crisis was my fault. I told Wendy it was absurd to think this was her fault. I'd reassured Mrs. Adams that she was not to blame. I'd been my usual responsible self, going to my job to earn enough to pay the caretakers' wages and feed everyone, yet it bugged me. I'd spent all these years trying to comfort my confused mother, then just like that I misplaced her.

Likely as not, my Disputatious Neighbor will scold me for that too, the same way he'd scolded me over Jade.

"Yikes!"

I hadn't meant to speak, but fear jolted through me when the right side of the road suddenly dropped off into a canyon as we rounded a curve.

"What?" Jade jerked in alarm.

"Just startled."

"Trust me," he said.

Driving the twisting highway took all of Jade's attention. The snow fell and then accumulated. It turned cold enough that the crummy shimmied on the steeper curves. You'd think the crummy's weight, vibration, and noise would assist traction. The weight did demand frequent shifting of gears while traveling uphill. The signs on the S curves usually read 30 mph or 25 mph, but the crummy had to take the curves at five miles per hour below that.

We reached the intersection with Hyatt Prairie Road, which meant we'd passed through most of the hairpin turns. At Green Springs Inn, Jade poured Pennzoil into the crankcase. Howard went inside the inn and came back with our coffee thermos refilled, plus beef jerky and a family-size bag of Fritos corn chips. I went to the payphone and used Jade's international calling card to check with the state patrol for news.

There was none.

—

"Can we talk while you're watching the road?" the voice beside me asked.

Back on the road, Jade ground the gears, seeking second. When he reached third gear, the crummy again chugged along to the beat of Canned Heat. I reached for the player's controls, pressing Off. In the back, Howard crunched corn chips.

Not talking while seated a mere eighteen inches from each other was…uncomfortable. Yet at the moment virtually everything was uncomfortable, so it might be a good time to let Jade talk, since he kept asking. And it wasn't doing any good to fret about Ruby; we were doing all we could.

If only I'd made up my mind about whether I wanted to keep living shoulder to shoulder with him residing next door. I couldn't decide between *not having* to see him every day versus *not being able* to see him. I focused on my current dominant feeling: my bones rattling while the crummy shimmied and shook along Highway 66.

I bravely said, "Becca asked me to warn you about the Green Springs Highway. But she also said to tell you that this might be your chance. What did she mean?"

"Oh gosh. Well, Sasha." Jade spoke my name, then took several moments to say more. "I've been trying to talk to you. But you've evaded me for the last week."

"Winter melon and tofu." That sounded resentful even in my own ears.

"What? Gosh, I forgot how you do that, speaking Chinese out of nowhere. Translate?"

"It means unforeseen circumstances. I didn't intend to be rude by not stopping to talk with you." I *had* been rude, but Jade had such a knack for showing up just when I was already too stretched.

"Like last weekend?" he said. "On Friday, you said you'd sleep in Saturday morning. But when I came by, you blew me off."

"Yeah, you knocked on the door just after the mailman had me sign for the news that my dissertation had been plagiarized." I sucked in a breath. I keep thinking I'm over it, but shock and grief kept finding cracks to seep through. "When you found me by the creek, I was swallowing a second dose of bitter gall, after my dissertation advisor told me to give up."

"Gosh. I wish you could—no, you couldn't have trusted me. I hadn't asked about your dissertation because it seemed private."

I waved that off. "Yeah, but discourse on Cantonese popular culture puts most people to sleep. Kevin's the only person I know who can tolerate it even in small doses."

I took a breath, then recounted the obstructions and complications each time Jade had appeared. The Monday call with Claudia prompted a lot of questions.

"Your sister-in-law Claudia? Alex's mother? I've run into her several times in New York. Her agent knows my agent."

"She only told me once about meeting you." Why must the Heavenly Immortals keep pushing Claudia deep into my story when I hardly know her? "She's suing to seize guardianship for the twins and Ruby, because I made Alex turn gay."

"Wait. What?" He whipped his head around to look at me.

"Watch the road!" I grabbed the armrest, which threatened to come off in my hand.

"Alex? Alex isn't gay." He watched intently out the windshield, a puzzled note in his voice.

"Yes, Alex. Who told me that you explained the path to gay enlightenment. Though you should have sent him to me."

He shrugged, dismissing my claim. "I hope to do better next time. What happened Monday morning?"

"I was on a conference call with all the lawyers. When you knocked on the door, Claudia had just said," I paused to recall exactly how she'd attacked me, "'Our children should not be exposed to the perverse elements of Rik Eliot's inclinations.'"

Jade grasped the crummy's huge steering wheel, his knuckles white. "Is that why Wendy showed up?"

"Sort of. Wendy called to tell me she isn't on Claudia's side, and I learned that her life's falling to pieces. She needs a boost."

"Which you always give when anyone needs it. And that's why," he slapped the steering wheel, "you had a little dog in the kitchen when I was whining about the weather forecast."

"Also on Monday," Being compulsive, I had to finish explaining my week from hell, "Willie asked to marry my mother. Then we had Xavier and the fake gun. It's been…quite a week."

"Then you aren't avoiding me, Sasha?"

Despite the jolting and noise, Howard began to snore. So I had to watch both sides of the highway. I swiveled, looking left, then right. I asked, "Do you want me to tell the truth?"

"Yes, dammit." Jade glanced over at me, frowning, then he had to pay attention to the road again.

Wound up tight as a clock over both Ruby and the crummy jolting along a slick road, I couldn't untangle the knot in my gut. But part of that knot was ordinary trepidation for how I might humiliate myself when I explain to Jade why he should move out of the cottage. Or that I wished he wouldn't move.

It had to be said.

"I feel a certain trepidation about bringing up the subject with you." There, I said it, just as we hit a major untended uplift of blacktop that made me bite my tongue. It took a moment to speak again. "I know you want to talk to me about renting the cottage after October. Or are you giving notice? My next-door neighbor says you need more space."

"Rent?" Jade's voice rose a tone. "Rent? You think I want to talk about the damn rent? That's why you're avoiding me? Are you fucking kidding me?"

There, that's Jade's vocabulary as I remember it. "What else do you and I have to talk about besides that?"

"Fuck, Sasha. I want to…" Jade swerved to avoid a ground squirrel darting across the road. "I have volunteered to be the one to beg you not to move to Hong Kong."

"What?" The crummy roared. I wasn't sure I'd heard right.

"Your friends at Chez Margot thought Becca should do it, but that made her uncomfortable. So I volunteered to do it, to save her. They agreed because they think I have no stake in the matter." He glanced at me.

I pointed insistently to the highway, directing his attention, while the crashing, crackling Dragon's Blood crystals scrambled up into my throat so I couldn't speak.

He tapped the steering wheel. "I'm asked to say that they worry you won't find good friends in Hong Kong. They very much wish that you'd remain here with your real friends."

"But...But...they..."

The roar of the crummy took over my breathing and all my major organs. I coughed.

"Goodness, Sasha. What's wrong?" He down shifted. The gears ground. The engine roared. Howard snored.

"They eat dinner with me and sit at my table late at night to talk about...things." Like love and hope. My voice sounded small in all that noise. "I've been talking about going to Hong Kong for years. No one ever hinted that they think I'm fucking up."

Well, Becca says so. But not about Hong Kong.

"Sasha, they know you're passionate about returning to where you were once happy. But since your dissertation was stolen, it's not the same. So they are worried now." He shifted down for a tight curve. "Becca says you'll insist it's not anyone else's business."

"Yes, I've warned her before." Like when she tried to talk me into dating the guests in my cottages.

He made it another half-mile down the road without speaking while I had only crummy noise and Howard's snoring to substitute for the scream I repressed.

"You should go visit first. Feel it out." Jade stared through the streaked windshield like he expected demons on the road. "Go see your master and your friend Kai."

Those crystals clotted in my throat. This was far worse than how I imagined *can we talk* might turn out.

"Sasha, your friends don't want you to run away to live with strangers in a strange land."

"Run away." I repeated the idea, mumbling the words. I'd held onto this compelling dream, my next step after the twins graduate, after I finish my PhD. "All this time, my friends were thinking my Hong Kong plan is just running away?"

"No, this is recent. They see it in a different light now, given the shakeup around your dissertation. I argued that it's too soon, too confusing to be making new plans. But they want—"

"I'm not confused." I think not. If only I could hear my own thoughts over the crummy's roar. "Why would I be confused?"

"Has it even caught up with you yet? It's only a few days since you learned about your dissertation. Kevin and Becca insist that you need to see right now that leaving Ashland would be a mistake. So I'm supposed to beg you not to move to Hong Kong."

He glanced my way, then back at the demanding highway.

"Sasha, I know your family commitment expires come spring. And since Becca says she's not going to Hong Kong with you, then doesn't that mean your thing with Becca expires too? And—"

"What thing with Becca?"

"I've been wondering just that, but Claudia said—"

"Claudia? What does she say about Becca?"

"Every time Claudia sees me in New York, she says the same thing. That you're still living with a woman, which is so very good for you and the twins."

I choked, starting to say, "Living with—"

Jade held up his hand, didn't let me finish. "Now that I've been here for forty-five days, I think Becca only has a room in Chaos House and is not your lover, even though I've seen her kiss you and say she loves you."

"Becca is obviously in love with Gaye. We're just friends."

"Yeah, I think maybe Claudia—"

"Lied to you?" When I next speak with Claudia, I'll need Nick to protect me from my outrage—if this damned crummy and what Jade kept saying didn't break my head into a hundred pieces. "What is it about me that sets Claudia off her nut?"

And what about friends who think I'm fucking up.

"Let's go back to where we started, Sasha. The part where you messed with my head, talking about the rent." Jade ground the gears on an incline. "You said you're afraid to talk with me. I find that distinctly unpleasant."

"I said I feel trepidation." All the damn day, every day. "It's because our…" I wrote a dissertation on it. Why can't I just say *friendship?* "Because the world broke into pieces and cannot go back together, I must strive to keep from being…unhappy. Since you came here, I thought…I feared—"

"You *are* afraid of me."

"No. Until last night, I thought you had a boyfriend."

"What boyfriend?" Jade glanced over at me, eyes wide.

I held my breath, and not because of the polluted, overheated interior of the crummy. How humiliating now to say, "Timothy."

"Timothy? He's barely old enough to vote. He's…" Jade tapped the steering wheel again. "Why would you think that?"

"He's beautiful. He's nice. You're always with him."

"To protect him. You let Timothy hang out at your house."

"Because you asked me to watch out for him."

The ponderosa pines and Douglas fir began to give way to juniper trees. Occasional stands of sugar pines and incense-cedars appeared. We were descending into the more arid side of the mountains, while the crummy burned enough oil to destroy anything pristine about this forest.

"Okay, Sasha. Now that we understand all about Becca and Timothy, and I've repeated what your friends wanted me to say, can you and I talk?"

"I don't know." My chest was tight again, like I'd run too fast up a too-steep hill. "I feel in my bones that there's an abyss that cannot be crossed."

"An abyss? I have waited fucking years for you to finish doing Ruby and Wendy's karma." He braked for a logging truck that entered the highway from a side road. "But it's taking forever. Kevin says he'll kick my ass if I don't fix this. Becca and Stephen say I should have fixed it weeks ago."

"Kevin? Becca? What do they—"

"They all say I have to start by apologizing."

"For what? Talking to me about going to Hong Kong?"

Jade pounded the steering wheel again. "Okay, here we go."

On the next steep hill, Jade downshifted to second, then ground the gears shifting back to third. I had that breathless sensation, pressure weighing on my chest like when a rollercoaster mounts the first rise and plunges down.

—

Jade watched the road, not turning my way, which relieved my anxiety about the road but heightened my anxiety about what he was about to say.

"I thought…no, I *believed* I was being all noble, not coming to you till now. That it's been my responsibility to make it easier for you to do what fate forced you to do. When Inez asked me to sub during her sabbatical, she said you were leaving for Hong Kong next year. I worked like a mad man all summer to push through grants so I could afford to come here, since I had to cancel and refund a bunch of contracted projects."

"You couldn't just call me?"

"No. I was a dolt, believing you had a girlfriend."

"You feared my entirely imaginary girlfriend might answer?"

"And also, I didn't know if you'd want to see me. I thought if I just appeared, it'd seem more like fate."

"Why didn't Inez tell me you were coming to Ashland?"

"I wanted to surprise you. That wasn't a good idea, was it? But I know you and—"

"Stop saying that. You say you know me, but then you say pure crazy stuff. I mean, Becca?"

That must have been the weird note in every conversation since the morning when he found me in my skunk-shirt above the wall. I clutched the dash to keep the crummy from shaking me loose and sending me off into the void.

"You didn't come talk to me either, Sasha. I wanted to give you space and to be patient until things came together. Which I thought would be…which I believe is inevitable. I mean, c'mon, Sasha. We know each other. Think how long it took us to come together the first time. You're shy and I'm half-witted."

"This is what Kevin and Becca want you to apologize for?"

"No. I mean, I *am* sorry I'm an asshole and half-witted—"

"Neither is true. I reject your apology."

"Dammit, Sasha, I'm sorry I left when you fell into a hard time." Jade's voice was nearly lost in the roar of the crummy. "I should not have let that first Fulbright pull me away."

"No, you should *not* have come back. You did what we'd planned for months after I wrote the proposal for your first Fulbright. I'm the one who bailed on the plan and…and hurt you." I stammered the last part because I'd twice been slapped upside the head by Lt. Col. J.J. Smith.

While he spoke, Jade watched the road, which was halfway comforting, because it kept us from dying in a crash. "No, not true. When your long letter came—it was so rational about how you had to do this thing—I walked around swearing and punching things. Then I sent you that inane postcard! *Que sera sera.* But I lied. And I'd forgotten how to be alone. So I wanted to believe it when Claudia told me I was a hero for staying away."

I was getting brain freeze each time I heard her name. Why had the Heavenly Immortals given Claudia a speaking part in my family's Tennessee Williams tragedy?

Jade took one hand from the steering wheel and pretended to suck on a cigarette, then imitated Claudia's cigarette rasp: "'Thank you for not luring Ricky away since he has his hands full.'"

I said, "Why is her head screwed on ass backwards? That Christmas Eve was the first time she met either of us."

"Beats me," Jade said. "I've never done her an evil turn."

After we crossed the Klamath River and came to Keno, the landscape opened onto pastures and hay fields. The highway sound came less noisily through the floor.

I said, "I'll have to thank Claudia, that she kept you from doing something nuts."

"Yeah?" Jade didn't sound convinced. "But also, Sasha, she said, 'Wendy wouldn't leave her lover for the twins. It's noble that you chose to do what's best for the girls.'"

"That's—"

"And she said you were happy, Sasha."

"Wendy left because she was seriously cracking up. And I wasn't noble. It was just my turn to do what had to be done." And I had not been happy.

"If I was noble," Jade said, "I'd have scrapped my Fulbright and come back. I wanted to. I should have."

"Chuck your Fulbright? What could you possibly do in Ashland? Make coffee mugs to sell at the Oregon Country Fair?"

"I don't know. But I'm not done apologizing for being the biggest dolt in the twentieth century."

"I remain outraged at the very idea of you discarding that Fulbright." I punched his shoulder so hard that he rubbed it, making me nervous since he needed both hands on the wheel.

"Ow, stop it, Sasha. Don't hit me for being a dolt."

"I do not accept your apology, Jade Solberg. In no possible universe should you have come back here. The adults in my family cannot manage their own lives or spin their talents into success. You can and you did."

"Then if I don't have to apologize, what do we do next, Sasha? We still know how to be friends, right? We work at the site every day. We eat breakfast together. We're already comfortable again."

"No, we are not. I can barely croak *good morning* when you sit down at the Chaos table."

"Why not? What am I missing? Why do you keep talking about the abyss and a broken world?"

"Because you're…" I was about to plunge like the crummy crossing the Cascade divide. "You are one of the most beautiful men the old gods ever made. You're kind. You're talented. And graceful. You're more like a demi-god than a man."

"Goodness," Jade said. "Gosh."

I had to count breaths. Four cycles. He kept flipping every train of thought onto a chaotic sidetrack. Worst of all: *Gosh.*

He said, "But what is all this stuff about the abyss?"

I could barely muster what to say. "All this time, the world has told me I cannot have what I want."

He banged the steering wheel with his palm, then slapped my knee, which stung. "I just now learned that what I believed was utterly wrong. You too have to accept being just plain wrong. Because we're more than just friends. C'mon, Sasha. Please say yes to a better fate."

"You just fried my brain. I need a minute." To restart my heart on a regular rhythm.

It was late afternoon with a thick cloud cover, barely still daylight. We'd reached Route 140, headed toward Lakeview, and the road was now straight and flat. I scanned the ditches and farmers' driveways on Jade's side of the crummy.

"But it's turning out to be good, isn't it?" Jade asked.

"Yeah. For one thing, I haven't worried about Ruby for the past ten minutes. Thank you for that."

"Goodness, that's worth something. Glad to help." He flicked the wipers to swish away dirty splashes from the road. "Now, can we just be comfortable together? The way we know how to be, just doing whatever comes next?"

"You make it sound easy."

"It will be. Also, can we maybe fuck sometimes?"

My heart couldn't be coaxed back to its resting rate. A few beats went AWOL. Because I was ecstatic. I tried to answer, but it was like a dream where I must speak yet can't make sounds.

I pushed the words out. "I think maybe—"

Then Howard's deep voice rumbled from the back.

"Hey, boss, there's a white Datsun on the right."

Jade pulled onto the narrow strip that passed for a shoulder. The layer of snow wasn't thick, so the sudden braking of the crummy scattered gravel.

The Datsun was twenty feet past the shoulder in a field. No headlights shining. Strangely, that sight steadied my thumping heart. I could take action.

44: Birds in Flight

THE SNOWFALL HAD LET UP. The crummy's headlights showed the Datsun to be empty, its doors open, the dome light on.

Overhead, two flocks of Canada geese headed south, honking their hearts out just above us. I yanked at my seatbelt and jerked at the crummy's screwed-up door handle.

Jade grasped my forearm. "Whoa! No one's here."

"Did the police find them? And take them away?"

"Stay here." Howard jumped out, a flashlight in hand, and prowled around the Datsun, examining the interior. Then he was back inside the crummy, pulling the door closed against the cold.

"There's no sign anyone was injured, so don't worry about that. The crash, though? The windows aren't broken, but your car is totaled."

Ten deep breaths, the first five wheezed.

"What next?" My mind danced. Not like me. I'm the calm one in every emergency.

"Find a phone and call the state patrol?"

"Yeah." That was too little. I clenched and unclenched my fists, just to do something. Anything.

Howard said, "I'm taking one more look."

When Howard walked away, Jade grabbed my coat collar and pulled me across the crummy's wide bench seat, cradling my head in his hands. "I wish your Heavenly Immortals would stop dumping worries on your head."

Then Jade Solberg kissed me.

A burst of static burned my lips, made my eyes tear up. His knuckles scuffed my clavicle, rubbed open a hole so that my heart leaped out, crossed the chasm to his hands.

His lips throbbed, the same beat as my pounding heart.

The Heavenly Immortals do not yank your soul from your body, but I swear we floated a mile above this mortal plane. Music of the spheres played, like chimes on a summer wind, and lights flashed from heavenly bodies, revealing that not even a crack separated our souls.

—

In the real world, red-and-blue lights flashed from behind us as a patrol car pulled up.

Jade pulled away, though remaining close enough to arouse each cell's memory of those pillowy lips.

Howard hiked back up to the crummy while Jade cranked down his window, which was a chore. Likely that window hadn't opened since the Seventies.

The patrolman shined a flashlight in Jade's face.

"Are you Rik Eliot?"

From the highway's shoulder, Howard said, "It's the other dude in the front. We're looking for his mother."

"Ah, yes." The cop nodded, his flashlight bobbing. "When Dispatch called your house, they said you went out looking and gave us your license plate so we could find you. Rest assured, sir, the state police have found your mother."

"She's safe?" My voice cracked. My entire being was cracking.

"She was transported to the local hospital for observation. The driver had a heart attack, which is why the car went off the road. He's in serious condition."

Howard said, "Tell us how to get to the hospital. She needs me. And she needs you too, boss, of course."

I'd been so wrapped up in…myself…I'd failed to see how stressed Howard was. He cared about Ruby. It wasn't just his job.

It was only twenty minutes to the hospital. For the entire ride, I couldn't find my fear for Ruby. Instead, I felt only that peculiar exhaustion that comes when you've cried for ninety minutes. Though I hadn't cried all day.

The snow stopped falling and the temperature didn't keep dropping, so the layer of snow hadn't crusted over. It squeaked under our boots when we tramped across the parking lot. A breeze loosened snow from the sugar pines at the edge of the lot. The mercury-vapor lamps lit the clouds that hung low overhead.

Why am I still cataloging useless details, even in a crisis?

I must have spoken out loud because Jade said, "It helps with the tension. I count stones in the square I'm working on."

At the desk, Howard got directions to Ruby's room.

Jade said, "I'm going to find out about Willie."

As we came down the hall, Howard said, "Hey, boss man, it can feel rocky with the IV and the monitors and seeing what dehydration can do to a person in a real short time. The fluorescent lights will make it weirder."

He opened the door, blocking my view as he boomed out, "Hi, Ruby. How you doin', sweetheart?"

When he stepped into the room, I saw her. I understood he'd been trying to prepare me.

She'd never looked this bad. She was whiter than the bedsheets. The insertion of the IV into the back of her hand had caused an enormous bruise, where I let my attention settle since her face was also bruised. My guess: she'd slapped herself when the Datsun stopped abruptly. Her blue eyes were watery and red-rimmed.

"Hi, Chris. I missed you at lunch." She wagged a finger. Her hand shook violently. "Mustn't be late, dear. It's bad manners."

Then she held her shaking hand out in greeting.

To Howard.

"I'm so happy you're here, Chris. Can you make them stop poking me?"

We pretended to have a conversation, Ruby and "Chris" and an absolute stranger.

When the doctor came, he checked her briefly, and kindly. Howard and I followed him into the hall.

"She can be released tomorrow," the doctor said, "but she must be in a care facility. She cannot go home. In fact, I'm surprised to hear that she's been under home care."

Several decisions happened, mostly guided by Howard. First, we needed a care facility as a destination.

"We got that covered, boss." Howard had a worn piece of paper in his wallet that listed care facilities in the Rogue Valley. "This isn't my first rodeo."

I pointed to the facility where I'd arranged for Ruby to live next May. I made the call from a pay phone, with Howard at my elbow telling me the questions to ask.

"You want to know if they have a bed for acute care, boss. We'll ask about long-term next week."

In a few minutes, we had a bed. Then we had to arrange transportation. The hospital gave us a contact number for a service that could bring her to our side of the mountains.

Halfway through my questions on the phone, Howard took the receiver from me.

"Don't beg," he said. "It's a service."

It took Howard less than three minutes to confirm they could manage a memory care patient.

"I'm her caretaker. I'll be riding with her." He put his hand over the receiver. "Doncha think it's better if I go with her, boss?"

I nodded.

Howard was grinning, satisfied with what he'd managed.

"It's all gonna be okay, boss. I'll sit with Ruby until they throw us out. Could you get me a cup of coffee?"

He had a hand on my elbow and raised the other for a high-five. I grasped that hand.

"Howard, I am so grateful. You've been more than a good friend to Ruby. You—"

He pulled his hand free, waved me away "Hey, boss. After you find coffee for me, go find your boyfriend. See what's up with Willie Smith."

—

Jade sat cross-legged on the sofa in the little family waiting room outside the intensive care unit, sketching in his pocket notebook. They had a real coffeemaker there, so I dumped the bad coffee I'd brought for him, and let Jade pour me a freshly brewed cup.

The endless beeping and soft intercom calls differed from the sounds in the wing where Ruby had a bed.

"They won't let me see him," Jade said. "I lied and said I was family, but it didn't get me anything. And I can't get his brother on the phone. The hospital has been trying every thirty minutes."

I tried to sip the coffee, but it was still too hot.

"Ruby is mostly dehydrated," I said. "Disoriented. Bruised. After we'd been there for fifteen minutes, the nurse said Ruby was a lot better than when she came in."

"That's good news." He touched my hand in that light way that has disconcerted me the past few weeks. "You okay, Sasha?"

I let my hand rest on his. It felt astonishingly natural.

"They're letting Ruby out tomorrow," I said. "We arranged transportation to take her to a care facility in Medford. Howard will ride with her."

"Shall I repeat myself? Are *you* okay?"

"Yeah. I stopped jittering from that ride in the crummy."

"I'll accept that answer." Jade closed his hand over mine. "Want to hear what I've learned? I called the state patrol and said I was you." He peered at me, as if checking I approved. I shrugged. So what? "A state patrol car was following the Datsun, verifying the license, when Willie plunged into that ditch."

I was far too able to envision Ruby's fear.

Jade continued, still clutching my hand. "One cop did CPR on Willie and the other helped Ruby calm down. It was only about ten minutes from the moment of the crash until our fleeing lovers were in an ambulance and on the way to the hospital."

Another residual dose of adrenaline unloaded into whichever of my organs was assigned to carry away the excess. Ever since we'd pulled up to the wrecked Datsun, I'd been watching a bad movie where Ruby is frightened, hurt, and confused.

"The state patrol had questions," Jade said. "I did my best as Rik Eliot to answer. First, do you want to prosecute Willie Smith for stealing your car?"

"What the hell? No."

"Good, I answered that one correctly. I also said no to prosecuting for either elder abuse or kidnapping."

"What? Who would do that?"

"Lots of people. Also, the state patrol agrees with Howard. Your car is totaled. They gave me a number for a tow truck."

"Can we just hope someone steals it?"

"Hmm. A good idea. But I already called a tow truck."

"You...you..."

"Yes, me. Remember? I said a couple of hours ago that it's my turn. You can count on me for a change."

The muscles that habitually resist? Couldn't.

"Thank you. It is good that we're friends. I agree."

He'd taken my coffee cup and was dumping three packs of sugar and two little plastic cups of cream into it. And laughing.

"Still," I said, "it'd be cheaper to let someone steal it."

"Yeah, might have been." Jade stirred the coffee with a wood stick and handed it back to me. "Sasha, I'm pretty sure you'll jump down my throat for this. But I gave the tow company my insurance and credit card." He held up his hand when I started to complain. "Let's worry about all that another day. Tomorrow morning, we'll get what you need out of that car."

I sipped the coffee. No, I slurped the coffee. Every cell yearned for its share of sugar and cream. I'd been thoroughly distraught while we drove over Green Springs. I was exhausted yet still anxious to take real action. "You and Howard are doing everything. I should—"

"Yeah, you should let your friends help. Becca says you have a bad habit of taking on everything by yourself."

"Becca has a bad habit of getting in my business."

"It's called friendship, Sasha. Do you want to hear what else I learned?"

"Please."

"The chihuahua bit one of the cops. Would not let them get close to Willie. They muzzled it and called animal control. It'll cost fifty dollars to get Willie's dog out of the pound."

"We'll let the lieutenant colonel deal with the dog. Let's try to call him again."

J.J. Smith answered this time. It was one of the most disheartening calls of my life.

"You won't come until Monday, Mr. Smith?"

"There's nothing I can do for him while he's in the ICU. I'll call the hospital to give them his Medicare number."

"And if they need you to make decisions?"

Silence from J.J. Smith.

I said, "Jade gave them your name as Willie's personal contact. We're leaving early in the morning, so it'll be the hospital that calls you going forward."

"I understand how these things work."

"It'll cost fifty dollars to spring Willie's dog from the pound."

"Fifty dollars for an old dog? Ha."

After I hung up, I dived for my cup of coffee-flavored sugar, just to have something to hold on to.

Jade was frowning. No, he was mad.

"What?" I asked. "I was as polite as that man ever allows me to be. I did my best."

"What an asshole. After seventy-two hours, they'll put that dog down."

I set my coffee on the side table and folded my arms. Closed my eyes. Felt how much I wanted to lie down and lose consciousness. That little barky dog had tumbled into the crater of worry I'd carried since midday. Since Wendy showed up. Since Xavier waved a gun at Timothy. Since Alex got picked up by the Ashland constabulary. A new movie played behind my closed eyes, now that I didn't need to worry about Ruby being alone and afraid: Molly and Ramona standing over my carcass after I'd let a dog be put down for something other than rabies.

"This feels sort of natural, doesn't it, Sasha?"

"What? An uncomfortable sofa? Weird noises from hospital rooms? Being tense all over, even though the crisis is over now? Haven't been in this space since you tumbled off the scaffold."

"No. Making decisions together. Getting stuff done that needs doing." He touched my hand again. Just barely.

I grabbed hold of his hand. Hard. Who knew this would be how the day turned out?

"Yeah. That's us now." I yawned. That's what I needed: oxygen. "We'll bail out the chihuahua tomorrow morning."

"After we find where your car was towed."

"I have to call my vice principal, since I won't be at school tomorrow. I'd better let Mrs. Adams and Danielle know what's going on. And the kids—"

"I already called Becca," Jade said. "She has it all handled. You've done enough today. Let's find Howard, get dinner, and go sleep somewhere."

45: Zhiji

WE ATE BURGERS AT A GREASY spoon, too tired to go more than two blocks to find food. Ditto for choosing a motel, one that time forgot, with only one room available, holding two twin beds.

"Saw that plot in *It Happened One Night* and a half-dozen romances." Howard chuckled, slapped Jade on the back. "But never one with a trio."

Room #5 assaulted us with a pungent smell of mildew and cigarette smoke. Who was I to complain? My hair and clothes stunk of rancid french-fry grease and 30-weight motor oil. And eight hours of sweating in anxious dread.

Howard claimed the bed closest to the bathroom, then cried dibs on the first shower.

Which left Jade and me with the other bed. We regarded each other across the worn pink chenille bed cover.

"I've waited eight years for this," Jade said. "It's everything that I have anticipated."

"Yeah. The ambience. The subtext. Motifs of transformation and desire manifested in the forlorn pink tufts of the bedspread."

Jade shed his sheepskin coat and wiped his face with his sweatshirt. "Goodness sake. Last time I smelled this bad was in a Boston drunk tank."

"Should I ask?" He was right about smelling bad. I think we were tied in that.

"Only if you want me to humiliate myself."

"I don't. Not even a little bit."

Jade got the next shower, returning in boxers and a t-shirt to lie down on the side opposite the wall.

The trickle of water from the mineral-encrusted shower head and the few remaining drops of shampoo were not refreshing. The hot water ended before I'd rinsed out the shampoo.

I crept under the covers on the side by the wall, my back to Jade's on a bed too narrow for two adults.

"Dry your hair," Jade whispered. "You'll catch cold."

"The towel is wet, and there's no hair dryer. I'm fine."

The electric baseboard heater hummed. Howard was soon snoring. I drifted, neither asleep nor awake, still seeing the white line and the canyons opening up alongside the highway. Speeding along. Falling, falling. My leg jerked me back to consciousness.

"Oh good, you're awake," Jade whispered. "Now we can talk again. What's your answer?"

"What?"

"Are we comfortable friends? We were interrupted before you said yes."

"The word you want is more meaningful than just friends. It's *zhiji* in Mandarin. It means 'the one who knows me.'"

"Then, yes?" He coaxed me to turn so we faced each other.

"Definitely."

"Even though I left you?" He was sincere. "Which I will keep apologizing for."

"Don't, please." I could swallow again. And that troublesome hollow behind my breastbone felt warm, like when the sun shines on you. "What happened back then shouldn't be called leaving. Didn't we both learn better today about all that?"

"Then it can be us again, just doing what's next? I mean, if you want me."

Oh, Heavenly Immortals, yes!

But I said, "Are you sure? My friend Michael says I'm massively fucked up and need therapy."

"I've taken that into consideration." Jade put his hand on my ribs, over my t-shirt, then nudged my arm so I touched him in the same way. "You're maybe slightly fucked up around the edges. Negligible, compared to everything else about you. Can we just say nice things to each other right now?"

"Sure. I admire you more than anyone I know." It wasn't the time to make an exception for my friend Michael, who'd dedicated his life to fixing broken children.

"It's nice of you to say so," he said. "I also admire you. As a teacher. As the kids' uncle. As a decent and good man."

It took a moment to get my breath, so I could say, "You're fantastically talented, Jade. You might even grow up to be a great and renowned artist someday."

"Aw shucks. Keep whispering nice things. Am I your flawless ideal?" His finger moved down my ribs as if counting them.

"No. When I stock the cottage kitchens, I can't help noticing you're a total effing slob. Always were."

"In Greece, I had a maid. That worked well."

"Yeah, that's how Ruby managed things in Hong Kong, but we don't have those here. My kids pick up after themselves."

"I'll change," Jade whispered. "I've done it before. Like, I don't get mad much. Except for Xavier Torres, who's an asswipe."

"I agree with that assessment."

"And housekeeping is merely a personal style."

"Rubbish." I felt his breath tickling me. We weren't touching, but he was about to make me laugh out loud.

"It's part of my creative process," he said. "Like you and your lists. You wouldn't be the great man you are without your lists."

"What do you know about my lists?"

"You leave them on the kitchen table. While I drink my coffee every morning, I'm forced to admire your meticulous handwriting—well, block letters—and your orderly and brilliant marshaling of space and time."

"I need to make a list of all the reasons I'm glad you're back in Ashland." I touched his lips, like I'd been longing to.

He touched my shoulder, just the knobby point, with only two fingers. But that knob must have been an acupressure point because, after a minute, I began weeping.

"Sorry," I whispered. The bed was shaking.

He cupped the curve of my shoulder with his warm hand.

"It's just…so sudden." No, it had taken an eon to get here.

Jade whispered, "Yesterday morning, you promised me it was all going to be okay."

"That was about the weather. And the mural. I didn't say…" I could hardly get the word out "…*all*."

I wished I wasn't crying. I wished I could stop. But I wept until I was wheezing and had to get up and find my inhaler.

"Sorry." I sat on the edge of the bed, waiting to feel that I'd inhaled enough albuterol to stop wheezing.

"I only worry that you'll end up dehydrated. I should have planned ahead and got some Gatorade."

"Stop trying to make me laugh."

"Okay. If you say so. Go to sleep, Sasha." When I lay down, he curled up behind me. "Tell me more about your Ziggy thing."

"*Zhiji.*" I said it as carefully and clearly as I could, given the amount of tear-sprung snot choking me. "Tomorrow."

He gently stroked my ear lobe. "I swear I'll be right beside you from now on."

—

When I woke, Jade stood at the motel room door. The curtains were open. The window showed only dark sky.

"Howard's already up, Sasha. He went out to scrape ice off the windshield. He wants to get to the hospital early, so we're there when the doctors make their rounds."

Dawn had lit a clear, cloudless sky by the time we got to the hospital. There's a rule, etched by the Heavenly Immortals, that if it snows too early in the season, the next day is bright and sunny, as if the demi-gods want to pretend it never happened.

While we ate breakfast in the hospital cafeteria and drank more bad coffee, I wanted to call home again. Jade argued that the kids didn't need me to help them out of the door, hadn't needed it for at least two years. He called both the school and the Festival to announce no site work that afternoon, and that the Saturday event was still on.

When the transportation guys showed up at eight thirty, we'd already signed all paperwork and received care instructions. By nine o'clock Ruby and Howard were on the way to Medford.

Jade and I stopped at the tow company. The owner came out, wiping his hands on a shop rag. "That beater has a hundred and fifty thousand miles on it. I can give you a hundred dollars for it. Your insurance covered the towing."

When we drove away, I expressed my sense of loss, capped with, "My sole personal possession for my entire adult life turns out to be worth only a hundred measly dollars."

Jade said, "Sadly, he'll make money by selling it for parts. It's too bad you can't stay here in Klamath Falls and sell it for parts yourself. Maybe you'd earn two hundred dollars. But then you'd spend it all on motel rooms and café food."

At the pound, we bailed Willie's chihuahua out of jail. They gave us two scoops of dog food and a leash, but we had to buy a carrier. Although the interior of the crummy was an environmental disaster area, rescued dogs have to ride in the back, in a dog carrier. I remain mystified throughout that trip: What caused that dog to bark for five minutes every twenty miles? I kept hearing it as an existential proclamation: *I am here. I am dog. Hear me roar.*

It's usually ninety minutes to Ashland from Klamath Falls on a good day. Enough traffic had crossed over Green Springs that the road was almost bare. Going west, we descended the curves, still steep, still posted for thirty miles an hour. However, going this direction, I looked out on the other, less terrifying side of the road.

The sun was out. I was feeling what might be called "happy" when Jade poked me. Actually he dug a finger in my ribs.

"You haven't said one word about Hong Kong today."

That fractured the morning's sunshine and happiness. I changed the subject. "I'm trying to get over being ticked at my friends for thinking I'm fucking up."

Jade started to pound the steering wheel, which I recognize as his personal form of punctuation. Then he gripped the wheel with both hands. "Sasha, there's a whole raft of other people you should be ticked at. But to keep on topic, I want to stay in Ashland. I can't act on that desire until I know if you're staying and that you can tolerate seeing me on the street."

"I thought…" The chihuahua yipped, distracting me for two heartbeats. "Last night, I thought you swore to stay beside me."

"Of course I did. But is that in Ashland? Because Hong Kong makes it kind of hard for me. I mean, I'll do it. I'm just saying it'll be hard. So…really? That's where we're going next?"

"Yes. No." The dog interrupted, yipping again. "Maybe. I don't know. It's only a few days since everything I've worked for got jerked away from me."

Then the chihuahua with no name started a raft of barking, competing with the roar of the crummy and giving me an opportunity to refocus the conversation. Which proved to be a mistake.

"What raft of people am I supposed to be ticked at?"

"First, we can fill the Angus Bowmer Theatre with the crowd of people who abandoned you. Your father, Ruby, Kai—"

"Kai is still my friend."

"You told me once that he picked an insipid wife who won't let him speak Chinese with you."

"Cantonese. And we do write to each other."

"Please let me get to my point. Wendy abandoned you when she ditched the twins. Claudia screwed you from here to Sunday, abandoning family loyalty. Your uncle Chan failed to notice your dissertation disappeared from his house. That's another kind of abandonment. And I abandoned you—"

"You just did what you had to do while I had to—"

"Yeah, yeah. My point is there's a crowd of us who caused you deep pain. You should be royally pissed off at each of us. Yet you just double down like a control freak, safeguarding the people around you and changing your plans to make it perfect for everyone else, even Ruby."

"That's your point? That I'm a control freak? It's what works for me. Are we still talking about Hong Kong? Have you been psychoanalyzing me with Becca?"

"No, absolutely not. My point is…Holy crap!" A car passed us on a curve. Mercifully, we didn't all die. "You've been avoiding me since I came to town because…"

"No, I haven't."

"You have. And it's because you won't just get mad at me for leaving. You should have socked me in the nose the first time I jumped into your space. You should have kicked me in the nuts every time I tried to make nice with you."

"I will repeat: you didn't leave me. My family's needs disrupted our half-assed plan to roam the world."

"Okay, maybe. But right now, when I hear that you want to move to Hong Kong, I feel that you want to run away from *me*—which I deserve after abandoning you."

No-Name Chihuahua howled, saving me the trouble of voicing my…thoughts?…feelings?…dismay? Yeah, that's it.

Jade didn't wait for an answer. "Back then, I walked around angry all the time, until I learned to stop. Maybe we swap now, and you get angry at the people who deserve it. Every single one of us."

"I don't see—" My no-name buddy howled again. At a higher pitch than what I felt. "What good would that do? Why would getting mad make sense?"

"Why does going back to Hong Kong make sense? Is that all you want to do in life once you don't have to make lists to take care of everyone else?"

"So you think my lists are weird, like Becca does?"

"No, I think they're beautiful. I just wish you'd put your own wishes on the list. Like, right now, tell me one wish you could add, just for you?"

"I wish..." No-Name Chihuahua barked, first sounding like he needed to warn off wolves, but then dropped a tone, sounding like the saddest dog in the world, as if tuned in to my karmic wavelength. "I wish I could be held and rocked like a little kid."

"I can do that, Sasha!" He sounded excited, stopped short of slapping the steering wheel. "I want to do that. Trust me."

"Um, no. I can't give up my habits. And I know you. We'd be eating dry cereal and running out of Band-Aids in a week. I will, though, accept comfort rocking. If we make it through Saturday."

"Will you tell me what you now think about Hong Kong?"

"What will you do in Ashland, Jade?" Do I get to question your plans the way you've questioned mine?

"Thank you for asking, Sasha." He rested his hand on my thigh for a second before he had to reach back to the gearshift. "To start, I invented three new designs for pasta bowls. And coffee mugs with matching drip cones. Plus a gravy boat that I'm rather proud of. And I'll offer classes, since crowds of California retirees are moving here. Just basic wheel work and coil pots. I also have an idea for a storefront where people can glaze premade porcelain slips. It's popular in L.A. for grade-school birthday parties."

I wanted to shout: *Are you out of your freaking mind?*

He leaned over to look at me. "Goodness! Your face, Sasha! I wish I had a picture. Are you still so gullible?"

"You jerk! Tell me your real plan."

"It's not fully baked yet. But I can ask my agent to find a gig in Hong Kong for late spring—you know, so we can all travel together when school is over. But I can only stay until September because I have a three-week artist-in-residence gig in Boston."

"The twins are going to Boston in August to start school."

"That's convenient. Will you go to Boston with me? And I have a three-month contract in Bilbao next October. Will you come too? I have to spend this winter preparing for that, which is why I need a bigger workshop. I'm planning big pieces and—"

"Balboa?" I was slow to catch on. "Panama? Newport Beach? San Diego? Columbia?"

"Bilbao." Jade repeated it twice. "Spain. Right now, Boston and Spain are my contracted stops next year. Hong Kong can serve as a good start for our Wandering Scholars itinerary."

"I'm not a scholar anymore." There, I admitted it. Out loud. It didn't hurt at all.

"No, you're a master craftsman who can do contract math better than my agent. You're a brilliant tactician. And Becca says you've been writing grant proposals for artists. Tell me that plan makes sense—at least, as far as I've gotten with it. Doesn't it sound right for us, Sasha? We can travel and teach together, and then come back here when we need a break. It'll be like in your Ziggy thing."

"Zhiji."

"Exactly. But to be ready for Spain, we have to find the right studio space now. Like, next week. And I need to order kilns. Can you help me set them up?"

"Jade, you're going too fast. My brain is stuck figuring how to afford a new car and how to get the house ready to sell."

"Am I? First, you should buy a truck. You know you want to. We can get a small car the kids can drive. Plus," he ran his finger up my arm, making me shiver, "I have more money than both of us can spend."

"Yesterday you claimed you had to scramble to afford to come to Ashland."

"That was just bad timing. My accountant made a chunk of timed investments, with huge penalties for early withdrawal. Money is not a problem for our plans. And money is 97 percent of what you worry about, isn't it?"

"I can't—"

"If you are about to be bourgeois and say, 'I can't take your money,' just don't. It's only what you used to call roommate math. Except we'll be business partners. We're a matched pair for that."

"Partners." Warmth flooded my veins, as if I'd run far in sunshine. I'd call it happiness, but unlike any I'd ever felt. "Okay, then. But we need to think seriously about the details."

"Great. You can start a list."

"Right." I was almost comfortable being somewhere I'd never been before. "The first item is, 'Figure out whether Jade's business ideas really make sense.'"

"No, that's the second item. The first item is, 'Figure out what Sasha really wants.'"

For a bit, we traveled in silence. I stayed busy being bourgeois, doing the math for how to pay for Ruby in managed care seven months earlier than my budgeting allowed. Jade kept looking my way any time he could take his eyes off the road. He'd repeat, "It's all good, right?"

Each time I stopped doing my budget-math to answer, I bit back my response: *If I can sell the house and get a good price.* But that wasn't what he kept asking. I have habits I don't know how to break. Yet I answered, every time: "Yes."

He pounded the steering wheel as was his habit. "We'll make it be good."

For the four-mile descent from Hayden Mountain Summit, the speed signs read 20 mph. It's one of Kevin's favorite rides as soon as spring weather allows it. I'd enjoyed being his passenger several times. But when the highway reached Buckhorn Road that morning, I was hugely relieved. So was No-Name Chihuahua, who barked the whole way we glided through that descent. I didn't enjoy the curves, though we'd enjoyed an intimate dispute, shouting our thoughts over the noise of the crummy. Jade remained quite cheery despite the demanding drive.

I said, "You didn't grind the gears once going this direction."

"My soul is on wings, Sasha. Don't you feel it?"

"Yes, I do. I'm elated." I'd separated the buzz of the crummy from how I felt. No internal crunching. The Dragon's Blood crystals had fitted themselves together and quit moving, like locked pieces in a Chinese puzzle that had been solved.

"I'm happier than you," Jade said. "I didn't spend any of this journey to the west worrying about how to pay for Ruby's care."

Apparently, I'd done my Ruby math out loud. But that reminded me of one more factor in the total sum. "I need to give the care workers at least two weeks' severance. I keep forgetting to put that in the total."

"We can manage that."

"We?"

"We already decided that you are no longer tackling the world all by yourself. Don't make me keep shouting about it over the crummy's racket."

We got back to Ashland in one hundred minutes. That meant I could make it to school for my last three classes. Jade argued that I should skip it, but I'd stretched the bounds of grace that a temp worker can expect. I stopped at the house to change, while Jade went to give the dog to Willie's brother.

Chaos House was eerily quiet. No TV in Ruby's room. No sign of Wendy and Pandora. Just Felix the Clock swinging his tail in the kitchen. When I came downstairs in chinos and blazer, Jade was back, dog carrier still in hand.

"I'll give you a ride to school," he said.

"Mr. Smith didn't take the dog? No, obviously not."

"He gave me a longer leash. I'll keep the poor fellow in my cottage until we figure out what to do."

So, all the way to school, I made verbal lists for Jade:

> Get dogfood from the bottom right kitchen cupboard.
>
> Find old dishes in the third lefthand pantry cupboard.
>
> Find a blanket in the second-floor linen closet.
>
> Avoid a showdown with Pandora.

"Should we take it to a vet?" I asked. "Do dogs have to go to the doctor if they've been in jail?"

"It's a little dog," Jade said. "I bet it managed its brief incarceration just fine."

I sneezed. Three times.

"Are you okay?" he asked. "Is our new dog getting to you?"

"Maybe. Or maybe I'm coming down with something."

After school, I walked home, stopping at Sally's house to leave homework and quiz papers with her. The walk home felt great for three reasons:

> One: Not being in a crummy, a hospital room, or a motel room the size of my kitchen table. I hadn't had a decent run since Saturday, and that run had not been any fun.
>
> Two: No mural site work that afternoon. I didn't have to shepherd a dozen teenagers or stir thin-set concrete with a wooden tongue depressor.
>
> And three: The sky was a beautiful, brilliant blue, and the sun shining on my face wouldn't set until almost six thirty.

No, I had a fourth reason for feeling so good: *Jade is the one who knows me.*

The only hitch? My body felt a shuddering sensation, as if the flu or the world's worst head cold might be just over the horizon, right when I'd begun to believe that the Heavenly Immortals had dropped good fortune on my part of the world.

46: In Defiance of Demons

DOWN WATER STREET, I RAPPED ON the Lazarus Cottage door, wondering how Jade had fared with No-Name Chihuahua. Disappointingly, there was no answer. I checked the patio, then came into Chaos House through the back porch, thinking I'd better repair the screen door. Heated voices came from the living room.

"I will discuss it with your uncle when he comes home."

"No, we'll talk now." Alex was angry, which doesn't often happen. "I don't need Uncle Rik to argue for me."

Claudia was in the Chaos House living room. She sat in the armchair, her posture as straight and stiff as a martinet, arms folded, an unlit cigarette between her fingers like a weapon. She always looks put-together, but her hair was too much like Margaret Thatcher's to be attractive.

A great angel restrained me. I stood on the back porch, soap powder tickling my nose, and watched the action inside through the open kitchen door. Jade came up behind me, slipped his arm around my waist. Held me so close, I could feel his heart beat.

"Sasha."

He whispered it so quietly it was like the wind at my ear.

Claudia flicked a lighter.

"You can't smoke in here!" Ramona held up a scolding finger, looking too much like me when I advocate for Rik's Rules. "You can smoke in the backyard but take your butt with you when you're done."

"No," Molly said, "go smoke in your car, Aunt Claudia. You only lit up to be rude to Uncle Rik."

"That," Alex said, "is what this is about, isn't it, Mother? Being mean to Uncle Rik? But he's never mean to anyone."

Jade tightened his arm around my waist. I wanted to tell him to relax. It's only the older generations of Eliots who are cuckoo. The kids are all right.

"This," Claudia said dramatically, "is all about proper care for all of you children."

Molly snorted a laugh.

Claudia shook a finger at her. "When your Uncle Rik gets home, our first discussion will be about his having abandoned you children alone for an entire night and day."

Ramona said, "We aren't little kids. And Becca and Wendy were both here all night. We've refused after-school daycare since we turned eleven."

"Why are you picking on Uncle Rik?" Molly said. "You're being ridiculous. You must know that."

"Uncle Rik does everything he can to make things right," Alex said. "He's kind and honest."

"But you," Molly said, "you're just being a wicked witch for no good reason."

"Do not call me names, Molly Eliot. I'll discuss that behavior with Rik, too."

Ramona grabbed her parka from the coatrack by the front door. "C'mon, Alex, Molly. Let's just go. Uncle Rik can deal with this…this *person* when he gets home."

"No," Alex said. "Uncle Rik has to deal with everything all the time. He's been chasing Grandma Ruby for two days."

"And Aunt Claudia wants him to eat a shit sandwich," Molly said. "He won't eat it, but he'll know what's best to do."

"I know what to do," Alex said. "I'll deal with this, not Uncle Rik. Mother, I am not going back to your house. You cannot force me to come with you."

"I certainly can, young man."

"No, I actually have rights. But I don't want Uncle Rik to spend a fortune on lawyers just because you got your tit caught in a wringer."

"Alexander Eliot!"

"Oh stuff it, Mother. I'm staying here. I'm getting good grades, even in math. I'll graduate in May. I have friends. You can't prove it's bad for me to be here. Instead, everything good is happening." He lowered his voice, instead of raising it. A power trick teachers use. "Uncle Rik stopped the lawyer from claiming you're mentally abusive. So don't be. Or else."

"Are you threatening me?"

"I'm telling you to stop. Respect that." Alex's voice was firm, low, and strong. I felt tears welling up again, feeling so proud of him. Jade pulled me a fraction closer.

Claudia slapped her palm on the table. "But Rik Eliot is a danger and—"

"So help me," Molly crossed her arms, "if you say one more bad word about Uncle Rik, I'll throw you out on your butt."

Alex said, "And you just want to bully me. If you keep acting like Grandma Ruby, you won't see me until you're…you're *old*."

The front door burst open, banging into the credenza, rattling the glass panes of the door.

"What's going on?" Wendy came in, dropping Pandora on the floor along with six shopping bags. "Oh Great Goddess, *you're* here? Well, hello, Claudia."

Twenty-four hours earlier, when I'd left, she'd been woeful. Now she looked 75 percent better. She'd showered, washed her hair, trimmed her bangs. Found lip gloss and eyeliner, likely from the twins' bathroom. She wore freshly washed jeans with a well-starched shirt. Ah, those were my clothes. So she'd dried the clothes from last night's Mount Wendy. She'd also found my old Keds, so her put-together appearance frayed at floor level.

Pandora headed straight for Ramona, jumping up on her leg for attention.

"Hi, Wendy. Aunt Claudia drove up in a Mac truck to dump cow shit on Uncle Rik," Molly said. "Bet she brought some to dump on you too. She's big on taking a dump on other people."

"You little brat!" Claudia stood up. "After everything I've done for you."

Time to intercede. First, I had to peel away Jade's arm. "Enough." I came in through the kitchen. "No calling names. Rik's Rules. Please apologize, Molly."

"We're sticking up for you," Ramona said.

"I have this handled, Uncle Rik," Alex said. "You don't need to rescue me."

"I see that you're doing fine," I said. "I'm proud of you. Hello, Claudia. It's good to see you. Now, Molly? Your apology?"

Molly glowered, struck an obstinate stance I hadn't seen since she turned thirteen, fists at her side. "Dearest Aunt Claudia, I appreciate all you've done for us, letting us eat TV dinners at your house for a month every summer. And sending us matching sweater sets for Christmas. I apologize for saying you're a wicked witch. Even though you flew here on a broomstick."

She pushed past Wendy and out the open front door, not taking her parka. Pandora tried to follow, but the screen door slammed before the dog could get through.

"Hi, *kaukau.*" Ramona scooped up the dog. "Welcome home. Oh, hi, Jade. I didn't see you there."

"Rik! You're back," Wendy exclaimed. "Is Ruby really okay? I thought Jade was just trying to make me feel better when he called last night." She bent to pick up her packages.

"Ruby is safe and cared for," I said. "Ramona, Alex, please find Molly. Take her parka so she doesn't freeze and don't come back until dinner time. That will be at seven o'clock. I have to go finish business at Ruby's care home."

Alex, on his way out the door, said to Jade, "Can me and Quinn rehearse in the garage?" When Jade nodded, Alex added, "And can Quinn stay for dinner, Uncle Rik?"

"He has to ask his mom." Tonight, Quinn at dinner would be a terrible idea, but likely his mother would say no, since she'd often told him that the SAT exam was crucial to his future success. She'd want to feed him herself.

After the kids closed the front door, I turned to the two women. "This is where I offer tea. Or, if you prefer, coffee. But I have only five minutes to play host."

"This is your chance to practice, Sasha." Jade turned on the kettle. As if he lives here. "Kick some gonads."

"It's Friday," I spoke to Claudia, ignoring Jade's prompt to be angry, "so I'm short on snacks. But it looks like Ramona made protein bars."

Jade lifted the dome off the cake stand, like he did each morning at breakfast. "This batch has chocolate chips."

"Do you have chamomile tea?" Wendy asked.

The last few minutes had rolled over my sister with no effect. She claimed to be used to living in chaos in that dick-guru's commune, where people shouted and said unkind things. It was extremely unusual, the kind of chaos happening here this afternoon. Not one of us should get used to such turmoil.

Wendy headed for the kitchen table. "The protein bars are great, Claudia. But no eating in the living room. Or smoking."

"Rik's Rules," Jade said.

"Yes, I do have chamomile tea," I said. "It's what Mrs. Adams drinks." I had to rummage in the cupboard to find the box. "Coffee or tea, Claudia?"

"Darjeeling, please. Do you have milk?" Claudia did not seem to notice that Jade hulked, seething, apparently intent on transferring his anger to me. But what's the use in getting mad about Claudia, who looked beleaguered?

"You're in luck," I said. "I do."

I hung my blazer on a chair in the corner and rolled up my sleeves. Timothy had missed two breakfasts, so we had plenty of Darjeeling. I hoped Kevin was taking care of him, perhaps convincing him to eat properly.

—

Jade said, too brightly, "Chamomile is a swell idea, Wendy. I need an antidote for all the hospital coffee we drank. Hi, Claudia, it's been a while. Last time was for drinks at P.J. Clarke's, wasn't it? On Third Avenue?"

Claudia mumbled a hello, as if not wanting to give Jade attention. It'd been two years since she and I had seen each other in person. She didn't look older so much as haggard, despite being as meticulously groomed as ever.

Jade went on, cheerily. Was I the only one who noticed his eyes were on fire? "Are you here for the media event tomorrow? Alex will be thrilled to show you his work on the mural."

"No," Claudia said. "I'm here for—"

I interrupted. "It's fortunate you're here. We all need to discuss the details of Ruby's long-term care. The doctor insists that she must remain in care."

"I came," Claudia stressed, "to take Alex home."

"Just stuff it, Claudia," Wendy said. "Don't you get it? If you push, Alex will run. I'm walking proof that neither California nor Oregon cops look for teenage runaways. Give it up."

Besides the shower and makeup, Wendy had made the strongest assertion since she'd arrived, and it wasn't about her or Pandora. It seemed time to confirm that the problems Claudia had raised were already solved.

I said, "Alex was clear just now that he chooses to stay here. Since he's not in any danger, he gets to decide. We have Ruby's business to discuss. I have to sell this house no later than January."

"Sell the house?" Wendy echoed.

Claudia's frozen hypercritical expression thawed to curiosity. She'd been sidetracked. At last.

Jade said, "It alarmed me, too. But then, I listened to Sasha doing the math all the way from Klamath Falls."

He and I had talked about more than nursing-home math.

"Why so surprised?" I focused on Claudia. "It's been the plan for years to sell the house when Ruby moves to long-term care. Yesterday's crisis just pushed up the timing."

"Where will I live?" Wendy pleaded.

"We'll figure that out, I promise. But Ruby's social security is a pittance, and this house is her only asset."

Claudia said, "We have to discuss Ruby's guardianship."

"If you want to take it over, you're welcome to it." I stood, awkward as it is to get up from the bench at the table. "But I have an immediate legal duty. I must sign papers before the care home's business office closes at five. Meanwhile," I took a breath, "please believe I intend true kindness for you, for Alex, and for Ruby. Give up being mad at me."

"But—"

Jade pursed his lips, clearly not wanting me to be so nice.

I said, "Dinner is at seven if you want to join us, Claudia. I'd offer to let you stay for the night, but I haven't had a chance to clean any of the free rooms. Now, don't smoke in the house, and don't let Pandora into my room or up on the sofa."

I grabbed my blazer and walked away without waiting for an answer, happy to have been as polite as I'd demanded of Molly. Most of my pleasure came from the image of Alex standing up for himself. And Claudia's open-mouthed amazement while Alex made his case. If only I'd ever managed that with Ruby.

I was almost out the front door. Jade lingered, saying, "It will take me a while to find true kindness, Claudia. You lied to me."

Outside, the sky was still a brilliant blue, but the sun had dipped behind the mountains. To the east, Grizzly Peak glowed golden save for a thin crown of gleaming white. I admired the shining peak while listening to Jade.

"Rik says you believe things about Alex that upset you."

"It's not your business, Mr. Solberg."

"Oh, I'm Mr. Solberg? Now that you aren't having cocktails and lying to me?" He didn't wait for an answer. "Whatever might have been said in a heated moment, I will tell you the truth, since I teach undergrads and often meet young men who are finding their way out. Alex is a sensitive, talented artist."

"It's not your business to explain my son to me." Claudia's voice was scratchier from cigarettes than in past years.

Wendy said, "It's not your business, Claudia, to jump on Alex's shit. Or Rik's, even though Rik is gay."

Jade said, "Yes, thank heavens, Sasha is gay. I am a lucky boy. But we're talking about respect for Alex."

Claudia couldn't smoke, but she was steaming. "It's not any of your business to—"

"It's more my business," Jade interrupted, "than when you lied to me over and over about Rik. I've been with Alex every day since he came to Ashland. I've watched him become sure of his place in the world. You can see it in how he walks and carries himself. His artwork shows new confidence too."

"His art?" Claudia sounded puzzled, knocked off track.

As much as I was enjoying all that, I wanted to grab Jade out of there. But just then, that infernal scrub jay dived at my head. I waved my arms against the startling sensation that I was in *The Birds,* a nightmare erupting. It squawked and settled back in the oak tree to bitch at me. A simple moment. But then, a nightmare had erupted every time I'd almost enjoyed myself for the past week.

Two dogs barked behind the house. Pandora had met No-Name Chihuahua. Wendy called, "Come, Pan-Pan. Leave your new friend alone. He's shy."

47: Beyond Care

I HEADED TO THE DRIVEWAY for my car, struck for a moment by its absence before recalling that I no longer own a car.

"I'll give you a ride." Jade was again right behind me. Close.

"Can I bear twenty more minutes in the crummy?" I pretended to complain, but I had no alternative.

"I returned the crummy to the guys I rented it from. Found something better." He pointed up the street to a mid-Seventies Ford Econoline van, with a primer-gray left rear quarter panel.

"You were busy while I was teaching."

"I lost patience with the crummy. You can borrow this van when you need it."

By the time we left the city limits and passed the 55-mph sign on Highway 99, the engine hump between us had squealed in three distinctly different ways.

"Guess this beast needs a tune-up from the collective on Oak Street." Jade sighed.

"It needs more than a tune-up." I couldn't put off talking about what happened five minutes earlier. "Jade?"

"Yes, Sasha?"

"Last night in the Mildew Motel, you swore to be there with me going forward."

"I did promise. I'm good for it."

"Nice. But you didn't have to jump straight into my business with Claudia."

"I jumped into Alex's business. And my own. Do you disagree with what I said?"

"I agree completely. Yet I should assert those truths for him."

"Sasha, you stomped out right when she was hankering for a fight. And two things bear repeating. One, Alex wants to stand up for himself, which is one point I made with Claudia. You don't have to carry everyone else's burdens. Second, I only offered Claudia a simple lesson in reality. I am eligible to do that since I have a personal relationship with her, which she abused by lying to me on several occasions."

Another squeal from the engine hump.

"Might be the fanbelt," I said. "Or something worse."

"Don't change the subject. You can't let people like Claudia off the hook. Your younger family considers you a demi-god. I've joined *that* branch of the family and so feel called upon to join with them for anything within the realm of my experience."

"Demi-god? They think I'm a pain in the ass with a morose sense of humor, no ability to dress, and bad taste in music."

"They think you're a good cook," Jade said. "And I agree. Also, you look good in jeans, the tighter the better. I'm so glad you aren't following current fads."

"Turn right by that sign. There's the home."

The nursing-home administrator was prepared, with all the papers lined up and little clips to show where to sign. They'd forewarned me about payment processes, so I had the checkbook for Ruby's expenses. They were modern enough to have the paperwork for setting up automatic payments for whatever Medicare doesn't cover. Since she owned a house, she wasn't eligible for government money.

The manager gave us a small tour on the way to Ruby's room, showing us the chapel, dining room, and sunroom. Then Jade peeled away, saying he'd wait in the lobby.

Ruby's room was painted a peaceful blue, with windows looking out on a garden. She'd be sharing it, but the previous patient had gone home that day. Howard sat in the guest chair, listening to Ruby, then interrupting to coax her to drink water.

She looked better than yesterday, better than this morning. Someone had fixed her hair, and she wore lip gloss.

Howard stood. "Hey, Ruby. You've got company."

I started my usual conversation with her: the weather, what's interesting out the window, what's on television. But she watched my mouth move, not hearing what I said.

"It's nice here," I said. Howard made a cut sign. Yeah, I know better than to make her aware she's in an unfamiliar place, which would send her into a state of deep confusion and fear. "What can I do for you, Ruby?"

"You can stop sticking me with needles," Ruby said. "I can swallow a pill. I'm not crippled."

"Uh, okay."

Howard had the same pitying look as when I first saw her in that hospital room. Pity for me, that is.

"Chris, look." She motioned for Howard, not me. "I told you the male nurses here are good looking. But they're all Mexicans. He must be very poor."

"He looks happy." Howard did what we know how to do, redirecting her attention.

Ruby said, "This Mexican nurse boy is so handsome, I bet he can marry a rich white girl."

Howard's eyes flicked to me. His mouth twitched. He offered her the straw, kept hold of the cup. "Ruby, you got to drink more water. So they won't poke you again."

A care worker appeared with a dinner tray. "Are you ready for dinner, Mrs. Eliot?"

"You can call me Ruby," she said sweetly. "What do you think, Chris? Should I have dinner?"

She was asking Howard, not me.

I said, "Have a good supper, Ruby. I'll see you soon." I'd made it to the door when she called after me.

"Goodbye, you beautiful man. What's your name?"

I turned back. "Sasha. I'm called Sasha."

"Bye, Sasha." She gave me a wave like a little girl's. "Chris, where's Willie? He promised to come for lunch. He's always here by now."

"I'll go ask," Howard said.

He followed me out of the room. "Sorry, boss. Sometimes I'm Chris. Sometimes I'm her father or a guy named David."

"That's my father."

"Yeah, I guessed as much. I'm used to her drifting, especially when she's tired. I'd say it's worse after yesterday's adventure. But she's already much better than last night. She's been going on about Willie since she woke up."

"It's good you came over with her, Howard. I'm worried how she'll be in the night. Do you think I should stay with her?"

"Naw, I'll stay tonight. The doctor in KFalls sent along some Valium. By tomorrow, I'll have the whole staff understanding what she needs. The on-call doctor will see her come morning. We'll get her regular doctor involved next week."

"Thanks for staying. And thanks for everything."

"It's my job, boss."

"We both know you're going beyond that." I shook his hand.

"You best get home, boss. I bet you promised the kids dinner, and everyone's going to a fight movie tonight. Am I right?" He jutted a finger at Jade, who'd come in from the lobby and lingered by the door. "Take care of the boss man, even better than he takes care of everyone else."

"Trust me," Jade said. "I've got it covered."

When we passed the office, the clock showed fifteen minutes before the weekend closed off any possibility for business.

"Jade, can you wait for me for a minute by the van? I have to ask a question."

Once the front door unlocked for him and Jade was out of the building, I went to the office, pulled out my wallet, and did a thing I've never done before: used a credit card that didn't belong to me, without permission.

—

In the parking lot, Jade grabbed my arm, firmly enough that it hurt. He pulled me into the arbor vitae hedge and wrapped me in his arms. Hugged me hard.

"I'm okay," I said when he let me breathe. "Likely I have to cry really hard one more time, but I'm not doing it in a hedge. And I'm not doing it while that fanbelt squeaks. Why did you rent yet another a wreck of a beater like this?"

"I bought it. It only cost two hundred dollars. Aren't you proud of my thrifty ways?"

"Okay, make me feel guilty."

"Never," he said, looking puzzled.

I handed back his credit card and long-distance calling card, which I'd had since we bailed No-Name Chihuahua out of doggie jail. "You just paid for a room and transportation to bring Willie over from Klamath Falls when the hospital discharges him. I'll pay you back, though likely it only means getting the billing straight with Medicare."

He pocketed the cards. "I'll get it back from J.J. Smith. He thinks he's my friend, but he was mean to you and to his own brother. I intend to persuade him to take care of Willie."

Back on Highway 99, we headed south-by-southeast. Jade didn't ask more about the business with Willie. I was busy not thinking about how Ruby doesn't know me but remembers that rascal she met a month ago. I was not inspecting the unhealed injury Michael talked about. And anyway, that hole isn't a raw wound; I don't need first aid. My mother left me long before now.

It was time to let go of all of it. I have other people who still need my care and attention more than I need to dwell on Ruby's failings.

Plus, there was now this man beside me whose attention I'd longed for.

Jade, tapping the steering wheel, broke the silence. "Sasha, who were you with in Chez Margot on Tuesday?"

"My friend Michael, the adolescent therapist."

"He didn't look like a teenager."

"A doctor for teenagers, Mr. Pedant."

"That's Mr. Wandering Scholar, please."

"Michael was here from San Francisco for just a day. Why?"

"You had the most haunting look on your face. I've worried about it ever since."

"He told me to put my mother in care and get therapy."

He again tapped the steering wheel, that now-familiar habit. "Do you agree, Sasha? Do you need therapy?"

"Probably. Like you said, my mother and father abandoned me. My family was cruel for no good reason."

"My parents died and left me an orphan."

"Not the same thing."

"Yeah, I suppose." He slowed for the speed limit at the Entering Phoenix sign. "I shouldn't joke. If you go to therapy, do I go with you, since you and I have that Ziggy thing?"

"That might be confusing. And the word is *zhiji*."

"Why confusing?"

"Several years ago a therapist told me I shouldn't enter into a relationship until I'd resolved the issues around my mother. And that it might take years."

"It's been years since then. But why should your mother be given yet another chance to rob you of all joy?"

"I didn't think of it that way." Rob me of joy? Huh. Just what had happened. "That therapist said I'd likely transfer all my neediness onto any new personal relationship."

Jade smacked the steering wheel and pointed at me. "Then it's a good thing we don't have a relationship, Sasha. Though if we did, I'd tolerate you being needy."

"We don't have a relationship?" My stomach sank an inch lower in my belly, though I knew he was teasing.

"No, we'll just do what we do, Sasha. Eat at the same table. Share friends. I'll still pay you for the raku kiln work. It's just our life, not some bourgeois relationship."

"That's it? That's what we'll have?"

"Plus the usual. Laugh. Cry. Celebrate. Go to bed at night. Get up and drink coffee. You make better coffee than I do, but I promise I'll clean up after."

"Truly? My kitchen won't look like Lazarus Cottage?"

"I've become a responsible adult. So voilà! No needy bougie relationship. Just the guy who knows you."

I sat back, tickled by the engine vibration coming through my seat in the van, which diverted other sensations. I didn't want more tears for a while. But this was a difficult conversation to have over a squealing fanbelt. Or whichever belt it was.

"*Zhiji* is more than that," I said. "It's letting yourself be known to the other person, however uncomfortable. It's mirroring each other's soul, all action in unity and selfless devotion."

"That too." Jade nodded, tapping his thumb at the top of the steering wheel. "Also, if you get a new therapist, don't forget to say that you've already reached one of your life's goals."

"What's that?"

"You're a much better man than that stranger, your father."

If he didn't have that ridiculous grin, I'd be crying again. Something snapped in my body.

"What's wrong?" Jade said when I shuddered beside him.

"I keep feeling like I'm getting a virus or something."

We'd passed the sprawling Lithia Motors car lot and reached the Entering Ashland sign when Jade said, "Wasn't Willie taking your mother to church on Sundays? I heard him ask one day when I was stalking you."

It took me a moment to restart my brain after hearing his last few words: *When I was stalking you.*

"I don't remember the name of the church," I said. "It's a non-denominational outfit south on Siskiyou Boulevard."

"Let's call and see if they have friends in Klamath Falls. Someone should visit Willie. It's been bugging me that he's all alone."

48: Two Fish, Swimming Together

WHEN WE GOT BACK TO Chaos House, Ramona was making a salad. Alex carefully brushed melted butter and garlic over a split loaf of French bread. I smelled lasagna from the oven, so who knows what they ate last night. Molly was noisily vacuuming the stairs. When she saw me, she turned off the vacuum.

"Is Grandma okay?"

"She's as well as can be. Howard is staying with her tonight to help her get comfortable."

Ramona said, "Can we go visit?"

I said, "Howard says to wait until Sunday. And I don't have a car anymore. We'll have to take the bus."

Jade said, "You can take my van."

I glanced at him in a speaking way: *Your van is a piece of junk.* But I meant it in the friendly manner of close companions who know the song of each other's heart. He pressed a finger hard on his lips, though I saw that my speaking glance made him laugh.

Claudia said, "I'm not leaving for home until Monday. We can go in my rental."

Her voice had changed; it was lighter. She'd surrendered her martial posture. The kids were also moving around differently. Freely. Normal.

Jade, however, responded harshly to Claudia's offer. "No need, Claudia. I've promised all the transportation Sasha and the kids need until he finds a new car."

Claudia's hackles rose again. "What right do you have to meddle in family business?"

He leaned toward her. "What right did you have to tell me a pack of lies about Sasha? You said he was happy. He was not."

"I meant—"

"Do not say that you meant well, Claudia." Jade shook his finger at her. "Please recognize that Sasha and I are partners who share all our business mutually."

Molly made a squeaky sound. Ramona grabbed her sister and swung her around.

"Yes!" Alex slapped the kitchen table with enthusiasm.

"What in the world?" I asked but in Cantonese dialect. Not too helpful. No one answered.

Molly said to Jade, "Since you're part of the family, what do we call you?"

"Maybe big brother?" Ramona turned to me. "*Dahgo?* That's the word, right?"

"Maybe just Jade?" he said, sounding reasonable, while I felt that jolt of panic which comes when control slips away.

I said, "It's not clear that he'll be living here."

"He already does." Ramona pointed to the dishes stacked on the kitchen counter. "He leaves his coffee cup on the rack with the breakfast dishes every morning."

Alex said, "He spends more time in the garage than I do. I'd call that living here."

Molly said, "If Wendy moves into one of the cottages—"

"Then Jade can have Stephen's room," Ramona said.

"Or Ruby's," Molly said.

"Why do we need a new arrangement? I like Lazarus Cottage," Jade said. "It's like home to me. I'll pay rent after the Festival arrangement ends."

No one but me paid attention to his question. I nodded.

"Mother," Alex waggled a finger at Claudia, "this is where you say, 'I'll pay Alex's rent.'" He tugged my sleeve. "*Suksuk,* can Mother stay in one of the cottages when she comes to visit?"

"That sounds good," I said. It sounded maudlin. "Except I have to rent out the cottages. Our cashflow remains precarious."

"I didn't say I'd pay. Or visit." Claudia looked over at Jade, pursing her lips. Sulking. Because she had totally lost.

Alex stood over her, hands on his hips. "You have to pay my room and board. You can make up your mind about visiting later. Like, say, tomorrow."

Ramona said, "Aunt Claudia, it'd make Alex really happy if you visited. If you don't like staying at Chaos House or the cottages, you could stay at the hotel."

A lot must have happened since I'd gone to Medford. Yet I didn't ask. Talking more about it should wait until people cooled off. And it shouldn't happen over dinner. Or until I'd slept all night. I'd rolled Sisyphus's karmic stone uphill every single day that week and twice last Saturday. That Sisyphean stone is hardly round and hence difficult to roll.

"I'll think about it," Claudia said, which was a significant surrender compared to last Monday's assault by attorney.

The oven timer went off. Molly called for Wendy to join us, and we all sat down to supper at the Chaos House table.

"Oh Ricky." Wendy could not lose my ancient nickname. She sat down on the other side of Jade. "I found a tree frog in the dryer. I took it to the upper duck pond in the park. Tell me I did a good deed. It wasn't your pet, was it?"

—

After supper, I sent the kids off to get milk, bread, and eggs for breakfast. I went upstairs to change out of my teacher clothes. Before I could close the door, Jade was in my room, standing there with his thumbs in the pockets of his jeans.

"What?" I took off my blazer and put it on a wooden coat hanger. My blazer needed brushing, but it'd wait for weekend chores. I unbuttoned my teacher shirt and dropped it in the laundry basket.

Jade pressed Play on my tape player. Which resumed blasting 'Straight to Hell.' Right at the plea: *mama, mama, mama.*

"Goodness." He switched it off.

"Goodness? How did that end up in your vocabulary?"

"I worked with Muslim students on that Fulbright in Turkey. So I had to end all my bad habits."

"Oh. That's obvious if I'd thought about it." I pulled my t-shirt over my head.

"Gosh, no, that's you being beautiful."

When I emerged from under my t-shirt, Jade was unbuttoning his own shirt. He said, "I'm going to work all night on the mural. I might finish. I hope."

"Do you want my help?"

"Yes. First, you can help restore my depleted energy. Since ancient magic can be brought to earth by the Holy Immortals—"

"They aren't holy. Only Heavenly. It's a class distinction."

"Whatever. Stop talking." His shirt half off, dangling from his wrists, he touched the same knob on my shoulder as he had in the Mildew Motel.

"You're all ropey, Sasha. Like an ancient woodcutter in a fight movie. Are you working out in a gym?"

"No, just plain working."

I wiggled out from under his touch to pull off his shirt, but his cuffs were buttoned. In the tangle, he wrapped his arms around me and tumbled us both onto the bed.

"Don't resist." His voice resonated through the bones behind my ear. "I shall let you have your way with me. Like in a romance."

His warm breath traveled down my neck. He mouthed rows of kisses all along my clavicle, then tongued that hollow behind my breastbone. Everything had fallen still behind those bones as if the dragon's crystals had been lulled into peaceful sleep.

A dog barked. Another barked. I couldn't yet tell one from the other. They joined in a small-dog duet.

"Are we supposed to be watching the dogs?" I failed to block my automatic inclination to take action.

"No," Jade said. "We are scholars undertaking a serious scientific study of whether human intimacy is restorative or exhausting. Our experiment is time-sensitive and cannot be interrupted."

—

Later, other details aside, Jade got his clothes back on more quickly than I did. While I dressed, he inspected my room, picking up the faux Roman ceramic disk showing a laurel-crowned young man, fingering the red silk robe hung over the back of my chair. He sat at my desk and read the top page of my manuscript aloud:

> These are stories of the grace and complex gestures of men who literally give up their lives to the person who best understands them.

"Is this about us, Sasha?"

I pulled on jeans, then sat down to put on socks, not looking to see his reaction to my writing. "Do you think a sweatshirt is enough for tonight? Should I bring a coat?"

"Gosh. This must be five hundred pages, Sasha."

"Only four hundred. It's a great soporific if you can't sleep."

"When the weekend is over, I intend to sleep for a week. But I want to read this first, Sasha. It's a major scholarly work."

"My advisor thought it had promise. It was at least good enough to steal."

"Are you going to go ahead and publish it?"

"Yeah, I'll try. I haven't got another project for this winter."

He was laughing, still reading the synopsis cover page that I'd made for Kevin.

"'If he did happen to read this, he'd skip to the conclusion.' So you do know me."

"That lay under the entire endeavor. Let's go figure how much lumber the dog's fence needs. Then I'll help you finish the mural."

He wouldn't let me out the door without another embrace.

"For the sake of science," he whispered.

—

Downstairs, a grocery bag was folded on the counter. The eggs and milk were in the refrigerator. The kids must have departed for the evening since all the skateboards were gone from beside the front door. No sign of either Wendy or Claudia.

Jade and I went out with a tape measure to decide how to fence the backyard for Pandora. And No-Name Chihuahua, I guess. We flipped on all the outdoor lights to see about well enough to take measurements.

"I only want to know how much lumber to buy. It's eight feet between posts, so..." I estimated the number of posts with basic mental math.

"We're doing pickets, right, Sasha? Painted white? Those little dogs don't need a six-foot-tall fence."

"Pickets don't go with the style of the house," I said. "And it's just the backyard."

"But pickets make a place feel like home."

"Jade, I can't read the tape measure. Stop twisting it."

"How can I read the tape without twisting it?"

"Your end says 'one.' You don't have to read anything. Just hold it against the corner of the house."

"I'm not used to being the go-fer. On my projects, I take the measurements."

"This is my project. We'll use wire instead of pickets. And we want a gate on each side of the house, plus one at the back that goes down to the woods by the creek."

"We'll spend all Sunday digging post holes, won't we?"

This felt so normal, as if we'd practiced, including the squabbling and Jade bitching about the work before just doing it.

I said, "To get a jump on Sunday, I'm going to buy the lumber tomorrow morning."

"How will you haul it? In my brand-new van?"

"I could, I suppose. I was going to get them to cut the posts in half at the lumber yard. You know..." Why hadn't I thought of this before now? "I should get a pickup instead of another car. It'd be worth the investment in the long run."

He laughed, pointing at me.

"What? Talk instead of laughing."

"'In the long run.'" He imitated me. "Your robust plan was to sell everything and move to Hong Kong. Now, 'in the long run,' you want a truck. But in the short run, you need to haul more than one person in your new vehicle. I'm not sure it's legal for kids to ride in a pickup bed, like we did when I was a kid."

"Oh, yeah." All week, the ruination of my robust plan had felt like a canyon opening before me. Now, a horizon has opened, and I want to explore what lay beyond. "Guess we haven't figured out much yet. Even Sunday is a rough sketch."

"It's just...if you're still moving to Hong Kong, I need to know so I can adjust for such a drastic change in my plans. What do you think it costs there for a thousand square feet of industrial space? I need that much for my workshop and kilns. I know Inez makes do with four hundred square feet, but I have different processes that require a great deal more space."

"I don't—"

"What's the exchange rate for Hong Kong pounds to U.S. dollars? Or is the rate the same as British pounds?"

Claudia came out the back door. She settled in a chair by the patio table, holding a cigarette but not lighting it.

"Do you agree, Claudia," Jade asked, "that the dogs want a picket fence, not a six-foot-tall fortress?"

"I don't know about dogs," she said.

"Not pickets," I said. "Too much work. Just posts and wire."

"Is that the appropriate aesthetic, Claudia?" Jade asked, though who knows why he was bugging her to answer. "Do you want to see pickets or wire when you come to visit?"

Oh dude, what the—

"I don't care." Then she stirred and changed positions to look at us. "Rik restored the house and cottages. He can make good design decisions. Especially for resale value."

"See, Sasha? Claudia agrees. Pickets have resale value."

I waved him off, given that he has no idea of what enhances resale value. Instead, I was direct.

"Claudia, seriously, Alex would appreciate it if you'd visit often. We can make room."

"Thank you. I'll have to review my writing schedule."

Jade clapped. She looked up startled, then saw he was smiling, as if he approved. She dipped her head for a moment before she said, "Rik, Alex insists that I apologize to you. They all ganged up on me because they're worried about you. I do apologize. It was wrong of me to try to solve the problem the way I did."

"Thanks," I said. "Peace?"

She nodded, held her hand out to shake mine.

"And?" Jade prompted. "The rest of it?"

"The rest?" She hesitated.

Jade gestured, prompting her, his voice arch. "Screaming at Alex? The perverse elements of Sasha's inclinations?"

"Just let it go," I said, preferring not to push Claudia further than she volunteered to go. This partner stuff is going to take getting used to.

Jade said, "You are counting on Sasha to let it go, aren't you, Claudia? Even though you hurt him. But neither Sasha nor I will let you off the hook for having hurt Alex."

"I'm sorry about what I said, Rik."

She lit that cigarette, her hands covering her face, hiding her expression.

"It's in the past," I said. "We can forget it."

"No, we can't," Jade said. "People can't go around saying hurtful things and then just being sort of sorry."

"I want to forget it, Claudia," I said. "I would, though Jade thinks I ought to be righteously angry. But you acted as insanely mean as Ruby. This whole month of your…shit behavior has only been about *your* feelings, not about what Alex needs. Rather than be angry, I'm just begging you not to hurt Alex or abandon him."

"See how nice Rik is?" Jade didn't sound nice at all. "But Alex needs more from you, more than just apologizing to him. You have to figure out how to get right with him, right enough to last for his lifetime. I'll see that kind of action on your part as karmic payback for what you owe, after what you did, lying to me."

Just then Wendy burst through the back door, apparently her natural way of coming and going. Pandora escaped out through the door, following her. "The kids got vanilla ice cream when they went to buy milk for breakfast. Who wants some?"

"Actually, Wendy," Claudia said, "let's us girls go get a drink. Want to walk up to the hotel with me?"

"Wow!" Wendy said. "That's another advantage to not living ten miles up a dirt road. We can walk to a bar."

When she rose to go, Claudia said, "I will consider your advice, Jade." To me she said, "I'll pay the attorneys. And prepare proper guardianship papers for you."

Jade called after Wendy. "Don't leave the dogs with us. We are on our way out for the night."

"Danielle said she'd watch them," Wendy said. Yikes, I hadn't yet told Danielle she was no longer employed. "She agreed since she's staying in tonight and doesn't have to take care of Ruby." Wendy followed Claudia, then turned back. "Ricky, are you going out to celebrate with your friends?"

"What does Rik have to celebrate?" Claudia asked. "That we aren't quarreling anymore?"

"No, silly," Wendy said. "Ricky doesn't have to get out of bed anymore when Ruby has nightmares."

49: In Defiance of the Heavens

WE WEREN'T GOING OUT TO celebrate. We were going to complete as much of the mural as possible before dawn. Or die in a mutual auto-combustion pyre while trying.

I hadn't heard the phone call that arranged it, but we were met by two guys from the Festival stage crew who'd helped with the Sunday mural work. They'd set up Klieg lights and unlocked the wire cage around the boxes of tiles and work gear.

When the lights were switched on, I was standing by the lower right of the mural where Ramona had been working. Edgar as Tom o'Bedlam was 95 percent done. And looked nothing like me.

Of course it didn't. I'd seen the plastic-encased ID drawings that specified the colors and placement of the stone-and-glass pattern that was Edgar's face. Quite different from the crumpled trash I'd picked up last week.

"What's wrong, Sasha?" Jade was right there. "Are you going to mix cement? We're ready to start."

I hadn't heard him call me. I pointed to poor grieving Edgar. "I found the Lear drawing you threw away. Where the figures all had Eliot family faces."

"Goodness." He had his hand on my shoulder, gripping it. "You weren't supposed to see that. No one was. I'm sorry."

"Is that how you think of me? A crazed Tom o'Bedlam?"

"No, of course not. I drew it after I saw Ruby in the garden with Willie. It was just a cartoon."

"But pretty harsh." I still didn't know how to feel about it.

"I had to vent, Sasha. I can't understand what you feel about how your mother is…mostly gone but still poking at you, while you are taking care of her."

He squeezed my shoulder harder. I tightened up, resisting the old fight-or-flight rush coursing through me. Then I relaxed, as if he'd found an acupuncture pressure point. "Yes, but now that nightmare of grief is over."

"Does it happen that fast, Sasha?"

Alex and Quinn appeared, skateboards under their arms.

"Hi, Rik—I mean, Mr. E!"

"Hello, Jade!"

Molly, Ramona, and two other girls from the mural crew came up behind them.

"Can we join your night crew?" Quinn asked.

Jade immediately agreed. "Yes. I'm working till dawn."

That left me to be the bad guy.

"You," I circled to encompass all the kids, "need to be home by eleven o'clock. The SAT is tomorrow morning."

"We have frequently been reminded of that," Molly said.

The kids got ready to work faster than I could get to each pair with fresh thin-set cement. It took half an hour for me to get into a work rhythm, since the previous night in the Mildew Motel had been good for my soul but not exactly restful for my body.

However, it took Jade no time at all to be busy. He cruised like a sprite through conversations with each pair of workers about what they should try to achieve before eleven o'clock, admonishing them to go slowly. "Go for quality, not speed," he said several times. However, once he began working on Lear's face, he united speed and quality.

The music that Jade set to play—Depeche Mode, Nektar, Joy Division—had to be turned off at ten o'clock, I think because of some deal the Festival had with the people who live nearby. So after ten o'clock, we worked in silence.

Actually, that silence produced a great deal of sound: metal palette knives scraping cement from aluminum palettes onto the concrete wall; tiles tinkling while an artist picked the next two or three stones; shuffling tennis shoes on the scaffold; quiet words traded between paired artists; soft *chink* and *oh no!* when tiles fell to the ground; *hey Mr. E!* when a pair called for more cement.

When the kids had to go home, Jade shook hands with each of them, proclaiming them artists and heroes and making sure each knew to appear for the Festival's reception was at two o'clock.

"We'll have a private party afterward!" Jade proclaimed. "Only artists know how to party!"

Then it felt too quiet, like sweeping up after a major life's festival. Jade, though, just went back to work. I cleaned up spilled tiles and washed the kids' tools and palettes, then checked the grouting around the newest work, which I knew Jade did after each mural work session.

An hour later, our working quiet was shattered again, though it was past Festival curfew time.

"The wanderers have returned!" Stephen called. He led most of the late-night Chez Margot crew from out the back door: Becca, Kevin, Timothy, Nick.

Stephen had sandwiches; Kevin had orange juice and cola from his bar mixers. I'd been drinking water all evening, but the smell of toasted sandwiches reminded me that it'd been many hours since dinner on a day with no lunch.

I greeted Timothy, who stood closest to me. It was nice to see him looking unguarded. Happy, even. I felt mortified that I'd had less than kind thoughts. "Hope all is going well."

"It's going good," Timothy said.

"It's better than good," Kevin said, his arm around Timothy. "He's been cast in a new play. And I'm still doing workshops, though *King Lear* won't be on the playbill next summer."

Becca said, "The Festival asked Xavier Torres to leave. But you knew that would happen."

"Fantastic!" I lifted my hand to high-five Timothy, but he didn't pick up on it. My hand hung in the air. Kevin slapped it.

"How was Green Springs?" Kevin asked. "I assume that's the route you took to Klamath Falls. My favorite."

Jade had to swallow a bit of sandwich, then said, "It wasn't my favorite yesterday. Snow and logging trucks. Not pleasant."

Kevin said, "Did Rik gasp and scare the crap out of you at every hairpin turn? He's like that."

"Only where the road dropped off steeply on his side." Jade tipped his hand, waving it to indicate an inconclusive answer.

"That's every curve on the way east," Kevin said.

Stephen said, "I want to hear about the whole adventure."

"Yeah," Becca said. "Stolen bride. Snow hazard. State patrol. Happy ending. Tell us all."

"Nothing beats a first-person narrative," Kevin said. "Trust me on that. I was a Lit major."

Jade told the story, but it wasn't the pins-and-needles, life-and-death experience I'd endured. The way Jade told it, not much had happened. He left out the part where he'd turned my life around and pointed it in another direction. He finished the story and his sandwich at about the same time.

Kevin said, "So Rik white-knuckled it over Green Springs and back again. Per usual for him."

"Did you fulfill your mission?" Becca asked Jade, obviously fishing for the outcome of his *don't go to Hong Kong* assignment.

"In the end," Jade said, "Ruby Eliot is happy with her new digs, and Sasha has two new dogs in his backyard."

That ending obviously left Becca unsatisfied.

"Now," Stephen said, "can we help?"

"I'm grateful that you offered," Jade said. "But Sasha and I need to work quickly. There's no time for me to supervise"

"Will you come to the unveiling tomorrow?" I asked.

"The event is today," Becca said. "And it's mandatory for my job. I'll make sure the makeup team is here early."

"Why?" I asked.

She pointed to me, and then at Jade. "That color under your eyes is called charcoal."

Kevin was last to leave us, calling to Timothy that he'd be there in a minute, then turning to whisper to me. "You have three hickeys on your neck. Consider covering up out in the light of day."

When they'd all departed, Jade stepped back to the center of the plaza. I was beside him, the Klieg lights casting long shadows behind us.

"We're going to make it," he said. "Though Lear's face will take a good four hours to finish."

"I feel," I said, "as if we've been here before. More than once."

"Yeah." Jade agreed. "But we were always tripping balls back then. Let's get to it."

50: Fools and Madmen

IT'D BE FUTILE TO TRY TO coax Jade away. He surrendered on his own when the eastern horizon was growing lighter. At home, he drank coffee while I made waffles and bacon. I had cocoa ready when the kids shambled into the kitchen. Jade cut and squeezed oranges and then poured juice for each scholar.

At eight thirty, the trio accepted the freshly sharpened #2 pencils and the protein bars wrapped in waxed paper. They politely covered their mouths instead of laughing at me directly.

The girls were already out the door when Jade put his hand on Alex's shoulder.

"I know you, young Eliot. You are intelligent and crafty. You will ace this."

As they started down Water Street, Jade pulled me onto the porch, his arm around me as we watched them walk away.

"They grow up so fast," he said, sounding nostalgic.

"I suppose," I said. "Though that was the longest eight years I ever lived through. Why get emotional this morning?"

"I'm pretending I'm not ticked that their mothers didn't get out of bed to see them off. The twins might be blasé about the test, but Alex is scared. The kids have been talking all week about how the SAT would affect their futures."

"Kids who ate dinner here have heard my reassurances. And I coached Alex on how to take the tests." I'd taught the girls how to take tests years before.

"What you say might be real," Jade said, "but there's also what they *feel,* which is also real. Wendy and Claudia should have been here to wave them off to battle."

"Don't look for more grudges. The kids are all right."

We had separate tasks for the day. I set off to borrow the Oak Street collective's flatbed truck. Between ordering and waiting at the lumber yard, and then unloading and returning the truck, I made it through morning chores without surrendering to fatigue.

I next saw Jade for about five minutes at noon, when I was preparing lunch and awaiting the return of the SAT scholars. He grabbed an untoasted cheese sandwich and departed, calling only, "See you later."

I didn't fare much better when the kids returned after the test. The best I coaxed from them about their test experience:

> Alex: Half the math was in a foreign language. So I just guessed.
>
> Ramona: Aced the essays. The lit excerpts were trite.
>
> Molly: Multiple choice was boring.
>
> Alex: What's for lunch?

They had forty-five minutes between coming home and being required to be at the site ahead of the event. Hence, I saved my questions about the test for later—when they'll have forgotten what else they'd experienced beyond nervousness and boredom.

—

At the wall, a scrim had been hung over the mural. After all, the event had been dubbed an unveiling.

I spied Jade in the press gaggle. He wore black jeans and a black leather jacket over a black t-shirt. His crew was also all in black, with zippered sweatshirts. That left me, Mr. E the Chaperone, as the only member of the team dressed like people in the audience, since I wore my teacher clothes, but with a white turtleneck (as

Kevin advised). Only my black Converse court shoes marked me as a team member.

Valerie had come with Julio. He immediately glommed onto Alex, who must have swung Julio into the air a half-dozen times in the lead-up to the event.

A few minutes before three o'clock, the crew began urging parents and friends to sit down, then they milled near the wall, where two-step risers had been set up, like for a choral performance. When Jade gave his signal for their attention, Julio grasped Alex's shirt tail and couldn't be coaxed away.

"Hey, cowboy," Jade said. "Long time, no see. I need Alex right now. Can you go sit with your mom?"

Julio shook his head solemnly.

Hence, when the crew lined up along the risers and cameras began flashing pictures, the back row of the black-clad chorus included a pint-size figure in a vibrant blue Underdog t-shirt, stuck to Alex like Super Glue.

I slipped into the rear of the crowd, to the standing-room section, just before the Festival director stepped up to introduce Jade. The director recited more of Jade's artistic biography than I'd known about. Then, whatever the Festival expected from this event, Jade took the mike, welcomed people, and made a couple of dumb Shakespeare jokes, starting with a quote from *King Lear* about fools and madmen and then bridging to one I recognized from my remedial liberal arts courses as a *Macbeth* quote:

> I have no spur
> To prick the sides of my intent, but only
> Vaulting ambition, which o'erleaps itself
> And falls on the other.

He pointed to one of the Festival stage crew guys at the end of the scrim, who then gestured to his partner at the other end, and the scrim was dropped.

Most in the assembled audience clapped politely. Friends of the crew clapped, stomped, and shouted cheers. Our crew glanced at each other while their friends cheered, finally smiling at that enthusiastic reception.

Then, for the next thirty minutes Jade introduced each of his mosaic artists, who came over to stand with their partners near the portions of the mosaic they'd worked on. When introduced, each artist accepted the penlight from Jade, pointed to their part of the mural, and described what they'd learned from the venture, often including portions of Jade's mini-lectures.

Alex spoke first, repeating his talk on the Golden Rectangle, but with much more polish and greater animation than Quinn at his most eager.

The most interesting thing at that moment wasn't Alex's presentation, since I'd heard most of it before. Instead, I watched Claudia while Alex spoke. She sat in the third row of folding chairs. One minute into Alex's talk, she clapped her hand to her mouth, astonished. Two minutes in, she fished a handkerchief from her bag. I think—no, I'm sure she was crying.

Jade had guessed it: she didn't know this side of her son.

All the kids were great. It's not just prejudice but my true belief that Ramona and Molly were the most poised. Each kid concluded their talk with a solemn thank you to a funder or institution that backed the project. They held notes, surreptitiously checking which name they were assigned. After each such acknowledgment, the whole crew clapped, hands extended to the target of gratitude, like actors or musicians clap for their director.

After the conclusion of the formal event, the kids remained with their work partners, posing for pictures at the mural. Insubstantial refreshments (punch and cookies) were served from tables near Chez Margot.

"A total success," Becca said to me in passing. "Jade's a star." I agreed while having no idea when Jade pulled off organizing and coaching for the event. I'm paid to be present whenever the crew comes together, but that coaching hadn't happened while I was around. And most of those kids had been swimming through the SAT rapids that morning.

While the crowd was departing, I watched Jade, who was still enmeshed with a couple of reporters and, judging from their clothes, three pairs of funders. Molly and Ramona were a few steps away from Jade's confab, showing Wendy the sections they'd worked on. Jade turned to them, said a word, and brought the twins into his interview.

Behind me, I heard Alex speak. He was only inches away, but I politely did not turn around and intrude.

"Mother, let me introduce you to Quinn's mom. That's who he's talking to over there."

"In a minute," she said. "Alex, I had no idea. I'm ashamed for thinking that drawing was just your little hobby. I didn't respect your work or even know what you're up to. I am so sorry."

"It's fine now, Mother. Please don't cry."

I stepped away. I didn't need to be in their most intimate business. I headed toward Jade, for no reason other than his magnetic pole pulled me in that direction. I dodged a clutch of Festival people, including Becca and the stage crew who'd helped with the Klieg lights. They'd been among those called out with gratitude. One asked me if I'd be at the after-party. "It's Jade's idea. But Becca's been working on details. You'll be there, right, Rik?"

"He's the school chaperone," Becca said. "He has to go wherever the kids go."

"If Jade's there," I said, "I'll be there."

From the look Becca gave me, that must have sounded dumb. I laughed, feeling deep joy at voicing my true state of being, not just something I'd signed a contract to do.

Becca looked at her watch. "We'd better free Jade from the press gaggle and herd everyone down to the party."

While most people who remained began drifting down the passageway toward Lithia Plaza, I followed my internal pull toward Jade, who was talking with the stage crew about packing everything up for the night.

"Rik, a moment." It was Claudia.

"Hi, it's nice to see you here." I sounded like I meant it, and I was glad, for Alex's sake. "Are you coming to the after-party? Parents are invited."

"I'm headed home. I like driving at night."

"Alex will be disappointed."

"Mmm, I think not," she said. "We've already said goodbye. He made me promise to ship his things next week."

"Yeah," I said. "I think he especially misses his dirt bike and his other guitar."

"Rik, you were right. I didn't understand Alex or what matters most to him. I had no idea—"

"That Alex possesses the genius of an artist?" Jade was behind me, so close that I smelled bay rum and felt his heat.

Claudia's eyes shot his way. Her professional face closed off whatever feeling she was about to share with me.

She said, "I promised Alex that I'd come for Christmas."

"Good idea," I said. "That gives everyone time to breathe and think about everything."

"Alas, I'll miss you." Jade wrapped a hand around my waist. I resisted looking around to see who noticed. "I have a four-day seminar at Cooper's Union over the holidays."

Oh? We hadn't yet discussed the full calendar of plans. And Jade was talking about leaving Ashland.

Impulsively I said, "Then we should all go to New York for the holidays."

His arms tightened around my waist. "That's a fantastic idea. We can take the twins to see Boston U. And I'd love to take Alex and Ramona to the Met and MoMA and the Guggenheim."

I nodded, as if enthused. "Let's just do it. It can be a surprise for the kids." The surprise for me would be how to pay for it. To be considered later. "Will you join us, Claudia? I'm sure Alex will want you to come."

"Yes, Claudia," Jade said. Sugar dripped from his tongue. "Do come along. You and me together in New York again? Like old times?" He moved to pull me closer, but I was already as close as it's possible to be.

"I don't think so." Her lips thinned as she forced a smile. "I'll come to Ashland at Thanksgiving then."

"Sure," I said, not doing my best job of sounding gracious.

"Oh rats, I'll miss that." Jade slipped both hands around my waist, under my blazer. "I have a one-day event in Berkeley."

I leaned into feeling his hands on me. My shirt was thin; I felt their heat. "Then we'll all go to the Bay Area for the holiday."

"Four days together?" Jade sounded excited. "Do you mean that everyone can go?"

"The kids would love it." I'd have to win the lottery to afford plane tickets, but…to be considered later.

"Claudia, instead of Thanksgiving at Chaos House," Jade said, "why don't you invite us to your house? It's in Berkeley, right? We'll be right there since my workshop is the next day."

"Yes–s–s." Claudia stammered an agreement. "The twins can stay at my house, I suppose."

"Wendy too?" Jade asked, then said to me, "It's a chance for you and me to enjoy better accommodations than the Mildew Motel. Alone together."

"I'll have to persuade Wendy to come." I didn't mention her fear about the dick-guru guy wanting her arrested for assault.

Jade shrugged. "We have a few weeks to work on details, but we'd better get plane tickets on Monday. Right, Claudia?"

"Yes. Well. I need to be on the road."

She glanced between us, surely seeing a united pair. If only I'd been that strongly aligned with Jade when Claudia met him at the Bad Christmas. She shook my hand, apologized again, and headed up the plaza to Pioneer Street.

"Let's go!" Jade released his hold on me, already walking away. "Can't be late for the party. I am totally freaking starved."

I scrambled to tag after him across the brick plaza. "Uh, Jade? I can't afford to fly everyone to San Francisco."

"I bet Claudia will pay for Alex," he said.

"And New York is far beyond me."

"Gosh! You, in an act totally unlike you, just joined with me in jerking Claudia's chain. But now you're worried about money?"

"Of course I'm worried. We're flying how many people all over the place?" I started counting on my fingers, though I'd done the math in my head.

"We can afford it. Didn't I explain that to you? And I will not spend the holidays away from you and everyone else." He dug an elbow into my side. "I thought you'd feel remorse for being mean to Claudia. Especially since I had my hand up your shirt, right in front of her." He stopped walking, caught me by the sleeve. "Wait! Did you just make a spur-of-the-moment commitment, but you don't actually want to do it?"

"No, I just..." Heavenly Immortals, I had to suck back the unexpected, lonely feeling I'd had moments before. "When you said you'd be going away, I rushed to make promises to fix that."

"Sasha, I swore to stay with you. And we can nag at Claudia some more over Thanksgiving dinner. With enough practice, we might get good at it. But if you don't really want to go to New York with the rest of us, I'll handle the details." He tugged my shirt, teasing. I caught on a bit more quickly this time. He dug a knuckle into my side, laughing at me. "If you give me a list of what to do."

"Am I supposed to get used to this?" I complained. "We start off in one direction, then end up somewhere else?"

"Yes," he said. "You can cry 'Stop!' each time I go too far. Or do we need a special safe word? Like, if I'm bullying you into something you don't want to do? Though I think you wanted to join me in being mean to Claudia."

"'Stop' might be enough." There was much more to say. I didn't want to be bullied into anything. And I didn't want any of what's happening with us to stop.

Jade put his arm around my shoulder. "Hmm. Better add this to your list of all the stuff we have to figure out in our new plan. But there's plenty of time for that. All the time we want."

As we started down the steps to Lithia Plaza, he added, "Except I do need to find a new studio and order kilns next week."

—

At Jade's behest, Becca had rented the pizza place just across the creek from downtown and had pre-ordered twenty-five pizzas. Each of the kids brought a friend plus their parents or guardians Which meant fifty people were inside when we arrived.

Valerie was just inside the door and greeted us first. "Hi, Rik! We should have dinner together soon. I've missed you."

"That's a possibility," I said, "now that the mural is done."

At least as far as most everyone was concerned. I'd heard on the way here that Jade intended to inspect every inch in the next week to be sure every single glass bead and tile is set tight.

She said, "I'm here because I can't pry Julio off Alex. He's swung Julio around enough to give them both motion sickness."

I said, "Guess we have to make sure there's bread for Julio."

"Becca took care of that." Valerie excused herself; someone she knew waved from across the room.

Jade was eating bites of pizza while circling the room, shaking hands, and greeting the adults who'd come with the mural crew. I crossed the room to where Molly and Ramona were introducing Wendy to their friends' parents. Ramona said to Quinn's mother, "Wendy is here while writing her next book."

Mrs. Hargadine bent forward, curious. "Are you Wendy Eliot who wrote *Girl on the Sidelines* and *Bad Reputation?*"

Wendy nodded. Color rose in her face, as if recognition made her blood flow more freely.

> Quinn's mom: I read *Girl on the Sidelines* when Quinn was four. It kept me from going out of my mind.
>
> Wendy: Thank you for saying that.
>
> Quinn's mom: I know Alex's mom is a writer too. But I don't get that minimalist stuff. What are you writing now?
>
> Wendy: The working title is *Demons and Destiny at the Cloud Café.* But publishers never let you keep your title.
>
> Quinn's mom: I cannot wait. I'm Donna, by the way. Do you want to get coffee one day next week? Or a drink?

More evidence of my dim-witted self: I didn't know Donna's first name until that moment, and I had no notion Wendy was still a writer. Unnerved from eavesdropping—no, only surprised since I was too tired to have emotions—I went to sit by Alex, whose parent was on I-5, already past Hilt and nearing Yreka. I sat down just when Jade made it to our side of the room.

"Hey, it's my favorite cowboy." Jade again greeted Julio, who remained stuck to Alex. "Eating pizza tonight, hombre?"

Julio started to shake his head, but Alex said, "Sure he is. All my cowboys eat pizza." He called down the table. "Pass a slice of cheese pizza to my buddy here."

I'd tried every possible temptation over the two years that Valerie lived at Chaos House, but in one night, Jade and Alex got him to eat nonwhite food. It was mostly Alex though, who applied gentle wannabe-peer pressure.

I managed to scarf down two pizza slices while greeting parents who wanted to thank me for their child's extraordinary experience. After Jade had greeted everyone, he stood beside the room's fake fireplace and made his hand signal for attention.

"It's time for awards." He pulled covers off a pair of cartons and picked something from the first one. Then he called Zooey's name. "The first award goes to Zooey Helman for perfect attendance and for the most positive attitude."

She came up, stooped in her shy tall-girl posture. Her award was a framed ID sheet with one of the drawings that had guided her work. The frame trailed a blue award ribbon with her name hand lettered. All team members received a similar award, each signed by Jade with a personal note.

"So that's what Jade was doing in the garage," Quinn said.

"Or half of what he's been doing," Alex said. "But what do you think he's making those giant boxes for?"

After twelve awards were handed out, Quinn called, "What about Mr. E? Doesn't he get an award?"

Zooey called, "At least for perfect attendance?"

I'd dodged attention through the main event, but the kids began chanting *Mr. E! Mr. E!* and clapping their hands. So I stood when Jade motioned for me to join him. He bent to retrieve a frame from a carton.

"Yes, there's a reward for the best thin-set concrete man in the business, who faithfully brought us our daily bread."

Cameras began flashing when he handed me the award: a peanut butter sandwich pinned on a TV-dinner tray with a palette knife, dipped in resin like egg foo yung in a Chinatown café window, and framed in a shadow box. My trailing blue ribbon had a rosette, like a prize at the state fair.

That spawned just what one might expect if one had spent any time around high school kids: raucous shouts and whistles, followed by the mural crew singing and stomping to the first lines of 'We Will Rock You.' The parents clapped politely.

When I sat down again, Alex leaned over and said, "That was Molly's idea. It was also her idea we all wear black."

Later in the celebration, I had to beg at the counter for a cup of coffee. Jade wandered by just when I grabbed a paper napkin to cover a set of sneezes.

"Are you sick?"

"Dunno. Maybe I just need Benadryl." Though I hadn't been around our new dogs for six hours.

"I hope that's all."

Still possessing boundless energy, Jade continued around the room, speaking at length with each adult about their kid's special contributions and what he knew about their college plans. Two sets of parents captured me into a conversation about the possibility of private math tutoring for their students. I listened, offered advice for what they could do on their own, and promised to discuss the notion again after Christmas break. I'd begun to like the idea of three free hours after school and so didn't respond immediately to the idea of additional income.

One might think it had to end soon, but this was a peak event for these kids, and they weren't ready to let go. At nine o'clock, Valerie tried to coax Julio into leaving. He was having none of it. A few minutes earlier, new food options had been announced: ice cream sundaes.

Alex said, "Please let Julio stay. He can spend the night with us at Chaos House."

A wave of emotion passed over Valerie's face. Joy won out. "Sure. I'll come pick him up early tomorrow." She left Julio, his blue Underdog shirt now stained red, between Quinn and Alex.

Every kid in the room was elated with what they'd achieved since early September and how it had been recognized that day. Julio, who had compromised his long-held principles that night, might be the happiest.

51: Wandering Scholars

AFTER FIFTY GOODBYES OUTSIDE THE pizza party, Jade avowed he was still vibrating too hard to go home. I wanted to go to bed and sleep past dawn. Yet I also wanted to stay with Jade. If I've learned anything, it's how to manage two opposing desires, so I hiked with Jade up to Chez Margot. He seemed carefree. However, I was about to appear before the jury of my peers who'd been so concerned about my future that they'd sought an intervention.

Most of our usual crew was present, including Gaye, who didn't start her shift at the radio for another hour. Valerie, sans Julio, sat at the end by Stephen. Only Frankie and Inez were absent from our usual crew. The last dinner settings had been cleared, and the kitchen crew was cleaning up.

We sat in the empty seats in the exact middle of the bar, as if people had left space for us. Jade sat by Timothy. I sat beside Becca, but I leaned past Jade to greet Timothy.

As Kevin made my usual drink, he said, "You'd better tell him, Timothy."

"I guess I'm supposed to give you notice, Rik," Timothy said. "I won't be returning to the cottage." He glanced shyly at Kevin, who smiled, which illuminated Timothy like bright sunshine. "I think we'll be in L.A. for the winter, then come back here when rehearsal begins for the new play."

Jade sipped the drink Kevin placed before me, made a face, and said, "Jack Daniels neat, please."

I excused myself and went to the men's room. When I came out, Nick cornered me in the short hall by the kitchen.

"So no more Eliot family squabbles? Your sister called late yesterday afternoon. No, she's your sister-in-law, isn't she?"

"Claudia called you?"

"Alex called, then put his mother on the line. So I owe you. Your effort on my windows was greater than my efforts on Alex's guardianship issues."

"It's not a big deal. It'll balance out."

"Yeah, and this time I won't have to track down the sleazy attorney who helped Ruby seize your trust fund."

"I wish I had amnesia about that whole episode." I headed back to the bar with Nick following me. "There's more work coming for you. I have to sell Chaos House as soon as possible, to pay for my mother's care."

"Sell Chaos House!" Becca exclaimed, looking wary.

"You know that's been the plan for a long time," I said. "The plan just needs to move up to January."

"You'll get a better price in the spring," Nick said. "It's a rule of thumb for real estate."

"Sasha did the math all the way from Klamath Falls," Jade said. "He's convinced he has to sell sooner rather than later."

Gaye clinked her glass against Becca's. "That settles it, my love. We have to find our own place. I win that argument."

Becca turned to me. "But you'll have to rent somewhere. That won't be easy with three kids."

"And Wendy," Jade said, then dropped his voice. "And me."

Everyone must have heard. No one blinked.

I said, "Maybe I can get a deal to rent back the house until the kids graduate. I bet no one who buys that monster wants to move in immediately."

Stephen said, "Rik, you said you'd give me the first chance come spring. I'm not sure I can arrange financing by January."

Again, Jade got involved without first asking. "I now know the big-money people in the Rogue Valley. I bet I can help you find interim financing, especially since a major work of contemporary art is involved."

"Do you mean that creepy *Lazarus* painting?" Kevin asked.

"Indeed," Jade said. "Stephen, do not paint over *Lazarus*. You should sell me that wall."

"Not sure I want to sell it," Stephen said. "They say large-format art brings good money with the right buyer, if you hold onto it and hit the market right."

"It's my wall." Despite the fatigue and happiness enveloping me, I could at least assert right of first possession. "It is not part of the deal when the house is sold."

They pretended not to hear, and I sipped my innocuous drink while Stephen and Jade dickered. My face felt so hot, I must look flushed. It took me a moment to feel my way through the symptoms of the disease pursuing me. My head and my upper chest burned. Surely people could see heat and light coming off me.

Ah, the heat was merely relief. I wasn't used to my problems being resolved with so little effort on my part.

Nick held his glass out to Kevin for another drink. "We cannot be talking real estate in a bougie bar like freakin' California yuppies. Let's talk in my office on Monday."

"After school," I said. Stephen nodded.

The conversation then went the way it always does at Chez Margot: all over the place. The director of the new play Timothy had joined wasn't predatory. Gaye and Becca were finishing production on their audio gig, and public radio had expressed interest after hearing a sample. Nick was dating a United Airlines flight attendant, and they planned Christmas in Hawaii.

And no one asked why Jade had a finger hooked in my belt loop the whole time.

Becca was sitting close beside me, so I felt her increasing impatience, like she had her own fire burning. After Gaye left for work, Becca smacked her hand on the bar.

"Stop delaying. Jade, tell us. Did you carry out your mission?"

"I did," Jade said, "amid our many travails on the search for Ruby and her paramour."

"And the result?" she prompted.

"I am doing as my friends suggest." I pointed to Kevin. "Especially for the strongest recommendation I've heard."

People settled back to listen, expectant looks on their faces.

"My goal has long been to finish my PhD and teach in a Hong Kong university. But what Kevin told me is right. I don't need a PhD to find other kinds of teaching positions."

They were nodding. I hoped to hypnotize them with logic.

"Hence, as Kevin recommended, I plan to spend the winter making a solid, achievable plan to publish chapters of my dissertation as books and monographs. Failing to reach my PhD goal brought an enormous sense of loss, but I hope to overcome such feelings while following my new direction."

"Yes!" Kevin raised his hand in victory.

"No!" Becca punched me, hard enough that I mashed up against Jade and he had to let go of my belt loop to catch me. "You know I'm asking about Hong Kong."

"Oh, that part. I did listen closely to the plea Jade made on your behalf. I understand that you are all worried about my future plans, and I'm seriously touched by your concern." I nodded my gratitude to each of them, Becca last because I wanted to torture her. "So now, I want to assure you, I will not go to Hong Kong and end up alone."

Becca praised the lord and patted her heart in relief. Stephen and Kevin high-fived each other.

I held up my glass. "I salute your concern as good friends. Now, to resolve the potential problem you identified in my plan, Jade is starting a search for industrial space for his workshop. I have a fair idea about which neighborhoods in Hong Kong might have what he needs."

Becca's face lost all expression. The others looked confused.

Timothy, who always looks like he doesn't know what's happening, said, "Is Jade going to Hong Kong with you?"

"If he keeps his promise."

Jade tucked two fingers inside my waistband and pinched me. He pursed his lips, thoughtful. I hope he was pondering how much he likes me jumping into business without asking first.

He tossed back the rest of his shot of JD before speaking. "It's true. I am seeking industrial space for a workshop. I did swear to stay by Sasha's side, but it was late at night after an arduous drive." He turned to me. "I'm not sure that 'in Hong Kong' was attached to my real estate goals or that promise."

"Rik!" Becca pleaded. "What?"

I grasped her hand. "As you and I have discussed over many late-night talks, my long-term goals are focused on becoming my true self. Don't you agree?"

"Uh...yes?"

"In my life as I'm living it at the moment, I'm busy reconstructing my true self amid drastically changed circumstances. Such a reconstruction of self takes a great deal of psychic energy."

"Oh brother," Kevin said. "You can steal a dissertation from the scholar, but you can't purloin the pedant from his heart."

"The pedant is part of that scholar's true self," Jade said.

I agreed, in order to press toward my point. "Given all that, I decided to not decide anything right now, especially since I spent this week living through upheaval with no sleep. I promise to tell you, Becca, as soon as I know what's next."

"You can't move away, Rik," Becca said. "That just makes no sense now. Maybe it never did."

Kevin said, "I'm sure he'll take your opinion under advisement, Becca. But you should recognize that he's jiving you."

I still held her hand. "I am touched that you care about my future." I leaned over to whisper in her ear. "Jade was slow to make that promise because he's been waiting for you and me to break up. He feared he'd be breaking your heart by stealing me away."

She blinked, leaned past me to gape at Jade, and—as I'd hoped—ceased bugging me.

"It's almost midnight," Nick said. "The Varsity is showing *Drunken Master* with Jackie Chan."

Timothy and Kevin chimed in, eager to go. Becca guessed she might come along. Stephen said he'd lock up, but he and Valerie were heading home.

"*Drunken Master* is a true classic," I said. "But I've seen it."

Becca said, "You've seen it at least six times, Rik. That's never stopped you."

"The last..." I counted on my fingers "...sixty-two hours have been particularly demanding. I have to call it a night."

Timothy asked, "Are you coming with us, Jade?"

"Not this time. The last couple of days took a lot out of me. I need my beauty sleep."

Kevin watched as Jade dropped dollar bills on the bar then hooked a finger in my belt loop again. "That's how it is?"

"That's how it is." Jade stood up, the light of the chandelier crowning him like an angel.

I felt butterflies in my core. Please, I begged the Heavens, don't make this be the flu.

—

"Who knows what chaos there'll be at home this time," I mused.

"Let's not hurry back, just in case. I want to talk to you without the roaring crummy, the screaming fanbelt, our nosy friends, and a house full of Eliots who..." He paused. "Jiminy Christmas, as my dad used to say. Your sister and your sister-in-law are...um, difficult. I guess I already knew that."

Jade and I ambled down Main Street. I jittered, but my balance was fine. Not a virus? After the adventure of the last few days, fatigue felt like it had physically incarnated, like a shaggy beast that walked alongside me, occasionally nuzzling close and tripping me. Also, I'd been so keyed up all week, the absence of apprehensive tension left me giddy.

When we reached the plaza, the same streetlights were shining as a week ago, but now the cityscape wasn't imbued with a Fifties film noir atmosphere.

"We must be coming to the plaza from a different angle." I explained to Jade how the dark streets had felt the night Alex kicked a hacky sack footbag while in the wrong place at the wrong time.

Jade glanced around the shadowy plaza. "Makes me yearn to come here at two o'clock in the morning and sketch it."

"Not this morning, I hope."

"Nope. I have other plans." He smirked.

He pointed toward the park, tilted his head as an invitation. We walked around the lower duck pond. Many of its inhabitants, like the mean-spirited mute swans, live here year-round. Half the mallards slept in a row, their head rotated backward, bills resting on their backs. The others paddled around the pond, as if aimless.

"Do you still feel like you're catching something?" Jade asked. "Is it a virus? Or just dog allergies?"

"I'm okay. I haven't been assessing my body signals correctly. Since you came to town, I've been expecting chaos to break loose. Now that the future's here, it's the opposite of bad. I've instead arrived at an exotic, unexpected destination. I have to readjust my internal organs to a new equilibrium."

I was babbling. A duck shuffled out from the bushes and stood at the edge of the pond as if undecided about the next step. I shared the feeling.

Jade sat on a park bench. Well, he sprawled like he usually does, legs out. When I sat beside him, he rested his arm on the back of the bench behind me, his finger stroking my ear lobe.

"You know, Sasha, I came here seeking the fire I had in my life years ago."

"So you said."

"But I wasn't looking to find it in a mosaic of Lear or two sections of Ceramics 101 and a 300-level ceramic methods class. It's you. You made the world crazy and wonderful."

"It was the other way around."

"I have a hundred examples of your wild ways, Sasha. You scored some Owsley acid and dragged me off to see *The Horse's Mouth* at the Varsity. That *Lazarus* wall? Your idea."

"Hardly."

"Who had the notion for the Patroclus and Achilles mural? You got all excited about it at the Greek café on University Ave, the one with great avgolemono soup. I owe every innovative idea in my MFA project to you."

"Jade, none of that started with me."

"Your memory is failing in your old age. Yet I recall it clearly."

"Trust me, no nascent creativity came from me. When I'm running, I've pored over details of those adventures. You were the instigator, and I was your acolyte."

"Trust you?" Jade laughed. "I stalked you for forty-five days and you never knew."

"How long will you tease me about that?"

"I'll stop now. I do want to talk to you."

He stood, dragging me up with him, and we walked the well-groomed dirt trail again. The wakeful duck at the edge of the pond scuttled away, plopping into the pond.

"What is it?" I felt curious, free of trepidation. I'd learned not to dread what Jade might say. "Are you unhappy because I told our friends that we're moving to Hong Kong?"

"Are we?"

"No." I had to stop hedging. "They were right. I'm tossing my Hong Kong plan onto the trash heap of history. Still, I do want to visit again after the kids graduate. Will you come with me?"

"That'll be us, just doing what's next. Every single day."

"Mmm." Yeah, I hummed. That thought was so delicious. "What do you want to talk about?"

"You." He'd gotten half a step ahead of me. He stopped, making me stop, then looped his finger in my belt loop. "Sasha, you're always the caretaker. You cook, make repairs, manage all the business for a boatload of people."

"Yeah?"

"I said it yesterday. Let me carry your burdens for a while. Do your teaching gig and cook dinner, but otherwise, lay down your burdens. Take a rest."

"I don't have burdens." I stumbled over a tree root intruding on the narrow trail. Jade caught me. "And I don't want to end up eating dry cereal at breakfast."

"You just set down caring for Ruby. I bet it takes months to recover from that. But then you added caring for Wendy. The dark circles under your eyes match the swatch for ash on a color wheel."

"That's allergies. And shades of black and white aren't on any color wheel you ever made."

"Don't be difficult, Sasha. How can I help you construct your true self if you're too exhausted to lift a hammer?"

This wasn't the right conversation for my sixty-third hour without sleep. "I surrender. I can agree to less fretting. Plus I have a few extra hours each day now. I could—"

"Rest?"

"Go on longer runs. And run after school so I can sleep at least an extra hour in the morning."

He was silent for too long. At last: "Okay. I won't try to change you or your habits. That'd be wrong. Just don't try to make me take up running."

He steered me off the path by the pond and back to the paved walkway that leads to Lithia Plaza. He stopped at the fountain to drink lithia water, I guess because he's perverse. I wandered up the plaza. Rotten-egg–scented water is not my favorite.

When he joined me again, Jade said, "Will you go on a date with me, Sasha? Next Saturday?"

"A date?"

"Yeah, you know, when people who like each other go out and do something special together."

"Next Saturday?" I asked, dull-witted with fatigue.

We paused outside the Log Cabin tavern across from the fountain. I stepped aside to let late-night customers move past us. The mercury-vapor lamp overhead made Jade's eyes glow with ethereal light. He talked rapidly, excited about our date.

"A Jackson County highway crew is putting in a new culvert up past Eagle Point. They're excavating on Friday, and I'm taking my 300-level ceramics class out on Saturday to dig clay. The County crew has big diggers that can go down ten feet, so we expect to find clay that contains no organic matter. It's bound to be the best opportunity this year."

"I'm honored to be asked. Casual wear, I assume? Red Wing boots or Chuck Taylors?"

"You know these woods. You tell me."

He grabbed my elbow and tugged, pulling me out of the way of a clutch of Log Cabin denizens, all bearded and dressed in an assortment of denim and cowboy boots. We rounded the corner into the pedestrian alley that runs behind the stores across from the plaza. He shoved me up against the brick wall.

And kissed me.

He tasted of whiskey and pizza.

Those familiar full, pillowy lips? Soft, warm. Too many senses came to attention. My mind raced. How do I deserve this? Will I lose it in a heartbeat? Is it real?

Then the thousand nerve endings in my face wiped away all rational thought.

Our teeth clinked. The sound unlocked what I knew in every tissue of my being. I shamelessly ravaged his tongue. He hummed, a deep vibration that tickled my lips and palette. I released his tongue and attacked his lips and face with a hundred butterfly-soft kisses. Afraid to breathe.

His finger stroked my earlobe. Then he pulled my hair.

I taught him that. I got the idea from watching *Women in Love,* but didn't have a chance to try it until I met Jade—well, several months *after* I met Jade.

Heavenly Immortals, I was such a naïve boy. For such a very long time.

52: Rain and the Heart's Melody

JADE STEPPED BACK FROM OUR kiss, looking as intoxicated as the couples and trios wandering out of the tavern. He'd pretty much bruised my lower lip, sucking on it.

"Uh." It took me a second to be able to speak. "I don't do this out in the open in Ashland."

"I miss your long hair." He tugged at a fistful again.

"It caused problems on my handyman gigs. What happened to your long hair?"

"Set it on fire at an open-pit kiln in Britain. It smelled bad and scared the bejeezus out of me."

"Ah, hazards of a Wandering Scholar's life." I laughed, only a little jealous of yet another foreign adventure I'd missed.

"I hope you aren't laughing at me, Sasha. I never did figure out why I was paid to recreate a neolithic pottery method in an Iron Age hill fort. It was fun though, until I was burning like a witch. Want to see the scar?"

"Maybe later."

"Yeah. Not out on the streets of Ashland."

We crossed over to Water Street, where our shoes crunched on the sandy granite road surface.

"Do you feel okay?" he asked.

"Given the last five minutes, I feel expansive. Like I stepped into Ashland Creek and became part of the flow."

"Then tell me, Sasha, what do you want—that no longer involves moving to Hong Kong?"

"I just…" I cleared my throat to get the words out. "Hong Kong was where my real life was supposed to begin after all these years as a substitute teacher and handyman, never having any adventures. But now, you look like the next adventure."

"Ah." Jade sighed. "Can we do the plan we talked about yesterday, where we travel for adventure and also stay here? Ashland would be so easy for me to call home."

"Home." I repeated the word, but in a Cantonese dialect.

The familiar crunch of the gravel on Water Street told me it wasn't Hong Kong I'd been homesick for in Seattle. It wasn't Hong Kong I'd been plotting to get back to all this time. It was the Chan family dinners. Which I'd recreated, first at Fermat's Last House, then at Chaos House, because Chan-suk gave me the model for everything I'd missed in my own family.

"I want to stay at your table, Sasha," Jade said. "Can we figure out how to have a new table, right here?"

For whatever reason, the Immortals led me to hear my grandfather's voice: *Stay where you belong, Ricky.*

As happens with profound—and obvious—enlightenment, I tripped on a pothole. Water Street is full of them. Jade caught me in his arms, so I didn't crash down on the sandy roadbed. He held on for too long, clutching me.

"Uh…" I felt a tickle. The long-feared virus? Or trepidation rising from the dead? "I built a whole life here and never let anyone see my fear. I guess that's another habit I have to break. But yes, we can have that."

"Maybe we can move the Chaos table to a new home."

We arrived home well after midnight. Chaos House was silent, all the lights out except for the front porch. I assumed the kids got in on time, since they'd kept Julio with them.

Jade said, "I think Lazarus Cottage would be best tonight."

He must have seen doubt on my face under the porch light.

"One, I cleaned the cottage," he said. "And two? As I recall, you're noisy. Anywhere else would be a second mistake."

"I don't recall that." *It's been so long.* "What other mistake?"

We paused on the front steps while Jade unlocked the door. He grinned like a wide-eyed figure in a Caravaggio painting. He said, "The biggest mistake I made was thinking that the choices were only *either, or.* Either I travel and do art, or I stay home with you. If I hadn't listened to Claudia, maybe the choice might have been *both.* That's what we're choosing now, right?"

He pushed the door open, and we stepped inside. Lazarus Cottage had never before glowed with such warmth. The usual wild havoc was gone from his living space.

"Sasha, we'd better drink a raft load of water if we don't want to feel like warmed-over hell in the morning. It has to be water. The refrigerator is empty."

We sat at the tiny linoleum-and-chrome dinette table, sipping from our glasses, Jade watching me with a tempting smile.

"Jade? *Both* would still have left me here while you played Wandering Scholar. Ruby took away my trust fund, which made it impossible for me to wander."

"She took…What?"

"On that Bad Christmas night, while Ruby was insulting you and harassing Wendy, she told me she'd revoked my trust fund. I didn't have money to travel with you on your Fulbright, even if the twins hadn't steered me in another direction."

"I don't like your mother."

"She did tend to beg the whole world to resent and fear her."

He touched my hand in that way that leaves me ready to die of bliss. "Not like us."

"No, not like us."

My dissertation explains the adventures of bonded pairs of heroes who know each other, with all that stuff about devotion and debt, blood and fidelity, promises of constancy and unity.

Two Fish That Swim Together.

Immortals Hidden on Earth.

In this new beginning, our efforts had fit together in natural ways over the last two days. We made decisions with ease, moving of a single accord. At this moment though, sitting at the dinette table, I felt awkward and dull with fatigue.

"What will I do?" It nagged me. "Just trail after you? Find a local substitute teacher gig when you go to Outer Mongolia or Mumbai? Being your business manager won't fill my time."

"You can choose where we go half the time. We can be partners in actual projects. Like right now, I'm making a mess of the boxes I'm building in the garage. You'll have a better idea."

"What are the boxes for? Shipping crates?"

"Partly. My next project for Bilbao is a set of children's figures and faces in porcelain. I'll create most of them here this winter. Then onsite, I'll use the boxes to recreate an archeological dig where the faces are emerging from a gravel-and-cement matrix."

"Fercrissakes, are you insane?" I jerked back in my chair. The screech as the chair scratched the floor emphasized my exclamation. "You can't do that in Spain! Franco hasn't even been dead for ten years. It'd be heartless…cruel."

"I'm not heartless." Jade batted at my hand, as if scolding. I must have touched a nerve. "It's crushing, hearing people's stories about the civil war. I found it overwhelming when I taught in Barcelona, whenever I could coax someone to talk about it."

"Whose life will be made better by seeing artistically contrived dead children in dirt? Surely you can conceive of better."

"What? I've thought about this project a lot. I want it to be a tribute, lifting souls after loss. When I work on archeological digs, I always feel like we're resurrecting lost life. Honoring it."

I drained my glass of water, got up to fill it again. I shut my eyes to envision the porcelain children, then squeezed them tighter to keep from falling asleep on the spot.

"Portable altars," I said. "Like they have in the Victoria and Albert Museum. Make the wood look old, sanctifying your porcelain children. Maybe with miniature porcelain friezes showing the children alive and at play."

"Goodness, Sasha." His empty glass clattered on the linoleum tabletop. "Didn't you just refuse to admit that we used to be creative partners? Your idea is better, except it's beyond me to manufacture anything more than shipping crates."

"I can do it." I picked up the sketchbook Jade had tossed on the table before sitting down, his pencil clipped to the cover. I flipped to the back and began outlining a folding triptych. "We can use discarded construction wood, maybe from that remodel down on Oak Street. Make it look like polished rosewood and ebony, with your figures like the relics of saints and—"

"Stop." Jade seized my hand, shook it so hard that water from my glass spilled over both of is. "You're killing me."

"You don't like the idea?"

"If you say any more, I'll want to get started in the garage right away. First, I need to find a better workshop, a permanent one. But before that, we need to figure what being partners means. And before that—"

"We need to sleep."

Jade traced the curve of my hand, from thumb across the crook, up my index finger.

"Or at least go to bed together," he said. "I am a human kiln burning at 2400 degrees, ready to fire porcelain."

"I am the human incarnation of momentum conservation, just before an explosion."

"Oh Sasha! Can I love a mathematician?"

"Didn't you answer that long ago? It's too late to be second-guessing yourself."

The dogs began barking. No, starting a riot. In the backyard.

"They haven't been this excited before," Jade said. "Though I feel the same. Just not barking about it."

"I hope they wake my Disputatious Neighbor."

Jade said, "I'm surprised Ramona isn't offering comfort."

Which instantly made me worry that the twins weren't home yet. So I jumped up to fix it. "I'll go find out what's going on."

That's what I do—fix things. However, in the case of barking dogs, I have no relevant experience. I went into the backyard, wishing Wendy or the twins might come deal with this. No-Name Chihuahua and Pandora, both out after curfew and without adult supervision, barked and danced around each other, a different kind of excitement but equally as playful as Jade and I were—except for the barking.

I picked up Pandora, put her in the Chaos kitchen, called for Wendy, and closed the back door.

No-Name Chihuahua had huddled under the Chaos patio table by the chair where Willie used to sit. "How did you get out?" I murmured as I approached. He turned his head away when I softly said, "Hey, puppy, come."

The chihuahua played hard to get, while shaking and looking woeful. I had to hunker down to reach under the table and wrap my hands around his tiny body. "We need to get you somewhere better." I fetched the key to Xavier's deserted cottage and coaxed the dog in. I filled a dish with water, then got a pillow and blanket from the miniscule bedroom to make a bed. I coaxed the dog onto the pillow and tucked him under the blanket.

"It's just for tonight, amigo. We'll solve it all tomorrow."

What else could I do? I'm too allergic to cuddle the critter to comfort him. But it didn't feel as if I'd done enough. As my final idea for the night, I turned on the radio, so No-Name Chihuahua could listen to Gaye's after-hours music broadcast. She was playing a David Bowie retrospective. I left the chihuahua with the reassurance that he might be a hero, just for one night.

I stepped out the back door. Ramona appeared, still in her leather jacket, as if only now arriving home.

"*Kaukau,* let me take him. Just for tonight. He must be lonely and frightened."

So No-Name Chihuahua didn't get to spend the night with David Bowie. I was softly singing 'Ramona'...*come softly*...when I went back into Lazarus Cottage.

Where Jade had fallen asleep stretched crosswise on the bed, still in his Converse shoes, black jeans, and leather jacket.

I was no longer capable of making decisions. I'd worn my critical capabilities to a nub, having slept too few hours for more than a week. And my nose twitched, histamines rushing forth from having offered No-Name modest comfort.

I pulled the trailing end of the blanket over Jade, turned out the lights, and went up to my own room at Chaos House.

—

The windows in my room had been closed for two days, so the air felt stale, parched. I opened the window just as rain began to fall, and that delicious odor—petrichor—wafted over me. The rain got serious. The wet-dirt perfume of creosote bush replaced the fresh-rain odor.

Because Wendy had taken Pandora with her when she hid in my room on Thursday, I stripped the bed and remade it with fresh sheets. Then I undressed and collapsed, pulling the quilt over me just as lightning struck. The second strike was closer. Fire season had ended, so the flash and thunder felt more thrilling than worrying. I expect I only imagined that the small hairs on my neck stood on end, drawn to the electricity.

It took half a minute lying there to figure out what I was feeling. It came to me before the next lightning strike. Since I'm a runner, I recognize serotonin release. That feeling roaming around inside me was not disease but euphoria.

Lightning struck for the third time, flashing several times. I was counting seconds to determine the distance of that strike when the door to my room banged open. The repeated flashes of light showed a large form that crossed the room in the subsequent darkness and then slumped beside me on the bed.

"Yikes, Jade. You scared the crap out of me."

"The windows are rattling in the cottage. My fingers tingle so much, it attracts the lightning."

He shoved my quilt aside.

"Jade, do not get into this bed in your clothes. Or shoes. I just changed the sheets."

"You are so fussy."

He stripped faster than I've ever seen a man do. Then again, how much do I know about how fast men strip? Yet he ended up hopping about on one foot. The lightning flashed again.

In the fried ozone air—I think that's what sucked away the oxygen—I said, "A sane person takes off *both* of his shoes before dropping his jeans."

"Yes, Sasha. You're right."

"Are you afraid of lightning?"

"No. But all the electricity in the air got trapped in my body. I'm tingling all over. Then it made the clouds crash."

"It doesn't work like that."

He lay beside me, first trapping my hands between us.

I wiggled to get our limbs sorted.

He flipped me over and held my hands over my head. "How does it work, Sasha?" He breathed the words into my face.

"The lightning heats the air instantly. The rapid expansion of the air creates a sonic boom and—"

He kissed me. My fingers tingled. When I could breathe again, he'd numbed my lips.

"We should talk." It was me asking now, instead of avoiding.

"Okay, Sasha. Talk. I will always listen. But do not talk about the relationship that, for the sake of psychotherapy, we are not having. We are a bonded pair, which is pure science."

He only let me get out a word or two, every now and then. And I struggled, having no glossary to help find the right phrase. The correct nuance. I was stuck with repeating simple nouns, alternating pronouns.

My family...Your family.
My house...Your house.
My table...Your table.
My bed...Your bed.
My heart...Your soul.
My mirror...Your—

"Shh, Sasha. Don't be afraid. Don't cry now."

"I'm not crying, you dolt. I'm chanting."

"How am I supposed to know that? You're speaking Chinese."

"I'm inventing a litany that marries all the ideas to be hammered into shape since we're staying together far into the future." I repeated the chant in English.

"That's lovely." He had his hand over that place where the crystals now rested behind my breastbone. "Still, it's rude to converse in a language that other people in the room don't speak."

"There's no 'Chinese,' just a congregation of many dialects. For example, I speak Hong Kong Cantonese."

"Yes, *sifu*."

"Wait. You're laughing at me."

"But in English, *sifu*."

He kissed me. Just a smack by my lips.

"There is no culturally appropriate situation in which you kiss your master."

"Yes, *sailou*."

"That means little brother. I'm at least six hours older than you. So the respectful diminutive is —"

"As you say, dear heart." His lips stopped mine. His breath tickled my ear. "It's us, just doing what's next, every single day."

Another flash of lightning etched the maple tree's limbs on my wall. I counted to thirty before the thunder came our way.

"Tell me more about how the clouds aren't colliding, Sasha."

He curved around me, draping his arm over my shoulder, his hand near where my heart beats. Wrapping himself around me like that, he could kiss only the back of my neck.

I felt compelled to adjust for a better position.

THE END

EPILOG:
Every Single Day

After the Rain

In Chaos House, opportunity.
Improbability.
Homework.
— Alex Eliot

53: The Sanctified Table

AT SEVEN THIRTY SUNDAY MORNING, the sun should have broken the horizon. We know the sun rises every morning, but the cloud cover was still too thick to verify that the sun rose on *this* day. Unfortunately, last night's rain wasn't sufficient to delay the fence work I'd promised for Sunday.

I had a crick in my neck from a now regrettable sleeping position. My brain felt as thick as the pancake batter I was stirring. I'd chosen a stainless-steel bowl. The screech of metal spoon on metal dish tore at my ears. I reached for a wooden spoon.

Molly came into the kitchen, spent twenty seconds watching me work in slow motion, then pushed me aside to take over. I broke eggs into a ceramic bowl, then found the whisk scratching kiln-fired pottery was also annoying.

Ramona came in the back door with the dogs on her heels. Both obeyed her command to sit, then waited while she filled two bowls with dog food. They knew her to be their incarnate goddess Hecate. If I correctly recall remedial liberal arts mythology.

"*Kaukau.*" Ramona wasn't asking a question, just seeking my attention. "Given the precedent that Wendy has set, along with the fact that I am quite responsible in my habits, I believe it's appropriate for Stanley to spend nights in my room. I will make sure he doesn't run free in the common spaces."

"Who's Stanley?" *Ramona is dating? And wants to sleep with a guy?* How long have I been totally out of it?

She pointed to No-Name Chihuahua. I had to nod, only as acknowledgment; she wasn't asking permission. Entirely fair.

Alex came in, Quinn behind him, Julio tagging after, still in his pizza-stained shirt.

"Get the chocolate chips, Alex," Molly said. "And the maple syrup is on the same shelf."

"Where?" he asked. "Which cupboard?"

"Don't pretend to be helpless," Molly said. "You've lived here too long for me to be tricked into that. Quinn, please make coffee for Uncle Rik."

"He drinks it black, right?" Quinn said.

I pulled it together enough to get Julio up to his usual place at the table. The Cheerios box hadn't been opened since Valerie moved out. Only half a bowlful remained. And no more milk. I let him pour what was left of the cereal.

"Sorry, amigo. We have to hope your mom comes before you starve to death."

Unfazed, Julio began lining individual Cheerios up on the table, which isn't usually allowed. But heck.

"Is there coffee? Please?" A voice begged. It felt as if music just began playing.

Jade emerged from the stairs looking hung over, though we hadn't been drinking. He wore the white turtleneck I'd worn the day before, hair wet from the shower and half combed, . And also, to my eyes, utterly glorious. He sat on the bench, sandwiching Ramona between us. She said good morning but remained bent over her sketchbook, like she had been since she'd claimed care of Stanley.

If I'd made a conscious choice and sat on the other side of the table, I would not have seen Jade emerge from the stairs and everyone wouldn't have been able to see the first unguarded expression on my face and this moment would not have been a confession or a coming out. But I sat on this side of the table, so everyone could see me light up as though the morning sun had emerged from behind the cloud cover.

Yet no one was looking at either of us. Good, because that borrowed turtleneck covered up only half of the revenge hickeys.

"Hey, cowboy," Jade said. "It's you again. Good morning."

Julio responded in the polite way he'd been raised. Then he said, "I'm going to be a fireman. Not a cowboy."

Jade nodded solemnly. "Do you have to sell your horse?"

"I don't have a horse. But I'm getting a dog. Like Ramona. She has two dogs."

Alex called from the pantry, "There's no syrup. And the bag of chocolate chips is almost empty. Do you want carob chips?"

"No!" the twins cried in unison.

Molly sprinkled water on the cast-iron griddle, bent her head to listen for its sizzle, then began spooning batter onto the hot pan. "We'll just eat them plain, like grownups. Get the peanut butter and jam, Alex. Or the honey."

"Nada," Alex said. "An almost empty jar of lemon curd. The honey is crystallized."

Quinn put a cup of coffee in front of me, another by Jade, who beamed, then said, "You, sir, are a gentleman and a scholar."

I sipped the coffee. It was hot. And tasted like dirty water. "This is decaf."

"It's all there is." Quinn protested innocence.

"May I have more Cheerios, Uncle Rik?" Julio gazed up at me like a Dickensian waif.

"There isn't any more, amigo. It's pancakes today or nothing."

I lifted him down from the table since it'd be a few minutes before pancakes arrived. He ran slow circles around the table, keeping a sotto voce siren going at every turn.

Wendy came in, dressed again in my jeans and shirt. She sat opposite me at the table, saying good morning to the general crowd. When she called her dog, it didn't look up from snarfing the last of its food until Ramona called its name and pointed to Wendy. Then Pandora shuffled over to sit at my sister's feet.

"There's only decaf," I said. "So don't get your hopes up."

Alex dropped a plastic bag of granola on the table. I can't remember when Ramona might have made it. August? He also set down jars of peanut butter and boysenberry jam that each held a single spoonful. He poked his head in the refrigerator. "There's half a jar of apple sauce. And a quarter stick of butter."

"No one did the shopping yesterday," Molly said.

Ramona said, "One might say that all of Rik's Rules have been abused grievously for several days."

"Not all," Molly said. "I haven't gone with college boys or done drugs or conceived a child. The rest of the rules?" She made a *poof* motion.

The mathematician in me saw proof of a theorem: chaos ensues as a consequence of giving up control, even for just a few hours. The liberal arts scholar in me was too exhausted to produce either an appropriate quotation or a metaphor.

"*Sailou.*" Wendy spooned the last bite of lemon curd from the jar and didn't say more until she'd eaten it off the spoon. "I borrowed your typewriter last night. I hope you don't mind. I like to write in the darkest hours, and you weren't around to ask."

"Sure, I—"

"Ah ha," Alex cried. "There's chocolate syrup and ice cream left from Friday night. That ought to do it." He laid all the rest of the depleted options on the table, like evidence for a court case proving my sloth.

Quinn said, "We could stuff the scrambled eggs in the pancakes and eat them like tacos."

"That might do it." Jade got up to look through the spices on the counter. "Is there chili oil?"

"I'm committed to not judging anyone's choices," Molly said. "But save some ice cream for me."

Ramona inspected her sketchbook, not making choices.

Julio saw Molly dishing scrambled eggs into a serving bowl. He switched off his fire alarm and called, "Everyone go wash your hands and sit down. *Right now*!"

However, before I could get Julio back to the table, Valerie and Stephen were at the door. They (wisely) refused Ramona's invitation to join us at the most barren table in this house's history. With only modest coaching, Julio said thank you to Alex for inviting him. Jade high-fived Julio as he motored past.

On his way out the door, Stephen said, "See you tomorrow at Nick's office."

Which would have launched another *you're selling the house* conversation, except no one was paying attention to anything but their own business.

When Molly carried the bowl of scrambled eggs and a plate of pancakes to the table, Alex slipped a tape into the kitchen boombox and clicked the Play button.

Dead Kennedys. *Fresh Fruit for Rotten Vegetables.*

"Good choice, young Eliot," Jade said.

I said, "Alex, I'd deeply appreciate it if you'd please move the volume slider over to the fourth notch."

"*Kaukau,*" Molly said, "when did you get so old?"

"This old man needs to drink tea." I pushed aside the cup of decaf and started to get up.

Ramona put her hand on my shoulder. "I'll get it, Uncle Rik. Darjeeling?"

"He's not Timothy," Molly said. "Give Uncle Rik the hard stuff. Lapsang souchong."

When Ramona stood, Stanley creeped from under the table to follow her. Jade said, "May I look at your sketchbook, Ramona?"

He couldn't see the alarmed look that flicked across her face, like a small animal startled in the underbrush. But she nodded. "Of course you can."

While Ramona filled the kettle and set it to boil, then clattered in the cupboards to find tea, Jade slowly turned the pages. I couldn't help but see pages and pages of delicate, intricate nature drawings: the trees in our yard; the more exotic winter ducks in upper Lithia Park; wrens, chickadees, and nuthatches at our feeders. And pointillist landscapes: a long vista toward Pilot Rock; a series of low waterfalls in the park, framed by new undergrowth taking root where the creek banks had been torn by spring floods.

I had no idea.

"Do you want a critique, Ramona?" Jade said. "Or just a stern warning that you'd better not waste your genius? These are marvelous. And each is better than the last."

"Thank you." She spoke softly; her face flickering with relief and pleasure. "Later this week, will you look at the portfolio I'm planning to submit? Give me advice?"

"Yes!" Jade was enthusiastic. "I promise. Where are you applying? What's your favorite school?"

"San Francisco State," Ramona said. When she brought my tea, she sat beside me, so I had to scoot down close to Jade. "That reminds me, *kaukau.* Molly and I have the forms to submit our SAT scores to other schools. But we each need a check for that."

"I'll do it tonight." After I've recovered from learning about new college choices. "Where else are you applying, Molly? San Francisco too?"

"No, University of Washington," Molly said. "I don't have a major yet. The UW seems like the best place to figure it out. Eugene is such a small town, so UO is out. And everyone I've met from California is a giant a-hole. No offense, Alex."

He offered a no-blame gesture. "Just happy I talked you out of Boston. No use going to school in a foreign country."

I'd failed us all, bringing chaos by neglecting my lists. The day's chores now appeared infinitely complex. I got up for paper and a #2 Ticonderoga pencil to write a list for Sunday:

Build fence—add outside shelter?
Move Frankie's stuff to Inez's house.
Week's shopping.
Clean Ruby's room; pack stuff for care home.
Clean west and middle cottages.
Sunday dinner—seek requests (have no idea).
Pick up math papers from Sally; prep for Monday.
Begin proposals for Cantonese pop-culture books.

Ramona read my list, which lay right in front of her. She said, "Wendy, if you're moving into the west cottage, you should clean it. Can you do the middle one, too? Molly and I can tackle Grandma's room. Will Danielle know what needs to go to the care home?"

"Hmm." I hadn't thought that far. "I'd better call Howard."

"We can call," Molly said. "If we had the Datsun, we could go shopping instead of you and then take Grandma's things to her."

Ramona said, "We can take the old red wagon to the co-op."

"You can borrow my van," Jade said. "That is, if you have a license and can handle a three-speed shift on the column."

After I calculated the few blocks to the co-op and whether that panel van could make it, I chose not to interfere.

Wendy said, "I'll do the cottages later. I'm going to clean up the raised beds this morning. Really, Ricky—"

Jade held up his hand. "Can you call him Rik, please? You are the only person he lets call him by that name. However, it reminds me too much of Ruby. So maybe don't use that name?"

Wendy slapped her mouth. "Dick me like a duck. You are right." She turned to me, while I was still coping with her language at the Chaos table. "You, little brother, should be ashamed of letting an asset like the garden decay. Does anyone else want to help rescue the herb garden?"

Molly and Ramona glanced at each other. "We will. But first, come with us to the co-op and help with the shopping."

Wendy agreed but then lifted a finger with a sudden idea. "Doesn't this division of labor fall into patriarchal stereotypes?"

"Anyone can dig post holes who wants to," I said. "Or staple the wire fencing."

Alex said, "Uncle Rik, you don't have tonight's study hour on your list. Aren't you going to check my math homework?"

"Goodness, young Eliot," Jade said. "When Sasha was your age, he was taking courses in differential equations and modal logic, and no one ever checked his homework."

"How do you know?" I asked. "You hadn't even met me then. You were still in high school."

"I saw your transcript once," Jade said. "I didn't understand it. But then, I met you in Ceramics 101 for latent liberal arts majors, where you never did learn to throw pots properly."

Molly began to clear dishes but stopped and folded her arms. "Is this the way it's going to be now?"

God I hope so.

"Pretty much," Jade said. "Probably every single day."

"Are there rules for this?" Ramona asked. "Uncle Rik's old rules seem pretty out of date."

"Do you want new rules?" I asked.

"No!" all three kids answered.

Ramona said, "Don't we already know how to figure out what's right? Wasn't that the point all along?"

In minutes, the dishes were cleared, the kitchen clean, and leftover scrambled eggs divided between two dog dishes. The three women discussed what to do with the dogs, deciding that the dogs' care could be trusted to the rest of us while the women made the grocery trip.

"Alex, do you have boots?" I asked. "It's time to learn a skill that might serve you well later in life. Converse won't do."

"Guess we'd better get to it," Jade said. "Those holes won't dig themselves."

"Quinn," I said, "you're welcome to dig post holes, but you have to get permission from your mother."

Quinn ended up going home because learning to dig holes was not on his mother's list for their Sunday's activities. Alex went to find better shoes in his room.

Jade kissed me the moment the kitchen emptied.

"See what happens?" I wrapped my arms around him. "I gave up control for a day, like you begged me to. And now there isn't even dry cereal or coffee in the house."

"I bow to you. I acknowledge your superlative ability to keep order in our lives." He touched that sensitive place, near the hollow behind my clavicle. "I long to plumb the depths of your control. Did you have a teaching moment prepared for digging holes?"

"Hush," I said. "We're just doing what's next." I adjusted the day's list, putting stars by the items that were no longer mine. "No one made a shopping list."

"Someone else can worry about what's missing," Jade said.

"I hope they remember to get coffee." That's the sole anxiety I could muster. "My brain is not fully functional. We are lucky that the fence job is just applied mathematics and physics. "

The dogs, who'd stood at the front door for a while after the women left, came back to sniff under the table for what might have fallen—besides Cheerios, which neither wanted.

"Sasha, do you remember that hollow feeling after being tits up on acid for three days?" Jade said.

"I do."

"I'm just realizing it was only lack of sleep," he said. "Yet did we ever accomplish as much in three days of staying awake as we have since Wednesday? You didn't have half of it on your last list." His hand rested on mine so I couldn't read my revised list.

"What did I miss?" I disengaged my hand to revise my list.

He nuzzled my ear. "The last list didn't have the part where we change the world and do a bucketload of karma."

Alex banged open the door from the basement. "I'm ready to dig post holes."

"You'll find gloves in the toolbox on the back porch."

I drained the last of my tea, then sat on the sofa to put on my Red Wing boots.

"What music shall we have?" Jade unplugged the boombox, tucked it under his arm. "What's appropriate for the art of building a dog fence?"

I said, "Something that pisses off Mean Mr. Mustard."

He and Alex debated albums, ranging from *Bela Lugosi's Dead* to *Under the Big Black Sun.* Alex darted to his room to find tapes.

Me, I was going with the flow.

But first, I had to fix the broken screen door.

THE NEW BEGINNING

Jade the Wandering Scholar. Read some journal entries from Jade's first year wandering at: anniepearson.com/chaoshouse/

Rik's Dissertation. Rik is a meticulous scholar who relied on physical copies for all his research material. But I made up many of the untitled stories he tells. However, the authors and directors of books, movies, and comics cited in Rik's synopsis are real and can be found via casual web searches. You can read Rik's synopsis at: anniepearson.com/chaoshouse/

Ashland Shakespeare Festival. Go, you won't regret it. However, there is no *King Lear* mural near the theatres.

Cantonese Romanization. The romanized spellings for food are taken from English-language recipe sites. I also wanted to use terms of endearment that children might have learned as expats in Hong Kong in the 1960s. I used the romanized spelling for these terms based on the Yale method as found in the "Hong Kong Government Cantonese Romanisation," and then supplemented it with notes from native speakers on message boards. Unless you're writing a scholarly treatise, you can use Wikipedia to find more resources about this topic.

CETA Funding. As an economic recovery effort, the federal Comprehensive Employment and Training Act (CETA) was created as an extension to the 1930s' Works Progress Administration (WPA) program. CETA began as a general job training program, but modifications included artists. From 1974 to 1980, the program gave full-time jobs to 20,000 artists and arts support staff in public and not-for-profit agencies.

Give My Heart to the Hawks. Rik refers the title of a Robinson Jeffers poem: allpoetry.com/Give-Your-Heart-To-The-Hawks

Hoedads. To learn more about what was once the largest worker-owned cooperative in the U.S., see the brief primer at: wikipedia.org/wiki/Hoedads_Reforestation_Cooperative

Lithia Springs. You truly do not want to drink from the lithium fountain in downtown Ashland. However, it's likely your curiosity will win out over my warning.

McCarley's and the Dahlia vs. Chez Margot and Chaos House. This story is not historical fiction. Most research was done via pseudo-AI queries into my own memory. I've verified names and locations of real businesses used in the text. However, Chez Margot is a fictionalized stand-in for a former Main Street restaurant. Water Street was mostly industrial land at the time of this story. The Victorian-turned-B&B that I used as a model for Chaos House was on North Main. If you have corrections to suggest, please write to me care of Jugum Press.

Queer as a Clockwork Orange. Please see what Anthony Burgess and Stanley Kubrick had to say about that early twentieth century Cockney phrase. Here's one link: bit.ly/3MSt5wt.

Upper Lithia Pond. The eagle and the menagerie are long gone. None of the plans made to rescue the eagle ever came to fruition.

Writers and SO[S]C. Young Wendy says, "No one who goes to college here becomes a writer." Wrong! I did. So did others.

Xavier freaking Torres. Although the Oregon Shakespeare Festival and the city named Ashland exist in the real world, the character called Xavier Torres is purely fictional. Nothing in this book reflects any real-world occurrences at the Festival.

Zhiji. I recommend *One Who Knows Me: Friendship and Literary Culture in Mid-Tang China,* by Anna M. Shields (Harvard University Asia Center: Cambridge, MA, 2015). See also "...Let's Have a Conversation About Soulmates" and "...Let's Talk About Knowing in The Untamed" by the blogger hunxi-guilai on Tumblr at: hunxi-guilai.tumblr.com.

Composition Song List: Lucinda Williams, Dave Alvin, the Clash, the Blasters, the Cure, David Bowie, *The Untamed* and *Word of Honor* OSTs, king.org.

Acknowledgments: My profound thanks to Jacyn Stewart, Susan Urban, Laurie Cropp, Curt Colbert, Carol Buckmiller, and Martin Fossum for critical reading, and to Jane Dow for editing. Special thanks to Ajax Bell for close reading.

Character List

Family:

Rik Eliot a.k.a. Sasha, Ricky; born: Aldrik Alexander Eliot.

Alex Eliot: Rik's nephew; named after grandfather.

Christopher Eliot: Rik's older brother; Alex's father.

Claudia Eliot: Rik's sister-in-law; Alex's mother.

David: Rik's father.

Lex Eliot: grandfather's pen name.

Molly Eliot: smaller niece.

Ramona Eliot: taller niece.

Ruby Eliot: Rik's mother.

Wendy Eliot: Rik's sister.

In the Chaos guest cottages:

Jade Solberg: a ceramics artist.

Timothy Bonham-Day: actor.

Xavier Torres: visiting director.

Tenants and Chez Margot friends:

Becca Lee: tenant; Festival administrator.

Eddie: Chez Margot bartender.

Frankie Weiss: printshop manager; former tenant.

Gaye Verlaine: DJ; former tenant.

Inez Saint: art professor.

Kevin Emery: Chez Margot bartender; former tenant.

Nick Lawrence: Rik's attorney.

Stephen Garland: tenant; owner of Chez Margot.

Valerie Ortega and Julio: tenants.

Ruby's caretakers:

Mrs. Adams: morning caretaker.

Danielle Nickels: live-in night caretaker; student.

Howard Curtis: evening caretaker.

School and mural crew:

Jacqueline Urquell: administrator.

Quinn Hargadine: Alex's friend.

Sally Ogden: math teacher.

Mrs. Solon: unseen art teacher.

Zackary Helman: Molly's friend.

Zooey Helman: mural crew.

Neighborhood:

Dharma: from women's collective.

J.J. Smith, Lt. Col. (retd): Disputatious Neighbor.

Mrs. Hargadine: Quinn's mother.

Willie Smith: next-door neighbor.

Hong Kong friends:

Kai: Rik's best friend in Hong Kong.

Chan-suk (Chan-sinsang): Rik's teacher in Hong Kong.

Cheung Bai Shing: a professor.

Wendy's friends:

Dikshant: enlightened master.

Jophiel: lover in Big Sur.

Mimi: unseen nanny.

Zane: Wendy's friend.

Out-of-town friends and mentors:

Eugene Randolph: PhD supervisor.

Gerard Crowe: Michael's partner.

Michael Lyle: friend; doctor.

About the Author

ANNIE PEARSON lives in Seattle and posts about fiction and eclectic project planning at: www.anniepearson.com. Follow her on BlueSky: @anniepearson.bsky.social.

WRITING AS ANNIE PEARSON:
Chaos House
Demons & Destiny [forthcoming]
Restoration Rules Series
No One Dies
Reap Justice
Call the Reavers
Rain City Incidents Series
The Grrrl of Limberlost
Artemis in the Desert
Nine Volt Heart
The Pirate King

WRITING AS E.A. STEWART:
Accidental Heretics Series
1: *Bone-mend and Salt*
2: *Trebuchets in the Garden*
3: *Crux Lunata*
4: *Song of Valerós*
The Mad Woman of La Catalane: A Novella
The Blue Door…and More Accidental Heretics Tales
Legends of Valerós Series
Wheel and Serpent
Traitor
Hero

Bad Reputation by Ajax Bell

After being caught in a backseat tryst with the mayor's son, Shane Fontaine is exiled from his small hometown. Alone in the city, he seeks solace in punk show mosh pits and bathhouse saunas. Rescued from a brutal beating, Shane is befriended by a Russian engineering student, launching a set of traumatic and ecstatic encounters. To survive, Shane must become a man who chooses to persist, do the right thing, and stand up for others.

Nine Volt Heart by Annie Pearson

Can you find true love without a nondisclosure agreement after your picture is on the cover of *Rolling Stone*?

He said, "I love you."

She said, "You don't know the real me."

He said, "Great title for a song. Key of G? Can we do it together as close harmony?"

Enjoy an electric ride through the backstreets of Seattle, where tourists never go.

Wheel and Serpent (Legends of Valerós series) by E.A. Stewart

To earn a place as a knight, Taresa of Valerós must get a message to the king of France. But crossing the Languedoc proves treacherous: Taresa and her friends are hunted as rebels after a murder at a Templar house. Amid the chaos and cruelty of the crusade against the Cathars, Taresa sets forth to save her friends, armed with wit, loyalty, and her absent lover's third-best sword.

www.jugumpress.net

www.ingramcontent.com/pod-product-compliance
Lightning Source LLC
Chambersburg PA
CBHW021212260626
47172CB00002B/386

* 9 7 9 8 9 8 8 2 8 6 2 1 9 *